Josh shrugged the strap of his bag more firmly on to his shoulder. 'Are you coming?'

Miriam shook her head. 'Not yet. There's a full moon tonight and I want to watch it from up there.' She pointed to where the great rock mass that was Sharp Tor rose stark and grey above the moor. 'Why don't you stop and see it with me?'

'No, I must get back for supper. Mum will be wondering where I am.'

'Mummy's boy!' Her voice mocked him as he scrambled from the gully and set off home across the moor.

'Josh! Josh Retallick!'

He turned to see her standing wide-legged on an uneven rock above the gully.

'If you come up to Sharp Tor with me I'll let you kiss me.'

'I don't want to.' He turned his back on her and walked away.

'You will one day, Josh Retallick. You will one day!'

Chase The Wind

E. V. Thompson

WARNER BOOKS

A *Warner* Book

First published in Great Britain in 1977
by Macmillan London Ltd
First paperbacked in 1979 by Pan Books Ltd
This edition published by Warner Books in 1998

A CIP catalogue record for this book
is available from the British Library.

ISBN 0 7515 2485 9

Typeset in Palatino by
Palimpsest Book Production Limited,
Polmont, Stirlingshire
Printed and bound in Great Britain by
Mackays of Chatham plc, Chatham, Kent

Warner Books
A Division of
Little, Brown and Company (UK)
Brettenham House
Lancaster Place
London WC2E 7EN

History lives on in these ruined walls
Sagging with age and troubled thought.
Stone-wept tears around mossed feet.
Yesterday's hero. Apart. Forlorn.

Once proud and tall above the moor,
Its chimney smoke would chase the wind
High over mounds of broken ore
That gave to man his daily bread.

But who was last to close the door?
Did he look back with sad regret
Or, turning, laugh and hurl the key
And climb towards the setting sun?

But no man lives who knew it then
And gaping doors no secrets hold.
While scouring time and moorland gorse
Eradicate our yesterdays.

Chapter One

Ninety fathoms below grass, in the darkness at the bottom of the main vertical shaft of Wheal Sharptor copper mine, Joshua Retallick stepped from the ladder on to the ore-strewn floor. He took a couple of shaky steps, his legs trembling from the climb down.

Above him, so far up that the clean, star-studded sky could not be seen, was a small rough-square hole. Through this was hoisted the copper ore that would make one man rich and send fifty more to a premature grave.

Josh moved to one side as boots scraped on the wooden rungs above him. The night shift was coming on duty. As each man stepped to the floor he would flex his arms, easing the muscles in his shoulders. Muscles knotted by the fear of falling that made a man grip each rung just a little too tightly.

The miners passed through the openings into the tunnels that sloped gently away from the main shaft. They stooped, automatically but unnecessarily, used to smaller tunnels than these. Once inside they paused to light the yellow candles that each man relied upon to give him light by which to work and warning of foul air.

Josh followed one of the miners along the tunnel where he knew his father was working. At first, the tunnel was narrow,

with water oozing from walls shored up in a haphazard
here-and-there manner. Then, suddenly and dramatically, it
opened out into a huge vault, eighty feet wide and thirty
high. Here there had been a seam of near-pure copper. Now
it was a rock-walled emptiness – the ore long since fed into the
belly of a Swansea smelting-house and disgorged as blocks of
gleaming metal, each tinged with the colour of the furnace,
to be shipped in tall-rigged vessels to a world eager for
high-grade Cornish copper.

In the vast chamber clouds of dust hung on the heavy air.
The shadows of the new arrivals flickered and were distorted,
moulded by the smoking flames from two candles standing
in niches in the rough-hewn wall.

A dirty sweating figure, stripped to the waist, appeared
from a small tunnel, pushing a laden wheelbarrow ahead of
him. Seeing the new arrivals he rested the wheelbarrow, added
another streak of dirt to his face with the back of his hand and
called back down the tunnel from which he had emerged.

'Time to wrap it up, Ben. Night shift are here.'

The call was taken up by unseen men in other tunnels,
'Knock it off! Night men are here!'

Men cramped in unnatural postures gratefully eased their
way back from exploratory borings and headed towards the
main shaft to begin the long climb to air and home, to
comparative comfort and company, where there was not a
million tons of rock and earth packed above them.

The miner who had first signalled the arrival of the relief
shift grinned at Josh. ''Tis a bit late to be coming down to help
us. Has Preacher Thackeray given up trying to learn you? Does
he think you should be working below ground wi' us?'

'No.' Josh grinned. 'There's a meeting of the Benefit Union
at the chapel tonight. Lessons ended early.'

'I wouldn't mention anything about it to your dad. He's not
too happy wi' talk about Thackeray's "Union".'

Budge Pearn towelled his body with his rough-spun shirt
before pulling the crumpled garment over his head and
tucking the end inside his trousers. At eighteen he was four
years older than Josh. His mother had died in childbirth. When

his father was killed in a mining accident Budge was seven years old and had been taken into the Retallick household.

'When are you coming up to see Jenny and the baby?' He pronounced it as 'bebby'. 'She's right handsome now. Plenty of hair, too.'

'I know. Jenny brought Gwen down home today. That reminds me. You'd better not be late home. Mum gave Jenny some boiling bacon for your supper.'

'I'll be up on the moor before your dad sets foot on the ladder.' Budge pocketed the stubs of half a dozen candles. 'Give my love to your mum.' Then with a cheery wave he was gone.

Further along the tunnel, Ben Retallick welcomed the arrival of the night shift with grateful relief. At thirty-five years of age he was reckoned an 'old man' by mining standards. It was an era when a miner who had seen his fortieth birthday below ground was something of a rarity.

Climbing over a heap of newly dug ore he crawled backwards along a tunnel scarcely three feet high and only as wide as his shoulders. It would be widened eventually – the copper seam was quite broad here – but he had been burrowing his way forward in an attempt to determine its direction and value.

Ben Retallick had been working in Cornish mines since he was ten years of age and was one of the most experienced miners on Wheal Sharptor. He had worked two-men shallow streamings on the high moor and the great labyrinths that extended beneath the sea in the far west of the county. He might well have been a captain for one of those tin mines had not Theophilus Strike asked him to come and work as a tribute worker on the newly discovered copper seams of the Wheal Sharptor. This meant that Ben Retallick would become a free-lance miner, contracting on a piece-work basis for the right to remove the ore for the mine-owner at so much per ton. This was why it was so important to know the direction and value of a seam of ore.

It was said that Ben Retallick could follow a rich seam even when it leap-frogged a twelve-foot barrier of granite. He would not be deluded by a tempting stretch of momentarily rich ore which petered out within a few yards.

Outside, in the wide tunnel, Ben Retallick stood upright slowly. The cramped muscles had knotted his limbs into a crouched position, and it was a painful adjustment. The damp from the walls of a mine worked its way into a man's joints and caused them to swell.

He looked up to see the sympathy on Josh's face and grimaced. 'A boy shouldn't see his father when he's fighting the cramps, Josh. What are you doing down here?'

Josh shrugged and tried to sound nonchalant. 'My lesson finished early. I thought I'd come down to meet you.'

Ben Retallick saw the half-filled wheelbarrow and the long-handled shovel cast hastily aside and frowned. Budge Pearn had been in a hurry to finish work. It was time he learned that a man always emptied his own wheelbarrow below ground. Then Ben smiled at his own thoughts. Budge had plenty of time to learn. With a pretty wife and baby daughter waiting for him at home there was more reason for a young man to be on the surface than trundling barrow-loads of another man's ore down here for three pounds a month.

'Come on, son. Let's go up top and taste some fresh air.'

At the foot of the ladder there was a great deal of good-natured banter and jostling between the men working another seam. Ben put a hand on Josh's shoulder and stood back from it. At the end of a shift he had neither the energy of the youngsters nor patience with them.

Another man also lacked patience. Heavy-browed, dark-eyed and scowling, Moses Trago elbowed his irritable way through to the ladder. Broad-shouldered and brutal, he cared for no man's opinion, using his fists in arguments where other men would use words. Behind him, walking in his brother's shadow, the quieter John Trago loomed just as large.

The arrival of the two men put an end to the outburst of good humour and Ben and Josh shuffled forward with the other miners.

This was the part of mining that Ben found more difficult with each passing day. From ninety fathoms down there were five hundred and forty ladder-rungs to be climbed before a man's head rose from the hole in the ground. Ben knew the number. There had been a time when he would count them. But no more. These days he gritted his teeth, kept his face turned downwards and climbed numbly. Occasionally the man above him might be climbing too slowly, or would slip because of his own weakness and step upon Ben's fingers. Then he would feel an unreasonable fury – almost a black rage – against the unseen miner. The feeling would sustain him, drive him on until he stumbled out on to earth that was open to the sky.

Once on the ladders all talking ceased. A man would regret each mouthful of wasted air when he arrived, lungs roaring for oxygen, at the top of the shaft.

Josh was aware of this and he climbed steadily and carefully ahead of his father.

Never a pleasant experience, tonight the climb suddenly became a frightening nightmare. Josh and Ben were on the fourth ladder, almost fifty feet from the bottom of the shaft when there was a blood-freezing scream from high above them and the confused shouts of men.

Josh had no idea what was happening, but it was an experience that Ben had known many times before. His ''Ware below!' rang out and he used the same breath to clamber up to share a rung with Josh. 'Swing behind the ladder,' he hissed. When Josh obeyed him hurriedly, Ben Retallick closed his arms about his son and held him tight against the ladder with arms and knees. His back pressed against the uneven rock of the shaft.

Most times a falling man would mercifully smash his head against the side of the shaft and know no more. This one was not so fortunate. The scream had died to a low inhuman sound in his throat as he flailed past Josh and his father, but he remained conscious until the moment he crashed on to the floor of the shaft. Josh would remember the sound of it for as long as he lived. His hands about the ladder gripped so tightly that his nails drew blood from his palms.

For two full seconds there was silence. It was broken by the clattering of boots as the men on the lower ladders scrambled back down.

'Ben! Ben Retallick!' The cry went up as Josh followed his father down.

'I'm here. Who was it who fell?'

'Budge Pearn.'

'Oh my God! His poor maid.'

Josh heard the agonised whisper from his father as his own legs threatened to buckle beneath him. The miner dropped to the floor of the shaft where flickering candle-light added to the gruesome scene, then turned back to shield Josh from it. He was only partly successful.

'Wait for me at the fifty-fathom level, Josh,' he said.

Josh could only nod his agreement. He was not sure whether the lump in his throat would make him cry or be sick.

Ben put a hand on his son's shoulder. 'Go on up. There's nothing you can do here.'

Josh turned and climbed blindly, the lump still lodged in his windpipe. Budge Pearn had been as a big brother to him.

Behind him, Ben looked down at the smashed body. Miraculously, there was not a mark on Budge's face. Reaching down he closed the lids on fear-filled eyes. 'Poor maid!' he repeated. Though only a few weeks past her seventeenth birthday, Jenny Pearn was now a widow with a baby to support. Like Budge she was an orphan, her father having died in an identical accident. Ben looked down at the body and thought of the young wasted life. He felt suddenly old and tired. The boy had so much to live for.

Tom Shovell, the shift captain, swung off the ladder and bent down over the body. Then he looked sympathetically at Ben. 'You get on home. We'll do what's necessary here. Budge will go up in the ore-sling.'

Ben nodded numbly.

'We'll take him on to the chapel from there. I'd be obliged if you would take it on yourself to tell Jenny. You – or Jesse.' Jesse was Ben's wife. 'I needn't tell you how sorry I am, Ben. He was a well-liked lad.'

'There's little comfort in that for poor Jenny.'

Ben Retallick began the climb to the surface once more. At the fifty-fathom level Josh joined him and they completed the climb in silence.

There was a chill east wind blowing on the moor. Normally Ben would have shivered and hurried along the path to his cottage when the breath had returned to him. Tonight there was no speed in his legs. The small group of miners clustered around the top of the shaft murmured their sympathy, but that was all. They saved their questions for those who came to the surface behind him.

It was early March and quite dark as they took the path that wound over the shoulder of the tor towards the small cluster of slate and granite cottages huddled against the wind in a shallow depression on the east-facing slope. As they walked they could hear the heavy hollow thudding of the great pumping engine at the Wheal Phoenix in the valley beyond the cottages. Once, there was a red glow which flared up behind church-like windows as one of the furnace doors was swung open.

'How . . . how do you think it happened?' Josh asked, speaking for the first time since they had both stood by the shattered body in the shaft.

'I expect Budge was in a hurry. Probably trod on a loose rung. It's an easy thing to do. I've seen it happen too often.'

'But why to Budge?'

He had to make it sound fierce or his voice would have betrayed him.

'I don't know the answer to that.' Ben put an understanding arm across his son's shoulders. 'Why do so many men die in the mines? You're the one getting the schooling. Think of some way to save miners' lives and you'll be blessed by every mother and wife in Cornwall.'

He stopped talking as they heard the sound of someone running and stumbling along the path towards them. The footsteps were too light to belong to a man.

'Who's there?' Ben called.

'Ben! Is that you?'

'Jesse! What are you doing out here?'

'Oh, Ben! Thank God you're safe! Thank God!' She clung to him, shaking violently. 'They told me there'd been an accident. That you'd fallen.' She buried her face in his rough shirt, grasping the material tight with her fingers.

'Who told you that?' Ben put his hand beneath her chin and lifted her head.

'Moses Trago. I left everything and ran. Your dinner! It will be ruined.'

'Moses Trago is quicker to carry bad news than to offer help.' Ben Retallick was angry. Moses Trago must have heard his name being called and assumed that it was he who had fallen.

'Then there was an accident. What happened? Was anyone hurt?'

'It was Budge, Mum.'

Ben felt Jesse stiffen in his arms as Josh spoke. 'He fell from the ladder.'

'He's dead, then.' It was a statement of fact rather than a question.

'Yes,' said Ben gently. 'Jenny hasn't been told yet. I was going to see her myself but it might be better if you did it.'

Jesse was silent for so long that Ben thought she might not feel capable of breaking the news to Budge's wife. Then she burst out, 'Why? Why did it have to happen to Budge? The two of them had found so much happiness together. Oh! Poor Budge! Poor Jenny!'

'It was an accident, Jesse. They happen.'

'It's that damned mine. Worn ladders, frayed ropes . . . !'

'Enough now, Jesse. It gives us our living.'

'Try to tell that to Budge – God rest his soul.' She sobbed once. A long uneven breath. But she slipped from Ben's arms when he tried to comfort her.

'I'll go to Jenny now. Before she hears the news from someone else.' She paused alongside Josh. 'If you ever become a miner, Joshua Retallick, I'll never forgive you.'

She moved away along the path, and her voice came to them from the darkness.

'Ben?'

'Yes?'

'I'm not forgetting to thank God it wasn't you.'

As she hurried away Ben said, 'One day you'll be looking for a wife, Josh. If you find one who is half the woman your mother is you'll be a lucky man.'

His own parents would have disputed that when he first told them he was going to marry her. They were staunch Methodists and had brought Ben up in the same faith. Jesse shared the same religion – up to a certain point. But she possessed an impetuosity, a disconcerting habit of saying exactly what she thought when the thought came to her. It was not kindly accepted by her elders. It did not happen so often now; the years had mellowed her. But once in a while she would say, or do, something to remind Ben of the girl she had been when he married her. Wilful and stubborn his parents may have thought her, but Ben loved her for it and had never sought to change her.

In the kitchen of the small granite cottage Josh swung the cooking-pot off the fire while Ben eased his boots off. Small, but spotless, the kitchen served as dining- and living-room. There was one other downstairs room where all the 'best' possessions were housed. It was kept for special occasions and the formal visits of people outside their immediate circle of friends.

Josh ladled stew into two bowls, and they sat at the table eating in silence. Josh was thinking of having more when the door banged open and Jesse Retallick bundled inside a thin pale girl who looked hardly old enough to be the mother of the kicking, wailing infant she clutched to her. Jesse kept an arm about Jenny and took her straight through into the 'best' room.

A minute later she was back in the doorway. 'Josh. Upstairs and move your things into our room. Make yourself up a bed on the floor. Jenny will be moving into yours. Ben, bring some fire into the other room.'

She went back to look after Jenny, and two chairs scraped back as Ben and Josh moved to carry out Jesse's orders.

As Ben was filling a bucket with live coals from the kitchen stove, Jesse came back into the room and deposited a pile of baby-clothes on a chair.

'Hurry and get in there with her, Ben,' she said. 'She hasn't started crying yet. When it comes it will be all the worse for the waiting.'

When Ben took the coals in, Jenny was seated on the faded horse-hair sofa that had been a wedding-present from his father. Dry-eyed and taut, she was not even aware of his presence and continued to stare vacantly in front of her.

He poured the coals into the fire-place and piled wood on top of it before standing up and looking down at the pathetic young window. He wanted to say something to her, give her some words of comfort; but she was as cold as rock, totally withdrawn from the world of the living.

'Is that fire going?' Jesse swept into the room and, picking up the baby, placed her on the floor in the corner of the room. 'Leave us now, Ben.' She moved to the sofa where Jenny was sitting unseeing. With a last pained look at the girl, Ben returned to the kitchen.

Josh made his bed – an untidy heap in a corner of his parents' bedroom – and climbed into it, pulling the blanket up to his chin. He was lying there, his face turned away from the door, when his father came into the darkened room. Ben saw the glitter of tears on his cheek.

He said nothing but walked to the window and looked down into the valley where Henwood village lay. There was light shining from the large windows of the chapel, and he guessed the body of Budge Pearn had arrived there.

Then he heard the sound from the room downstairs. It startled him before he realised fully what it was. Starting as a low moan it quickly swelled and expanded until it burst out as a sob. Then Jenny began crying noisily. Painful as it was to listen to, Ben yet felt a sense of relief. Now Jenny was a young girl who had lost her man. A widow with a small child. Someone with whom to feel sympathy and for Jesse to comfort. Before, she had been unapproachable, locked away in a place where no other human could join her or share her pain.

Ben went downstairs, put on his boots and coat, and let himself out of the house to walk to the village.

Despite the darkness and the chill east wind a great many villagers were gathered about the entrance to the chapel. The insularity of the small moorland communities had been changed by the influx of miners from other parts of Cornwall – and even from beyond the Tamar. But a fatal accident, like any other deviation from the norm of everyday life, was an event to be shared by all.

There were enquiries from all sides about Jenny as Ben strode to the chapel door. Some stemmed from mere curiosity, but most from genuine concern for her. The women in the crowd knew that tomorrow, or the next day, it might be their turn. The mines were notorious widow-makers. Accidents were all too frequent. Even when a man thought he had won, and gave up the life of a miner, he discovered that the mine had passed on a fatal legacy to him. He had spent years toiling in air sometimes so foul it would scarcely support life, breathing in dust for the whole of a shift. Then the sudden change of temperature at the end of a shift when his labouring lungs exchanged the heat of the mine for the chill of a winter night. They all took their toll of him. Few ex-miners survived to spin yarns of their exploits to their grandchildren.

The inside of the small chapel was clean and starkly bereft of ostentation. Ben was surprised to see the preacher inside, distributing hymn- and prayer-books thinly along the benches.

The Reverend Wrightwick Roberts was not a resident preacher. He rode the North Hill Methodist circuit. Methodism was still a young religion, dependent entirely upon the Sunday collections for its income. Only the larger mining communities like St Cleer, where Josh went for his lessons, could afford to support a resident preacher.

The North Hill circuit minister was himself an ex-miner and his shoulders were almost as broad as Moses Trago's, but when he spoke his voice was strangely soft coming from such a big man.

'It's a night for grieving, Ben. The Lord's ways are beyond

the understanding of mortals.' He nodded towards a closed door at the far end of the chapel. 'Budge is through there. Mary Crabbe is with him.'

Mary Crabbe had been taking charge of births and deaths in the district since before Ben was born. He nodded his acknowledgement. 'It's been a sad day, Wrightwick.'

The preacher doled out the last of the prayer-books. 'Every mine accident brings sadness to someone. How is Jenny taking it?'

Ben sat down on the end of a bench. 'Hard. But Jesse is looking after her.' He suddenly felt old, and the preacher saw it in the sag of his shoulders. 'Josh is taking it badly too. They were like brothers.'

'And you, Ben?' The preacher asked the question softly. Ben and Jesse had looked upon Budge Pearn as another son.

'Yes, and me.' It was as much as he would ever say on the subject and more than any other man would hear from him. 'You'll see to things, Wrightwick? Take the service for him? I'll be paying.'

'And what about the men on the mine? Don't they collect for such happenings?'

'Sharptor isn't the Caradon – or even Wheal Phoenix. We are still small. I want whatever is collected to go to Jenny. It won't be much. A few guineas aren't going to go far with a baby to feed and clothe.'

'Then what about Theophilus Strike? Won't he give anything?'

Ben managed a faint smile. 'That sounded like young Preacher Thackeray talking. Theophilus Strike pays wages, Wrightwick. Jenny will collect whatever was due to Budge – and a guinea or two besides.'

Wrightwick Roberts frowned at the mention of William Thackeray. The fiery young St Cleer preacher was fast establishing a reputation as a miners' champion, and the younger men flocked to hear his sermons on Sundays, packing the large St Cleer chapel to capacity.

'Why do you let Josh stay at Thackeray's school, Ben? He's not a good influence.'

Ben shrugged. 'His lessons are cheap – and good. Josh has learned to read the Bible and can work out sums that leave me with my jaw hanging. Is that bad, Wrightwick?'

'No. But that isn't what I am talking about. Thackeray teaches things that you won't find in any schoolbook. He feeds his ideas to young miners who know no better. Telling them to band into a "union" and demand more money is dangerous talk, Ben. It shouldn't come from a man who serves God.'

'All I've heard is rumours. None of them from Josh,' said Ben, standing up. 'But I do know the boy is learning things I would dearly love to have been taught. I am grateful to Preacher Thackeray for that. Josh will have a chance in life, Wrightwick. He won't have to go down a mine because he knows nothing else. And he won't end up on a table in your chapel with Mary Crabbe straightening his broken limbs.'

He stopped and drew a deep breath. 'I'll be away now before I say more than I should.'

'We've been friends too long for me to take offence,' said the preacher. 'And I'll walk up with you. I'd like to see Jenny.'

He held open the door and followed Ben outside. There were only a few of the older women still waiting and they bobbed their heads at the preacher.

The two men walked side by side along the street and on to the twin-rutted track that climbed towards the mine, passing close to the Retallick cottage.

Ben's tiredness was telling on him now, and the preacher slowed his pace to stay with him.

'How many years have you been mining now, Ben?'

'Most of my life, it seems. I've been underground since I was ten.'

'It's the underground part that takes it out of a man,' said Wrightwick Roberts. 'Don't you think it's time you thought about a surface job?'

Ben snorted. 'For what? A woman's pay?'

Wrightwick Roberts knew better than to pursue the matter. For Ben to give up working below ground would be an admission of defeat, an acknowledgement that he was too old to beat the ladders. But it was always the ladders that scored the final victory.

'How about an engine? Is the Sharptor going to get one?'

'I don't know. Only Strike can answer that. If it means spending money the answer is "No". Besides, we won't need one for a year or two.'

'What's money got to do with it? With the mine and its shop Theophilus Strike is making more money than he knows how to spend.'

'Likely you're right,' replied Ben. 'I wouldn't know.' They had arrived at the cottage. Ben opened the door, and both men went inside.

'How is she?' asked Wrightwick Roberts as Ben sat down gratefully.

Jesse had been bustling about the kitchen when they arrived and she said, 'As well as any woman who has just lost her man. And when she begins to get over it she'll begin to worry about the future for herself and the baby. She's no home because the cottage belongs to the mine and she's no family to turn to.'

'She has us,' said Ben. 'She can move in here. I hope you didn't wait to hear it from me to tell her.'

'No, I didn't. But it's nice to hear you say it.'

Wrightwick Roberts left the kitchen, and as Ben leaned back in his chair, relaxing a little, an unintelligible murmur started up in the other downstairs room.

'It will be strange having a baby about the house again.'

'Budge would be happy to know we are looking after the pair of them,' said Jesse. There was a break in her voice. Ben reached across to where she was standing by the table and took her hand.

The inquest on Budge Pearn was a brief perfunctory affair. It was held in the chapel, and the coroner was feeling the cold. It was his second inquest into the death of a miner that day and there were two more that afternoon.

He was experienced in dealing with mine fatalities, the previous year having supplied him with seventy-four – twenty-two of them the result of a single disaster.

Such fatalities were no longer of interest to even the most morbid, and the newspapers gave them only a passing paragraph. This being so, the coroner wasted no time in accepting the facts as they were presented to him. He recorded a verdict that one Budge Pearn, miner, had met with an accidental death whilst leaving his place of employment, namely the Wheal Sharptor. Then, there being no local gentry in the mining village of Henwood, the coroner immediately set off in his trap to lunch at Linkinhorne vicarage.

Budge Pearn was buried that same afternoon, on a day as grey as the occasion. The persistent easterly wind helped tears flow the more easily for the women and made casual mourners restless to return to their firesides.

But Wrightwick Roberts was not a preacher to cut corners at a man's funeral. Budge Pearn went on his way to the hereafter with as good a reference as any man could receive. In the same sermon the preacher damned a mine that allowed a man to fall to his death and then failed to send a representative to his funeral.

In all fairness, Theophilus Strike *had* delegated someone. His senior mine captain had been told to go, but Herman Schmidt could think of better ways to spend an afternoon than standing on a windswept hillside, listening to a sermon in a language he barely understood in praise of one of the workers he regarded as little better than animals.

Instead, Schmidt was shut inside his house in the nearby town of Liskeard. He was already in a state of alcoholic stupor. He was in the habit of spending much less time at the Wheal Sharptor than Theophilus Strike was aware of, but Schmidt's knowledge of mining had been learned with a Germanic thoroughness.

There was little that any man in Cornwall could tell him about copper-mining.

Once a week Herman Schmidt carried out a full inspection of the mine, and it was a day the miners had come to dread. If he found the slightest thing that was not to his liking, there would be miners seeking work elsewhere on the following day. There was very little that escaped his attention and, if his hangover was worse than usual, he was quite capable of inventing a reason for dismissing a man.

From his weekly visit the mine captain was able to compile his reports and direct the operations that kept Wheal Sharptor a profit-making mine.

Captain Herman Schmidt was a brilliant mine captain. He was also a foreigner, an atheist and a drunkard. The miners of Wheal Sharptor hated him.

Chapter Two

'Very well done, Josh. Your reading is greatly improved. Keep it up.'

Josh looked down in embarrassed pleasure at the book from which he had just finished reading. The Reverend William Thackeray was not given to handing out unearned praise to his pupils. They were all, like Josh, the sons of miners – each of them eager to learn, grateful for the opportunity of receiving the education denied to their fathers.

Starting these classes had been one of the first tasks William Thackeray had set himself upon taking up his appointment at St Cleer. A slight, stooped, consumptive-looking figure, he had accepted many years before that he was no physical match for his fellow-men. So he had chosen words as weapons to fight his way through life. Then he had discovered the Lord and recognised in him an unending source of ammunition. Sent to Cornwall, he saw the abject poverty so many miners lived in, the appalling rigours of work below ground. It was inevitable that he should become a social reformer. With his power of oratory he quickly earned the enmity of the mine-owners and 'adventurers' – those who held shares in the mines. He cared little for any of them. His sermons drew men to the chapel. Once inside, William Thackeray made sure that some of the Lord's teachings got through to them. He had also followed the fortunes of the 'Chartists' with considerable interest. Preacher Thackeray advocated the formation of a 'union' of miners in Cornwall to pursue the same quarry – the betterment of the working miner.

He spoke to Josh again. 'Yes, young man, you have it in you to become as educated as anyone in these parts.'

He suddenly stopped and jabbed a long sensitive finger at the air an inch from Josh's nose. 'But that is only the beginning. The important thing is *what* are you going to do with that education?'

The question and the finger took Josh by surprise. 'I don't know, sir – but I'm not going to be a miner.'

The menacing finger was lowered. 'I am pleased to hear *that*.' The preacher glowered around the room. 'How about the rest of you?'

He began pacing the width of the room in front of the class with short jerky steps. 'You are all the sons of enlightened men. Miners who started their life without the benefit of any education whatsoever, but who are determined their sons will be better equipped to go out and earn their livings. You will not have to go underground to support a family simply because you are unable to do anything else. Never forget that you owe it to your fathers to make something of your lives. You owe it to *me*. To *yourselves*. And you owe it to *God*! Never forget to thank him for giving you a preacher who is also a teacher. But the best way for you to show your gratitude is to take full advantage of your education.'

He stopped in front of Josh once more. 'Now, I will ask you once again. What will you do when your education is completed?'

'Well . . . I think I would like to be an engineer.'

William Thackeray's eyebrows rose an inch. 'An admirable ambition. Does any other boy know what he would like to be?'

The hands rose hesitantly and sporadically.

'H'm! We seem beset by uncertainty.'

He thumped the table in front of Josh with his fist, making him jump again. 'But to become anything worth while in this world you must *work* and *work* and *work*!' The words were emphasised with his fist, and at each thump Josh blinked involuntarily.

William Thackeray's eyes were aglow with the fires of enthusiasm. 'If a half – no, only a quarter – of those who raised their hands became teachers and educated the sons of working men, I would fall on my knees and thank the Lord for bringing success to my mission.'

He looked around the room at the tousle-headed ragged boys, and the fire dulled. 'But, for all my teaching, I have no doubt most of you will waste your knowledge – using it to count barrow-loads of ore, or perhaps to work out the percentage of copper to the ton.'

He shrugged. 'At least you won't be cheated by a dishonest mine captain. All right, boys, school is over for today. I will see you at the same time tomorrow – Wait!'

The sudden noise died away again as the twenty-two boys in the class closed their eyes and stood with bowed heads.

'Lord, may the wisdom and learning I have attempted to instil into these boys be used always to the glory of Thy name and the benefit of those who, though created in Thy image, have dug deep into the good earth Thou gavest to us and moved closer to the Devil and his evil ways. For the sake of Jesus Christ, our Lord. Amen.'

There was a mumbled 'Amen' in answer to his prayer, the briefest of pauses, and then a flood of boys surged out through the door. Leaving William Thackeray alone in the room with his thoughts.

The track wandered aimlessly in the general direction of Sharptor, skirting the Caradon mines and dipping down to where the great shaft of the Wheal Phoenix yawned deep in the shadowed valley. Josh ignored the track and went straight across country. Avoiding the few walled fields, cleared of gorse and fern by forgotten generations of farmers, he toiled up on to the high lonely moor.

This was the place that Josh loved above all others. It was a vast landscape of sweeping emptiness, uncompromising in its seasonal moods. The stunted bushes, bowing to the east, were evidence of the prevailing winds of winter. Now the gorse was a tangle of yellow blossom. Here and there a lacework of streams left the turf soft and sponge-like underfoot. The whole tangled moor was criss-crossed with the tracks of centuries of badgers and foxes. Above it all, blunt-winged buzzards circled remorselessly in search of their live prey.

That was how Josh saw the moor today. With the scattered houses, mines and creaking ore-wagons out of sight he could think, create his own future. He wondered what life was like away from the mining community, beyond the valley of the Tamar, further even than the dark highlands of Dartmoor dominating the horizon twenty miles to the east.

He had told Preacher Thackeray he wanted to be an engineer. In truth, he knew little about mechanical things. He had looked at the engines in the Caradon and Phoenix mines and had been very impressed by their size and noise, and the power of the hissing steam, but he knew nothing of their workings. He decided he would find out.

Josh was on the high moor proper now. He skirted the roofless ivy-clad engine-house and gaping shaft of a mine abandoned a few decades before owing to insurmountable drainage problems.

He paused to watch the aerobatics of a buzzard which had strayed into the territory of a pair of crows. The large black birds were working as a fighting team. While one harassed from close range, the second bird climbed high above them, dropping into the battle area with wings closed in a vain attempt to decide the issue. The buzzard, sure in the knowledge of its superiority, continued unhurriedly on its course. Only occasionally did it take a positive stand. It would roll on to its back to meet the threat from above with outstretched talons, capable of bringing the battle to an end with one ripping blow. Then it was the turn of the crows to take hurried evasive action. Courageous they were, but they knew the limited extent of their harassment.

Josh liked to see the buzzards. They enjoyed complete freedom of the great moor. A freedom he would dearly love to possess. But, except for the long summer evenings and occasions like this, there was little time for exploring. In the morning he worked at the mine, dressing the ore at the surface with the women and other children. In the afternoon he attended the school at St Cleer. Most evenings he would help with the household chores before settling down to more schoolwork, often working by the light of a tallow candle until bedtime.

The evening schooling had become more difficult since Jenny and the baby had come to live with them. He found the noise from the kitchen distracting wherever he was in the house. Usually he worked in the bedroom he now shared with his parents, but baby Gwen was put down to sleep in the next room. She had begun to cut her first teeth and cried a lot.

Josh could see the small group of cottages well down on the slope from the moor. Another ten minutes and he would be home. But first he had to pass the Tragos' home – and Morwen Trago was sitting astride a long rounded boulder outside the entrance.

The Tragos were a strange brooding family and their house very much in keeping with their image. It was comprised of a number of gigantic slabs of rock. Those for the front and side walls were laid upon their edge with three more balancing on them to form the roof. The rear of the roof, together with the back wall, was buried in the hillside. The doorway was a crevice between the rocks with an odd-shaped wooden frame surrounding a door seven feet high and designed to fit the space. Here lived Moses Trago and his wife and children, together with his unmarried brother John.

The 'house' had not been built by the Tragos. Some of the older inhabitants of Henwood could remember when Moses Trago's father had moved into it. Superstition had it that it had once been a burial-place for the 'old men' whose shallow diggings scarred the moor.

Morwen Trago was the eldest son of Moses. He was almost two years older than Josh. Sliding from the rock, he took up a position straddle-legged across the path in front of him.

Josh approached him warily, stopping when he was still ten feet away.

'What do you want, Morwen?'

'What do I want?' The bigger boy feigned surprise. 'I live here, Josh Retallick. There's nothing that says I can't stand outside my own home if I want to.'

'Then you'll let me past?' Josh's face felt taut.

'Of course I will – once I've seen what you have in that bag.'

Josh's grip on his canvas schoolbag tightened. 'It's only school-books. They belong to Preacher Thackeray.'

'Do they, now? A preacher's books! Preachers ought to look after their own books. Not use them to stop other folks from working. Religious nonsense, that's what books are.'

Morwen was echoing his father's words. They had been accompanied by a stinging cuff on his ear when Morwen had asked him whether he could take reading lessons with Preacher Thackeray. That had been when Morwen was working on the surface with Josh and some of the other boys. Since then Moses had found work underground for his son. Morwen was on the morning shift at the Wheal Phoenix where Moses and John now worked.

'Books are only nonsense if you can't read them,' Josh retorted. 'And they are staying in my bag.'

'We'll see about that . . .'

Morwen began to advance towards Josh along the path. He stopped when Josh stooped and picked up a broken piece of granite weighing about two pounds.

Morwen Trago looked at Josh standing with the piece of stone in his hand and weighed up his chances of tackling him. Just when it seemed he might ignore the odds, a barefoot girl with tangled long black hair and wearing a tattered dress ran between them.

'Stop it, you two! Josh, put down that stone.'

'No. Not until I'm past Morwen.'

She turned to the other boy. 'Let him go, Morwen. You're older than he is. Ma wouldn't like it if I told her you were bullying.'

Miriam Trago was the same age as Josh, but her shrill young voice carried the air of authority that came with being her father's favourite.

'He won't stop me,' said Josh defiantly. 'If he tries, I'll hit him with this.' He raised the hand holding the stone.

Morwen Trago looked from his sister to Josh. With a scornful shrug of his shoulders, he said, 'Keep your books. Only cissies and preachers read books.' He turned away and strolled towards the rock house.

Josh dropped the stone to the ground and mumbled, 'Thank you, Miriam – though he wouldn't have stopped me.'

'I don't care about that. I didn't want to see Morwen's head split open. That's all.'

With a look almost as scornful as her brother's she too turned away and walked towards her home.

'That's not true, Miriam Trago.' Josh called after her. 'You stopped us from fighting because you thought I might get hurt. You can't help being a Trago. You just don't want people to think you're nice, that's all.'

Miriam swung round to face him and glared for perhaps five seconds. Then she bent down, took hold of the bottom of her ragged dress and raised her hands above her head.

She was wearing nothing beneath it.

Josh's face went scarlet. He turned and fled down the path with Miriam's derisive laughter chasing him most of the way. Miriam Trago was as wild and untamed as the moor itself.

Chapter Three

The wet cold days soon gave way to warmer ones as the spring advanced into summer. The seasons of the year made little difference to the miners. Below the ground it was hot and wet the whole year round. But it did mean that when they climbed to the top of the ladders at the end of a shift they sucked in warm air. Consequently fewer of them contracted pneumonia.

For Josh, the longer days meant he was able to spend more time on the moor. Far more than he had in previous years. He rarely came home from the chapel school by the same path and, as the evenings stretched out, so did his walks. He avoided the Trago home as much as possible, but would often see Miriam in the distance. If she were close enough to recognise him, she would wave. He ignored her greetings. Miriam had wandered the moors from her earliest days and knew the whole wild area better than any man, woman or child. She worked a full day shift with her mother on the grading-floor at the Wheal Phoenix, but her evenings were spent out on the moor. There she felt free – free from her home environment, and free from the disapproving looks of the women in the village, who frowned at her bare feet and her lack of meekness and modesty.

Although Josh and Miriam would occasionally see each

other on the moor, the next encounter between the Trago and Retallick families occurred at a more senior level. It was a brief and violent meeting.

The Sunday evening was warm and pleasant. Ben, Jesse and Josh, a few paces ahead of Tom Shovell, Jenny and baby Gwen, took a slow walk homewards from Henwood chapel. Along the way they occasionally paused to chat to other miners and their families who were also making the most of an opportunity to feel the sun on their faces.

At the edge of the village the Reverend Wrightwick Roberts caught up with them. His perspiration was as much the result of a fiery sermon as it was due to the weather.

Ben Retallick said as much.

'It could be, Ben. It could be!' The preacher mopped his face energetically. 'But it's the Lord's work. I can't put less into it than you put into digging out copper ore for Theophilus Strike.'

Ben smiled. 'From the look of the collection we are digging copper for the Lord too, Wrightwick. There was no silver there.'

'It's a poor community, Ben.' The preacher carefully folded his damp and lifeless handkerchief before tucking it away into a jacket pocket. 'There is precious little money left over when a family has been fed these days.'

'I'll agree with that.' Jesse was walking with Josh. 'Unless something is done soon a month's pay won't buy a bag of flour.'

The two men nodded their agreement. 'It's a bad law that prevents corn from entering the country then sends half our own corn elsewhere,' said Ben bitterly. 'Unless Parliament does something we'll see the troubles of twenty years ago with us again.'

'We don't need any troops in Cornwall,' said the preacher.

Josh, his imagination fired at the thought of seeing mounted and uniformed troops riding into the village, moved closer to hear their talk.

'Parliament's never been slow to send in troops against the Cornish, Ben. You must know that.'

'But we've got a young queen on the throne now. She won't want to start her reign by spilling the blood of her own people.'

'She's only a girl,' replied the preacher. 'She will do what her advisers tell her. But we'll need the Lord's help if ever troops are sent in. We've got a hundred thousand miners, and hotheads aplenty to rouse them. There are even some of the Lord's servants who use His house for such unholy work.'

He looked accusingly at Ben. 'By sending Josh to learn from Thackeray you give him support, Ben. Don't you worry that Josh might get mixed up in the politics of his teacher?'

Ben shrugged. 'Let Thackeray preach what he wishes to men. He teaches schooling to children. It's thanks to him that Josh is able to read the Bible to us on a Sunday evening.'

Wrightwick Roberts chose to make no reply.

They reached a steep part of the track and, taking baby Gwen from Jenny, Tom Shovell tucked the infant into the crook of one arm. He made light work of the gradient, despite the extra pounds that Gwen had put on in recent weeks. In sharp contrast, Jenny had wasted away since Budge's tragic death. She was thin to the point of frailness, and her skin had developed a translucent paleness that attracted attention wherever she went. She had been a pretty girl before. Grief had changed her into a woman possessed of an unusual haunting beauty.

When they arrived at the cottage, Ben, Jesse and Jenny went inside with the baby. Josh stayed outside with the preacher, who was talking to Tom Shovell.

They had not been there for many minutes when a bellow from the direction of the higher moor brought their conversation to an abrupt halt. They turned to see Kate Trago, the wife of Moses Trago, running wildly towards them. Her long hair streamed behind her and the left half of her dress was ripped to the waist, exposing a distended and emaciated breast flapping pendulously as she ran.

Fifty yards behind her Moses Trago lurched around a turn in the path, running unsteadily with a wide-legged gait.

Kate Trago stumbled and fell in front of the startled group.

As Wrightwick Roberts went to help her she heaved herself up from the ground. They saw that one eye was swollen with an ugly graze beneath it.

Taking the preacher's arm, she pulled him towards the house. She signalled the others to come with quick movements of her free hand.

'Hurry! Get into the house,' she pleaded. 'Moses is mad drunk. Get inside or he'll kill me – and you!'

The preacher freed his arm. 'Take her into the cottage and you go with them, Josh.'

'Let me try to reason with him,' said Tom Shovell. 'I know him, Wrightwick. He'll listen to me.'

'He won't listen to anyone in his state. Get everyone inside. Quickly!'

The door banged at his back as the preacher turned to face the drunken miner.

Moses slipped on the same patch of mud as his wife, but steadied himself palm downwards on the path.

'Get out of my way. I want my wife.' Moses Trago's eyes were as unsteady as his voice.

'Go home and sleep it off, Moses.' The preacher's voice was pitched low and coaxing.

'I said I want my wife!'

'Leave her be. She's inside talking to Jesse Retallick.'

'I don't care who she's talking to. She's a lazy idle slut. No, she's worse than that. She's a thief. A thief!'

Moses lurched forward. He stopped so close that Wrightwick Roberts winced at the gin fumes the drunken miner belched into his face as he spoke.

'You know what she did? Do you want to know what that bloody woman did?'

Wrightwick Roberts avoided the thick dirty finger waving only inches from his nose.

'I'll tell you what she did.' He screwed his mouth up and blinked stupidly. 'I'll tell you what she did. She took money from my pocket. That's what she did. Took it when she thought I was asleep. What do you think of that, Preacher Wrightwick-bloody-Roberts?'

'I expect she had need of it.' The preacher's voice was calm and even, though Moses had thrust his face to within inches of his own. The sickly smell of the cheap alcohol made the teetotal Methodist preacher feel like retching.

'You expect she had need of it?' The miner's unshaven upper lip curled back in a sneer. 'I'll tell you what she has need of. I don't have to go to chapel to learn how to run my life. I'll do it my way. So will she!'

He lunged towards the door, but Wrightwick Roberts was too quick for him. He stooped under the other man's arm and, as Moses fumbled for the latch, put his shoulder beneath his armpit and heaved. Moses Trago took eight or nine uncontrolled backward paces on his heels before crashing to the ground.

Rolling over quickly he looked up at the preacher, sheer rage sobering him momentarily. 'I'll kill you for that!'

He came up from the ground with unexpected speed. Quick as he was, someone else was faster. The door behind the preacher was jerked open, and he was thrust aside as Ben Retallick took the headlong rush of Moses Trago with outstretched arms, closing them around the drunken miner as the two men came together. Finding his arms pinned to his sides, Moses Trago opened his mouth to roar. Ben Retallick's muscles strained and he cut off the sound.

Moses Trago was no stranger to fighting and he was not to be overwhelmed so easily. In an effort to break the other man's grip he staggered around until he tripped on a stone. Both men fell heavily to the ground.

Ben Retallick fell awkwardly, and his grip slackened for an instant. It was enough. Flinging his wide shoulders back, Moses Trago broke the encircling grip and scrambled to his feet.

Ben was still on his knees when Moses Trago's boot took him on the shoulder and knocked him rolling down again. The kick had been aimed at his head, but drink and exertion had taken their toll on the burly miner's faculties. It was fortunate for Ben. Had the viciously swung boot connected with its target he would not have risen again. Moses Trago moved quickly around him as he tried to rise, kicking him in the ribs, in the kidneys, aiming for his head. It was one of Moses Trago's wilder kicks that proved his undoing. It missed completely. Ben was quick enough to grasp the foot and with a twist and a heave he sent Moses Trago crashing to the ground once more.

Ben Retallick was on his feet in an instant. As his opponent began to rise he crashed a rock-hard fist against his temple. The miner fell face first on to the earth. It must have been a purely reflex stupidity which brought him half on to his feet again. This time Ben's punch swung up into Moses Trago's face. The force of it straightened him up before he dropped backwards to lie prostrate with arms flung wide.

'Now there's as fine a punch as ever I have seen,' said Wrightwick Roberts in admiration. 'It would have felled a bullock.'

'It needed to,' replied Ben, rubbing his knuckles. 'Moses Trago is a powerful man. But a man always fights harder on his own ground.'

He kneeled down beside the unconscious man. 'Bring some water, Wrightwick. It worries me to see him lying here like this.' He put an ear against Moses Trago's chest and looked relieved. 'His heart is going like a stamp-hammer. There's little enough wrong with him.'

Jesse came out of the house with a bucket of water and unceremoniously flung the contents over Moses Trago's face.

'There's no need for you to stand around here as though Ben had done something wonderful, Wrightwick Roberts,' she said. 'So you can take that unholy grin from your face. I don't approve of a man fighting in front of his family. On a Sunday too.'

Wrightwick Roberts' jaw dropped. 'He did it to protect his family,' he protested. 'If Moses had got into the house he would have smashed it up; he was fighting drunk. You should be thankful that the Lord was on Ben's side!'

'Ben has never needed anyone on his side when it came to fighting,' Jesse said, her jaw thrust out. 'You should remember that, Wrightwick. You knew him before we were married.'

This was all new to Josh. He looked at his father with new admiration.

'Anyway, a man protecting his family is one thing. There's no need for him to look as though he enjoyed it.'

Her words were harder than the look she gave her husband before she went back inside the house.

It took three more bucketfuls of water to make Moses Trago stir. It was like watching a young child wakening from a deep sleep. He twitched, shuddered, rolled his head from side to side and then slowly sat up. The last movement was almost too much for his abused body. It sent a protest via every nerve to the brain. Moses Trago clutched his head between his hands and let out a loud groan.

'You may think you are suffering now, Moses. One day you'll have to answer to the Lord for your misdeeds. This drubbing will be as a gentle tap on the hand compared with what will happen to you on that day.'

Moses Trago's reply was an expressive oath accompanied by another groan.

'If I hear any more of that sort of language from you, I'll forget I am a preacher and do the Lord's work for him . . .'

Moses Trago got unsteadily to his feet. He stood swaying and glaring at Wrightwick Roberts, Ben Retallick and Tom Shovell.

'I won't be forgetting this day in a hurry,' he said. 'You'll live to regret it, Ben Retallick. So will you, Preacher.' He raised his voice to be sure it carried into the house. 'You can tell that woman of mine if she dares show her face inside my home I'll break every bone in her body.'

He turned and staggered away along the path towards the high moor. Only Josh saw a small tangle-haired figure in a torn dress slip from the bushes on the far side of the house and vanish into the ferns on the hillside.

'You'd best be careful of him, Ben,' said the shift captain. 'Moses is a dangerous man. He cares little for the standards other men set for themselves.'

'Tom is right. You keep clear of him or he'll do you a mischief.'

Kate Trago had come from the house peering painfully through her one good eye. The swelling about the other had caused it to close completely.

'I'll not upset Moses. Neither will I go out of my way to avoid him,' declared Ben. 'He'll be all right when he sobers up. We were boys together, Kate. I know Moses Trago as well as any man.'

'No!' Kate Trago shook her head. 'Moses is not the man you once knew, Ben Retallick. He's changed. In the last few years he's changed. Oh, I know he's always been a rough man with his fighting and drinking; but there's more to it now. He's turned sour inside. He believes he's owed something. He'll never get it because he doesn't even know what it is! It's money and yet more than money. He envies you more than anyone else, Ben. You've got all the things that Moses hasn't. Respect. A house. You're part of something that we don't belong to. I know it must sound stupid but he really hates you for being something that he's scorned to be all his life.'

She stopped talking abruptly and there was an uncomfortable silence.

'I've said far too much. Take heed of it and I'll have thanked you for helping me. I must go now.'

'You can't go yet!' Ben Retallick protested. 'Moses is still raving drunk. He'll kill you if you go near him.'

'He won't.' She shook her head. 'He'll go home, stumble on to his bed just as he is and sleep until morn. Then he'll get up and go to the mine. That's all there is in his life. Drink, sleep and work. But he won't hurt me anymore.' There was a gleam of a tear in her eye. 'Besides, I'm his wife. I've got to go back to him.'

She started off up the path, pausing to call back, 'Thank you again for your help. Thank you.'

She went on her way without looking back. In spite of her cheap and well-patched clothes there was something about her walk that was too proud for one in her station of life. Only Jesse Retallick might guess at her innermost thoughts and she could have wept for her.

*   *   *

Three days after the fight Miriam Trago waylaid Josh on his way home from the St Cleer chapel school. She must have been watching for him from the top of the tor to have known which way he would come. She stepped out from the tall fern into his path when he was on the high flat moor, hidden from the cottages on the other side of the tor.

'Hello.' It was a casual greeting. As though the meeting were completely accidental.

'Hello.' Josh's reply was more cautious. His small feud with Morwen Trago had exploded into something far more serious and violent now their fathers were involved, and he knew Miriam had seen the fight.

But Miriam had not sought him out to extend the feud.

'Have you been to the chapel school?' It was an unnecessary question. They both knew it.

'Yes.'

'What do you learn there?'

'Oh, lots of things. Reading. Writing. Sums.'

'Do you like it?'

He nodded his head. 'Yes, I do.'

'I wish I could learn to read and write. I'd like to know how to write my name.'

'Why don't you ask your dad to let you go?'

She shook her head. 'I did ask him. He says there's no need of such fancy ways for girls. They should get out and make money before they get married. Not waste time on such things. That's what he said.'

The mention of Moses Trago brought about a long uncomfortable silence.

'He's not all bad, you know.'

'Who?' Josh was anxious to avert a clash with this naturally wild girl who was behaving in an uncharacteristically polite and quiet manner.

'My dad. He's not all bad.'

As she spoke she looked down at her dirty toes. Her bare feet had long been a subject of disapproval among the villagers of Henwood. They boasted that, no matter how poor they might be, there was not a child in the village who did not have boots for its feet. Had they voiced their disapproval to Miriam she would have been genuinely astounded. She enjoyed feeling the springy turf of the moor beneath her feet.

'He drinks – but so do lots of miners. And he doesn't hit me very often. When he does he's always sorry afterwards.'

Josh said nothing.

'He works hard. Even your dad says he's a good worker.'

'So he might be. But he gets very quarrelsome when he's been drinking.'

Her head came up and her dark eyes clashed with his. He thought he ought to have maintained his silence. Then the challenge subsided.

'That's his way. He doesn't mean anything by it.' She touched the corner of one of the books that protruded from his canvas shoulder-bag. 'What's this?'

'It's a writing book.'

'Writing? Show me. I want to see what your writing looks like.'

Josh hesitated. Despite Miriam's excitement and apparent interest he was wary of her. She could be trying to trick him into something.

'Please!'

'All right.' He extracted the book from the flat canvas bag with exaggerated carefulness. Flicking through the pages, he opened it to disclose a handwriting that was small and not too neat.

The untidiness meant nothing to Miriam; she was very impressed. 'There's such a lot of it. Did you write it all?'

He nodded, absurdly pleased at her praise. 'There's lots more. Almost a whole book full.'

She extended a long brown finger and gently touched the written words with the tip of it.

'What does it say?'

He turned the book up the other way and began to read: '"He said unto him, the third time, Simon, son of Joseph, lovest thou me? He saith unto him, Yea Lord . . ."' Josh read two pages before closing the book.

'That was from the Bible,' he said, embarrassed by the adulation on her face.

'It was beautiful!' Her expression was full of wonder. For the first time he noticed that she had very dark eyes, fringed by the longest eyelashes he had ever seen.

'I wish I could read and write.' There was no doubting her sincerity now.

'It wouldn't take you long if you took lessons.'

'Could you write my name – Miriam?'

Josh nodded. 'Yes.'

'Then write it for me. Please, Josh! Write it for me.'

'All right.'

He rummaged in his bag and came out with a scrap of paper. 'I need something to rest this on.'

'I know just the thing; it's a flat rock.' She took his hand and, full of excitement, pulled him after her as she left the path and plunged into the ferns and bushes.

'It's a secret place. Nobody but me knows of it.' Miriam took him uphill, through patches of undergrowth where tall ferns touched Josh's face and brushed coarse fingers through his hair while tangled brambles threatened to trip him.

When they reached an apparently impenetrable barrier of gorse, she released his hand and dropping to her knees signalled for him to do the same.

'Follow me.'

She disappeared into a low gorse-tunnel. As he followed her a carpet of blunt gorse-needles attacked his knees and the palms of his hands.

The dark tunnel twisted and turned for twenty feet before he was out into sparkling sunlight once more. Thick gorse was all around, but here in its centre was a large flat rock. Two others leaning against one another formed a small triangular cave. When he stood up he could see the whole of the Phoenix valley through the thin top branches of one of the gorse-bushes, but it would have been impossible for anyone to see the two children from below.

'Here, rest the book on this rock.'

She sat cross-legged on the granite, her skirt tucked between her legs, the thin thighs and calloused knees as brown as a gipsy's.

Josh unslung his bag and taking out a book placed it on the rock. Then he smoothed out a piece of paper and laid it upon the book. Taking out a thick-leaded pencil, he knelt down beside the rock. Carefully and elaborately he wrote the letters, calling them aloud as he went.

'M-I-R-I-A-M. Miriam. There you are!'

She had been watching him, hardly daring to breathe. Now she took the paper from him as though it was a magic formula for all the riches of the world.

'This really is my name? It says "Miriam"?'

'Yes.' Her reaction was most satisfactory.

'Can I keep it?'

'Of course you can. It's of no use to me.'

'This is the first time I've ever seen my name written down. I'll keep it for ever and always.'

He thought it was a small enough thing to give her so much pleasure.

'I'll teach you to write it for yourself if you like.'

Her reaction alarmed him. For a second it looked as though she might throw her arms about him. Instead, she dropped down on to the rock beside him and gripped his arm.

'Oh please!'

He first had to show her how to hold the pencil; then how to form the letters, with his hand clenched over hers. Her hair was very close to his face and it smelled like the fern.

It took a long time and the final result was far from satisfactory. Although Josh insisted that it was fine, Miriam knew better.

'No,' she said, clutching the piece of paper with Josh's effort on it. 'This is much better. But I'll do it properly one day, if you'll learn me.'

'I don't know,' said Josh uncertainly, not wishing to sacrifice all the long lone summer evenings on the moor he had planned.

'You can use this place for your own,' she persisted. 'And, if you'll try to learn me, I'll show you a badger's set.'

Josh wavered. Sensing the weak spot in his determination, Miriam prised it wide open. 'The badgers have babies.'

Josh's resolution crumbled and blew to the wind.

'All right. I'll teach you reading and writing. But I want to see the badgers first.'

'Come on, then.' Miriam was elated. For months she had watched Josh returning from St Cleer. Her whole being ached with wanting to learn the things he was learning. Her father would not allow her to attend the chapel school, so she had decided her only chance to achieve an education lay with Josh. She had been prepared to offer him anything in return for lessons. He had settled for a sight of the badgers. After the big build-up to this moment in her own mind it had come as an anti-climax. But she was still very happy.

Josh followed her through the gorse-tunnel once more and they headed across the moor, away from the Phoenix valley. Miriam took him on a direct course, deviating only once in order to avoid a patch of bog. He would not even have seen it but for her warning.

'If you got in there, you'd never get out,' she said. 'I saw a sheep caught there last winter. It was too far in for me to help it. In five minutes it sank out of sight. It was horrible!'

Josh shuddered. He took careful note of the position of the bog for his future ramblings. A little further on they dropped into a deep gully, about forty feet wide with a weed-covered stagnant pool at the far end of it. This, Miriam said, had once been a gold mine. Worked by the 'old men'.

'We must go quietly now.' She laid a hand on his arm and Josh edged forward, holding his breath, expecting to be confronted by a badger at any moment. He was apprehensive of the outcome as he had never seen a badger. His scant knowledge of them came from the tales of other boys who most probably had never seen the animal for themselves. In their tales the badger was as strong as a ram, as bold as a fox, and armed with claws the length of a boy's fingers.

'Here, sit down by me and don't say a word,' Miriam whispered as she pulled him down beside her on to a rough grassy bank with the level of the moor overhanging twelve feet above them.

Josh did as he was told and furtively looked about him. He could see nothing.

'Where are they?' It came out as a hoarse whisper.

'Shh! Their set is over there.' She pointed to a spot twelve feet away, where a sprawling thorn-bush grew from a substantial mound of earth. 'See the paths?'

Now she had drawn his attention to them, Josh was able to see three – no, four – well-worn tracks leading into the bush from four different directions. They were so well defined they could have been made by the feet of men.

'But where are the badgers?' His whisper was as low as hers had been.

'They'll be out soon. Usually they don't come out until after dark but lately they have been bringing their babies up for a while at this time of day.'

They sat in silence for a long time, but it was difficult to become too impatient. The evening was warm and peaceful, the drone of a bumble bee and the far high song of a skylark the only sounds that could be heard from the gully. Josh even found it pleasant being seated arm to arm with Miriam. There was a nice smell to her. It was not only her hair. The whole of her carried the scent of fern and heather. It was as though, while still retaining her human status, she had become a part of the moor on which she spent so much of her time.

He gave her a sidelong glance. Perfectly relaxed, she sat with her eyes half-closed, the long dark lashes almost meeting. Her thick black hair fell around her shoulders, as wild and unruly as a blackberry thicket.

Her eyes opened suddenly and she clutched at him. 'There! Did you hear that?'

'No. What am I listening for?'

'That thumping noise below us. In the ground. It's the badgers; they always do that. There, now!'

He heard it this time. It was like the warning thump of a rabbit far below them, deep in the earth.

'That means they'll be coming out now.'

Josh stared at the bush intently, not daring to blink until the whole bush swam before his glazed eyes. Then Miriam's grip on his arm tightened painfully and his eyes focused again. From the hole in the bush a long head, clearly marked with wide black and white stripes, came into view. The badger raised its nose and sniffed first to the west, then to the north and finally to the south. Satisfied so far, the animal advanced a foot from the bush, bringing its long-haired grey-brown body into view. The badger peered around cautiously but not timidly. It was larger than Josh had imagined. As large as a medium-sized dog. Suddenly, as quickly as it had appeared, the badger turned and was gone.

'It saw us!' exclaimed Josh, bitterly disappointed.

'Shh!' Miriam's fingernails dug into his arm again. 'It didn't see you. I don't think badgers can see anything very well. It always does this to make sure it's quite safe for the babies. They'll all come out now.'

She had hardly finished speaking when the badgers did exactly as she had said. There was no hesitation this time. The male badger lumbered straight out from the bush closely followed by two cubs. The female, rather more cautious, brought up the rear.

Josh held his breath until he thought he would burst. The badgers moved along their chosen path for about twenty feet before the male paused for a prolonged scratch. The two cubs took this opportunity to explore a nearby forest of ferns. It was Josh's efforts to follow their progress that brought the badger-watching to an abrupt end. He felt the stone turn beneath his hand as he leaned sideways. He grabbed at it but was not quick enough to save it. The stone bounced down the small embankment. With a startled squeak the female badger sent the cubs in headlong flight back to the set. She was close behind them. The male quartered the ground after them, emitting grunts and squeaks. He paused when level with Josh and raised a reproachful nose in his direction. Then he too was gone.

'I'm sorry,' said Josh sheepishly.

Miriam jumped down to the floor of the gully. 'It doesn't

matter. I've seen them lots of times before.' She looked at him suspiciously. 'But I showed them to you like I promised. You'll still learn me to read and write?'

Josh nodded. 'Yes. You meet me on my way home from the chapel and I'll give you a lesson. Not every day, though.'

'How many days, then – four?'

Josh shook his head. 'No. Two perhaps.'

They finally settled for three days a week and Josh shrugged the strap of his bag more firmly on to his shoulder. 'Are you coming?'

Miriam shook her head. 'Not yet. There's a full moon tonight and I want to watch it from up there.' She pointed to where the great rock mass that was Sharp Tor rose stark and grey above the moor. 'Why don't you stop and see it with me?'

'No, I must get back for supper. Mum will be wondering where I am.'

'Mummy's boy!' Her voice mocked him as he scrambled from the gully and set off home across the moor.

'Josh! Josh Retallick!'

He turned to see her standing wide-legged on an uneven rock above the gully.

'If you come up Sharp Tor with me I'll let you kiss me.'

'I don't want to.' He turned his back on her and walked away.

'You will one day, Josh Retallick. You will one day!'

Josh need not have been in a hurry to get home. Nobody had noticed how late he was. Besides, the family knew he was in the habit of deviating from the direct route. But this evening they hardly acknowledged his arrival. The house was full of people. Among them were most of the miners from Ben Retallick's shift, including Tom Shovell. Also there, and looking uncomfortably out of place inside a house, was Nehemeziah Lancellis, the mine hostler who had no home of his own and shared the stables of the horses he tended. Small of stature, he had ridden horses for gentry in his younger days. Until a fall left him with an ill-mended broken leg.

Wrightwick Roberts was also in the room. It was his booming voice that met Josh's ears when he went in.

'I am not happy about this trip into Bodmin. To go to see a
public hanging is shameful enough. With it taking place on a
fair-day there will be all manner of sinful things to entice our
young men.'

'But it's a holiday,' argued one of the men. 'And it's a double
hanging of miners. Men from the Kit Mill mine. Some of us
know them, have worked with them.'

'There's nothing to be proud of in knowing convicted murderers,' retorted Wrightwick Roberts. 'There are more than
enough Christians you *don't* know!'

'It's too late to stop it now,' said Ben Retallick quietly.
'Theophilus Strike has agreed to loan us the horses and
ore-carts for the day. Even though Captain Schmidt was
against it.'

Nehemeziah Lancellis nodded vigorously.

'Best accept it, Wrightwick,' went on Ben. 'See it as a chance
to say a prayer for the souls of the two men who are to be
hanged.'

'I can do that in any one of my chapels,' snorted the
preacher. 'If every man here came to chapel instead of Bodmin,
we'd pray the both of them straight into heaven.'

'They'll make it, even without our prayers,' said Jesse
Retallick from the kitchen doorway. 'From what I hear, others
were more to blame than them for the killing. A militiaman,
wasn't it?'

There was a growl of assent from many of the miners.

'There can be little excuse for killing a man, Jesse,' said
Wrightwick Roberts. 'A man's life is sacred.'

'And so is a man's family!' Jesse Retallick retorted, her face
flushed with emotion and hands planted firmly on her hips.
'Did the adventurers worry about that? Didn't they lock the
men out? Stopped them from working, then wouldn't give
them the money they were due? It's not surprising the miners
got angry. But even then the adventurers wouldn't stand up
to them like men. They called in the militia to do their dirty
work for them.'

'These are things you don't understand, Jesse,' said Wright-wick Roberts, and Ben Retallick looked up at the ceiling, waiting for the explosion he knew the preacher's words would provoke. 'The men wanted a charter. They spoke of uniting all the miners in the district. It's dangerous talk, Jesse. Such things are bound to lead to trouble.'

'I may not understand about charters and uniting the miners, Wrightwick Roberts. I do know how a man would feel if he saw his family starving, knowing the adventurers' store was full of food and them owing him money. I wouldn't give a snuffed candle-flame for the chances of any man who tried to stop him. There isn't a miner here who wouldn't do the same. That includes my Ben.'

The murmur of agreement grew louder, and Jesse raised her voice to say, 'You be there to lead the prayers for their souls, Wrightwick Roberts, or I'll shame you by doing it for you.'

Red-faced, with eyes flashing angrily, Jesse Retallick turned her back on the crowded room. Josh slipped into the kitchen before she slammed the door shut.

'I could have told you it wasn't wise to tell Jesse she "didn't understand". Not when she feels so strong about something,' chuckled Ben Retallick. The preacher ran a handkerchief around the inside of his collar, and conversation in the room got under way again.

'Better an honest direct woman than one who hides her thoughts and practises slyness,' said the preacher. 'It says so in the good book.'

He put his handkerchief away and held up a big hand for silence. 'All right, men. Now we've decided to go to Bodmin . . .' – he paused until the spontaneous laughter died away – '. . . we'll get down to details. Nehemeziah, how many wagons will we have? You've done the trip by wagon before, haven't you? How long will it take?'

Nehemeziah was not used to being at the centre of a discussion, far less being called upon to speak, but he did his best.

'Ah! Well, now. There's Bessie and Flower can take the oldest ore wagon. Tinker and Satan – begging your pardon, Preacher.

That's the name of the horse. He's called that 'cos of an evil temper. I didn't name him, o'course. Called that when I bought him from Liskeard market, he was.'

Satisfied that he had made his point, Nehemeziah Lancellis continued with the list of horses and the wagons they would pull. It was an impressive tally. The Wheal Sharptor had more than forty prime horses and half that number of wagons, ranging from the great ore wagons usually pulled by a team of six to the small governess-cart in which Herman Schmidt was riding to the execution.

The talking dragged on until late in the evening. Josh had his supper in the kitchen with Jenny and his mother, who was still smouldering after her outburst.

'Do you really think a union is a good thing, Mum?' asked Josh between mouthfuls.

'If it will force the adventurers to treat a miner as a man – then, yes, it's a good thing.'

'That's what Preacher Thackeray says. He told us that man is made in God's image and so we are all equal.'

'Equal? One man kills himself in a hole in the ground to make money while another man sits in a big house thinking up ways to spend it. That's being equal?'

There was a sudden outburst of noise from the next room and Jesse Retallick said, 'Listen to them! You'd think we were going off for a month instead of a day. It's always the same with men. All they've got to do is hitch up the horses and take us to Bodmin, then bring us back in the evening. They'll spend hours talking and arguing about it when they already know what has to be done.'

'Have you been to Bodmin before?' asked Jenny.

'Oh yes!' replied Jesse Retallick. 'This will be the fourth time.'

'What is it like?'

'Well . . . it's hard to describe. Lots of houses. Streets full of carts and carriages. Drunkenness. More people than we'd see hereabouts in a lifetime. Then there's the prison. A huge, ugly, grey place – enough to give you the shivers to look at it. I always think of the poor wretches kept inside for years.

It must be awful for them. But why don't you come and see for yourself?'

Jenny shook her head. 'I don't want to go to see two poor men die. No, me and Gwen will stay here and enjoy the sunshine. It will be nice and quiet with everyone else away. There'll hardly be one person left in Henwood village.'

'No, all those who can walk will be in Bodmin. Even Mary Crabbe – tho' I would have thought she'd seen enough dead men.'

'How about the Tragos?' Jenny asked.

'Miriam and Morwen are going,' replied Josh without thinking. 'But Moses Trago has some business to attend to.' He was repeating what Miriam had told him during one of her lessons on the moor.

'His business will be with the innkeeper,' retorted his mother. 'But how is it you know so much about the doings of the Trago family?'

'I expect it's that Miriam,' teased Jenny as she saw the colour creep up into his face. 'A pretty little maid for all that she's a bit wild.'

'You keep away from that family,' warned Jesse Retallick. 'They'll bring nothing but trouble. Every one of them.'

Another upsurge of sound from the next room indicated that the meeting was breaking up. Taking advantage of the distraction, Josh murmured his 'Good night' and made his way upstairs to bed.

Chapter Four

The day of the execution dawned bright and clear. The sun rose on the wagons loaded with miners and their families, being pulled by the toiling horses up the steep track from the Sharptor mine. There was an air of subdued excitement among the passengers. It was rare indeed for them to get together in this way for a social outing. The chapel-goers were used to praying together, the drinkers often found themselves in each other's company in one or other of the inns in nearby villages, but no one could remember them all going out on such a jaunt as this.

Even today there was a dividing-line between them. The chapel folk had possession of the front half of the convoy, and the standard deteriorated towards the rear, the last two wagons being filled with the younger miners, among whom bottles of gin were already being passed. Such behaviour did not pass unnoticed. The bonneted women in the leading wagons tuttutted disapprovingly, and old Nehemeziah Lancellis cursed the fact that he was in charge of the very first wagon. He would make certain he brought up the rear on the way home.

Most of the older children were riding in two wagons. Josh found himself sitting close to Miriam and her brother Morwen. But this was a different Miriam to the one he met on the moor.

True, she wore no shoes on her feet, but her hair had been brushed back tidily and the dress she had on was made from new calico. But it was her manner that Josh found so strange. He had said, 'Hello,' to her when he climbed aboard the wagon and she had scarcely answered. Morwen scowled deeply and succeeded in looking very like his father.

Miriam stayed quiet when the other children were talking and singing. They swayed together in gleeful exaggeration whenever the driver got a trot from his heavy horses on the rutted and pot-holed track.

Halfway to the Assize town the wagons passed a tin mine which was still operating, although it was a county holiday. There was much catcalling and ribaldry from the rear wagons, especially when they saw the women and girls at the shaft-head sorting the tin ore.

'You'll never find out what you're seeking there, m'dear,' shouted one wag. 'Come over here and I'll let you share what copper-mining's given to me.'

'I'll show 'ee what tin'll do for thee,' shouted the girl and, as the young miners whooped with laughter, she picked up a piece of rock the size of her fist and threw it hard and high. Her aim was good. As it plummeted down into the crowded wagon there was a great commotion. Some of the young men were pushed over the side by the efforts of those within to escape the missile.

The women laughed and cackled. The laughter changed to shrieks of simulated terror when a Sharptor lad shouted, 'Come on. We'll show these tinner-girls what a real man is.' The young men leaped from the wagons and began chasing the fleeing girls and women.

It was unfortunate that half the underground shift of tinminers were still in the boiler-house, changing their clothes before going below. As the Sharptor lads passed the engine-house the tinners spilled out amongst them. In the free-for-all that followed most of the young men from the other wagons jumped down to assist the hard-pressed Sharptor miners.

Morwen Trago was among them. When Josh tried to follow he was deliberately tripped – he suspected it was by Miriam

– then sat upon, his arms and legs pinned to the floor of the wagon.

'Let me up! Get off! I'm suffocating!'

'Shut up!'

One of the village girls, a buxom seventeen-year-old, raised the edge of her skirt to look at his face. 'Better dust in your nose than a lump of tin in your teeth.'

Jesse Retallick called from the next wagon, and to Josh's eternal shame the well-proportioned girl shouted. 'It's all right, Mrs Retallick! I'm sitting on him. He'll learn more down there than some of they fools over there.'

Josh fumed impotently at the shrieks of laughter that went up from the women.

After a few seconds the edge of the skirt was lifted again. This time it was Miriam's face peering anxiously into his own. 'Are you all right really, Josh?'

'No!' he hissed between clenched teeth. 'She's caving – my – ribs – in.'

'Oh! So you're saying I'm overweight, then?' said the fat girl. She bounced up and down on him, making the breath rasp noisily from his throat. So concerned was Miriam that she pulled the big girl backwards by the shoulders. She fell with her feet waving in the air and her skirts tumbled about her wide hips.

The others pinning Josh down were dealt with equally effectively. As Josh struggled up, sucking the breath back into his lungs, Miriam helped him to the front of the wagon. She sat him down with his back against the high board beneath the grinning driver.

The fight was over at the pit-head by now and the copper-miners were jumping back into their wagons. Morwen took his place in the rear wagons with them.

With her brother gone Miriam was her usual self. Once she had made sure that Josh was all right she kept up a steady stream of chatter. The chagrined Josh said little in reply.

Soon the wagons began passing many people afoot, all of them heading for Bodmin town. There were couples and families, old and young, miners and ploughmen, shepherds and pig-farmers, cowmen and hostlers. Others, tinkers and musicians and the traders and pickpockets, were already there.

When someone called that Bodmin could be seen up ahead, Josh was as excited as Miriam. He knelt up beside her, looking between the straddled legs of the driver on his high seat.

Over the broad sweating flanks of the horses they saw the slate roofs and jumbled streets of Bodmin town.

The wagon swayed and jolted down off the dirt track and on to teeth-rattling cobbled streets. The shod hoofs of the blowing horses struck sparks from the stones as the wagoner held them back down the steep approach to the county town.

Now there were sights aplenty to be seen as the slanting rays of the morning sun woke a million window-panes. The streets were at times so narrow that the upstairs of the houses leaned towards each other as though sharing a secret. Here and there the streets opened out into squares where stalls and sideshows, tinkers' carts, and livestock of all descriptions tangled together. To one side of the town stood the gaunt grim walls of Bodmin Jail. But above all there were people. Thousands and thousands of people! They were everywhere. Like disturbed ants. And still they poured into the town.

All this Josh and Miriam saw all too briefly before a town constable, perspiring in tall dark hat and heavy blue uniform, waved the mine wagons off the road. They trundled down a lane that led them away from the town again until they turned into a churned-up field three-parts full of wagons.

The unfamiliar and overwhelming nearness of the town had overawed the mining people. They milled around in their groups talking unnecessarily and laughing loudly and nervously, all waiting for someone to take the initiative.

Once again it was the young men who showed the way. Whooping and shouting, they moved off in a rowdy bunch, eager to sample the delights of the town – delights which the Reverend Wrightwick Roberts feared would prove sinful. He watched them go with a sad heart.

'Now, Josh, what are you going to do? Will you come

with us?' Jesse Retallick broke away from a small party that included Ben, Wrightwick Roberts and Tom Shovell.

'No.' Josh was aware of the disapproving look his mother was giving to the barefooted Miriam, who was pretending to be too interested in the town to notice. 'I'll have a walk about the town and see what's going on.'

'Well, you mind you behave yourself and don't go getting into any mischief.'

Jesse looked at the girl again and sniffed. 'Miriam, have you got any money to spend?'

'Money? No. But I don't need any,' she hurriedly added as a purse appeared in Jesse Retallick's hand.

'Nonsense! Everyone needs money on a fair-day. Here's threepence for you. Josh, have you still got that shilling?'

He held it out towards here, grinning happily.

'Good. Don't lose it. Off you go now, you two. Enjoy yourselves and be back here at six o'clock.'

Miriam transferred her astonished gaze from Mrs Retallick to the copper coins in her hand. 'She gave me money! Your mother gave me some money!'

'Don't sound so surprised. Mum is like that. She may sound a bit gruff at times but she never means anything by it.'

'And I thought she never liked me!'

Miriam's gratitude was beginning to be embarrassing.

'Oh, come on. Let's look around Bodmin. Everyone else has gone.'

Certainly, all the Sharptor and Henwood residents had gone, but more and more wagons were trundling into the field, and the roads from the surrounding countryside were jammed with people.

Josh and Miriam found themselves moving into Bodmin with the human flow. They passed stalls and shops that displayed everything imaginable for sale. From shoes to saddles and sweets to horses. Miriam spent a farthing at the first stall on some sweets which turned out to be even stickier than they had looked. They wandered along in bulged-cheeked silence until they found themselves before a great iron-studded gate, set into the high grey wall of the prison. Here the gallows had been erected on a raised platform and two oiled and pre-stretched ropes hung from the stout cross-beam, their noosed ends swinging gently and ominously in the faintest of breezes.

It was here, where the morning shadow of the gallows fell across the earth, that the crowd was thickest. Not everyone had been drawn to the spot by morbid curiosity. Wrightwick Roberts was not the only preacher with the idea of being on hand to pray for the condemned men's souls. Four or five Methodist ministers from the mining communities and many of their parishioners were also there. They formed a party of about two hundred strong, occupying the area immediately adjacent to the gallows platform. Their presence did not please the officer in charge of the military guard. He paced about on the platform, shouting to keep a clear passage between the prison gate and the gallows.

He eventually called to a sergeant. During the course of an earnest conversation they looked often towards the group of Methodists who were on their knees praying.

Nodding in acknowledgement, the sergeant turned away and walked to where his soldiers lounged against the prison gate. There was still a long time before the execution, but at the sergeant's shouted command the soldiers ceased their lounging. Unslinging their muskets, they moved to take up positions surrounding the platform. Significantly, there were twice as many soldiers on the side nearest the praying Methodists as on any other.

As nothing else seemed to be happening, Josh and Miriam took another walk about Bodmin and returned shortly before noon. The crowd had swelled to fill the whole vast space in front of the prison and overflowed halfway up the slope of the opposite hill.

At five minutes to twelve the huge studded prison gates swung open. Led by a single drummer, two columns of soldiers resplendent in bright red coats and white cross-belts marched slowly from the dusty courtyard within, the sun gleaming on the steel bayonets fixed to the ends of their long muskets.

Shuffling between the lines of soldiers were the two wretched miners, heavily manacled and chained to each other, clothes ragged, eyes fixed on the ground at their feet.

Their appearance was the signal for a murmur of excitement from the crowd. It quickly gave way to a growl of anger from the miners when it could be seen what condition the unfortunate prisoners were in.

The condemned men paused at the steps leading to the platform, aware for the first time of the vast size of the crowd. A soldier prodded them none too gently and one of the two tripped, dragging his companion to the ground at the very edge of the platform.

The crowd's growl became a roar, and the soldiers fingered their guns uneasily. The sergeant helped the prisoners to their feet with more sympathy than they had received at the hands of the soldiers, and the angry noise from the crowd died away. The hangman now stepped forward. Keeping his hooded head turned from the crowd, he moved to the men he was soon to execute.

'Brothers!' The voice of Wrightwick Roberts boomed out so loudly that there could have been few of the vast crowd who did not hear him. 'Brothers! Join me in a prayer for these two sinners who are nearing the judgement of the Lord. Let us appeal for His mercy. Pray that their sins be forgiven, their punishment end here on earth. Down on your knees and pray with me.'

There was a rippling movement through the crowd as all of the women and most of the men dropped to their knees or, as they were wearing Sunday clothes, squatted so as not to be conspicuous above the others.

The two condemned men also fell to their knees, grateful for the extra few minutes of life Wrightwick Roberts had won for them.

Josh was kneeling with the others but he had to reach up and pull a bewildered Miriam down beside him.

'Kneel down!' he hissed at her.

The voice of Wrightwick Roberts boomed out his thanks to the Lord on behalf of the two men. 'Lord, we thank thee for this opportunity to ask Your forgiveness for these miserable sinners . . .'

'What's happening?' Miriam asked in a hoarse whisper. 'Aren't they going to hang them after all?'

'Of course they are going to hang them. Just keep quiet!'

'Why is Preacher Thackeray thanking God, then?'

'Shut up!'

A woman kneeling in front of them turned her head to give them a withering glance, and they fell silent. Preacher Roberts' prayer was a long one, and when he had finished he ordered the crowd to stand and sing a hymn with him.

As the words of the hymn rose from ten thousand throats the officer of the soldiers found it difficult to contain his impatience. The whole thing was a nightmare for him. The sooner it was over the happier he would be. He looked for the hangman and saw him standing beside the condemned men. His hands were clasped in front of him and his chin thrust forward inside his hood. He was behaving as though he was in chapel.

When the third verse began, the officer spoke to the sergeant and the two prisoners were thrust forward until their faces were touching the rope of the nooses. The hangman was aroused from his religious fervour and persuaded to place the nooses about the necks of the two men. His action caused the voices of the crowd to falter. As he tightened the nooses and carefully positioned the knot beneath the left ear of each man the singing died away altogether. While the hangman was doing this the sergeant unlocked the chains that bound the men together and their arms were pinioned securely by the soldiers.

The officer stepped forward. His voice, nerve-tight, had but a fraction of the strength of Wrightwick Roberts'.

'Silence!' He called. 'Silence in the name of the Queen!'

The noise from the crowd subsided quickly.

'It is my duty to see that the sentence of death passed upon Thomas Arthur Sleedon and William Joseph Darling is carried out in accordance with the laws of this realm. They have been found guilty by a jury of fellow-men of the murder of Henry

Talbot, a militiaman, whilst he was carrying out his duties. Her Majesty's Judge of Assize has ordered that they be hanged by the neck until dead. Before the sentence is carried out they may speak their last words. May God rest their souls.'

'And may he rot yours and the souls of all those who oppress the miners of this county.'

An astonished Josh recognised the voice of his teacher, William Thackeray. The preacher was not a big man. He could not be seen in the midst of the group of agitated miners who stamped and shouted less than twenty yards from the gallows.

There was a murmur of agreement from the crowd, but William Thackeray had more to say.

'The militia is supposed to uphold the Law – not carry out the orders of the adventurers who keep miners poor in order to line their own pockets.'

The response this time was a roar of approval that alarmed the officer.

'What would we do if our families were starving? If food was deliberately kept from them? Wouldn't we take it?'

'Yes! Take it! Take it!' replied a thousand voices.

'The wrong men are on the scaffold,' shouted William Thackeray. 'It should be the adventurers! The mine-owners!'

'Take them down! Release them!' The cries came from all parts of the crowd as it seemed to sway forwards towards the gallows platform.

The officer rapped out an order and the soldiers brought muskets to their shoulders. At the same time the hangman reached forward. His shaking hand gripped a large wooden lever set close to one of the uprights of the gibbet.

Above the shouting and general hullabaloo a woman's voice could be heard screaming, 'Thomas! Oh God! Thomas!'

One of the condemned men, a look of anguish on his face, took a step forward – and trod into eternity. The trap-door dropped down on oiled hinges and the condemned men fell until the rope jerked them to a fatal halt. They hung with heads and shoulders visible to the crowd, their heads sideways as though listening, while the taut ropes quivered above them.

So sudden was the moment of execution it was seconds before the crowd fully appreciated that it was over.

When they did there was a sudden hush as though the world had stopped breathing. Then the woman who had screamed for Thomas Sleedon let out a long animal howl and Josh became aware that Miriam was clutching his arm, her fingernails biting into his wrist painfully.

A great gust of sound broke from the crowd and fists were waved angrily in the air.

'It was horrible! Horrible!' Miriam began sobbing. 'Why did they do it? Why did the officer kill them?'

Josh tried to tell her that it was not the officer's order but the court's, but too much was happening about them. The crowd was angry. Their feelings, like Miriam's, were turned upon the officer. As the soldiers cut down the two dead men a stone flew through the air, landing with a thud on the platform. It was followed by another – and another. Soon the air around the gallows was thick with missiles.

As the soldiers carrying the two bodies retreated towards the prison gate, the hangman cowered down alongside them. The remainder formed a tight line facing the crowd and retreated step by step. As they neared the gate those on the extreme ends of the line came under attack from the bolder young miners. This provoked their officer into showing them the authority of the Army. With blood trickling from a cut on his face, he snapped out an order. The line of soldiers stopped retreating and half of them dropped to one knee, their muskets pointing at their tormentors. As the crowd faltered, those exposed to the soldier's aim pushing back against the others behind them, the officer raised his sword. It fell, a flash of silver in the sun, and the muskets spoke.

At the last moment the soldiers raised their weapons and the musket-balls sped harmlessly above the heads of the crowd. But the volley had a salutary effect. The mob was thrown into near-panic, the frightened screams of the women nearest the soldiers leading those further away to believe they had been shot. Long before the truth became known, thousands were fleeing the field, while the soldiers and their grisly burdens were secure inside the prison. Indeed, there were many folk who never did know that the shots had not been aimed into the crowd. Tales of the murdering soldiers who shot at unarmed Cornish folk swept the county from end to end, doing nothing to enhance the fast-flagging popularity of the military.

Holding Miriam's hand, Josh ran with the crowd, not stopping until they reached the safety of the narrow thoroughfares.

His feeling of relief was almost immediately replaced by a sense of foolishness. No soldiers were pursuing them and there had been no second volley. But Miriam's tear-stained face was real enough. She was in a state of near-shock.

'Oh, come on,' said Josh, more harshly than he intended because of the discovery that he was still holding her hand. 'It's all over now.'

Miriam drew the back of her hand across her eyes and succeeded in producing horizontal smudges to add to the perpendicular ones.

She could not remove the sight of the hanged men from her mind. One minute they had been alive, men with thoughts and feelings; the next . . .

She had been watching the face of the one who had taken the pace forward at the moment the hangman pulled the lever. She had seen his utter surprise. Horrified, she had still been looking when the rope snapped taut and death displaced surprise. She would have nightmares about it for the remainder of her life.

'It's all right now. I'll buy you some more sweets – and we'll go in to watch the dancing bear.' The animal was just one of many entertainments on offer in the crowded fair.

They saw the bear, an unhappy, degraded and flea-bothered animal, and they bought more fruit and sweets. By late afternoon Miriam had succeeded in pushing thoughts of the hanging to the back of her mind.

As it was a special holiday the town's inns were open all day. There were many who took full advantage of the fact. Drunken men, and not a few women, became commonplace as the day wore on. In the ale-houses the loud and ribald singing drove smoke and the sweet heavy smell of beer and gin out through open windows and doors.

Those who had already drunk too much, unused to the town's brew, lay sprawled outside in the gutters amidst the litter of the day. The lucky ones were those who fell drunk in the main street. They were quickly removed by friends or the constables specially sworn in for this day. Those who were not so fortunate staggered far enough away to fall in some more inconspicuous alley. Here they were quickly relieved of everything of value by the gangs of young villains who followed them from the inns, fighting off similar-minded rivals.

There were many other fights for lesser reasons. The miners would be talking about them for weeks to come.

Josh and Miriam saw Morwen Trago in one such brawl and Josh had to drag Miriam away while she shrieked at her brother to stop. He was only just in time. A band of the special constables came on the run, laying about them with their long staves, driving off the able-bodied and arresting those who lay unconscious on the ground. Morwen was one of the runners.

But it was trouble of a different and unlooked-for kind that caught up with Miriam and Josh. It came in the person of Herman Schmidt, Sharptor mine captain.

Yet another fight had erupted in the town's main street. Josh took Miriam down a narrow alleyway in an attempt to bypass the trouble-area and return to the main street closer to the country dancing being held at the far end of Bodmin town.

The alleyway led into another – and yet one more until they were lost. Josh was about to suggest they turn around and retrace their steps when they saw a thick-set man standing straddle-legged close to the wall of a house. He had his back towards them and a stream of urine ran past him to the gutter.

Josh's instinct was to hurry past as fast as they could, but the man heard them coming. Turning, he blocked their way in the narrow alleyway. It was Herman Schmidt and the German had not bothered to button his trousers.

'Well, well! And what have we here, eh?' The accent was

thick and guttural and in no way helped by the amount of alcohol he had drunk. He peered down at them drunkenly and took a staggering step forward.

'What you want?' He was talking to Miriam. 'You looking for a man? All right, Cornish whore. How much you charge, eh? How much?'

Josh edged backwards and tried to pull Miriam with him, but the German reached out and took her arm in a grip that made her draw in her breath with pain. 'You hear me, Cornish whore? I am more of a man than your peasant farmer or poor miner. How much do you want?'

'One guinea.'

Josh looked at Miriam in amazement, unable to believe he had heard her correctly.

'A guinea! What you take me for? One guinea! It is maybe made of gold, Ja?' He snorted derisively, then stooped down to look more closely at her. The gin fumes on his breath were enough to make Josh wince and he was half a pace behind Miriam.

'Um! You are young, still. You have a room?'

She nodded.

'Then I give you half a guinea.'

'A guinea.'

'Half a guinea!' the German roared. 'No woman is worth a whole guinea. Not even a German virgin.' He cursed in coarse German and spat upon the ground.

'Miriam, what are you saying? Come away.'

Without turning around she waved her free hand behind her back, signalling for Josh to go. The mine captain, fumbling in a waistcoat pocket for a half-guinea, paused and spoke to him.

'What are you doing here, boy? Go away.' He peered at Josh, trying to focus his bloodshot eyes. 'Don't I know you?' He shook his head heavily. 'I should know you, perhaps. But go away. Run off.'

But Josh stood his ground. The mine captain pulled a golden coin from his pocket. He had no more success focusing his eyes upon it than he had trying to identify Josh. He held the coin up before Miriam's face. 'Here. Is this a half-guinea?'

She snatched it from him. 'Yes.'

'Come on, then. We are wasting time. Where do you live?'

Josh caught Miriam's hand, thoroughly alarmed. 'Don't go with him, Miriam. He'll hurt you. Don't go—'

Herman Schmidt said angrily, 'When I give an order it is meant to be obeyed.' The back of his heavy hand swung and caught Josh on the side of his head, knocking him off balance. He thought he heard Miriam scream, but the sound was lost in the blaze of lights that flashed in front of his eyes as his head struck a wall. Then everything went black.

When he opened his eyes he believed that he had been only temporarily dazed, but Miriam and Schmidt were gone. He felt sick. Whether it was from the blow to his head or the thought of what the German and the small girl were doing together he did not want to know.

He scoured the alleyways in the immediate vicinity, but there was no sign of them. Soon he found himself out on the main street again. The shadows were beginning to grow long when Josh gave up looking. There were still far too many people in Bodmin to make anything like a thorough search possible.

Despondently he made his way back to the field where the wagons were parked. This too was a scene of some activity now. The Sharptor contingent was not the only one to have travelled a considerable distance to witness the execution. Wagons were trundling off, late-comers running to get themselves hoisted aboard.

A couple of the Sharptor wagons had already left. In others there were drunken miners, placed there by their friends to sleep off their excesses. The wagon on which Josh and Miriam had come to Bodmin was empty. Josh clambered on to it and squatted near the front, the tall driver's-box blotting out his view of the noisy loathsome town. Gloomily he looked out across the fields towards the moor that lay between Bodmin and home.

Gradually more and more of the Henwood and Sharptor villagers arrived, but it was nearer eight o'clock than six o'clock when they were ready to move off. He had seen his

mother and father arrive, Jesse flushed with the excitement
of the day and carrying lots of packages of once-in-a-lifetime
frivolous purchases. She looked for Josh, saw he was safely
on a wagon and waved cheerily. He raised his hand in
acknowledgement, glad that she did not come across to talk
to him.

Suddenly from the corner of his eye he saw a flash of
brown skin and the familiar long black hair of Miriam as
she scrambled up beside him. He stiffened involuntarily,
not sure whether he was relieved or angry. But Miriam was
bubbling over with happiness, as though nothing untoward
had taken place.

'Oh, Josh! You don't know how glad I am to see you. When
you fell I thought Schmidt had killed you. As soon as I could
I came back to look for you, but you'd gone. Where have you
been? I've been looking everywhere for you.'

There was no stopping her. The words just poured out.
'Look! I've been shopping. I bought a comb for my ma. Some
tobacco for Dad. A new cap for Morwen – he's always wanted
one. There's some ribbon for me . . .' She paused. 'And I've
bought this for you.'

She held something out towards him. When he made no
move to take it from her she took his hand and dropped the
object into it.

He tried not to, but he had to look down at it. It was a
pocket-knife. A bone-handled knife with two spring blades
that folded into it. He was tempted, very tempted; but stiffly
he returned it, dropping the knife into her lap.

'I don't wan't it.'

Miriam's mouth dropped open in surprise. 'But it's a present
. . .' Her eyes suddenly opened wide. 'You don't think . . . ?'
You don't believe I went with that – that *animal*?'

A couple of women looked around at the vehemence of her
words. After giving them a withering look Miriam lowered
her voice. 'I wasn't going to let him get away with the things
he said to me. I took his money – and it was a whole guinea,
not a half-guinea. When I found a house with the door open
I took him inside and told him to go upstairs and wait for

me in the bedroom. It was quite a big house. I expect he's
still there.'

She smiled, epecting Josh to smile in return. That would
make everything all right again. But Josh's thoughts were in
a turmoil. He wanted to believe her. He did believe her. But
Miriam had led Captain Schmidt on.

'Taking his money was stealing. You should have come
away with me when I wanted you to.'

'It was *not* stealing. Not after what he said to me. Besides, he
hit you. He deserved to pay for that. Anyway, he had hold of
my arm, remember? I couldn't have got away. If I'd struggled
he would have hit me too and then something bad *would* have
happened.'

The wagon had filled up fast and now the wagon-driver
returned and made them all crowd closer together to allow
even more passengers to get on. When he thought there
were enough he climbed on to the seat and cracked his
long whip over the backs of the horses. With many 'Hups!'
and 'Heave hos', the horses strained into the harness. As the
wagon creaked its way out on to the road to begin the climb
away from the town the lights were beginning to glow in the
windows of the houses. On they went, up the track to the
high moors where a light hazy mist was beginning to blunt
the craggy tors.

Everyone was in a very happy mood – everyone except
Miriam and Josh. The singing rolled back and forth along the
line of wagons.

In the crowded swaying wagon, Josh sat with his arms
wrapped around his drawn-up knees. Miriam could do little
else but lean and bump against him, miserably staring in front
of her. Once or twice Josh stole a glance at her face, half-hidden
by her straggling black hair. Although it was not possible to
be sure, he thought he saw tears trembling on the brink of her
eyelashes.

He was thoroughly miserable. It was made all the worse by
the belief, hidden beneath a lot of other feelings, that Miriam
was right. Captain Schmidt *had* been holding her arm. He
would certainly have been violent had she tried to run away.

A dull ache at the back of Josh's head was proof enough of that. The captain also deserved to be separated from his money – that too Josh accepted. The thing that bothered him most was that Miriam should have been immediately aware of what the German was talking about, when Josh himself had not been really sure. He was still vague on some of the issues raised by the incident.

He thought of the mine captain, tricked into entering somebody's house; tried to imagine what had happened when he discovered his mistake. Perhaps he had been found in the house.

He looked again at Miriam but it was too dark to see her face now.

'Miriam, I'm sorry.'

There was no reply.

'I don't think you did anything wrong – and the knife is a lovely present.'

She grasped his hand, sniffed noisily and heavily, then rubbed her eyes against the shoulder of his coat. Without a word the pocket-knife was replaced in his hand.

'I wonder what old Schmidt is doing now?'

It was a very shaky laugh, but she managed it. He squeezed her hand awkwardly. 'I wasn't much help, was I?'

'That wasn't your fault,' she said indignantly. 'He hit you.'

There was silence between them for a few minutes and a new song was started in the next wagon. The wagoner cracked his whip for the horses to close up on the sound. Ahead of the first wagon a miner had jumped down and was leading the way with a lantern swinging in his hand.

'Do you really like the knife?'

'Yes. It's the best present I've ever been given.' He meant it.

'It was the first present I've ever bought for anyone.'

'I bet it cost a lot of money.'

'Yes, it did, but I've still got half a guinea left.'

She contorted her body and retrieved the coin from somewhere beneath her clothes.

'Here! You can have it. I don't need it.'

The warm coin was pressed into his hand, but he pushed it back and closed her hand about it.

'No, you keep it. One day you'll want to buy yourself something special.'

She contorted again, and the coin was gone once more.

She hugged his arm between both her hands. As the singing gradually died away only the soft clumping of the horses' hoofs and the squeak and creak of the wagons broke the silence of the night. Her head drooped to rest on his shoulder.

'Josh?' Her voice sounded sleepy.

'What?' he whispered.

'I wouldn't do bad things with anyone, Josh.'

'No?'

'No – only with you, and they wouldn't be bad then.'

There were strange stirrings in his young body and he felt very grown-up and protective towards the young but disturbingly mature girl who slumbered quietly on his shoulder as the wagons rolled homewards.

Chapter Five

William Thackeray rode back to St Cleer in an excited mood. He knew his words had stirred the huge crowd. Had the soldiers' officer not acted so quickly, he might have incited them to storm the gallows and release the two condemned miners.

The thought that he might have been partly responsible for the act which had sent them to the gallows never crossed his mind, although he knew they had attended the meeting he had called at Kit Hill when their troubles first started. But Preacher Thackeray was to be found wherever the miners had trouble. He would address them in the open air, hemmed in by the gorse and fern, or within the stone walls of a barracks-like sorting-shed. He cared little for his surroundings as long as there were men who would listen – and there were always men ready to listen to William Thackeray. Every Sunday he attracted huge congregations. It was as much for this reason as any other that his church did not withdraw him from Cornwall, for the words that he preached were not all drawn from the Bible. Not for Preacher Thackeray the comfortable meaningless jargon that country parsons had served to their flocks for generations past. He was concerned for the souls of his people, but he saw no reason why they should suffer unnecessary hardships in this life in order to enter the same heaven to which their far more comfortable employers were bound.

And so Preacher Thackeray urged the miners to join together to improve their lot in life. This was why he preached 'union'. This was why he was feared and hated by mine-adventurers and those whose fortunes were swelled by the poverty of the miner. 'Union' was a word he used in every sermon he preached. Union with the Lord. Union against the practice of paying miners with mine tokens redeemable only in the mine's own store. Union with every other Cornish miner. They needed it to negotiate terms of employment that would raise the status of the miner from near-serfdom to valued employee, with due recognition for his skills.

Thackeray advocated that the men should fight for their rights in any and every possible way. If it were necessary to use violence, then Jesus Christ himself had set a precedent. If a few tables had to be overturned – then so be it.

It was for this type of preaching that men came to hear him. He was as popular with miners as he was unpopular with mine-owners and Cornish gentry – for his preaching was not directed against the adventurers alone. He slated the Government for its short-sighted agricultural policies – policies which sent food prices soaring. He pointed a stern finger at farmers who took advantage of bad laws to withhold corn from the markets, raising corn prices to a level that miners' families found impossible to afford.

There had been little enough of Preacher Thackeray physically when he first crossed the Tamar into Cornwall. His continuous crusade among the mining communities of east Cornwall trimmed his weight still further. As Jesse Retallick once remarked, he had no more flesh on him than a weasel. It was a good description. Small and wiry, he possessed boundless energy. He also had the weasel's uncanny ability to hold the attention of an audience when he so wished.

He was almost halfway to St Cleer when he met up with one more group of men travelling in the same direction as himself. He would have passed through them with no more than an echoed 'Good night' had not one of them called to him.

'Is that Preacher Thackeray?'

'Unless I'm mistaken that's John Kittow. What do you want with me?'

The small group of miners closed about him, and John Kittow lowered his voice, for sounds carry far at night on the high moor.

'We'd like a word with you, Preacher. Somewhere quiet.'

'I'll meet you any time you like, John. Won't it do here?'

'No.' William Thackeray could detect the shaking of heads around him. 'No, Preacher. Better if 'tis said where there's light to see who's listening and walls to stop them as shouldn't be.'

'Then you'd better make it the chapel. Tomorrow night?'

'Right after the late shift comes up, if that suits you.'

'That's all right with me, John.' His horse threw back its head and danced sideways. Thackeray yanked it to a halt again. 'But won't you tell me something of what it's about?'

The movements of the horse had taken him a little distance from the men and there was a noticeable hesitation before the voice came from the darkness.

'Corn, Preacher. That's it in one word. Corn!'

Herman Schmidt did not put in an appearance at the Sharptor mine next day. There was nothing out of the ordinary in this and no one – with the exception of Josh – would have thought anything of it had not Theophilus Strike called in at the mine in the late afternoon. Then the word went around like chaff in an east wind. The German mine captain had been arrested by the Bodmin constable and kept in the town's lock-up overnight. It seemed he would have been there still, had he not got word to the Sharptor mine-owner of his plight.

Theophilus Strike had gone straight to Bodmin and eventually managed to smooth over what would otherwise have been a very serious situation for the German. He had been arrested on a charge of entering a dwelling-house with intent to commit a felony. There was also an additional charge of assaulting the constable called to arrest him.

With a great deal of diplomacy, backed up by a few gold

coins, Strike had persuaded the tenants of the house where
Schmidt had inexplicably found himself to withdraw their
complaint. The constable too was a reasonable man, appreci-
ative of the purchasing power of a brace of guineas. He had
the additional satisfaction of knowing that, whereas the wild
swings of the mine captain had not found their target, his own
beefy fists had left their mark on Schmidt's features.

Herman Schmidt pleaded 'guilty' before the magistrate to
a charge of being drunk and disorderly and was fined five
shillings, the magistrate adding a stern warning for him to
steer clear of the Bodmin hostelries in the future.

During the time his battered face was healing the mine
captain kept away from the mine as much as possible. For
what remained of that summer he was a quieter, more reasonable man. Nevertheless, it was some weeks before Josh
was able to see the mine captain's approach without a sinking
feeling in his stomach. He need not have worried. Herman
Schmidt could remember nothing of the events that had led
to his arrest

The lights were burning until well into the night in the St Cleer
Methodist church for the meeting between Preacher William
Thackeray and the miners of Caradon led by John Kittow. It
should have been one of the nights when Josh stayed late for
his studies but he was ushered out by the preacher and, after
looking at the faces of the men who began to arrive while he
collected his books together, he wasted no time in going.

Only selected miners were allowed into the hall that evening.
Others who called to see the preacher found the door guarded
by two burly Caradon men. They were curtly told to conduct
their business on another, more convenient occasion. Nobody
questioned it. Far better to accept whatever the preacher was
doing and forget about it.

Even so, there were many who wondered about the secret
meeting, but they would not be kept in suspense for long.

The shortage of corn had been growing steadily worse
throughout England. It had not been helped by the government laws which prevented corn from being imported, in a

misguided attempt to protect the interests of the farmers. It certainly helped the farmer, but at the expense of the poor worker. He was unable to afford the astronomical prices the corn was fetching on the open market.

When Josh mentioned the unusual happenings at the St Cleer chapel to his father, the miner knew immediately what it was about. Rumour had been rife lately that miners' action was imminent. Ben Retallick was sitting in the doorway of the cottage enjoying the late-evening air and he frowned at the thought of more trouble. Thackeray's meddling with affairs outside the chapel did not please him. He could see nothing but trouble coming from it.

'You'd best forget you saw anything tonight,' he said. 'And be quite sure that I'm the last one you tell of it.'

The miners of Caradon had determined to do more than talk about their problems and had already formulated a rough plan of action. They were having this meeting with Preacher Thackeray in order to give his quick and clever mind a chance to work out the details and smooth out some difficulties. John Kittow wanted to be sure that as little as possible could go wrong, for it was a bold plan the miners were embarking upon. . . .

Callington market was smaller than many others in the county, being overshadowed by the nearness of the greater market-towns of Liskeard, Launceston and Saltash. But trade was usually brisk for all that, and lately it had become a collection centre for farm produce. From here it would be hauled to Cotehele quay and shipped down-river to the seaport of Plymouth.

This particular market-day began much like any other and, although the observant onlooker might have noticed an unusually high proportion of miners about the market-place, it excited little interest. The farming community deliberately avoided noticing them at all.

There had always been miners on the moor. For longer than there had ever been farmers, in fact. But those early miners – the 'old men' of legend – had done no more than scratch the ground and search the streams for their ore. They lived a solitary furtive life and had little contact with men outside their own kind.

These 'new' miners were a different breed altogether. They dug deep into the very bowels of the earth, raising mountains of rubble around their shafts. The thump and clanking of their steam-engines reverberated over the countryside, frightening cattle and worrying the sheep. Even at night they worked, the glow from their furnaces flickering along the ridges like the watch-fires of hell. Neither were they partial to the solitary life. Instead, they roamed the lanes in noisy boisterous groups. It was a brave countrywoman who would venture past one of the many inns frequented by them.

No, the miner and the farmer were different breeds of men and there was a wide gulf between them.

All morning the farm-wagons trundled into Callington loaded with produce and livestock and among the produce was – corn!

The corn-market was at the very centre of the town, outside a stone-built granary. Here a man's occupation was forgotten as miner, countryman and town-dweller crowded around the auctioneer as he called loudly for bids.

As the bidding began the calls came quickly and eagerly from those who most needed the grain. 'Sixty shillings! Sixty-five! Seventy!' There was very little grain allowed to be sold on the home market. At seventy-five shillings for a quarter the bids were still coming in from all sides. At eighty shillings men began to shake their heads. By the time it had made ninety all but the most determined had dropped out, including the combines of ordinary people who had pooled their cash in an effort to get at least some corn to take home. When the corn reached a calling-price of one hundred and five shillings only the merchants remained – and none of them was from Cornwall.

The bidding slowed down noticeably now, rising in pence. 'One hundred and five shillings and four pence I am bid. It is best-quality corn and will fetch much more in the city – or even in Plymouth. Do I hear one hundred and six? Who will bid one hundred and six?'

'Eighty shillings, and I'll take the lot.' The voice, deep and very Cornish, came from towards the back of the crowd.

The auctioneer smiled derisively. 'I'm sorry, sir, you're a little late. The bidding has reached one hundred and five shillings and four pence – or did I hear one hundred and six?'

'You heard eighty shillings, and that's all you'll be getting. I'll take the lot.'

John Kittow pushed his way through the bidders to the front and a broad wedge of miners split the crowd behind him.

'You can't do this! I've been bid more than one hundred and five shillings. I am honour bound to sell at the best price.'

'There's nothing honourable in keeping food from the mouths of those who need it. Nor in robbing those who can pay more. Eighty shillings is a fair price for a quarter and that's what it will be sold for.'

The auctioneer began to protest once more, and John Kittow pushed him from his auctioneer's perch into the midst of the miners. The man disappeared momentarily and re-appeared to be raised high above the heads of the miners. Too terrified to struggle, he was passed over the heads of the cheering men to the rear of the crowd.

'Now!' John Kittow put up his hands for silence. 'We're selling corn to whoever wants it. At eighty shillings a quarter. There will be no bidding. It's a case of "first come, first served". Is it agreed that eighty shillings is a fair price?'

There was a majority shout of assent, but one man called out, 'The farmers have made enough profit from corn. Sell it at sixty shillings. Forty, even!'

'There will be none of that talk!' John Kittow put a stop to the murmur before it spread. 'There's been work put into the growing of it. A man is entitled to his living. Eighty shillings has been agreed and that's what it will be sold for. Nobody will be turned away if he has the money to pay for it. Come on, now! What are you waiting for?'

The crowd surged forward to buy a bushel or two. It was an opportunity that was hardly likely to be repeated. Word went quickly through the whole market of what was happening, and crowds thronged to the corn-sale. It was not only the townsfolk and the miners who came. Stalls were left unattended as traders deserted them for the chance of buying corn. It had been missing from their diet for so long that there were young children in some families who had never known the taste of it.

A few of the farmers whose produce was up for sale protested at the unorthodox method of sale, but when sections of the crowd turned on them they withdrew, angry and sullen.

One or two of the more aggrieved among them decided to ride from the town to summon the military from Launceston and Liskeard. They got no further than the town's limits. Formidable pickets of miners armed with pick-axe handles guarded every exit from Callington. The corn-sale would continue in their way for as long as was deemed necessary.

The sale of immediate stocks did not last the hour, but then the shout went up that there was plenty more corn stored in the granary. In ten minutes the doors had been battered down and spilling bags of corn were being passed out to enable the sale to continue.

The whole affair was conducted in a most efficient manner, proving that the hours spent in discussion in the St Cleer chapel had not been wasted. The miners worked in threes – one man measuring the corn, the second taking the money from the customer and placing it into the canvas bag held by the third. Other miners, sweat running down their grinning faces, humped corn from the granary and shouldered it to the sellers.

John Kittow was acting as general supervisor, calling up more corn for this trio; directing eager buyers to another where they would be served more quickly. At one stage he saw an old woman, wrinkled face anxious beneath her widow's shawl, moving from one group to the next, watching the proceedings from the edge of the would-be buyers, but not pushing her way through to the front.

'Is it corn you're wanting, mother?' asked Kittow, taking her gently by the elbow. 'You come over here with me and we'll see that you get it without waiting.'

'Ah, will I now?' The woman's voice was as old as her face.

'And what d'you think I'll be paying you with? Wanting's one thing, m'dear – buying's another.'

John Kittow noticed for the first time the frayed patches of her shawl and the all-but-threadbare black cardigan beneath it.

'You'll be a widow, then, mother?'

'These twenty years,' she replied. 'And he went the same way that you'll go. With his lungs full of dust from the mine.'

'We'll all go when the time comes,' said John Kittow, guiding her forward once more. 'But there'll be no miner's widow leaving here today without corn to fill her belly for a day or two.'

He spoke to a miner who looked up from a half-empty sack. 'Some corn for a miner's widow. As much as she can carry away.'

He drew some coins from his pocket and threw them into the money-bag being held by another miner. 'If any more widows, or others in need, come for corn give it to them. Pay for it from your own pockets. You'll get it back from the mine fund. But make sure the money goes into the bag. I'll have no one saying there has been any dishonesty here today.'

John Kittow proved himself a man of his word. When the last bushel of corn had been sold the money was brought to him and he passed it on to the farmers who had brought in the corn. They grumbled that they would have received more from the merchants but were so relieved to be receiving any money at all that they made little fuss.

The balance of the money was counted with the granary agent and he reluctantly gave the miners a receipt for it, agreeing that it tallied with the amount of corn sold at the miners' price.

Their business concluded, the miners of Caradon withdrew their pickets from around the town and, as peacefully as they arrived, they quitted Callington.

The military was called out and a troop of soldiers rode into Callington the next day, but there was very little that they could, or would, do. The business had been conducted in a scrupulously honest manner. Though the price was not what the farmers expected, they still made a good profit from it.

There was another reason for the tardiness of the soldiers in taking action. They were due for a tour of duty abroad, where there would be a chance of 'real' action, with possibly battle honours for the regiment and a title for its colonel. He had no wish to blow up a relatively minor rural incident into a people's uprising. There was no glory to be gained in quelling a civil disturbance.

Chapter Six

The remainder of that summer went quickly and there were many who were glad to see it pass. For others – and Josh was one – it was a year to gather in and cherish, and he hoped it might never come to an end. But the long happy evenings spent on the moor with Miriam grew shorter and became memories. They had searched the bracken for nests, watched the badgers live out their ordered lives bringing up a healthy family, envied the gliding, circling buzzard and twice disturbed a fox drinking from brackish water in a moorland hollow. The fox displayed no fear and its slow retreat from them could have been interpreted as insolence. But on the second occasion, when they tried to follow it through the undergrowth, the animal vanished without a leaf or blade of grass trembling to show which way it had gone.

Miriam said the fox was probably a witch in one of her many disguises. Although Josh laughed at her foolishness, he was true Cornish and the countless generations of superstition that had gone into his breeding made him glance uneasily over his shoulder more than once as he hurried home in the dusk.

Then, almost before they realised it, summer had gone. The winter wind rattled the leafless branches of the hunch-backed bushes and laid the dry bracken flat to the ground, and the horses working the mine-whims blew steam from wide nostrils as they trudged around in circles on their long road to nowhere.

'It's hard to believe that Christmas is only two weeks away.'

Jesse Retallick beat up the mixture for the pudding she was preparing.

'It's Gwen's first Christmas,' said Jenny. 'I hope we will have some snow for her to see.'

'She's a fine baby. It's such a pity her father isn't alive to see her face when she opens her presents on Christmas morning.'

The deep sense of loss was still there, but it was now possible to talk about Budge to Jenny without having her dissolve into tears.

'I believe Budge *will* see her face,' said Jenny quietly with absolute conviction. Tom Shovell was a religious man and he had been a constant visitor to the house since the summer. His simple faith had restored a great deal of her self-confidence and brought her peace of mind, much to Jesse Retallick's relief. There had been a time when she feared the girl would never return to normal.

Jesse turned to Josh, who was sitting reading a schoolbook in a corner close to the fire. 'With Christmas over life will be very different for you, young man.'

Her manner was jocular but there was sadness deep inside. The year 1839 would see great changes in the Retallick household. Josh was going away on an apprenticeship. Thanks to his education, Theophilus Strike had offered him the chance to become a mine-engineer.

Josh would be away for close on three years at Harvey's foundry and engineering works at Hayle. There he would learn how to build and look after engines of the type Theophilus Strike planned to install in the Sharptor mine. An engine would not be necessary for three years because there was plenty of copper in the shallow drier levels. The mine-owner saw little sense in spending money to erect an engine to drain deeper shafts when the men could be digging out the existing ore and bringing money in.

As the Hayle foundry was to build the engine Josh would be involved with it from the beginning. When he returned he would possess a greater knowledge of engines than anyone in the district. His presence on the mine would avoid the necessity of calling out an engineer from Hayle when something went wrong. Theophilus Strike had costed the whole operation very carefully. Eventually, Josh's apprenticeship would save him a great deal of money.

He had not, of course, told Josh about this when he called him in for an interview. Instead, he had checked Josh's reading, his writing and his knowledge of arithmetic. Then, satisfied, he offered him the chance of three years at Hayle in return for an undertaking by Josh to work at the Sharptor mine for the following ten years. To his astonishment and Ben Retallick's dismay Josh had refused this offer. It was a desperate gamble. Josh now wanted to be an engineer more than anything else in the world. But ten years was a long time to be tied to one employer. He was now fourteen years old. It meant that he would be almost thirty before he was free of his commitment. Although he might not want to move elsewhere, the very thought of the restriction would be constantly at the back of his mind. It would always rankle. Five years' tied employment with the guarantee of a reasonable salary constituted his terms of acceptance.

Strike's astonishment had quickly turned to anger but it did not last. He knew there was not another boy available at Sharptor with Josh's standard of education, and without an engineer he believed it would be foolish to buy an engine. Without an engineer being readily available a major breakdown could spell disaster for a deep mine.

He agreed to Josh's terms. But Josh was left in no doubt about his part of the agreement. He was expected to return from Hayle with the best engine in Cornwall, and his commencing salary would depend entirely upon the report that Strike received of Josh's proficiency at the end of his training.

When Josh and Ben Retallick left the mine-owner's office the miner had taken off his hat and regarded his son with incredulous respect.

'I never thought I'd live to see the day when a son of mine would be offered the chance of a lifetime by a mine-owner and turn it down like that! And then to go on and call your own tune! Josh, if cheek is what matters you'll go far in this world.'

'It wasn't cheek,' Josh said, hiding his own elation. 'It was simple arithmetic. I know what I will be worth to Theophilus Strike. He knows it too. I could have asked for more without being greedy.'

It was true. He and Preacher Thackeray had spent a whole evening discussing the matter, and the preacher had finally proved his case by using simple mathematics. Thus Josh had been able to attend the interview armed with the same facts as the mine-owner. Josh intended to work hard during the three years he would be at Hayle, and Theophilus Strike would receive value for his investment. But Josh had plans for his own advance into manhood. Only single men could exist on low wages.

'I don't know, I'm sure,' Ben Retallick had said. 'It looks as though this schooling of yours is beginning to pay off already!'

Josh looked affectionately at his mother as she busied herself with the pudding mixture. 'Don't let's talk about my going away until Christmas is over.'

'And why not? It's something to be pleased about. You are getting a better chance in life than your father. Be thankful he doesn't want his son to follow him down the mine. There's many who can't wait to get their children below ground. Some of the mites are hardly big enough to hold a shovel. Moses Trago never wasted any time with his Morwen.'

There was silence for a few minutes, but the mention of Moses Trago had reminded Jesse Retallick of something that had been on her mind for some days.

'I haven't seen that Trago girl lately. Do you still meet her?'

'Miriam? Yes, now and again.'

This was rather more than a white lie. He saw her every time he came out from the chapel school at St Cleer. During the dark winter nights she was always waiting nearby in the shadows. They would walk together to their hideout on the moors where, by candlelight, he would teach her as much of his evening's lesson as he could remember.

Jesse Retallick knew that the two spent a lot of time in each other's company. She had seen them herself. Had she not, she would have known by the Henwood villages' thinly veiled innuendoes about it being 'unhealthy' for a boy and girl to spend so much time alone together, away from the influence of adults.

In a quiet indirect way she had found out from Josh about the schooling he was giving to Miriam and she approved of it. Miriam Trago had more about her than most other girls of her age. If she could escape from the influence of the remainder of the Trago family, then she wished the girl luck.

'What is she doing for Christmas?'

Josh looked surprised at the question. 'I don't know. Probably nothing at all. Miriam told me once they don't keep Christmas. Moses Trago says it's just another day.'

'Then it's time she learned different. Tell her that she's welcome here for Christmas Day. That's if you'd like to have her here?'

Astonishment and pleasure wrestled for supremacy on his face, and a stab of pain went through Jesse Retallick as she realised that he would not be a boy for very much longer. She doubted whether he would remain with his parents for very long after he returned from Hayle.

'Can I tell her now?' He slammed his book shut.

It was her turn to show surprise. 'At this time of night? You're not going up to that Trago place?'

He shook his head. 'No, she won't be there, but I know where to find her.'

Jesse Retallick bit back a refusal and began beating the pudding with unnecessary vigour. 'All right. But be back before your father comes home from the chapel meeting.'

He was gone by the time she had finished talking, and as the door banged noisily behind him Jenny smiled. 'Now, there's a young romance for you!'

'Nonsense! He's still a child. Both of them are.'

'Maybe, Jesse. But I was married when I was only two years older than they are now. There's nothing wrong with it. Despite her family Miriam is a good sensible girl, and she thinks the world of Josh.'

Jesse Retallick said nothing, but her Christmas pudding was stirred more thoroughly than it had ever been in any previous year.

It was dark on the hillside and a heavy chill hung in the air, but Josh was too happy to notice. He left the path a hundred yards from the cottage and followed a badger track up on to the high moor. There he struck off into the undergrowth and the going was harder. Twice he thought he had reached the hideout before he saw the faint outline of a boulder in front of him and knew he was there.

He crawled quietly and carefully along the tunnel through the gorse until he saw a soft glimmer of light ahead. It went out before he reached the end of the tunnel and he knew that Miriam was there and she had heard him.

'Miriam! It's me,' he called in a hoarse whisper.

Josh rose from the narrow gorse-tunnel and advanced into the space between the rocks. The candle was tucked into a small recess so that it was well sheltered from the wind and as little light as possible escaped from the hideaway. Beside the fat home-made candle were jammed a couple of books, old and in an advanced state of deterioration. Behind them was a pile of paper filled with Miriam's crowded untidy writing.

'What are you doing here at this time of the night? Is something wrong?' Her eyes were even darker than usual in the candlelight.

'No, there's nothing wrong. He held it back for as long as he could. 'I just wondered what you'll be doing on Christmas Day?'

She looked at him in amazement. 'You came all the way up here in the dark to ask me that? I've already told you. Christmas is the same as any other day for us. Except that my dad doesn't work. I expect he will be drinking all day.'

'Well . . .' He could not control the grin that threatened to split his face in two. 'How would you like to spend the day with us? Come to the cottage in the morning and stay all day? Have Christmas dinner with us and everything?'

Her expression made the journey in the dark worth while.

'Honest? Who said I could come? Your mother?'

He nodded.

Josh had become used to her impetuosity by now and, after submitting to the first onslaught of violent hugging, he broke free.

'You'll come?'

'Of course! As it's just an ordinary day for us I'll be able to come and go as I like. Nobody will ask where I'm going.'

'Then that's all settled. I'll go back and tell Mum you'll be coming.'

'Can't you stay for a while and help me? There are lots of long words in this book. I don't understand them.'

'No. Dad will be home from the chapel meeting soon. I don't want to upset him before Christmas.' He shivered. 'It's freezing cold up here. I don't know how you can learn anything in this weather.'

'Where else can I go? I don't mind the cold but I don't like the rain very much.'

She carefully placed her books in a tin box she had managed to acquire and tucked it well back into a crevice between the rocks. Then she snuffed out the candle and crawled through the tunnel behind Josh. Once out on to the moor she took his hand in a perfectly natural gesture. They often held hands when they walked on the moor in the dark. It was practical as well as companionable. If one stumbled or slipped, the other was able to prevent a fall. But once off the moor, or in daylight, Josh would not have been seen dead holding hands with anyone.

'Didn't your mother mind you coming out to see me this time of night?'

'Of course not. Why?'

She shrugged. ''Cos people talk. Do you remember one evening in summer we met Nehemeziah on the path below here?'

'Yes. One of his horses had got loose and wandered up here. What about it?'

'A few nights later I heard him telling old Mary Crabbe about seeing us together on the moor.'

'That doesn't matter. We weren't doing anything wrong.'

'*We* know that. I doubt anyone else would believe it. I know Mary Crabbe didn't. I heard what she said to Nehemeziah and she didn't care whether I heard her or not.'

'What did she say?'

Miriam did not answer immediately and Josh pulled her to a halt.

'What did she say?' he repeated.

A gust of wind from the west caught Miriam's long black hair and blew it forward, the ends of it flicking across his face.

She released her hand and pulled the hair back, knotting it behind her neck.

'She said I'd end up in trouble one day. She said if it wasn't you who laid me in the fern it would be someone else.'

'The nasty-minded old bitch!' Josh bristled with indignation.

Miriam took his hand again and squeezed it. They moved off along the path once more.

'Anyway, Mum doesn't believe that. She wouldn't have asked you home for Christmas if she did.'

'I've always wanted to have a *real* Christmas. What's it like?'

He told her. Of the holly-wreaths decorating the pictures and the mantelshelf. The small presents and the large meals. Prayers at lunch-time. The singing around the fire in the evening. And he tried to put into words the atmosphere of Christmas, of being part of a family and belonging. She listened in thoughtful silence until they arrived at the track that led downwards to the cottage and up to the Trago home.

'Are you sure I won't be in the way. If it's a family thing, I mean?'

'Of course you won't. You've been invited. Jenny and the baby will be there. Wrightwick Roberts will be coming in the evening. Tom Shovell too, I expect. Besides, I want you to come.'

'That's all right, then.' She was happy again.

'I've got to go now. I'll see you tomorrow at St Cleer – same time?'

'Yes.' She leaned forward and kissed him on the lips. For all the clumsy inexperience of it, he went hot inside.

'Good night, then.'

'Good night.'

Josh walked home without feeling the cold, as tall as any man.

Christmas came, as it usually does, with a great rush. After weeks of anticipation and fretfulness and much planning on the part of Jesse Retallick, all was very nearly ready. On the day before Christmas Eve a cart-load of miners' wives, Jesse Retallick among them, went into Liskeard market. They returned laden with meat, vegetables and mysterious parcels that were promptly tucked at the back of cupboards, accompanied by dire threats directed against anyone curious enough to want to seek them out.

Then, on Christmas Eve, just before dusk, the Sharptor mine ceased working. The men came to the surface to be greeted by Theophilus Strike, who handed to each man a large fat goose, freshly killed, and a half-guinea. Beside him was Herman Schmidt, his cheeks aglow with pre-Christmas drinking and offering his hand to each miner together with a guttural 'Merry Christmas!' But even at this time of goodwill he was not able to hide his contempt for the men under his control. It had been his intention to work the men until midnight, but there was not a miner in Cornwall who would remain underground after dark on Christmas Eve. This was the night when strange things happened in a mine; when mysterious lights cast their glow in the deepest and most remote tunnels and Christmas hymns might be heard, sung by choirs who had no place in the world of humans. The miners put the strange happenings down to the 'knockers', the little men who lived unseen beneath the ground and whose mining activities had frightened generations of mining men who had given these underground 'piskies' their descriptive name. But whoever, or whatever, was responsible for these Christmas Eve happenings not a single miner could be found who would stay below grass when dusk began to fall over the moor. Some of the older miners even went so far as to take extra food on shift with them and leave it behind when they quitted the mine for the Christmas period.

But, once on the surface, the miners put the mine behind them and trudged off down the hill, the married men to their homes and the excitement of Christmas, the remainder to the equally cheerful but less inhibited pleasures of the inns.

Ben Retallick had his meal and then went off to help Wrightwick Roberts prepare the chapel, leaving Josh and Jenny to decorate the house while Jesse prepared the food for the one day in the year when the menu was not controlled by economy. The large jar on the kitchen mantelshelf was the source of this annual bonus. Every week Jesse Retallick put a few pence into it, the amount dependent upon current commitments. This had been a particularly good year, Josh and Jenny adding their share. The young widow was now working at the Sharptor mine, sorting the ore with Josh. They had become very close of late, like brother and sister. It pleased Jesse Retallick. Josh was an only child and, although she and Ben had tried not to spoil him, he had received far more attention than was usual in that age and place. It was partly due to Sharptor's isolation. Up there on the slope there was nobody of his own age, apart from the Tragos. Jesse tried to make up for it by interesting herself in what he was doing. This isolation had made Josh used to doing things on his own and helped him to develop the love he had for the high lonely moor where he was so much at home.

This too was why Jesse had not discouraged Josh's friendship with Miriam, despite her grave misgivings about the wisdom of Josh becoming involved with any member of that unconventional family. They were wild and unpredictable like the tough shaggy cattle that roamed the moor with no control and scant regard for the boundaries that were set up for them. But she had invited the Trago girl to spend Christmas with them in order that she might start the new year with a better knowledge of her. Then she would decide whether the friendship should continue.

All this was going through Jesse's mind as she mixed pastry and rattled steaming pots on the kitchen range.

'There, now!' said Jenny, stepping back to admire the ivy that she had draped around the window-frame. 'Do you think that will please your sweetheart, Josh?'

He went red. 'She's just a friend, that's all.'

'Of course she is.' Her eyes twinkled and Jenny looked happier than Josh had seen her for many months. 'That's all Budge and I claimed we were. Right up to the day we married we were just "friends"!'

She laughed at his discomfiture. 'Don't worry, Josh. I won't make your cheeks go red tomorrow. Not in front of Miriam. Mind, I've found some kissing-berry for over the door. You'd best use it when Miriam comes into the house. It's the custom. We'll not have you breaking it.'

'It's a stupid custom!'

'No!' said Jenny firmly. 'Girls put great store by such things. You want Miriam to have as good a Christmas as any other maid, don't you? Never mind, you've got a few years to learn about what Miriam likes. Come on, let's go and try one of your ma's mince pies. If we stay here your face will set fire to my decorations.'

Christmas Day dawned damp and grey, with low cloud looking in at the windows of the cottage. Josh rose before first light to begin building up the fire in readiness for the day. Usually this was the time when the presents would be opened, but today they were waiting until Miriam arrived.

His mother was next downstairs. Then his father and finally Jenny, carrying the baby. Everyone was made to walk around the room with her so as not to miss the baby's reaction to the decorations. Gwen was fascinated most by the huge candle which Jesse had lit when she got up. It would burn until the last of the family went to bed that night.

'I hope Miriam won't be too late,' said Jesse Retallick as she began to fry breakfast on the kitchen range. 'I can't wait to see the baby's face when she opens her presents.'

Josh walked to the window and caught a glimpse of colour out in the grey mist. 'Here's Miriam,' he cried and went to the door. He opened it and stepped outside expecting to see her coming down the path. But he could see nothing. Puzzled, he walked out to the gate and once again caught the glimpse of colour that he knew was her best dress.

'Miriam!' As he scrambled up the slope from the path she came out from behind the gorse-thicket where she had been hiding.

'What are you doing up here? We have been waiting for you. We can't open any presents until you're there. Come on! The baby's busting to get started.'

Miriam shrugged her shoulders. 'You didn't tell me what time to come. I haven't seen you for a couple of days. I thought your mum might have forgotten she invited me. Or your dad might have said I couldn't come.'

'What would he say that for? Hurry up! Everyone's waiting.'

'Just a minute.' Miriam bent down behind the bush and picked up a small pile of badly wrapped parcels.

'What are they?'

Miriam hugged the packages close to her and her chin went up. 'They're presents. Everyone gives presents at Christmas.' She did not add that it was a custom unknown in the Trago household. She had gone to a great deal of trouble to ask questions of everyone with whom she could claim the slightest acquaintance in order to find out what went on in more orthodox houses at Christmas-time.

'What have you got for me?'

'Wait and see.'

Now that she was quite sure that she was going to spend Christmas in a house with people who celebrated it in a way she had only heard about, Miriam allowed some of her excitement to shake itself loose.

Only her mother knew that she would be spending the day

with the Retallicks, and the secret was safe with her. Miriam was up and dressed long before dawn to go to her hillside hideout where she had concealed the presents. Since then she had been waiting in the bushes near the cottage, willing Josh to come out and look for her, shivering with cold and anticipation.

Jesse stood in the cottage doorway watching Miriam coming along the path with Josh, and she understood far more of the girl's feelings than Miriam realised or would have been happy to have her know.

As they approached his mother Josh could see the uncertainty begin in Miriam's face and he touched her elbow gently. 'It's all right,' he whispered. 'They are all waiting for you.'

It was doubtful whether his reassurance did anything to make her feel more at ease. But Jesse Retallick's first words jolted her to an immediate halt.

'Stop there and don't come inside!'

Josh was as startled as Miriam.

'It's bad luck to have anyone enter the house with bare feet at Christmas,' said Jesse. She had been straight-faced until now, but seeing Miriam's dismay she smiled. 'So we'll just have to do something about that. Here, child, open this.' Reaching behind her she picked up a parcel from a chair just inside the doorway and handed it to Miriam. 'A very happy Christmas to you, Miriam.'

'Well, don't just stand there gawking like a loon,' she said to Josh. 'Take her parcels from her while she looks at her present.'

Speechless, Josh did as he was told while Miriam undid the ribbons on her present and carefully opened out the wrappings.

Inside was a pair of shiny black shoes, made in soft leather.

Miriam's eyes said everything. 'Thank you! Thank you, Mrs Retallick.'

Jesse sniffed. 'Well, put them on, then – and be sure they fit. It's time we went in to breakfast.'

Hurriedly Miriam placed the shoes on the ground, slipped

her feet into them. They were a good fit, and Jesse nodded her head in satisfaction. 'I didn't think they would be far out,' she said. 'And they are made of soft leather so as not to hurt your feet.'

'They're beautiful,' said Miriam happily, trying not to walk awkwardly in them.

'Come on in and have some breakfast, child, before we let all the warm air out of the house.'

As Miriam crossed the step, Jesse squeezed an arm about her shoulders. 'It's nice to have you with us for the day, Miriam.'

'Don't let her pass under that kissing-berry until Josh has done his duty,' Jenny called from the kitchen.

'I'd almost forgotten that!' exclaimed Jesse. 'Come on now, young man. Miriam is your guest. You'll do the proper thing or there will be no Christmas presents for you.'

With flaming cheeks, aware of the grinning faces of his father and Jenny, Josh gave Miriam a quick peck on her cheek.

'That wasn't much of a kiss,' said his mother, 'but I suppose it will have to do for now.'

From the kitchen doorway Jenny let out a loud groan. 'The young men of today aren't what they used to be, and that's a fact. If Budge had kissed me like that I'd have wanted to know what I'd done wrong.'

Miriam smiled happily at Josh as she was ushered into the kitchen for breakfast. The initial awkwardness had been broken through and Miriam had been made to feel completely at home.

Her appetite was astonishing. She cleared her plate of a meal that would have set a miner up for the day, and then she accepted the offer of a second helping.

Immediately after breakfast they all adjourned to the best room and it was time for the presents to be opened. The baby provided the centre of attraction, but to her young mind an empty box was equally as interesting as the coat it had contained.

Miriam had some anxious moments when each of the

presents she had bought was opened, fearing that it might not be acceptable. There was a leather purse with a picture of Launceston Castle embossed on it for Mrs Retallick, and Jesse was clearly delighted with it. The gifts for Josh's father, Jenny and the baby were equally well received. For Josh there was a neckerchief in bright colours.

'You shouldn't have spent so much money on such things,' said Jesse Retallick. 'I'm sure you work hard enough for it.'

Miriam kept her face averted from Josh, and he knew what had happened to the remainder of Herman Schmidt's guinea.

Presents were exchanged all round and Miriam received more small gifts from the rest of the family. Then Josh brought out his present for her, and Miriam knew by the way the others lapsed into silence that it was something special. When she held it in her hands she thought it felt like a book – a thick book.

It was. When the wrappings were taken off she held a beautiful leather-bound Bible in her hands. 'Thank you, Josh,' sounded totally inadequate but it was all she was able to say.

'Josh said you were learning to read. We thought it would be a sensible and useful present,' said Jesse.

'You won't find better reading than is in there,' said Ben seriously. 'Everything you will ever need to know about life is in that book.'

Miriam opened the cover. Inside was written, 'To Miriam Trago from Josh Retallick,' and it pleased her almost as much as the Bible itself.

'Talking about the good book . . . It's time to be thinking of chapel,' said Ben Retallick, rising to his feet. There was general movement in the room and Miriam felt uncertain about what was expected of her, but Jesse came to her rescue.

'We'll let them go off to the chapel,' she said. 'You can help me with the Christmas dinner.' To the others she said, 'And don't you let that Wrightwick Roberts ramble on until everyone in the chapel has a spoiled meal waiting for him at home. There will be nothing here for him to eat tonight if he does.'

Wrightwick Roberts considered it his duty to visit those of his parishioners who were either sick or too old to come to chapel, but his evening meal was something he shared with the Retallick family.

Those who were going to chapel were soon ready and as they went down the hill Josh turned to wave to his mother and Miriam who were standing in the doorway.

He knew that his mother had arranged things this way. By the time he and the others returned from chapel she would have thoroughly assessed Miriam's character. The thought of it kept him fidgeting all through a service which seemed to go on for ever. Actually it was hardly any longer than the regular Sunday service. Preacher Robert's sermons were notorious for lasting overlong but he had a lot ahead of him today.

Then, with the service over, it was as though everyone in the village wanted to say 'Merry Christmas' to Ben Retallick and Tom Shovell.

Jenny grinned at Josh's impatience. 'For a shy and backward lad you're a mite eager to be back with your girlfriend.'

He scowled and said nothing.

'Don't worry, Josh. Miriam and your mum will get on well. Jesse's bound to take to her. You'd go a long way to find a girl like Miriam around here.'

Ben Retallick and Tom Shovell said their last 'Happy Christmas!' and they made their way up the track into the low damp cloud that still hung around the tor.

'You're just in time,' said Jesse Retallick as they stamped on the mat and filed into the house. She was smiling, and the whole atmosphere in the house was evidence that whatever Jesse had been looking for in their guest she had found. Now there was one Trago who would find a welcome in the Retallick household.

The meal that Jesse served up was gigantic, with the stuffed goose as the centre-piece. Even Miriam had to admit defeat. Afterwards they sat around talking and playing word- and guessing-games – except for Ben Retallick, who sat in his chair by the fire snoring gently for most of the afternoon.

Wrightwick Roberts arrived in the early evening, stamping

his feet on the doormat like some great wagon-horse. His eyebrows were raised at the sight of Miriam Trago, but he made a point of singling her out for special attention later when they had eaten yet again and were gathered around the roaring fire to sing hymns. Miriam had never been to chapel but she knew snatches of the hymns and was quick to pick up a tune. The words she read from Preacher Robert's hymn-book.

'You sing like a lark, girl,' said Wrightwick Roberts. 'A voice like that should be singing the praises of the Lord every Sunday. You come to chapel and there's not a girl in the village but wouldn't envy you and wish she could sing half as sweetly.'

Miriam was glad he did not persist in his talk about her going to chapel; she would have found that difficult to keep from her father for very long.

All too soon Jesse and Jenny began yawning, the preacher and Tom Shovell put on their coats and went out into the night and it was time for Miriam to go home. Christmas Day did not have many minutes to run but it was probably the happiest day she had ever spent and she had been half-hoping that a miracle would come along to make it last for ever.

Before she left, Jesse Retallick hurried into the kitchen and came back with a basket laden with food which she had handed to Josh. 'Here, you carry this up the hill for Miriam. There's heaps of food left. It's a shame to see it go to waste.'

At the door Miriam's reluctance to leave was so apparent that Jesse's heart went out to her and she hugged her in a way that left nobody in doubt as to her feelings about her.

'I'm sorry you have to go, my dear. It's been lovely having you. Mind you come here often to see us. I shall be very hurt if you don't.'

Miriam kissed her impulsively and with everyone's 'Good night' ringing in her ears she set off with Josh into the darkness.

Once out of the light of the cottage she took Josh's arm and hugged it to her. 'Oh, Josh! It's been such a wonderful day! The best in my whole life!'

'Mum liked you a lot,' he said, his teeth showing white in the darkness.

'You really think so? She was wonderful to me.' Still holding his arm, she gave a happy skip. 'She promised to teach me to cook properly. On a stove.'

'Haven't you got a stove at home?'

'No.' She stopped skipping, and some of the happiness escaped from her. 'There are lots of things we haven't got at home.'

They walked on in silence for a while. Then she stopped. 'I'll take the basket now.'

'It's all right. I'll carry it all the way for you. It's heavy.'

'No. My dad or Morwen might not be asleep. I'll go the rest of the way on my own now.'

'What's the matter, Miriam? Have I said something to make you unhappy?'

'No, it's nothing anyone's said to me. It's been such a happy day. Too happy. Nothing will ever be quite the same again. Now I'll have to go back to doing all the same things as always.'

'You can come down to the cottage now, though. Whenever you like. Mum said she would be hurt if you didn't come. She meant it.'

'I know. I'm grateful to her for that. Good night for now, Josh.'

She leaned forward and kissed him hard on the lips. Then she was gone into the darkness.

He stood there for a full minute, until there was no sound but the wind blowing down from the rocky tor, then he turned and went home.

Miriam pushed the make-shift door aside stealthily and eased her way into the damp interior of her home. The sour smell of exhaled alcohol fumes greeted her. Noisy snores came from the corner where Moses lay. They were echoed from Morwen's bunk in another corner. Now he was working full time he was doing his best to drink like a man.

'That you, Miriam?' her mother whispered from the gloom.

'Yes.'

'Did you have a nice day?'

'Yes.'

'That's good, but don't tell your father where you've been. He brought a bottle home and was shouting for you to come and have a Christmas drink with him. He got into quite a temper because you weren't here.'

Miriam said nothing.

'You hear me?'

'Yes.'

'Well, just remember it or we'll all suffer. Good night now.'

'Good night, Ma.'

Miriam pushed the basket behind her rough mattress and undressed slowly. Then, sliding between her blankets, she lay on her back, eyes wide open for a few minutes before turning suddenly to bury her head in the straw pillow.

Chapter Seven

Christmas with the Retallicks was supposed to have been a secret, but Miriam was not clever enough to keep it away from the remainder of the Trago family for long and she suffered cruelly when Moses Trago found out.

It was Kate Trago who brought the news to the Retallicks. She knocked on the door of the cottage on New Year's Eve at the height of a rainstorm. Even then she would not have come beyond the doorstep had not Jesse dragged her inside.

'I'm not standing out there to catch my death of cold for anyone,' she said. 'If you've something to say, then for goodness' sake say it inside. Now, sit down by the fire and get warm. I'll give you a cup of broth. It will take the chill from your insides.'

She ladled out a mugful of steaming brown soup from the pot on the fire, brushing aside Kate Trago's protests. 'Get it down and stop arguing. You look as though you have need of it. Right, what's this about Miriam?'

'I – I was hoping she would be here.'

'Well, she isn't. What's happened?'

Josh was studying in the best room. Hearing voices he came through to the kitchen and was taken aback to see who it was.

Kate Trago gulped down a mouthful of soup. It was very hot and set her coughing.

When the fit passed, she said, 'It was Moses. He found out she had spent Christmas in this house and there was a terrible scene.'

'Oh! And who told him she was here?'

'He found the shoes you gave her. I tried to stop her saying anything about them, but she was too worked up to listen. All she kept doing was shouting at him to give them back to her. Then it came out. She said she'd spent Christmas Day here. It was the best day of her life, she told him. Said that your Ben had got a proper house for his family. And . . . but, oh! she said so many things. The more he laid into her the more she shouted defiance at him.'

Jesse listened as though it was herself taking the blows. Josh's face had gone the colour of chalk.

'Did he beat her bad?'

'I don't know!' Kate Trago was close to tears. 'I was screaming at him to stop, but when I tried to pull him away he knocked me down.' She paused and looked from one to the other. 'If it hadn't been for our Morwen I think Moses would have killed her.'

'Morwen stopped his father?' Jesse knew the boy was big for his age. Even so, he was no match for Moses.

'Yes.' Kate Trago's hand began to tremble so violently that she had to hold the cup in her lap with both hands to prevent the contents from spilling. 'He took a pick-handle to him. While they fought, Miriam was able to get out. I haven't seen her since.'

The whole thing was beyond Jesse's understanding. 'When did this happen?'

Kate Trago looked shamefaced, 'Night before last.'

'*What!* And you haven't looked for her before this? The poor girl could be dying somewhere.'

'I know – but I was so sure that she would be here.' Her voice broke and the trembling got so out of hand that Jesse had to rescue the cup of soup.

'Josh, have you seen Miriam?'

'No.' It was quite true. She had not met him for two nights; but, although not usual, it had sometimes happened before.

She would find some animal to watch by moonlight, or even have to work late at the Phoenix mine. 'But I think I know where to find her.'

He was already putting on his boots.

'Don't forget your coat. It's bitter out there.'

Kate Trago stood up.

'You're not going before you've seen whether Josh finds Miriam?'

'I must. I've left the younger ones alone up there. Take care of her – and tell her it's all right to come home. Moses won't touch her again. He's sorry for what he did. He wouldn't say it to anyone, but I know it. He's a hard man, Mrs Retallick, but there's some good in him still and he loves that girl.'

'We won't argue about that now.' Jesse's lips drew into a tight line, relaxing only to call to Josh, 'Go careful. We don't want anything happening to you.'

Josh banged out of the house and into the night. It was bitterly cold and the wind bit at his ears. He crashed through the undergrowth, and now that he had time to think he dreaded what he might find at the hideout. He blamed himself for not going there before tonight. He should have known that Miriam would not have missed seeing him for two nights with his departure for the engineering works only a couple of weeks away.

He found the faint path that passed close to the hideout and followed it, relying on luck rather than sight, although a pale moon occasionally slid out of the heavy grey clouds.

At the entrance to the narrow gorse-tunnel he paused and listened. He thought he could hear a sound from within, but when he called softly there was no reply. Halfway along the tunnel he was sure of the sound and when he came into the hideout he recognised it for what it was. A cold chill went through him. It was shallow, rasping breathing. He had heard it once before, when Grandfather Retallick was fighting his last losing battle with death.

Josh fumbled on the rock with cold useless fingers for the candle. When he found it he had even greater difficulty in lighting it. But it finally lit and cast its flickering light across the shadows. To Josh's imaginative mind the candle-flame had more strength in it than Miriam's body. She was slumped in a corner, sheltered from the wind, with her back against the rock and her chin resting on her chest. It was this that was the cause of her bubbling breathing as much as anything else, but Josh did not know this.

He believed that she was dying, and the state of her face was sufficient justification for his belief. Her left eye was puffed up like an apple and he could not see whether it was open or closed. A bloody graze extended from the bridge of her nose back across her forehead, and the dark shadows on her face had nothing to do with the dancing candle-flame.

He dropped to one knee beside her and, putting one hand gently beneath her chin, he lifted her head.

Weakly she tried to jerk it away from him and the movement caused her to groan painfully.

'Miriam. It's me. Josh.'

He could see now that both her eyes were swollen and tight closed. She must have been lying here, completely blind, for two days and nights.

'Miriam! Can you hear? It's me. Josh.'

'I hurt! I hurt!' She whimpered.

'It's all right now. I'll get you out of here.'

'I hurt!' She subsided into silence again. Her chin fell forward on to her chest as Josh removed his hand.

Telling her that he would get her out was one thing. Carrying out his promise was something else.

When he tried to lift her to her feet he touched one of her ribs, low down on her chest, and it grated beneath his fingers. Miriam cried out in pain.

The next few minutes were a nightmare. In dragging her to the mouth of the hideout he knocked over the candle. Then by dragging, pushing and heaving in the darkness he finally succeeded in getting her out on to the moor. Doing his best to ignore her half-conscious protests and nerve-racking dry sobs he got her on to her feet. With her arm hooked about his shoulders he staggered downwards across the slope of the moor, heading in the general direction of the cottage. More than once he fell, taking Miriam with him. Each time he climbed back to his feet. Brushing the stinging gorse-needles from the palms of his hands, he would heave Miriam up again and struggle on. Sweat began to run down his backbone, making a liar of the weather.

Then, during a swaying pause for breath, he heard someone. More than one person. They were crashing through the undergrowth towards him. Thinking that it might be Moses Trago or one of his family, Josh lowered Miriam quietly to the ground. Trying to control his laboured breathing, he sank down beside her. Whoever it was began to move away. Up the slope to his left.

'It must have been Josh; it was too noisy for a pony.'

Josh recognised the voice of Tom Shovell and then his father's soft-voiced reply.

'Dad! Over here.'

Within seconds two heavy dark shapes loomed out of the darkness in front of him.

'What are you playing at? Have you found the girl?'

'Yes, but I thought you might be Moses. Be careful; she is hurt badly.'

'All right, Ben. Gently now. I have her.'

The big shift captain cradled Miriam in his arms as though she were a baby.

Ben Retallick's hand found his son's shoulder, 'Are you all right?'

'Yes. But you – you wait until you see her. Her face. . . .'

The grip tightened. 'Don't worry. She'll be looked after now. Well done, Josh.'

Josh gulped back the tears that threatened to well up in his eyes. Now that Miriam had been given into the care of more capable hands, his knees felt weak and shaky and the perspiration that had soaked into the back of his shirt lay across his shoulder-blades like ice.

When they entered the cottage they were greeted with gasps of horror from Jesse and Jenny. As Tom Shovell laid his burden down on the sofa the bruises on Miriam's face showed scarlet and purple in the light.

Ben Retallick sucked in his cheeks with anger, and the heavy breathing of the shift captain had nothing to do with the effort of carrying Miriam.

'I think she has a broken rib,' said Josh. 'Low down on the right side.'

'She'd best have a doctor see her,' declared Jesse. 'Tom, will you go out for one? Get the man from the Caradon. He's more likely to be sober than the Phoenix doctor. Ben, put pots of water to boiling. Jenny and I will get this mite to bed.'

She began unbuttoning the tattered cardigan that Miriam wore.

'And you can stop gawping!' This to Josh. 'You've done your bit. Now we've got our work to do. I'll be making up a bed in our room. You'll have to sleep downstairs until she's well. Unless I'm mistaken this one will be laid up for a couple of weeks.'

Jesse underestimated by a week. For the first four days the mine doctor from the Caradon group of mines was a daily visitor. He strapped up Miriam's ribs – two of them were broken – and worked on Miriam's face. He feared that her nose was also broken, but when the swelling around her eyes began to go down he was pleased to acknowledge that he had been wrong.

On the fifth day Miriam could see from one eye and progressed steadily thereafter. News of her beating swept through Henwood village like an east wind. There was a steady flow of visitors to the cottage door bringing gifts. They consisted mainly of cast-off clothing, the donors angling for an invitation inside to have a look at Miriam's battered face. Thanks to the firmness of Jesse Retallick few of them were successful. Yet all of them returned to the village with wild descriptions of the injuries she was supposed to have sustained.

Kate Trago was a frequent visitor. She always came after dark and would sit next to her daughter's bed saying scarcely a word and wringing her hands nervously the whole time.

But when Miriam was able to sit out of bed for an hour or so each day she received a visitor who caused great consternation in the Retallick house. He too came after dark, but the very fact that he knocked gently at the door and waited quietly for it to be opened was sufficiently unusual in itself.

Josh opened the door – and as promptly slammed it shut again. Turning to his father in alarm, he said, 'It's Moses.'

Ben Retallick leaped from his chair and Jesse reached for the heavy iron poker kept alongside the stove. Moses knocked again. It was not an impatient knocking, but neither was it timid.

Ben motioned for Josh to move further into the room before going to open the door himself.

Moses stood before him, his hat held in his two hands. 'I've come to take Miriam home.'

It was a bald matter-of-fact statement.

'Then you've had a wasted journey.' Ben Retallick controlled his anger admirably.

Jesse was less reticent as she moved up alongside her husband. 'You take one step into this house, Moses Trago, and you'll feel this poker across your head. That girl has suffered enough at your hands. You'll not get the chance to do it again.'

'I haven't come here to quarrel, Mrs Retallick. What has happened is done. It can't be forgotten, but it won't happen again.'

It was an effort for Moses to appear humble before anybody, but he managed it.

'It won't happen again because she stops here,' said Ben Retallick firmly. 'When she's well enough we'll discuss her future. Not before.'

'Ben, I came here tonight determined to keep my temper. What I did was wrong and I'm sorry. I could blame the drink but I'm not using that as an excuse. All the same, Miriam is my daughter and I want her home.'

The poker wagged at him like an accusing finger. 'You broke two of her ribs, did your best to disfigure her for life, then let her wander off on to the moor – to die, for all you knew. And you stand here and talk of wanting her? Moses Trago, you are a hypocrite. A big, bullying, lying hypocrite.'

Moses Trago fought hard to maintain control of himself and

the strain showed. Then a voice from the stairs made them all look in that direction.

'Mrs Retallick, please let him come in to speak to me.'

Miriam's face was still discoloured and she clung to the hand-rail unsteadily.

'What are you doing up? You shouldn't be out of bed.' The poker was lowered and Jesse went to her.

'Please! Please let him come in.'

A look passed between Jesse and Ben, then Ben stood back from the door. 'You can go upstairs to see her. But, father or not, she'll not leave this house until she's well.'

Moses Trago stepped inside, his shoulders filling the doorway. There was movement behind him and he said, 'Morwen and brother John are outside.'

'They can stay there,' said Jesse brusquely. 'You're coming in only because it will upset the girl more to have a scene, but you'll not stay long. She's still a sick girl and I'm not pretending that you are welcome in this house.'

Moses mumbled something that might or might not have been his thanks, then he went up the stairs, following Miriam in to the room where she slept.

Downstairs the only sound for a long time was the crackling of wood on the fire and the murmur of voices from the bedroom.

Suddenly Josh said fiercely, 'He's not taking her with him.'

'Don't go climbing hedges until they are built,' said Ben.

'But he said he's come for her.'

'And we said she isn't ready to go,' said Jesse firmly. 'Miriam isn't fit to go, and nobody is going to force her.'

They heard the bedroom door opening, and Moses Trago came clumping heavily down the stairs.

He stopped in the centre of the room and looked from one to the other, finally settling his gaze on Jenny.

'She says she'll be coming home when she's well,' he said. 'Until then I'd be obliged if you'd have her here. I'll pay for her keep.'

'You'll keep your money and your insults to yourself,' retorted Jesse. 'She'll stay because we want her.'

'I owe you for the doctor too,' Moses persisted doggedly. He slapped two coins on the table. 'Here are two guineas. That should pay for everything.'

Jesse was on her feet and had thrust one of the coins back at him before he could say more. 'We'll take one guinea for the doctor. You caused her injuries. There's no reason why anyone else should pay for that. Whatever else we have done has been because we are fond of the girl. We want none of your money for that.'

'I pay my debts.' Moses Trago flushed angrily. 'I'll be under no obligation to anyone.'

'You have a debt to the Lord,' said Ben Retallick. 'It was only His will that kept her alive until she was found.'

'Then give this other guinea to the boy. I hear he found her.'

Josh felt his heart pounding inside him as he stood up. 'I did that for Miriam. Not for your money. Buy her some new shoes with it to make up for those you burned.'

He felt his mother's eyes on him. Kate Trago had not told her that during the fight in the Trago home Moses had thrown Miriam's shoes on to the fire in his rage. Miriam had told Josh and been more upset about it than she was for her injuries.

'You've got spirit but no money-sense,' said Moses looking at him from beneath shaggy brows. 'I've already promised Miriam some new shoes. I've also told her she can have schooling from that preacher at St Cleer. I don't like the Trago family being under obligation to anyone for anything. I've said what I came for. When Miriam is well enough to come home her mother and Morwen will come for her. Good night, Mrs Retallick. Ben. Boy.'

His look passed on to Jenny. He nodded, then turned and was gone.

'The cheek of the man!' Jesse all but exploded. 'Of all the nerve . . . !'

'Hush, now,' said Ben. 'Moses Trago cannot change what he is. Keeping his temper tonight cost him much. Give him credit for that.'

In the middle of their conversation Josh went upstairs to

find out from Miriam what had been said by her to gain such concessions from her father.

Jenny Pearn said nothing. Something in Moses Trago's eyes when he looked at her had frightened her. Tonight he had been reasonable enough. He was certainly more sober than she had ever seen him before – but there was an evilness about him that went much deeper than drunkenness. It was an animal brutality – and yet still something more. With a shiver, Jenny arrived at the conclusion that Moses Trago was close to madness and she feared what this might bring to all of them.

Chapter Eight

Miriam left the cottage and returned to the Trago home one week before Josh was due to begin his apprenticeship at Hayle. Both departures hit Jesse Retallick hard. She had become very fond of the girl. Her quick wit and an ever-ready willingness to listen and learn something new endeared her to the whole household. Even baby Gwen was always pleased to go to her.

It was like losing one of the family to watch her walking away up the hill with Morwen Trago beside her. Her brother felt awkward and was impatient at having to stop and wait each time she turned round to wave.

Then, with Miriam out of the house, it was time to pack and repack, stitch and iron, and generally prepare Josh for a stay in a town which, although hardly fifty miles distant, was as remote as the Highlands of Scotland to Jesse.

Josh himself put off thinking about it until the very last minute. He had finished his schooling with the Reverend William Thackeray, and as a parting gift the preacher had given him an old wood-and-leather chest to carry his belongings. He had also given him some words of advice.

They stood in the chill evening wind outside the little house behind the chapel where the bachelor preacher lived.

'You will be carrying my best wishes with you, Josh. But,

what is far more important, you will be looked to as an example of what education can do for every miner's son. You'll become a symbol of escape for every boy who longs for more from life than a daily shift in a mine. Don't let us down, Josh.'

They walked along the path to the gate and Preacher Thackeray opened it, pausing to look intently at Josh.

'While you're away you'll be learning new things and meeting new people. Never let them make you forget where you come from or the men who remain here – working and dying in wretched conditions. Always keep them in mind. If during the course of your apprenticeship you hear of something that might make life easier for them, then follow it up. Work hard at whatever you do. If you hear anyone at Hayle talking about a union of miners, listen to him. I would like to know the strength of feeling about it in the far west. Talk to the other apprentices, Josh. Find out about unions in other parts of the country. It's gained a strong foothold in some parts and I'm convinced that's where the future of the miner lies. With a strong union he could live a better and fuller life – that and brains like yours to seek ways to make his job safer. He would be able to take his place in the community, Josh, a proud man with a special skill, not some sort of animal to burrow in the ground all day and go home drunk to sire brats all night.'

He held out his hand. 'Goodbye and good luck, Josh. May God be with you.'

Josh made his way homewards filled with a resolve to work hard and justify the preacher's faith in him. He would also serve the miner in every way possible. It was a resolution that was to remain with him for a great many years.

His next farewell was with Miriam. Josh had not been looking forward to it. He had thought about it for a long time, imagining it as a parting that would be full of emotion. He could not have been more wrong. Miriam had caught a nasty cold in the few days that she had been home. It was this that was choking her, not emotion. The tip of her nose glowed like a blacksmith's iron, and she shivered and sniffled constantly as they stood together on the path between their two homes.

'I'll write and tell you all about Hayle and my journey as soon as I arrive,' declared Josh. He was travelling by sea from Looe harbour.

'And I'll write back straightaway,' Miriam said nasally.

'Well . . . I'll say goodbye, then.'

'Goodbye, Josh.' Her eyes were watering in the bitter wind. She shivered and felt thoroughly miserable as Josh held her briefly to kiss her goodbye. She turned her head from him and he kissed her cheek

'I don't want you to catch my cold to go away with.'

'No. Take care of yourself, Miriam.'

'And you, Josh. I shall miss you terribly.'

He realised that he was going to miss her more than anything else at Sharptor. He would have liked to tell her so but did not know how to begin. When he looked at her shivering he knew it would be cruel to keep her out in the cold until he found the right words. He turned and walked away. Looking back once he saw her standing on the path, a teeth-chattering little figure who waved bravely through tears and cold until he was out of sight.

That left only his family the following morning. Jesse fussed about him, tucking in his scarf and pulling up his collar as he sat on the driving-seat of the ore-wagon beside Nehemeziah Lancellis.

'You be good, mind. No fighting with the others – and write often.'

'Yes, Mum.'

The aged hostler flicked the reins and the wagon creaked away. Josh waved until the huddled group of his mother and father, Jenny and the baby, Tom Shovell and Miriam disappeared from view around a curve in the track. Miriam had been unable to let him go without seeing him once more, in spite of her cold.

As Josh had never before been away from home for more than one night he set off on the journey to Hayle with very mixed feelings. He and Nehemeziah were on the first wagon of the day to leave the mine for Moorswater. This was the inland terminal of the canal linking the mining area with the seaport of Looe.

As they bumped along he looked at the driver, huddled into his heavy coat beside him, but the strange old hostler had eyes only for the great steaming horses. Josh took advantage of the silence to collect his thoughts.

The silence lasted for almost two hours and then Nehemeziah cleared his throat noisily, spat over the side of the wagon and said, 'There be the canal, down the hill apiece. 'Tis a fair busy place.'

At the water's edge Josh could see pack-horses and wagons lining up to be weighed before discharging their loads into the long, blunt-nosed barges.

As they pulled into line behind another wagon Nehemeziah called to a little man seated on the leading barge with his arms folded across the stout tiller. 'There's someone to ride with 'ee today, Tom.'

'Oh? And who says so?' scowled the man past his pipe.

''Tis Ben Retallick's boy,' said the hostler. 'Going down to Hayle foundry on the *Helen and Stephen* from Looe.'

'Well, why didn't you say so in the first place?' The man on the barge stood up awkwardly. 'Any member of Ben Retallick's family is welcome to anything that Tom Taylor can do for 'em. Come aboard, son. We'll be away in a few minutes.'

Fascinated, Josh looked at the man's right leg. It was a wooden peg from the knee down.

'Ah! You can look at it, young man. If it wasn't for your father I wouldn't be alive to wear a peg-leg. Heave your things aboard and sit down on this side. Watch the dust don't blow all over you when the last load is dropped aboard.'

Josh swung his trunk on to the barge and raised a hand in farewell to the Sharptor hostler. So began the second stage of his journey to Hayle. Ten minutes later the barge was under way. It was towed by a sorry-looking barge-horse which plodded along, head down, on the canal path.

'And how are things at Wheal Sharptor?' asked Tom Taylor as the barge slipped silently through the water.

'The mine is doing quite well,' replied Josh. 'They have hit good ore in the new south-east adit and won't need to go any deeper for a long time. When they do they will need an engine. That's why I'm off to Hayle. I'm going to become an engineer. But how do you know the mine? I've never seen you there.' The visit of a man with a wooden leg would certainly not have passed unnoticed.

'It was before you were old enough to know about it,' said the bargee. 'And I know it all right. That's where I lost this leg.' He banged his knuckles on the wooden limb. 'Carrying out the orders of that drunken German and using his gunpowder. It was when the mine first opened. We were cutting the twenty-fathom level. The roof came down on me. If your father hadn't been there to dig me out, I'd be buried there now for all that Captain Schmidt cared about it. If Theophilus Strike had any sense, he'd have made your father captain of Wheal Sharptor years ago. Ben should have left Strike and gone to the Phoenix years ago, when they wanted him as their captain.'

This was news to Josh. Nothing had ever been said in his hearing about his father having the opportunity to take charge of the great Phoenix mine.

'He stayed at Sharptor more to please your mother than anything else,' the bargee went on. 'But he'd never admit it. Jesse's always loved it up there. So she should; it's beautiful. I can remember how it would be on a fine day. You could look from your door and see every part of Cornwall that matters. Half of Devon as well. As I remember, you were no more than a year or two old then.'

He pulled on the tiller to take the barge out slightly from the bank. 'We had one of the cottages alongside yours. Tom Shovell has it now. We liked it there too, the missus and me. Of course, we had to go after the accident. A one-legged man is no good to Strike and his German captain. Not a penny did I get from him, although it was more than a year before I got this job. But I've always said it was leaving that cottage that killed my missus. She loved it there. Just like your mother.'

Josh murmured his sympathy, but the bargee was not

listening. 'Yes, beautiful it were up there in the summer-time. With the swifts nesting in the eaves of the cottage and the flowers all out in the garden. . . .'

He fell silent for a time and then said, 'Perhaps Ben knew what he was doing when he chose to stay at the Wheal Sharptor, after all.'

The barge eased gently into a lock, and for some minutes the ex-miner was busy casting a rope up to the lock-keeper and easing the boat through the narrow lock.

The whole process of locking fascinated Josh. He held tight to the barge when the gates at the lower end of the lock were opened, expecting the boat to be swept out like a leaf in a moorland stream. All that happened was that the barge settled down to the new level. The horse took the strain of the barge-rope and they moved slowly along the peaceful waterway towards their destination once more.

All the way to Looe the one-legged ex-miner regaled Josh with tales of the 'old days' at the Sharptor mine. Most of his yarns had to do with the sudden deaths that had occurred. As though trying to prove – as much to himself as to Josh – how lucky he was to be a live bargee, when he might so easily have been a dead miner.

Every so often his memory would dredge up a name and he would digress to talk about him. Most he dismissed scornfully as being fit only to grade the ore and not skilled enough to dig for it. A few – Ben Retallick and Moses Trago were two – he regarded as experts in the field of mining.

'How about Mary Crabbe – is she still alive?'

Josh assured him that she was.

'She's a witch, if ever I've seen one,' said Tom Taylor seriously. 'She's there for the birth of every child and the death of every man. Yes, she's a witch, lad. I've known her to arrive at a house ready to lay a body out at the minute he takes his last breath. She knows when it's time but it's no human voice that tells her.'

He caught Josh's expression. 'You don't believe me? Well, never mind, but just remember what I've told you. One day you will see for yourself. Calls the raven her brother, does Mary Crabbe.'

It was after noon when they tied up alongside the ore jetty at Looe. It was a busy and noisy part of the docks – and a very dirty one. There was ore dust on everything above ground and thick as mud underfoot. With the rattle of tackle and the creaking of the cranes it was not surprising that the fishermen of Looe had fought hard to have the canal elsewhere. It did little to improve their livelihood.

'You'll find the *Helen and Stephen* over the other side,' said the bargee. 'One of the fishermen will row you across. Don't give him more than a penny, though he'll ask for more. And, lad. . . .' He looked embarrassed. 'Be careful of Captain Henry of the *Helen and Stephen*. He's an evil man. I wish you were travelling to Hayle on any other boat.'

Josh had no idea what the bargee was trying to tell him but he thanked him and assured him that he would take care; then, struggling with his trunk, he set off along the busy jetty.

Before he had gone twenty yards a boy of about his own age, wearing an oversize ragged fisherman's jumper, appeared alongside. 'I'll carry your trunk for you for six pence.'

'You won't,' puffed Josh. 'I could hire a horse for that money.' He put the trunk down and took a breather.

'You're no sailor,' said the boy, looking at Josh's serge suit and heavy miner's boots. 'But you're not from around here.'

'From up on the moor. I'm taking passage on the *Helen and Stephen* to Hayle.'

'Then you'll be needing my boat,' said the boy, 'and as you're from these parts it will cost you no more than three pence.'

'It's not your lucky day,' grinned Josh. 'I've heard there is someone hereabouts who charges only a penny. I'll wait until I find him.'

The boy groaned. 'All right, a penny it is. Now, I'd better give you a hand with this trunk or it will take us half the day to get there and I'll lose all my good fares. I heard that folk from up on the moor sewed their pockets up before they came down to the towns.'

The boat was a small aged affair with three inches of water slopping inside it, but the boy handled the boat well and it was not long before they were bumping against some stone steps in the lee of the *Helen and Stephen*'s weathered stern.

She was much larger than Josh had imagined she would be, and when he stepped from the high quay on to the dirty rope- and tackle-tangled deck he was awed by the height of the masts. For all that, this was an ore-carrying boat. A pack-horse of the coastal waters. There was nothing glamorous about her role or her appearance.

He had an ugly moment when, heeding the urgent shouts of one of the sailors, he ducked quickly as a cargo-jib swung inboard, missing his head by inches.

The dust rose in clouds from the ore that rumbled and thudded down the chutes into the hold and there was a choking pall hanging over the ship. The men on the deck were fully occupied with loading, and Josh felt at a loss, wondering to whom he should report his presence.

He was rescued by a small balding man who appeared from out of nowhere and took Josh's arm, propelling him towards the stern of the boat while he dragged the trunk behind him with his other hand.

'Come on in here, boyo,' he said in a sing-song voice, guiding Josh through a door. 'You'll find a ladder along there a little way. Go down it and yours is the cabin on the right.'

'How do you know—?' Josh began, but the other man broke in, 'How do I know you are Master Retallick? That's easy, my lad. First, you come on board with your trunk and stand in a place where you are likely to have your head knocked off by the loading-jib. That means you are no sailor. So you must be a passenger – right?'

Josh nodded as the man pointed to a ladder, 'Go down there. Now, secondly, a passenger is something of a novelty on board this scow. So you must be Retallick. Simple when you fit all the facts together, you see.'

He pushed a door open and heaved the trunk into a space that was scarcely six feet square. 'Here you are, now. Not up to

the accommodation I've known on East India Company ships.
But it's a bed, boyo. It's a bed!'

He gave Josh a lop-sided grin. 'I'm Taffy Williams. Steward,
cook and Captain's whipping-boy. Like this leaking old ship
I've known better days, but we both keep going. You make
yourself at home. I'll let the Captain know that you're aboard.'
His face took on a serious expression. 'That's if he hasn't been
drinking. . . .'

He gave Josh a thoughtful look. 'I think it might be better
if you stay in your cabin as much as possible while you're
aboard. I'll bring your meals down to you. There's too much
work going on up top at the moment, anyway. The Mate won't
want you wandering around.'

Everything was bewilderingly strange to Josh and, although
he did not relish the thought of being confined to the cell-like
cabin for the whole of the journey, he did not argue. Instead,
he asked when the ship would be putting to sea.

'Everyone is working in order to catch tonight's tide,'
replied the steward. 'But a lot depends on whether the
wind holds its direction. If it moves any further to westward
we'll be obliged to stay here for a while longer. Now,
you just unpack the things you're going to need for today
and tomorrow. With a good wind we might make Hayle
tomorrow night, but I've known us to battle it out for a
week or more – then end up closer to Ireland than to
Cornwall.'

When the little Welshman had left Josh sat down on the
edge of the narrow bunk and looked about him. There was
little to see. A bed, a stool and table, all securely fastened to
the floor, and a cupboard. It was as spartan as a hermit's cell.
There was not even a port-hole to look through.

When the Welsh steward returned to the cabin Josh was
lying on the bunk, reading.

'A young man of learning, I see!' The steward chattered
as he transferred steaming dishes from the tray to the table.
'How I envy you. You young men today have opportunities
that were never around when I was a boy.' The last plate on
the table, he said, 'Sit yourself down here and get some of

this food inside you. Good solid food it is. I cooked it myself.
Especially for you.'

He fussed around as Josh seated himself and began to fork
the food to his mouth. The steward was right. It was good.

'No, when I was a boy, schooling was beyond the reach of
the likes of me. And of course there was a war to be fought
then. That made things very different indeed.'

'Were you in the war?' Josh looked at the steward with new
interest.

'Was I in the war? Why, bless you, boy, I was not ten feet
from Admiral Nelson himself when he fell dying. Oh yes, and
many's the cup of gruel I've taken up to him at night when he
paced the quarter-deck while we chased the Frenchie Admiral
halfway round the world. "Taffy," he said to me many a time,
"Taffy, if it wasn't for you making sure I had me victuals I'd
forget for sure and one day I would collapse and die. Then
England would be lost." Ah. Those were glorious days, young
Master Retallick. England will never see the like of Admiral
Nelson again. There wasn't a dry eye in the Fleet when the
news of his death got around.'

Josh was suitably impressed.

'There's plenty I could tell you about the war. But it would
take longer than you'll have aboard this lump of driftwood.'

Then, although the door of the cabin was closed and there
was no chance that anyone could see them, Taffy Williams
looked over his shoulder furtively before pulling a bottle from
his pocket and pouring some of its contents into a mug on the
table in front of Josh. 'Here, have a drink of this. It's as good
a rum as you'll get anywhere. Captain Henry keeps it hidden
in his cabin.'

The fumes rising from the mug that Taffy Williams held up
to his face caused Josh to jerk his head back hurriedly. 'No,
thank you. I haven't drunk rum before.'

'You haven't drunk—? No man ever refuses good rum when
he's on board a ship! You get it down you. It stops you from
getting the scurvy. Necessary at sea, is rum.'

Josh had never heard of scurvy, but it had an ominous
ring to it so he obeyed the steward and lifted the mug to

his mouth. Doing his best to ignore the pungent fumes, he took a mouthful and swallowed. The liquid hit the back of his throat and there was a brief period of shock as the rum cut off the supply of air to his lungs. Then the blood rushed to his face and Josh choked and gagged and coughed all at the same time.

It was an incredible performance. As Taffy Williams pummelled his back the steward sounded satisfied. 'There, I told you it was some good stuff, didn't I, now?'

Eventually the fit subsided and Josh was able to wipe the tears from his eyes.

'I think you are trying to poison me,' he croaked.

'Now, there's a thing to say. The lop-sided grin was there again. 'I bring you a drop of the Captain's best rum – at great risk to myself – and you say that. Never mind, boyo. You get the rest of it down and it will keep the bad weather outside of you.'

Josh tried another sip. This time it did not choke him. It burned a fiery trail down his gullet, and he gulped air like a fish.

'That's better,' said the steward. 'We'll make a sailor of you yet. Mind you. . . .' He looked quizzically at the heavy miner's boots Josh was wearing. 'We'd better keep you below. If ever you went over the side wearing those on your feet you would sink like the ship's anchor.' He winked cheerfully at Josh and was gone, the cabin door closing softly behind him.

Josh decided he liked the little Welsh steward and his cheerful breezy manner.

Whether it was the rum or the excitement of the day Josh never knew, but he lay down on his bunk intending to read his book and it was not many minutes before his eyelids drew together and he fell into a deep sleep.

He awoke to an unaccustomed sense of movement, and sitting up he became aware of the creaking of timbers all about him. He swung his feet to the floor and stood up, only to crash against the opposite wall. Then, seconds later, he was tumbled backwards on to his bunk again.

They were at sea, and it was not a comfortable feeling!

Josh rose to his feet once more, only to be flung back immediately.

At the third attempt he clung first to the edge of the bunk and then grasped a stanchion before making it to the door. Twice he opened it, and twice it swung back on to his fingers. Then he lurched out into the passageway and, advancing hand over hand along the rail running the length of the narrow unlit corridor, he arrived at the ladder. Here he could feel the cold air coming down to meet him. At that moment a small figure clattered down the ladder and collided with him.

'Is that you, young Master Retallick?'

'Yes.'

The single word came out distorted, first drawn out as the deck dropped beneath him, and then clipped off as the ship rose as suddenly, compressing his stomach.

'I think I'm going to be sick.'

'I'm not surprised; the wind's a bit fresh. Come up here with me. No, you go first.'

The steward supported him up the ladder, holding him when the ship's antics threatened to throw him back into the corridor.

On deck there was a sharp cold wind, and spray stung Josh's face and tasted salty on his lips.

'Let me tie this around your waist.'

The steward passed a rope about Josh, fastening the other end to something at the top of the ladder. He was not a moment too soon. The ship heeled heavily to one side, Josh's feet shot from under him and he skidded down to the side of the ship to be brought up with a sudden jerk within inches of the sea that surged past below the guard-rail.

'What did I tell you about those boots?' Chuckling, Taffy Williams began pulling him in like a fish on a line, but before he had brought in his 'catch' Josh pulled away from him and, lunging as far the rope would allow, fell to his knees and threw up in the direction of the sea.

Three times he was sick. Then, trembling, he scrambled back to the top of the ladder and sat down groggily.

'You'll be all right now.' The steward's hand gripped his shoulder comfortingly.

'Is it going to be like this all the way to Hayle?' The words came out in rhythm with the ship's movements.

'Bless you, no!' Taffy Williams exclaimed. 'We are beating into a beam sea at the moment. Once we get past St George's Island and clear the Ranneys we'll be turning down-channel with the sea behind us. You won't know we're moving then.'

Secretly Josh doubted whether he would survive long enough to prove the truth of the steward's statement. But after he had suffered another rasping bout of sea-sickness the ship heeled over and lay at an acute angle for some minutes, then straightened up and was heading down-channel. Although it was by no means a smooth passage, the ship had lost most of the see-saw cork-screw movement and life was much more comfortable. Now Josh could hear the voices of unseen sailors raised above the wail of the wind in the rigging.

'Now, you come down below again and get into a warm bed. I promise you that by morning the wind will have dropped and you'll wish that you could spend all your life at sea.'

Josh felt too weak to argue and allowed himself to be led below. Getting into the bunk he did his best to ignore the motion of the ship, although it was emphasised by the flickering oil-lamp which hung from a beam above him and obeyed the law of gravity, while the ship danced around it.

But Taffy Williams had been telling the truth. When he bustled into the cabin the next morning carrying a bowl of steaming porridge, with two boiled eggs rattling together in a dish, the ship was gliding along steadily. There was only a gentle rocking movement to show that they were still at sea. The events of the previous evening could all have been part of an unpleasant dream.

Not only that, but Josh also discovered he had an appetite and the porridge smelled good.

'Where are we?' he asked as he swung his legs to the ground. 'Are we close to Hayle?'

'Why? Are you in a hurry to get there?' queried the steward.

'Because, if you are, you've chosen the wrong means of transport. A horse would have been quicker. No, boyo, you can't hurry the wind. It blew even stronger for a while after you had turned in and we had to go with it. We were almost at the Scillies before it died down and we were able to turn. We're heading for Hayle now but it will be after midday before we sight Cornwall, I shouldn't wonder. The wind must have blown itself right out. There's scarce enough now to float a feather on. But when you've finished your breakfast I'll take you up to see for yourself.'

He was as good as his word, and when Josh had eaten and washed in the hot water the steward left outside the door Taffy Williams came down for him.

'When I take you on deck we'll go for'ard. Beyond the cargo-holds. Then even if the Captain goes on to the quarter-deck he won't see you.'

'Why shouldn't the Captain see me? He knows I'm aboard, and Mr Strike paid my fare. There's no reason why he can't meet me.'

Taffy Williams avoided meeting Josh's eyes. 'Captain Henry is a strange man,' he replied. 'I've served in this ship a few years and I know. Just take my word for it and keep clear of him. Things will be better that way.'

Josh shrugged. His curiosity had been aroused by the way everyone spoke of the mysterious Captain Henry. But he would not be on the ship for very long and, if he did not meet him, it would not bother him. He followed Taffy Williams up on to the deck without saying any more.

Halfway along the main deck Josh was straining his neck to look up at the men working on the yard-arms when there was a loud bellow from behind them.

'Steward! What the hell are you doing? Come here!'

Josh looked behind and saw a stocky black-bearded man standing straddle-legged on a small raised deck beside the helmsman.

'I'm just attending to the passenger, sir. I'll see him for'ard and be with you right away.'

'You'll come when you are damn well called, mister –

and bring the passenger with you. He's entitled to meet the man who is responsible for his well-being and safety while he's aboard. It's common courtesy for a captain to greet his passengers. Come along. What's the matter with you?' he bellowed as the steward hesitated.

Reluctantly, Taffy Williams led Josh back along the deck towards the helmsman's position.

As they drew near Josh thought that Captain Henry was not at all the kind of man he had imagined the captain of a ship would be. His 'uniform' was a large blue sweater, frayed at the cuffs and with a hole in one elbow. It sagged low over a pair of dirty blue serge trousers. Most incongruous of all, the Captain wore soft carpet-slippers on his feet.

'I should think so!' Captain Henry rumbled as they approached him.

His hand was hot and clammy in Josh's and the dark-brown eyes that looked at him were red-rimmed. Above a dark beard, his cheeks were a skein of tiny blue and red veins.

'Now, there's a fine-looking lad,' said Captain Henry quietly. 'He should have been brought to me as soon as he came aboard, Williams.'

Josh wondered whether it was his imagination or if the Captain's words really did carry more menace than the shouting of a few minutes before.

'Well now, boy,' said Captain Henry. 'And how did you sleep last night? Was the weather too rough for you?'

'It was a bit,' admitted Josh. 'Is it often like that?'

'I wish it was,' said the Captain. 'That was little more than a good breeze. You don't get any bad storms around home waters. Down in the Antarctic, now, that's something different again. When I was down there whaling I saw waves as tall as one of your mine-chimneys. That's real weather for you.'

He broke off to glare at Taffy Williams. 'Come now, steward. Don't hang around here. You've got work to do.' Then, as the little Welshman turned to go, 'The boy will have his lunch with me in my cabin.'

Taffy Williams looked unhappy as he went away, but the

Captain turned back to Josh. 'Now, boy, is this your first time in a ship?'

Josh said that it was.

'Then we'd better show you what goes on.' He pointed to the horizon where a few low islands could be seen low down on the skyline.

'Over there you can see the Scillies. A dangerous place to sail close to. The further away they stay the happier any sailor will be.'

Captain Henry went on to tell Josh of the ships that had foundered on the Scilly Isles. When he had exhausted that subject, he talked of whaling in the Antarctic. He showed Josh how the compass worked and even allowed him to steer the vessel. It was not long before Josh was wondering why both Taffy Williams and the one-legged bargee had been so concerned about his meeting the captain of the *Helen and Stephen*. He was interesting and entertaining company.

It seemed no time at all before the ship's bell was clanging to announce midday.

'That's the signal for lunch,' said Captain Henry, clapping Josh on the shoulder. 'Come down to my cabin. We'll have a meal in surroundings more fitting to a fare-paying passenger than that hen-coop of a cabin you slept in last night.'

He led the way along the main deck and steered Josh into a short corridor. The corridor ended at a red mahogany door with a gleaming brass handle.

The Captain turned the handle and swung the door open, waving Josh inside. 'There you are, boy. You won't find a cabin to compare with this even on those new-fangled steamers that the big companies are playing with. It's a captain's cabin, as good as any on an Atlantic packet. When the sea is your home you have to make your own comfort. D'you like it?'

'Like' was a totally inadequate word. The cabin was more luxurious than anything Josh had ever seen. The walls were panelled in polished rosewood with gleaming brass lanterns spaced at intervals along three of them. The fourth 'wall' was completely taken up by a long narrow window. It must have been tucked tight beneath the stern of the *Helen and Stephen*.

There was a fine carpet on the floor, while the furniture, at first sight appearing sparse, was cleverly designed to blend into the cabin.

'You don't mind if I change before we eat?'

Without waiting for a reply the Captain walked to one of a series of cupboards cunningly built into one of the rosewood walls. He opened it to reveal a rail of clothes quite out of keeping with his present rough appearance and station in life. There were shirts and waistcoats of silk, breeches of fine linen and coats that a gentleman would have been proud to possess.

'Don't look so surprised, boy. You don't think I've always been skipper of a gash-boat like this, do you? No, I've been master of some of the finest ships ever to have voyaged to India. In those days no man was ashamed to say he'd been a guest at Captain Henry's table.'

'Then why are you on the *Helen and Stephen* now instead of in one of those ships?'

'Well you may ask,' said Captain Henry, pushing a silken shirt inside corduroy breeches. 'But it's a long tale and better left in the past.'

Josh had seen many men change their clothing at the mine. When they came up from a wet shaft most men would strip naked and towel off before putting on their home-going clothes. In the rough mine surroundings a naked man was a perfectly natural thing. Josh had scarcely thought about it before. But here in this sumptuous unfamiliar cabin it embarrassed him. He looked away from the Captain, examining the remainder of the cabin.

There was much to see. A barometer standing fully five feet tall and set in soft golden brass; a globe of the world with mountain ranges raised in relief and coloured as though there was snow on the highest peaks. Harpoons stapled to the wall. . . .

'Well? Is it, or is it not, the finest cabin you've ever seen?'

'It's a very fine cabin,' Josh agreed.

'You're damned right it is!' Captain Henry strode across the cabin and briefly draped an arm about Josh's shoulders. Josh stiffened instinctively.

'You're all right, boy.' The arm tightened momentarily, then was taken away, much to Josh's relief.

The Captain now moved to another cupboard. Pulling out a key that hung on a long silver chain about his neck, he inserted it into the cupboard door.

The Captain reached inside and with much clinking of glass lifted a bottle and glass tumblers on to the table.

'Now, this is something else I enjoy. A good drink – and I mean "good". None of your cheap wines for me. I learned about good liquor when I was a real skipper. I had passengers aboard the whole time then. Men and women of family and breeding – not a hold full of grubby ore. Hah! Those were the good days.'

He poured golden liquid into two glasses. 'You try this, boy. The best sherry from Spain. You won't find its equal anywhere.'

'I don't really drink. . . .'

'Nonsense! I take it as a personal insult when a guest in my cabin refuses to drink with me. Come in!' he called in answer to a knock upon the cabin door.

The door swung open. Taffy Williams, dressed in a once-white coat came in carrying two bowls of soup on a tray.

'About time too,' grumbled Captain Henry. 'All right, boy, sit up to the table. That's it; the chair over there. I'll sit here where I can see you. What wine do you want – white or red?'

Taffy Williams was standing behind the Captain's chair and signalling to Josh he mouthed the word 'white'. Josh accepted his cue, although he did not want any wine at all.

'White wine?' The Captain sniffed his disapproval. 'I never drink anything but red. But it's your choice to make.'

He swung around upon the little Welshman. 'Are you still here? Get off and bring us some wine. Move yourself! By God! One day I'll get a real steward to take your place.'

He lifted his sherry and with a single quick movement tossed the contents of the glass down his throat. He immediately reached for the bottle to refill it. Waving the bottle in his hand he called, 'Drink up, boy. Tell me whether it's to your liking.'

Josh took a sip and was relieved to find that it lacked the fire of the drink Taffy had given to him the previous evening. This was quite pleasant. He said as much.

'Good!' The Captain filled his own glass for the third time. 'You'll enjoy the wine too.' He picked up a spoon from beside his plate, and Josh followed his example. The number of knives, forks and spoons on the table bothered him. He did not want to make a glaring error in front of his host. He need not have worried. For all his fine wardrobe and affected gracious living, Captain Henry ate his food with a gusto that would have disgusted a fastidious eater. The noise of the soup disappearing into his mouth curtailed all intelligible conversation.

Taffy Williams returned to the cabin carrying two heavy flagons. One he put down before Captain Henry and the other in front of Josh. Then, without uttering a word, he turned to go.

'Come back here. I didn't tell you to leave!' Captain Henry's shout made Josh drop a spoonful of his soup on to the tablecloth.

'Pour the drinks. What sort of a steward do you think you are? I've had ignorant savages who could do the job better.'

'I don't suppose they had to do the cooking as well,' retorted the steward in his sing-song Welsh voice.

In the silence that followed Josh thought that fire would belch forth from Captain Henry's nose.

'Damn you, Williams!' His voice vibrated with anger. 'I'll have you off this ship when we reach harbour. There won't be a skipper in the country who will take you on. No, not even on a stinking Irish pig-boat!'

Taffy Williams appeared to be completely unconcerned at the Captain's outburst. He calmly filled Josh's glass from the flagon before leaving the cabin. Ignoring Captain Henry's malevolent look.

'Insolent lout. I'll have him flogged if he's not careful.'

Josh observed that the skin between the Captain's beard and his eyes had turned an ugly purple.

'Well, is the wine to your liking, boy?'

Josh lifted his glass hurriedly and took a cautious swig. His astonishment showed before he could conceal it, and the Captain thrust his jaw forward aggressively. 'What's the matter? Is it vinegary? Damned steward. I'll murder him.'

'No.' Josh took a large mouthful. 'It's fine. It really is. I like it.' He emptied the glass and refilled it from the flagon.

Captain Henry beamed. 'That's the stuff, boy. You drink it down.' He poured red wine into his own glass until it overflowed on to the cloth. 'Wine was never meant to be any other colour but red. However, each to his own taste, I say. Drink up, boy. There's plenty more where this came from.'

Josh breathed a sigh of relief and took another drink from his glass. He could match the Captain drink for drink with this 'wine'. Taffy Williams had filled the flagon with pure water.

As the meal progressed Captain Henry became louder in his speech and more careless with the pouring of his wine. During the brief silences that interspersed his outbursts he fixed his bleary eyes on his guest. It made Josh more and more uncomfortable. By now he was eager to get the meal over. Breathing a sigh of relief he laid down his last spoon. Captain Henry did the same.

'Enjoy your meal, boy?'

'Yes, thank you. It was very nice. I'll be going now. . . .'

'Sit down! Sit down! That was as good a meal as you'll get at sea. Better than the swill we feed to the crew, eh?' He laughed uproariously, hiccuped, then belched.

'Sit down, I say. You've got to let food digest properly. What you need is a brandy. *Williams!*' He bellowed like an angry bull and the steward appeared so quickly that he must have been standing just outside the door.

'Clear this filth away. And get out the brandy. The good brandy, none of your new rubbish. They haven't made a good drop of brandy in France since they packed Napoleon off to St Helena.'

Josh began to edge towards the door but Captain Henry's

eye caught him and pinned him to the spot like a harpoon. 'Come over here and sit down. When this Welsh layabout has cleared away and put out the brandy we'll have a drink and talk together.'

He propelled Josh into a seat by the stern window, stumbling on the way and leaning heavily on him for support. Josh looked at the steward, appealing silently for his assistance. But before Taffy Williams could show any sign of acknowledgement Captain Henry turned on him.

'Are you still here? Get out, you lazy good-for-nothing.' He lunged at the frail little steward, who promptly fled through the doorway. Captain Henry slammed the door shut after him and drove home the bolt. 'That will keep him out,' he said. 'I'll get the brandy myself.' He staggered to the liquor cupboard, leaning against the imagined roll of the ship.

Listening to the Captain muttering to himself as he sent bottles crashing against each other in the cupboard, Josh was thoroughly alarmed. Captain Henry was roaring drunk. Josh had begun to realise why he had been warned about him. He was no normal man.

Lurching back to the table, Captain Henry placed a brandy bottle and two pot-bellied glasses in front of Josh.

'Here we are! The best brandy you can buy. This will put fire in your belly.'

'I won't have any more, thank you,' said Josh, determined to keep his voice steady.

'Of course you'll have some!' the Captain's voice thundered out, his beard jutting forward once more. 'Do you want to be taken for an unsociable lout?'

For a full minute he glowered, and Josh did his best to meet his eyes. Then the Captain's manner underwent a complete change.

'You mustn't take any notice of me, boy. I wouldn't hurt you. Just have a small drop so that I am not drinking alone. You'll enjoy it, I promise you.' He slopped the brandy into the two goblets and reached across the table to place one beside Josh.

As his arm went out it rested on the table alongside Josh's

own. The contrast was striking. One arm dark and hairy, Josh's smooth and light brown.

'Look at that, now,' said the Captain, pushing his arm against Josh's to make the contrast even more noticeable. 'You wouldn't think both these arms belonged to men, would you, now?'

He lifted his hand and ran his fingers slowly along Josh's bare arm from wrist to elbow. 'Smooth, like a girl's. Soft, too, I'll wager.' He took Josh's arm between finger and thumb and gently squeezed it.

Josh looked up at Captain Henry's face and his stomach turned over at the expression he saw there. Pulling his arm away, he stood up hurriedly.

'I'm going out for some fresh air. I think I'm going to be sick.'

Quick as he was, Captain Henry was faster, and with his back to the door he barred Josh's way.

'You can't go now, boy.' His tone was wheedling. 'Here, sit down and drink your brandy.' Beads of sweat stood out from his temples, but Josh stood his ground and the Captain's eyes began to glitter angrily. 'Where do you think you can go if you leave this cabin? You are on my ship. I could have you brought back here in irons if I wanted to. I am the captain and my crew do as I tell them.' Then his voice became low and persuasive once more. 'But there won't be any need for that, will there? You're an intelligent lad; I can see it in your face. You be nice to me and I won't hurt you. More than that, you'll find I can be generous to those I like and I'm beginning to like you, boy. Come along. Be sensible.'

Josh's heart was thumping in his chest as he assessed his position. There was no way out of the cabin while the Captain stood against the door. Physical force was out of the question. He turned back to the table. 'What is it you want?'

'That's better. I knew you for a bright boy as soon as I saw you!'

Josh avoided looking up into the leering face.

'As to what I want. Why, nothing more than for us to be friends. Men on board ships need to have friends. It's a strange life at sea, boy. A man needs someone to share things with. To help him with his problems. You know what I am talking about.'

Josh sat down, and the Captain came across the room to stand beside his chair. Josh could smell the animal smell of the seaman's body. A hand came down and touched his forehead. 'You're hot, boy. So am I. Undo your shirt; you'll feel cooler.'

The hand moved down further. Past his face and down to his chest. Josh looked up at Captain Henry. His fingers closed around the brandy glass and suddenly he hurled the contents straight at the bloodshot eyes. The glass shattered in his hand as Captain Henry staggered backwards with both hands to his face. Josh dived for the door.

Had the bolt not been so stiff he would have had it drawn and been out of the cabin before the Captain recovered. But while he frantically levered it up and down Captain Henry leaped at him. Pinning his hands to his side, he swung Josh away from the door.

'I'll teach you to pull a trick like that on me. You'll suffer for that, boy. I'll break you. Have you screaming for mercy. Damned if I won't.'

He dragged Josh towards the bed in the corner of the cabin. Just before they reached it Josh kicked backward with the steel-tipped heel of his miner's boot. He felt it strike home and scraped it hard down the Captain's shin. Captain Henry's grip broke, but Josh's flight was blocked by the table. Before he could get around it the enraged sea captain once more barred his way.

Looking for something with which to defend himself, Josh seized the half-full flagon of red wine. As Captain Henry lunged towards him, Josh swung it. Face and flagon met with a sickening smash, and as the flagon disintegrated the captain crashed to the floor.

Josh wrenched open the door and looking back saw Captain Henry lying with his head turned to one side. Blood poured from a jagged wound on his forehead.

In the corridor outside the cabin he collided with Taffy Williams and the First Mate.

'I've killed him! I've killed him!'

'Shut up!' The Mate went into the cabin and Taffy Williams rounded on Josh. 'Go back to your cabin. Leave us to deal with this. Don't stop on the way and say nothing to anyone. Not a word. You hear?'

Josh stumbled out into the winter sunshine and took the few steps to the guard-rail. There he fell on to his knees and was more sick than he had been during the storm of the previous night. Oblivious of the ribald laughter of the crew he finally cuffed the back of his hand across his mouth. Getting to his feet he made his way to his cabin.

Once inside he closed the door and sat down heavily on his bunk. The thought of what had just taken place in the Captain's cabin caused him to bury his head in his hands. It had to be a nightmare. It could not really have happened. Then he remembered the blood on the Captain's face as he lay motionless on the floor. It had been only too real.

He recalled the public hanging at Bodmin, visualising a re-enactment of the same scene with himself standing on the scaffold, the noose about his neck. The shame of it would kill his mother. She—

There were footsteps outside the cabin and he started to his feet. It was Taffy Williams.

'Sit down. Sit down,' he said, and correctly interpreted Josh's expression. 'Oh, he's not dead! More's the pity.'

Josh could not believe him. 'But the blood on his face? His head . . . ?'

'Yes, he's got a nasty cut on his forehead,' said the steward. 'He'll always carry a scar to remember you by.' He chuckled. 'That's a different memory to the one he thought he would have, I'll wager.'

The relief was so overwhelming Josh had to sit down again. 'What will happen to me now? What will he do?'

'He'll do nothing – except perhaps consider himself lucky to get away with only a cut head. The Mate made that clear to him. He promised Captain Henry that if anything came of this he would end his days looking at the sea through the bars of a prison hulk.'

He grinned. 'It was the Mate's happiest day aboard this ship. He leaves us at the end of this trip to take over his own command. He has been waiting for something like this to happen. It gave him the chance to tell the Captain what he thinks of him without fear of reprisal.'

'This is what you and the bargeman were trying to warn me about. I should have paid more attention.'

'I don't know about any bargeman. I certainly was. Captain Henry's reputation is well known among sailing men.'

'Why do you stay with him?'

Taffy Williams looked embarrassed, 'Well . . . I suppose I'm getting on a bit now, you see. It wouldn't be easy for me to find a new berth.'

He turned to go but paused in the doorway. 'We'll be putting into Hayle at first light tomorrow morning. Stay in your cabin until then. I'll bring your supper and anything else you might need. You came out of this scrape well – but don't let that go to your head. It could just as easily have gone the other way. Sheer luck decided it. Remember that.'

Chapter Nine

As Taffy Williams had predicted, dawn found the *Helen and Stephen* riding the tide into Hayle harbour. Josh was anxious to go ashore, and his packed trunk stood in the passageway outside his cabin. He himself stood at the top of the ladder to the deck, sheltered from the gaze of anyone at the wheel. He shivered in the cold mist which drifted low across the wide glistening mud-flats of the Hayle river estuary.

It was a dull unprepossessing scene, flat and dreary. On the far bank were the ugly stone buildings of the works that was to be his home for the next three years. Smoke from the foundry and smelting-chimneys belched forth thick and dirty, darkening the mist. Although it was early, there was much activity on the foundry jetty. Another boat was going in ahead of them. Two others tied alongside hurried to batten down to catch the tide. The *Helen and Stephen* herself would be staying only long enough to off-load a small quantity of iron ore for the Harvey foundry. The bulk of her cargo was copper ore bound for the Swansea smelters.

With the help of a longboat, the ship edged in towards the jetty. At the last minute the unpredictable tide caused the ship to swing in hard. She met the jetty with a crash that had Josh clinging to the guard-rail for support.

He hurried down the ladder for his trunk, but Taffy Williams beat him to it.

'Leave it to me, boyo. I'll carry this for you.' When Josh protested that it was too heavy, the little steward heaved it up and got his shoulder underneath it with an ease that belied his years. It was indicative of many years' practice carrying passengers' baggage in earlier days.

With the tide not yet full and the *Helen and Stephen* low in the water, there was no need of a gangway to connect the boat with the shore. A section of the guard-rail had been removed and Josh stepped direct from the deck of the ship on to the stone jetty. He shot a quick glance back to the stern-deck of the ship, but Captain Henry was nowhere to be seen – only the First Mate, who raised an arm in a cheerful farewell.

At the far edge of the jetty the steward lowered the trunk to the ground. 'This is where I leave you, Master Retallick.' He held out his hand and Josh shook it warmly.

'I don't think you will forget your first sea trip in a hurry.' The Welshman grimaced. 'But don't judge all skippers by Captain Henry. Most of them are fine men.'

Josh felt that he had known the little steward a lifetime instead of a scant two days. 'Thank you for all your help. It's a good thing you were around. Without you I don't know what would have happened. Thank you again.'

Taffy Williams smiled. 'I should be thanking you. The story of how Captain Henry got his scar will grow with every telling. I shall be able to enjoy free drinks for the rest of my sea-time on the strength of having been there when it happened. Take care of yourself, young man. Learn all they have to teach you here. It isn't only the mines that need steam-engines for pulling carts along the rails. Steam-engines are going to change things. You are getting in at the beginning of something very important. I wish I was your age so I could do something like it myself.'

He was not used to making such long speeches, and with a half-wave of his hand he turned and was gone.

'You Joshua Retallick?' Although Josh did not recognise the accent it was pure Cockney. The voice belonged to a boy of about his own age.

'Yes.'

'You'd better come with me, then. Tom Fiddler's the name. I've been sent to meet you.'

He made no move to help as Josh picked up his trunk. Carrying it before him, Josh walked stiff-legged after the other boy.

When they reached the corner of the main foundry building Josh put the trunk down to take a rest. The other boy stopped with him.

'Didn't see Captain Henry on deck when the *Helen and Stephen* came in. Is he still in command?'

'I expect he was in his cabin.'

'Did you meet him?'

Josh met the curious blue eyes with a hard stare. 'Yes. Why?'

Tom Fiddler shrugged his shoulders. 'Just wondered. I've heard talk about him. A bloke I know of reckoned as how he'd got a few funny ideas.'

'He's still got them. We didn't get on very well.'

The other boy grinned at Josh, his manner becoming suddenly friendly. 'Pleased to hear it. 'Ere, let me help you with that trunk.'

Taking one of the handles he let the trunk swing at arm's length between them and chatted away as they walked on.

'You'll like it here all right. Harvey's makes the best engines in the world. Mind you, it's best to keep out of the way of the Copperhouse lot. They'll fight you to try to prove theirs are better.'

He pointed to the far end of the long narrow creek to the east. Black acrid smoke belched from a series of tall grimy chimneys. 'That's their works. Most of the river bank belongs to them. They had the only quay too and did their best to put us out of business. But Old Man Harvey showed them. He built his own docks here, then thumbed his nose at them. Never forgiven him for that, Copperhouse haven't.'

They skirted the edge of a huge granite-block building, treading a muddy path between piles of rough ore, rusting girders and new-cast boiler parts, pockmarked and heat-stained. As they passed an opening as wide and tall as a miner's cottage, a furnace door was opened. The heat and roar from within gave Josh an almost physical blow and sent him staggering. 'You'll soon get used to that,' said his companion. 'But at first you'll be gasping for breath whenever they open a furnace door near you.'

Before they passed into the building that served as a dormitory Tom Fiddler pointed out the house of the works manager. It lay between the dormitory and the gate. Tom said this made it well-nigh impossible for any of the apprentices to get past the house without some member of the household observing them.

The dormitory itself was comfortable enough. It even had a wood floor – a rare luxury for a single-storey building – plus a partitioned-off dining-area just inside the entrance. Along the whole length of the building, spaced out against the two long walls, were a dozen beds. A fair-sized locker stood alongside each.

Tom pointed out the empty bed and locker allocated to Josh. This would be his for the next three years. But Josh was not given any time to settle into his new surroundings. Tom Fiddler waited while he changed into working clothes, then took him to meet the works manager.

William Carlyon was a tall, hook-nosed, no-nonsense man who frowned at Josh as though he disliked all boys – and new apprentices in particular. Dismissing Tom with a peremptory wave of his hand, he kept Josh waiting for some minutes while he completed a letter and sealed it down. This done, he leaned well back in his chair. Placing his fingertips together in front of his chest he looked coldly at Josh.

'I understand you are a boy with a fondness for violence?'

Josh was momentarily startled and then his spirits sank. News of his encounter with the master of the *Helen and Stephen* had not been slow in circulating.

'Well, Retallick, is it true or is it not? Are you a young man who practises violence?'

'No, sir.'

It came out as an unhappy mumble.

'Speak up! You are saying that nothing happened on the *Helen and Stephen*? You never struck Captain Henry a blow that severely gashed his head?'

Josh searched desperately for the right words. 'I hit him with a wine flagon – but it was. . . . I didn't want to have to do it.'

William Carlyon nodded, his eyes not leaving Josh's face. 'Perhaps you would care to enlarge upon that statement?'

Josh hesitated and then shook his head. He did not want to relive the nightmare afternoon on the ship, even if it meant being sent home to Sharptor in disgrace.

'I see! You are quite certain you will not talk about it?'

'Yes, sir.'

'Very well.' The manager stood up and walked to the window that opened out over the untidy foundry yard and stood with his back to Josh.

'If you take my advice, you will maintain that attitude, Retallick. Knocking Captain Henry unconscious may make you something of a hero in the eyes of a great many people hereabouts, but I have no room for a troublemaker among my apprentices. However, Captain Henry has gained a certain unfortunate notoriety and the fact that he has laid no charges against you weighs heavily in your favour.'

He turned to face Josh. 'Do we understand each other?'

Josh could scarcely hide his relief. 'Yes, sir. Thank you.'

'Then we will consider the matter forgotten. Unless you yourself commit some act to remind me.'

He frowned again, but his face no longer looked quite so formidable to Josh. 'Now we begin the task of turning you into an engineer. All in three short years!' He sniffed derisively. 'That is scarcely enough time to teach you to work an engine, let alone build or repair one.'

He walked to the door, beckoning Josh to follow him. 'But we'll make a start and teach you your trade from the very beginning.'

An hour later, sweating and coal-grimy, Josh was helping a toothless old ex-miner to shovel Welsh coal into the greedy furnaces and bring them up to a heat that would boil iron.

For a week Josh carried out this task and developed muscles that had lain dormant until now. He learned that there was more to maintaining the correct temperature in a furnace than just heaving coal through the fire-door. The raking and banking, clearing and de-clinkering were of equal importance.

His return to the dormitory at the end of each working day was the signal for a great deal of good-natured banter from the other apprentices. They had each been initiated into the engineering trade in the same hard manner. The bantering was not as rough as it might have been. William Carlyon was not the only person in the Hayle engineering works who had heard of the fight on the *Helen and Stephen*. The news had earned Josh a cautious respect from the others. But, this apart, they were a friendly enough group of boys. They all worked a long day in different sections of the foundry. In the evenings they spent a couple of hours writing notes or studying plans of engines – past and proposed. Because of this there was little opportunity for Josh to get to know them quickly. The exception was Tom Fiddler, who took upon himself the task of teaching Josh the Harvey routine.

Every one of the boys was totally dedicated to becoming a steam-engineer. Listening to them discussing problems and theories in the evenings, Josh envied them their knowledge and seniority. It would be some time before he could get down to actual engineering. At the end of his week as a stoker he would be helping to load the ore into the furnaces.

Then he would learn how to handle the steaming molten metal that poured like a brew from hell into the waiting moulds. Following that he would become involved with the moulding itself. Boilers, pipes, beams and tramway lines, all were made at Harvey's Hayle foundry, in addition to the parts that were made in the works' own smithy – another link in the chain of Josh's learning.

The apprentices worked a six-day week, the seventh day being theirs to do with as they wished, provided they did not

miss the two-hour service held in Hayle Methodist chapel in
the morning.

Washed and wearing the best clothes they possessed, they
assembled outside the works manager's house to escort the
Carlyon family to chapel. William and Molly Carlyon had
wanted a son to continue the Carlyon line. Instead, they
had produced two daughters. Sarah and Mary. Sarah was
Josh's own age, but Mary was only six, spoiled by family
and apprentices alike.

Josh took an immediate liking to her and she to him. All
the way to the chapel she chattered away. He found himself
having more to say than he had for the whole of the time he
had been at Hayle. Before they fell silent to pass in through
the chapel door she had elicited details of his home, parents
and a great deal more besides. This information seemed to
interest her sister too.

Inside the chapel Josh had his first taste of the deep division
between the two foundries established in the small town. In
Henwood he had been used to sitting in the pews to the left
of the aisle and he instinctively went in that direction. He was
hurriedly pushed to the other side by Tom Fiddler.

'We sit over here,' he hissed into Josh's ear. 'That side's for
Copperhouse.'

Josh sat behind the Carlyon girls. He could not help noticing
the whiteness of the backs of their necks and the fair hair
drawn back in identical tidy plaits. Paradoxically, it made
him think of Miriam – of her brown skin and long, untidy
black hair. He wondered what she was doing at that very
moment. As the weather was fine she would most probably
be somewhere on the moor, scuffing her feet through the dead
brown fern; or perhaps she was in the hideout, reading, or
writing to him.

The service was long and boring. More than once Mary
Carlyon turned to smile at him, to be sharply elbowed into
conformity by her sister.

When the service finally came to an end the apprentices
were allowed to walk around the town until lunch-time. It
was during this period, according to Tom Fiddler, that they

enjoyed slanging matches with the Copperhouse apprentices, occasionally goading them into a fight. Despite Tom's enthusiasm Josh did not join them. He remembered William Carlyon's warning and had no wish to become involved in any fight.

He had thought to make his own way back to the engineering works, but the Carlyon family were only a short distance ahead and Mary saw him. She called out to him and they waited until he caught up.

Mrs Carlyon queried the fact that he was not staying in town with the other apprentices. Josh made the excuse that he wanted to write home. This was partly true. He knew his mother would be worrying about him. Miriam too. He would address the letter to his parents, and Miriam could read it to them. But it was difficult to think of letter-writing when he was surrounded by the Carlyon family. From them he learned that it was part of the apprentices' Sunday afternoon routine to have tea with the family.

When he left them and went into the dormitory the unaccustomed silence in the empty building was unbearable. He began his letter in a mood of homesickness that remained with him throughout the whole three pages. During that time he wanted nothing more than to be on the moor, wandering across the green wind-swept expanse.

The mood did not leave him until the others returned, noisy and happy. They had achieved a rowdy confrontation with the Copperhouse boys. No blows had been struck on either side, but in the verbal battle the Harvey apprentices were in no doubt that they had won the exchange of insults.

'They don't know nothing about engines,' scoffed Tom Fiddler. 'You could suck more water out of a mine with a straw than one of their engines could raise. And we told them so.'

There was renewed laughter when Josh asked what the reply had been.

'Their faces went as red as a runner's waistcoat,' said Tom. 'But they didn't have no answer. Harvey's engines are the best in the world.'

This was a belief that Josh was to find throughout the

works. From the old man who cleaned the clinker from the furnaces to the company's top designer, each and every man was genuinely convinced that Harvey's products had no equal.

Josh enclosed a brief note to Miriam with his letter, asking about some of the things that mattered only to them – or that mattered not at all. These few lines took longer to put together than the whole of the letter to his parents. He sealed them down and put them safely in his locker. Tomorrow they would go out with one of the ore boats to Looe, then up-canal with a bargeman to end the journey in the pocket of a Sharptor wagoner.

Josh had not been away from home a week; yet already, when the other boys were around him, Sharptor seemed like another world in another time. Tea in the Carlyon house, however, was one part of his new life he would gladly have forgone. He began to feel ill at ease when he sat down at the huge table with its white cloth, silver cutlery and ordered appearance. It might have had something to do with his recent experience of similar refinements. It would have been less of an ordeal had he been seated in the midst of the other boys. As he was the newest apprentice Mrs Carlyon wanted to find out something of his background. So he was seated between herself and Sarah.

This only added to his feeling of awkwardness and made him more clumsy than usual. During the past week coal dust had become engrained in his fingers and beneath the nails, and he tried to keep his hands beneath the table as much as possible. Because of this he quickly crammed his mouth overfull whenever he had to use his hands. This was always the moment when either Sarah or her mother asked him a question. He would have to gobble like a turkey and swallow greedily to give them an answer.

Mrs Carlyon quickly established that his father was a miner in one of the smaller mines and Josh would be tied to the same mine for a number of years after his apprenticeship. After that she lost a certain amount of interest. Not so Sarah.

To the Cornish of the far west, Bodmin Moor was something

vague and mysterious, shrouded in mist and legend. Sarah was curious to know more about it.

When he began to talk about the moor, Josh temporarily forgot his shyness. By the time he had finished telling Sarah about the badgers and their habits he found that the whole company had been listening to him.

'You know your badgers and Bodmin Moor well, Josh,' said William Carlyon. 'You also have the ability to talk about them. Take the same interest in engineering and Mr Strike won't be sorry he sent you to Hayle.'

He stood up. 'Now it is time to send you all back to your dormitory to prepare for tomorrow. Work hard during the coming week. We look forward to having the pleasure of your company next Sunday.'

During the next weeks Josh's life settled into a pattern that varied only in the work he was doing. Gradually he began to enjoy his Sundays with the Carlyons more than he had that first one. If Mrs Carlyon was not happy because Sarah spent most of the time talking only to Josh, neither she nor William ever mentioned it.

That was a mild winter. When it gave way without a struggle to spring, Easter had arrived.

This was a weekend that Josh had been looking forward to for two very good reasons. One was that after the weekend his apprenticeship would start in earnest and he would begin to learn about the working of steam-engines. The second was that the boys were being given a four-day holiday, and he was going home. Not by sea, but overland in a coach. Travelling with no less a personage than Francis Trevithick, son of the great Cornish engineer and inventor Richard Trevithick. Like his father, Francis Trevithick's influence extended beyond the field of mine-engineering. Richard had married into the Harvey family, and his son had learned his skills with them. He was currently working on steam locomotion.

It had caused more than a passing stir among the apprentices when they saw him at chapel one Sunday morning. Later they met him at the Carlyon house. It was there he made his offer to take Josh as far as Launceston in his own coach. He was travelling to Bristol where a Harvey steam-engine was to power a new transatlantic paddle-steamer being built in the Bristol docks. He was to act as an adviser on its installation.

Shivering by the gate of the works in the early Good Friday dawn, Josh began to worry whether Francis Trevithick might have forgotten his promise. Then, at hardly a minute past six o'clock, the carriage swung around the corner, pulled by a pair of fine horses.

Josh started to clamber up on to the driving-seat with the liveried coachman but the carriage door swung open and the gruff voice of Trevithick called to him, 'In here, lad. You'll freeze to death up there in those clothes. Besides, I want to find out whether they are teaching apprentices anything these days.'

Josh climbed inside and sat on the shiny black leather seat opposite the master-engineer.

'You'd better make yourself comfortable and enjoy the ride while you can,' grumbled Trevithick as the horses gathered speed and the coach swayed in rhythm with their gait. 'There's little enough good road this side of Wadebridge. Now, tell me what you've learned about engineering at Harvey's.'

Josh started to say that he had not been at the works for many months and had learned hardly anything at all, but Trevithick waved his excuses aside with an impatient gesture. 'Nonsense! You will have learned quite a lot, I am sure. How do you bank a furnace to get the maximum heat from it? And what do you do to keep it at the highest possible temperature using the minimum of coal? Then what about moulding – you've done some of that? Good, then what must you be most careful of when you pour into the mould? Presume there is a flaw in the metal, how would you know it was there if you couldn't see it on the surface?'

Josh gave Trevithick the answers he was looking for – briefly at first, but the engineer demanded more detail, probing the limits of Josh's knowledge.

'And what are you going to do when you leave Hayle?'

Josh told him about Theophilus Strike and the Sharptor mine.

'This mine of yours – it's still being pumped by a horse-whim?' Trevithick spat the question out. 'What depth has the mine reached? How many men are working it?'

Josh told him.

'Then Strike ought to be horse-whipped! What sort of a mine captain does he have to allow the mine to operate in such a primitive fashion?

'A German, you say!' He snorted. 'They've killed as many Cornishmen by their ignorance as the whole of the French Army with their bullets. What type of engine will you install there? Do you know?'

Theophilus Strike had ordered a beam-engine of proven performance. A type that had been used in local mines for more than thirty years.

Trevithick snorted derisively yet again. 'In three or four years' time all those engines will be as out-dated as the rag-and-chain pump. Any we have on the shelf will be sold off abroad. You listen to me, lad. If you can persuade this Theophilus Strike to buy one of the new-pattern engines – say a forty- or fifty-inch model, with a central-flue cylindrical boiler, he'll never regret it. What's more, he will save enough coal in the first year to pay the difference in price. Here, I'll show you what I mean.'

He pulled a small case out from beneath the seat and, producing paper and pencil, proceeded to illustrate his point, proving it with the aid of masses of figures. Most of the technical details were beyond Josh's understanding, but he realised that this was a unique opportunity and took possession of each sheet of drawings as Trevithick discarded it. He knew that one day it might prove invaluable.

When the engineer had exhausted the subject of the engine, he said, 'What provision is there for a man-hoist?'

Josh confessed that he had heard no mention of it – adding that he was determined to do something about it when he possessed more knowledge.

'Good for you. With a German in charge you will find it hard work. To him the Cornishman is of less importance than the horse on the whim. If he dies it is a nuisance – but no

more than a nuisance. How long does it take a man to reach
the surface from a deep shaft? Twenty minutes? Half an hour?
An hour even? By the time a man has climbed for that long
he is thoroughly exhausted. If his hand slips he doesn't have
the strength left to save himself. If he survives the climb to
crawl out of this hole like some sweating dirty creature the
cold air is going to tear at his lungs as though it were a
steel rasp. My God, boy! Our miners – yours and mine –
they deserve better than that. Look here. I'll show you the
way an ordinary pumping-engine can be used to bring men
to the surface without interfering with its primary purpose.
My father designed it. It's the simplest principle imaginable.
If the mine-owner needs any convincing, as most of them do,
I will give you some figures to prove how much energy a
miner expends on climbing *down* a ladder. That should make
him interested. Save that energy and he gets more ore for
his money. It will also prolong a miner's working life by
ten years. I am perfectly serious about this, young Retallic.
Get a man-engine working in your mine whatever else you
forgo. This is as worthy a crusade as any that has ever been
embarked upon. Persuade all mine-owners to provide a lift
for their miners and you are halfway towards forcing them
to accept that they are employing men. Here, look at this. You
don't have to be a fully trained engineer to understand it.'

Trevithick explained his father's idea in the simplest possible terms. He had been correct; it was an amazingly simple
idea.

'Why every mine does not have one is quite beyond my
understanding,' he said. 'I believe that it is worth any cost
involved to save one single life. Yet here is something that
costs very little and nobody wants to know it.'

Josh thought of Budge Pearn. Had there been a man-hoist
in Sharptor mine, Jenny would not be a widow today.

'Preacher Thackeray is always saying the very same thing,'
said Josh, now completely at his ease with the engineer.

'Preacher Thackeray?' frowned Trevithick. 'I've heard talk
of him. He's the man who wants all miners to unite. That's
dangerous talk, young Retallick. Help to make the miners' lot

an easier one by all means. That is Christian charity. But don't try to put ideas into a man's head that he is the equal of his employer. It's talk like that in the North that has caused so much trouble. "Unionism", I believe they call it. "Dangerous nonsense" is more like it. Put power into irresponsible hands and there is but one outcome. The sort of bloodbath that swept France not very many years past. I defy your preacher to stop that with words once it's begun.'

Francis Trevithick was merely saying what every middle-class man in England honestly believed to be true. Treat the workers as equals and they would turn and cut their employers' throats. It would be many years before the shadow of the French Revolution ceased to darken social progress.

'But politics holds no interest for me. Nor you, if you have sense. Do you understand the principle of the lift now?'

Josh did. The thought that he would probably be able to build one when he got back to Sharptor at the end of his apprenticeship filled him with enthusiasm. As well as preventing the deaths of miners like Budge Pearn it would stop scenes like those he had seen around the top of the shaft in winter. Miners coming off shift – his father amongst them – would sit or lie helplessly on the ground, coughing and gasping with pain as their labouring lungs drew in cold air. He asked a few questions. Trevithick answered him and drew quick live diagrams, cursing as the coach bumped and jolted, making the drawing of accurate lines impossible.

'There you are,' he said finally, handing his last drawing to Josh. 'Somewhere I have a detailed set of plans that my father once drew up. I will send them to you at Hayle. It is far too bumpy now for drawing. Tell me what little you know of the principles of a steam-engine.'

Helped along by Trevithick's sympathetic questioning, Josh discovered that he knew far more than he had realised. Most of it had been gleaned from the arguments and discussions that went on every evening in the dormitory between the more advanced apprentices.

And so the hours and the miles sped by until they arrived at the toll-gate at Bold Venture. Here Josh left the coach.

Trevithick climbed down with him, shading his eyes against the sun in a vain effort to pick out Josh's destination. All he could see was an apparently rugged moorland. When Josh explained that he would be striking straight across the moor to his home, Trevithick patted him encouragingly on the shoulder and got back into the coach.

Smiling through the open window he said, 'For my part, I would be as incapable on that moor as you might be designing a double-action steam-boiler. But you have time to learn. I doubt I have.'

He signalled to the driver, and with a crack of the coachman's long whip the coach heaved away. Josh waved goodbye to the engineer who, a few weeks later, had full sets of plans for no fewer than four different types of man-lift delivered to Josh at Hayle, each of them with details of its advantages and drawbacks listed in Trevithick's own handwriting.

When the coach was well on its way, Josh turned off the road on to a barely discernible track leading across the moor. It was not really necessary to follow any path, being too early in the year for the grass to have grown to any height. The fern that would soon be shoulder-high was no more than a series of large green staples pegging the ground. Only the gorse was thick and yellow-flowered, but this grew more sparsely when he reached the higher moor.

It was a bright clear day, and Josh could see the balancing stones by Sharptor from three miles away. He was not the only one able to see for such a distance. Before he had gone another half-mile a figure was running to meet him. A few minutes later a laughing, panting Miriam threw herself upon him.

'Josh! I knew it was you! I had been seeing cattle, sheep and ponies and all sorts of things that I thought were you. Then suddenly I saw you and there was no doubt. Let me look at you. You have grown taller and broader! You have, don't laugh.'

Josh hugged her, still laughing. He had not realised just how much he had missed her. There were changes in her too.

'What's been going on while I've been away? Your hair! You've had it cut.' It had been brushed so much it shone.

'And that's a new dress. You didn't have that when I left – and shoes! I must have been away much longer than I realised. You're not the same Miriam.'

'Josh Retallick!' Her expression was that of the other Miriam. 'Don't you think I might have done all this because I was meeting you? Because I wanted to look nice for you?'

'Have you? Dressed and made yourself look nice for me, I mean?'

She looked at him for a moment, then laughed. 'No. William said I must tidy myself if I wanted him to teach me.'

It came as a shock to realise she was talking of Preacher Thackeray. Josh had been taught by Thackeray for years without referring to him by his Christian name. Miriam was prattling on. '. . . Jenny washed my hair and cut it for me. This dress was one of hers. Do you like it?'

She pirouetted around in front of him, finally extending one foot in front of her. 'And my dad bought these shoes for me.'

She saw his face and stopped. 'What's the matter, Josh? Don't you like me as I am now? Do you want me to take off my shoes?' As she bent to untie them he stopped her. 'No, Miriam.'

'What is it, then?' she pleaded.

Josh wondered himself. 'I – I don't know. I think it might be because you have grown up so much while I have been away.'

'I thought you wanted me to grow up. Wanted us both to grow quickly.' She spoke quietly, but the unhappiness had fled and her dark eyes were shining.

'Yes.' Josh felt awkward, tongue-tied. 'It's come as a bit of a surprise. That's all.'

She took his hand and spoke, looking down at the ground. 'It's a special sort of surprise, Josh – and only for you.'

She squeezed his fingers. 'Come on, now. Your mother has a wonderful dinner cooking for you and I'm invited. Don't let it spoil.'

It was better then, walking home across the moor, linked hands swinging between them. Miriam told him of the badgers, and of the old blind pony that had started following her across the moor when she went for her daily schooling.

By the time they reached the cottage there was the same easy companionship between them that had always been there, and after a few minutes inside the house it was as though he had never been away, except that there was more to talk about around the table. His mother fussed about him excessively, unwilling to believe that he could possibly be fit and well after more than three months away from her care.

Ben Retallick said very little after his initial handshake, but he looked well satisfied with life and occasionally had a smile at the way Jesse was fussing around their son.

The remainder of the day passed very quickly. At dusk Josh accompanied Miriam to within sight of her home. On his way back along the path, whistling softly to himself, he saw someone standing ahead of him. He stopped whistling and took his hands from his pockets. He relaxed his clenched fists when his father's voice called, 'That you, Josh?'

'Yes, I wondered who it was standing there. I thought it might be Morwen.'

'I came out for some air,' said Ben Retallick. 'There's little enough of that down below in Wheal Sharptor. The sooner you come back with that engine the better. We are going down another twenty fathoms next month. I'll wager that we won't be far from water at that level.'

Josh slowed his pace to match that of his father.

'Haven't they dug another adit to take the water off?'

'No, and the horse-pump can't cope with much more than we've got now.'

'Whose idea is it to go down further? Schmidt's?'

'Yes. Don't you agree with it?'

'No. Do you?'

His father shook his head, and Josh went on, 'When I left Sharptor everyone was talking about the rich ore they had found on the present level. They said they wouldn't need to go deeper for years. So why go down now? Why not wait for the engine?'

'I don't know, Josh. Only Schmidt knows the answer to that.'

They had arrived at the gate of the cottage now and Ben Retallick stopped. 'I hear tell you ran into a spot of bother on the way to Hayle.'

Josh went cold. 'Yes.'

'Did that ship's captain hurt you?'

'No, I hit him first.'

'Good. That's all I wanted to know.'

Josh gulped. 'You heard what I did? I hit him with a flagon of wine. At the time I thought I had killed him.'

'Lucky it was you and not me who hit him. Likely as not I'd have made a job of it.'

Josh felt vaguely relieved. The thought of his parents finding out about the incident with Captain Henry had worried him.

'Does Mum know?'

'No! If she ever found out she'd be waiting for that sea captain with the kitchen cleaver the next time he came into Looe town. I think this is one secret we had better keep to ourselves. I wanted you to know that I believe you did what had to be done. We'll let the matter lie there and not bring it up again. If I thought too much about it, I might be the one waiting at Looe for him.'

The weekend went all too quickly. Most of the time was spent around the house with his family, or on the moor discovering the signs of spring with Miriam.

She walked as far as St Cleer with him on his return. From St Cleer he was travelling on the recently established coach service as far as Truro. The trip had been a surprise present from his father. The money he had saved was only sufficient for Josh to travel on the outside of the coach, but without it Josh would have had to set off at dawn and walk. Either that or trust to the generosity of farmers with their slow-moving carts. As it was, he would have a seventeen-mile walk from Truro to the works; but in Cornwall, in the early part of the nineteenth century, the ordinary Cornish man or woman was well used to walking.

At St Cleer they called in to see Preacher Thackeray and he

greeted Josh enthusiastically. He frowned when he was told what Josh's apprenticeship had consisted of so far, and said it was 'a waste of valuable teaching time'. But he waxed enthusiastic when Josh spoke of his conversation with Trevithick.

'He is absolutely right, of course,' said the preacher. 'I am glad to hear of a man of his standing in society so concerned with humanity. But why doesn't he express his views to the mine-owners – the adventurers? If he persuaded his relatives, the Harveys, not to sell an engine without a man-hoist being installed at the same time, every mine in Cornwall would have one in no time.

'It will come eventually,' he went on. 'When the men start pulling together for their mutual benefit. They proved what could be done when corn was short. If only they would join together in one strong union they could right all the wrongs in the mines.'

This was Preacher Thackeray's self-appointed mission in life, the crusade that he believed he had been ordained for. But there was no need to preach his beliefs to Josh. He had been converted long before. At this very moment he was wishing that the preacher might have had other business to attend to. It would soon be time for the coach to leave, and there were a few things he wanted to say to Miriam.

But Preacher Thackeray had no other pressing business.

'You learn all you can about those man-hoists while you are at Hayle, Josh, and about anything else that will ease the lot of men like your father too. It's a great opportunity that will never be repeated.'

'I wish I could do the same,' said Miriam. She had nodded her agreement while the preacher was talking. 'You are teaching me schooling. To what use can I put it?'

'That depends on the husband you choose,' said Thackeray. 'Marry a miner or a farm-worker and your education will be wasted. Education won't bring a baby into the world and it will not cook a meal. Find a man whose mind matches your own quick brain. Between you there should be no limit to what can be achieved. You must find a man who recognises that a woman is capable of thinking for herself – a rarity in these parts, I am afraid.'

'Miriam, can we . . . ?' Josh made a vain effort to get Miriam away, but it was already too late. From outside the inn the coachman's horn called on travellers to board the coach.

Josh shook the preacher's hand then walked the few yards to the coach with neither the time nor, of a sudden, the words to say what he had been wanting to say. Now it was too late and he was miserable.

'Don't you want to go, Josh?'

They stopped at the coach and he looked at her. She had been studying his face. There was understanding in her eyes.

'It's not that I don't want to go. It's . . .' He shrugged helplessly as the coachman sounded a final warning.

'Is it because of me?'

He nodded. 'Yes.'

'Then you've no need to worry, Josh. I will be counting the days until you are back. But quickly now; the coach is leaving.'

He snatched a quick kiss and jumped upon the coach as the coachman cracked his whip. The horses strained against the leather of the harnesses.

'I'll write, Josh. I'll write.'

Miriam ran to the corner after the coach, and he waved until the trot of the horses became a canter and St Cleer and Miriam receded over the brow of the hill. Josh dug his hands into his pockets and mulled over the words that should have been said.

Chapter Ten

There was little time for brooding in the days and weeks that lay ahead of Josh. William Carlyon was determined that the engineers trained at the Harvey works should match the engines for which they would be responsible. When he handed the plans for the man-hoists to Josh he asked him why Trevithick should be sending them to him. As a result of his reply William Carlyon not only saw that Josh received the fullest possible training as an engineer but also that he was fully conversant with all the latest developments in man-hoist design.

In his own way Carlyon was as enthusiastic as Trevithick had been, but for a different reason. The works manager saw that by getting miners to and from the working areas more quickly they would be extracting more ore and the mines would be going deeper. This is turn meant more pumping would be required. And pumping meant engines. It was not only Harvey's that depended upon rich and efficient mines. The whole economy of Cornwall was propped up by the mining industry, but as explorers and colonisers advanced across the face of the earth they were discovering huge deposits of copper and tin in areas where cheap labour was readily available. Thus the need for greater efficiency was becoming a very important factor in Cornish mining.

Josh did not mind the extra work resulting from his expressed interest in the man-hoist idea. If engineers are born and not made, then Josh was a born engineer. He had an instinct for mechanical things which was apparent to everyone responsible for his training.

His letters to Miriam and his family were full of his newly discovered skills and interests. Even on Sundays in the company of the Carlyon family he could speak of little else, and it did not always please Sarah. One Sunday in midsummer they were returning from chapel. He was in the middle of extolling the virtues of Harvey's latest thirty-two-inch engine which was proving to be far more efficient than previous engines twice its size. Sarah suddenly stopped and stamped her foot angrily. 'I am sick of engines! Sick of the sound of them. Sick of hearing about them and sick of living in the middle of a foundry. I'm surrounded by the smell of engines, bits of engines and men who work with engines. I *hate* engines!'

With that she lifted her chin and flounced off, leaving a stunned Josh staring after her.

Mrs Carlyon had caught the end of her outburst. 'My daughter has always been one for speaking her mind, Josh. It may not be a fault but it can be very disconcerting at times. Take no notice; she will be better tempered this afternoon.'

Since she had learned that Trevithick was taking a personal interest in Josh, and William Carlyon had marked him out as an outstanding future engineer, Mrs Carlyon's attitude towards him had warmed considerably. 'I understand her feelings, though,' she said with a glance at William Carlyon, who was trying not to smile. 'There are times when I feel like screaming too. All the men I meet here believe that the whole world revolves around the Harvey works. There are other things in a woman's life. Of course, you can't be expected to understand about that yet.'

It was with some trepidation that Josh went to tea that day with the Carlyons, but Sarah behaved as though nothing had happened. All the same, Josh was very careful not to talk about engines. Soon the conversation turned to horse-riding, Sarah's latest interest. The Carlyon girls had owned ponies for years,

but for her recent birthday Sarah had been given a full-blooded
hunter. It was a beautiful spirited horse. Sarah thought there
was no better horse in the county, but her mother was terrified
of it. She felt sure that Sarah would not be able to control it.

'Have you ever ridden?' Sarah asked Josh over tea.

'No. Except bareback on the mules and cart-horses at the
mine,' he replied. 'And then only when Nehemeziah wasn't
around.'

Then he had to explain about the little mine hostler who
shared the horses' stables and lived for little else but his
charges.

'Wouldn't you like to learn to ride properly?'

'Yes.' It was an unthinking reply. 'But I could never find
the time.'

'Of course you could.' Sarah had him firmly on the hook.
'Daddy, Josh says he would love to learn to ride but doesn't
have time. He could ride Pedlar on Sundays, couldn't he?'
Pedlar was the pony which had been succeeded by Hector,
as her new hunter was named.

'If Josh thinks he can fit it in with his engineering studies I
have no objections.' He looked from his daughter to Josh and
back again. 'Besides, I think it might do him a great deal of
good to have an interest outside his work. Providing, as I've
already said, that it doesn't interfere with his studies.'

The grins of Josh's fellow-apprentices were tinged with
envy. Quite apart from the break with routine, Sarah was a
very attractive girl.

'Tonight, then. Can we start tonight?'

'If you wish. But I won't have the stable lads turning to
because you want to go riding, Sarah.'

'There is no need for them to do anything. Josh and I will
saddle up and rub down the horses when we come back.'

'Then what are you waiting for?'

'I have nothing to wear for riding,' protested Josh. 'I can't
go as I am. Not in my best trousers. And I certainly can't wear
these boots on a horse.'

'Daddy, you never wear your riding clothes now. Can Josh
borrow them?'

'There is no need for him to borrow them,' said William Carlyon. 'He can *have* them. I doubt if I shall want to go riding again.'

He grinned at Josh. 'It's no use, Josh. Sarah has decided that you are to have a riding lesson. I would never hear the last of it if I were responsible for spoiling her plans. Come along with me.'

Josh followed him upstairs to return after a time wearing riding breeches that were a shade too large. Tucked inside tall shiny riding boots it did not show too much. The jacket was slightly overfilled across the shoulders, but the whole outfit looked quite smart.

The apprentices thought so too and whistled their approval, defying Mrs Carlyon's attempts to silence them.

'You look a right toff in that get-up,' said Tom. 'We'd better draw straws to see who gets his hands dirty on that old ninety-two-inch engine tomorrow. I can see it isn't going to be you – sir.'

Josh took a menacing step towards the grinning Cockney, and Mrs Carlyon hurriedly stepped between them. 'Now, you boys, just stop it.' She took Josh's arm. 'Take no notice of them, Josh. You look splendid.'

So too did Sarah when she came into the room where the boys were gathered. At that moment there was not one of them who would not have been eager to change places with Josh. The high-heeled boots she wore beneath her long dark-brown riding skirt made her look taller. She was a naturally slim girl and the effect was emphasised by the braiding of her long blonde hair at the back of her neck.

Josh felt awkward walking from the house in his newly acquired riding boots. He was keenly aware that the Carlyon family and the other apprentices were watching from the house. There was another chorus of whistles when Sarah took his arm to cross the slippery foundry yard, but once out of sight of the house Josh relaxed.

At the stables he saddled the two horses under Sarah's instruction. He had some trouble with Hector until Sarah took the thoroughbred's head between her hands and talked to him as Josh threw the saddle on to his back. After she had checked the girth-straps, Josh led the big horse outside and helped Sarah to mount. He then led out the pony and swung into its saddle. Wheeling it around he followed her out of the works.

They took the road which led away from the town, going towards Lelant Down, and were soon cantering across open grassy country.

Drawing in beside him, Sarah said, 'Why did you tell me you couldn't ride? You are doing splendidly.'

'It's just like riding the mine horses,' replied Josh. 'In fact it's easier; there is something to hold on to and somewhere for your feet.'

'Come on, then!' cried Sarah. 'I'll race you to the top of that hill.' She dug her heels into the hunter's ribs, and in three bounds it was as many lengths ahead of the pony.

Josh followed suit, and Pedlar responded readily. It was now that Josh learned the difference between riding a slow-jogging pony and trying to sit one that is galloping. He managed to stay with it but it felt as though his arms and legs were going in four different directions while his body bounced between them. At one moment, his face was buried in the coarse hairs of the horse's mane. The next, his head was jerked back on his neck and all he could see was sky.

Fortunately the pony found it almost as uncomfortable to have such an uncontrolled weight upon its back. It slowed, dancing in a half-circle, shaking its head, not sure what to do. Josh was able to bring it quickly back under control and he took it up the hill at a more leisurely pace.

Sarah had dismounted and was waiting for him, flushed from the gallop. Her hair had fallen loose and was hanging about her shoulders.

'I won! Why didn't you give Pedlar his head? He enjoys a good run.'

'He didn't enjoy it today,' declared Josh, swinging gratefully to the ground. 'I wasn't doing any of the things he is used to his riders doing.'

Sarah laughed. 'You'll learn. I'll show you on the way back

what you should have done. But look over there. Isn't that worth coming up here to see?'

She pointed to the north where the farmland sloped away to the edge of St Ives Bay and the sea beyond. A few red-sailed fishing-boats leaned away from the wind in the middle distance. Closer to the horizon two packets crowded on full sail without apparently moving and were overtaken by a wisp of lace-cloud.

'It's beautiful up here, isn't it?' said Sarah as Hector chomped grass behind her, reins loose over his head.

'Yes, it is,' agreed Josh. 'But you have to see the moor to really know what beauty is.'

'I've seen it,' said Sarah. 'We went to Barnstaple once and crossed over it. It's a bleak dreary place.'

'It isn't! I expect you took a road over a flat part of the moor. Get away from the road and you'll find the rivers and the tors and the valleys. The whole of it's alive with more animal and plant life than you will ever have seen in one place before.'

'You really love the moor, don't you?'

Josh nodded, thinking of it as it would be at this time of the year.

'And have you discovered all these birds and animals and plants by yourself?' Sarah was looking at him as she asked her question and she caught his expression. 'Who do you explore the moor with?'

He cleared his throat before answering. 'Sometimes by myself. Sometimes with Miriam.'

Sarah crouched down and stroked Hector's nose as he pulled the grass. 'Who is Miriam? What is she like?'

He tried to describe the wild moorland girl but was aware that his word-picture was a mere skeleton of the real girl. He did not know whether the fault lay in his telling, or because it was impossible to describe Miriam without having the moor near at hand. He never thought of the one without the other. It was the first time he had realised the fact. He thought it strange that the realisation should come now, when he was high on a hill, looking out across the sea in the company of another girl – a girl who was so different from Miriam.

'I think we ought to go home now.'

Sarah flicked the reins back over Hector's head and had swung up to the saddle before Josh could make a move to help her.

She was not silent on the return journey. She told Josh how he should hold himself and move with the movement of the pony, yet there was a certain reserve that had not been present before.

Back in the stable he rubbed down both horses and on the way back to the house he thanked her for the lesson.

'Will we be able to go again next Sunday?'

'Would you like to?' She looked at him, knowing that she was able to read his thoughts by his expression. Josh had never mastered the art of lying.

'Yes. Very much.'

Some of the sparkle returned to her. 'All right. We'll make it a regular Sunday treat. We can go out early, before breakfast, when everyone else is still in bed. That's the time I enjoy riding best. It feels sometimes as though there is nobody else in the whole world – especially up there on the hill. Come along into the house and have something to eat and drink before you go back to the others.'

And so riding became part of Josh's routine. He enjoyed both the ride and Sarah's company. The other apprentices grudgingly came to accept his good fortune and special relationship with the Carlyon family. If they did not resent it, then it was because Josh never let up on his engineering studies. More than that, it was apparent to everyone that William Carlyon demanded a higher standard of work from Josh than from the others.

During these first months at Harvey's boys completed their apprenticeships and went out to take their places in the world. Others joined the works and the cycle was completed. But it still came as a shock to Josh when Tom Fiddler's training came to an end in the late autumn, although he would only have stayed until Christmas anyway. Tom's father was an enterprising butler in the household of the Lord Mayor of London. It so happened that during the course of his duties the Mayor was called upon to entertain a very wealthy Chilean mine-owner, and the Cockney boy's father found an opportunity to talk to him. He spoke with such effect that not only did he secure a highly paid post for Tom in Chile, but the mine-owner also travelled all the way to Hayle to meet him. Before leaving he placed a large order for mine equipment. Tom would be required to accompany it to South America.

Until the equipment was ready Tom was going to London to spend the remainder of the time with his parents. Then he and the machinery would take passage in one of the huge steam-powered ships Trevithick and his contemporaries had helped to design.

Officially there was no such thing as a farewell party for an apprentice. But, on the day before the newly qualified engineer was due to leave, William Carlyon would let it be known that he had other business to attend to and would not be carrying out his customary 'lights out' inspection of the dormitory.

As soon as darkness had fallen the departing engineer and his closest friends would slip quietly from the dormitory. Scaling the high foundry wall via the roof of the stables, they would make their way to one of the many inns of the town.

John Wesley was still remembered by many Cornishmen around Hayle, and his Methodism was a powerful force in the county, but Hayle was a seaport as well as a mining centre. In spite of the many pressures brought to bear by the Methodists there were many hostelries that catered for the tastes of the non-religious miner, or the sailor intent on spending all his pay in one uproarious night lest his next trip prove to be his last.

The Boot Inn was just such a place and it was to this infamous haunt that Tom, Josh and three other apprentices made their way from the works. It was the first such visit for Josh, not because he held any deep religious convictions but because of his habit of studying hard – this and memories of his only previous drinking session, aboard the *Helen and Stephen*.

On the other hand, Tom boasted that he had not missed one farewell party during his three years' apprenticeship at

Harvey's works. This was borne out by the reaction of the pot-girl who came to swab off their table as they squeezed into an empty corner of the noisy smoke-filled bar.

'What, you here again?' she said to him. 'They must have apprentices piled two deep inside those walls, the number of farewells you'm having.'

'Ah! But this is a special one,' said Tom, giving the girl a lewd wink. 'It'll break your heart to hear it. It's for me, Rosie. I'm off to South America to make my fortune.'

'You'll never do that down any mine,' sniffed the girl, hitching up a shoulder of the dress that threatened to slip down and expose what little of her bosom could not already be seen. 'And as for breaking my heart! It will be a sight quieter around here, I dare say. I won't be going to bed with bruises on my backside where you've pinched me. If that's missing you, then good riddance to you, I say.'

Despite this off-hand speech the first ale that Tom had was a present from the pot-girl. ''Cos I'm so glad to be seeing the back of you,' she explained.

The boys, Tom especially, talked a great deal and made a lot of noise, but they were not drinking heavily. For one thing, their pockets would not run to it. In the main they came from homes like Josh's own. It was a sacrifice for their families to keep them at the engineering works.

Josh found himself fascinated by the other customers of the inn. Sailors for the most part. They were a loud and boisterous crowd, and the jokes they told were bawdy in the extreme.

Suddenly a hand was clapped on his shoulder, 'Well, I never did! If it isn't Master Retallick. And what might you be doing inside a place like this?'

Josh swung around to see Taffy Williams smiling behind him. The little steward looked much frailer than Josh remembered, and when he stood up he towered over the little Welshman.

'Taffy! It's grand to see you again. I've often wondered how you were. How long are you here? Are you still on the *Helen and Stephen*? But don't stand there, come and join us.'

'Well, there's enough questions for one breath. No, I won't

come and join you, thank you. I can see that you and your friends are having a little celebration.' He nodded to Tom and the others in a vague cheery way. 'Besides, I am with a friend over there at the end of the bar. He and I were shipmates on the American run when we were both no more than lads.'

'Well, at least let me come across and buy you both a drink,' said Josh, fingering the coins in his pocket, hoping he would have enough for the extra ales.

'I'll be back with you in a minute,' he said to Tom.

Taffy's friend was a small man with a permanent blink and a head devoid of hair except for a thin bushy fringe around the edges.

'Willy, I would like you to meet a young friend of mine, Josh Retallick.'

A limp hand was placed briefly into Josh's.

'H'm! He's a big lad,' murmured Willy in a soft disinterested voice, his sing-song accent indicating that he too came from across the waters of the Bristol Channel.

'He's the one I have told you about so often. The one who scarred Captain Henry.'

'Is he now?' The lack of interest disappeared immediately. 'In that case I am *very* pleased to meet you, young sir. You did something that should have been done many years before. I don't know how Taffy managed to stay with him for as long as he did.'

'You've left the *Helen and Stephen*?' Josh queried.

'No,' Taffy shook his head, 'but Captain Henry has. I think the Mate must have said something to the agent after he'd taken over his new ship. When we docked in Falmouth three weeks later Captain Henry was sent for by the owners. He never came back! When a new captain came aboard two days later we packed his gear, sent it ashore – and that was that!'

'Where did he go?'

Josh paid for the two tankards of ale and Taffy lifted his to Josh. 'Your very best health. Where's he gone, you ask? Now, that's a question, that is. He's certainly not sailing these waters. I've heard rumours that he's master of a small ship trading between the west coast of Africa and the Caribbean.'

There was a murmur from Willy. 'We know what cargo he'll be carrying on that run. Slaves. Battened down in a stinking hold. Treated worse than pigs from Ireland, they are. Yes, Captain Henry's found his place in life. One day he'll burn in hell for it.'

'I thought slave-trading had ended,' said Josh.

'It has in this country,' said Taffy. 'But they still have slaves in the Americas. There's a ready market for them anywhere over there. While there's money to be made and men like Captain Henry to sail the ships, the trade will go on.'

'Poor wretches,' sighed Willy. 'I once saw a slave ship come into New Orleans. The slaves, poor souls, were brought out of the hold chained together, all trying to protect their eyes from the light that they hadn't seen for months. And the smell! It was unbelievable. The crew kept a gap between the ship and the jetty when they berthed. As the slaves came ashore they were pushed into the water and held under with a long pole. I was surprised some of them didn't drown. But it did get rid of some of the smell. After that they were all taken off to be auctioned.'

Willy shuddered in an exaggerated manner, oblivious of the amused looks some of the seamen were giving him.

Josh made his excuses, shook hands once again with the two little Welshman and returned to the table to rejoin his friends.

'Where'd you dig those two up from?' asked Tom with great interest. 'They're bleedin' pansies. Faded ones at that! I shouldn't have thought they were your type?'

'I met Taffy on the *Helen and Stephen*,' said Josh, glaring at Tom. 'If it hadn't been for him I'd have been in real trouble. He proved to be a good friend at a time when I most needed one.'

'Fair enough! I'm sorry,' said Tom hastily. 'No offence meant, Josh.'

Josh relaxed and grinned. 'None taken, Tom.'

'Whew! I'm glad about that,' said Tom. 'For a minute I thought you might take me by the throat and shake me. Here, it's my turn to buy another round. It's no use you trying to make that ale last any longer. Rosie! Let's be having some service here. Can't have you getting fat and lazy.'

'I wish you was as particular about not wanting me to get fat for other reasons,' said Rosie, gathering up the tankards noisily. 'I could do with one of they chastity-belts, working in here. And a foundry-cast backside would be a help. If I had a guinea for every pinch I gets, I'd be able to buy an inn of me own.'

'It's a shame, Rosie,' said Tom, when the laughter had died away. 'But if you can't afford your own inn you can at least have a drink with me. Take for them all from that.'

He slapped a half-guinea down on the table.

'Thank you, Tom. I'll take the money and have the drink later, when things are bit quieter. But you mind what you're doing with your money. I'll wager this half-guinea was given you for your fare home. Spend it and you'll be walking to London. You miss that boat to South America and there'll be no fortune for you.'

'Don't worry about me, Rosie, my love. Tom Fiddler will never be short of money in his pocket.'

Rosie gave him a shrewd look. 'No, I don't suppose you'll ever want for anything, Tom. I can see it in your face. You'm born lucky – and that's sight better than being born rich. But what am I doing standing here talking to you? I'll find myself out of a job if I don't serve some of the other customers pretty quick.'

'Now there's an ambition for a man,' said Tom, watching her make her way across the bar-room away from them. The inn was very full now. As she elbowed her way through the noisy half-drunken crowd more than one hand patted her well-rounded buttocks.

'Hey! It looks as though that friend of yours is in some sort of an argument, Josh,' said lanky Nick Doid, the only other Cornishman among the Harvey boys 'There's quite a crowd about him over in the far corner.'

Josh tried to get a better view of what was happening, but it was Tom who exclaimed, 'It's the Copperhouse apprentices.' In an instant the five of them were on their feet.

The Copperhouse boys had probably been drinking else-where before coming to the Boot Inn. In the noise and general activity none of the Harvey apprentices had seen them arrive.

One of them, a large ginger-haired youth of about seven-teen, was mincing around the little Welsh steward, one hand held behind his head and the other on his hip. His com-panions whooped and shouted encouragement. The ginger-haired youth tried to persuade Taffy to dance with him. When he refused, another of the Copperhouse crowd pushed him from behind and sent him staggering forward. The big youth caught him and dragged him around in a rough imitation of a dance. Meanwhile Willy shrank back further into the corner, his eyelids fluttering frantically.

Josh waited to see no more. There had been a look of physi-cal pain on Taffy's face as the ginger-haired youth grabbed hold of him. Ploughing through the crowded bar, Josh's anger reached flash-point as he arrived in the midst of the Copperhouse party. Taking the ginger-haired apprentice by the collar he tugged him violently backwards, forcing him to release the steward. Then Josh swung him round and using him as a protesting battering-ram cleared a path to the door, and flung him headlong into the street.

Tom's cheers were echoed by some of the seamen who had watched what was happening. They were short-lived. The remainder of the Copperhouse apprentices were on Josh before he could return to the table. He was borne to the ground, fists and boots flailing, by the sheer weight of their numbers.

Within seconds the Harvey apprentices rushed headlong into the fray. As the grappling, fighting youths rolled around on the floor the other occupants of the inn became involved, accidentally or otherwise. In two minutes the inn had erupted into a heaving, seething mass of battling customers.

On his knees, Josh came face to face with Tom. 'Are you all right?' he shouted.

'Fine!' Tom bellowed in return. 'Look.' He opened his hand to reveal a fistful of coins. There was copper, silver – and even a gold piece glinting among them.

'They're all over the place!' He grinned. 'Look for yourself.'

A sailor reeling back from a blow fell over the outstretched arm and the coins were scattered to the four corners of the room.

'You bloody fool!' Tom shouted and struck out at the sailor as he regained his feet. The blow caught him behind the knee and he fell down again, cursing and flailing about him.

Josh got to his feet and was swapping punches with one of the Copperhouse apprentices when the cry went up that the town constables were on their way. There was an immediate stampede for the door. The constables were notorious for cracking heads and lodging disturbers of the peace in the lock-up for a night prior to an introduction to the magistrate. With the prospect of thirty days on the treadmill in Bodmin Jail looming over him plus certain dismissal from Harvey's Josh was one of the first through the door.

He ran through the darkened streets, over the foundry wall and down the sloping roof of the stable, not stopping until he was safely inside the dormitory. The others came in one by one until, in the dim light from a taper, Josh saw that they were all present. With the exception of Tom!

'Oh, you needn't worry about him,' said Nick Doid. 'I saw him going out through the back door of the inn with Rosie. There'll be little sleep for the rats in the hay-loft of the Boot Inn stables tonight.'

It was a sorry parade of apprentices who bade farewell to a smirking Tom Fiddler the following morning.

'I've never known such a night for accidents,' commented William Carlyon, turning Josh's head towards him in order to see his swollen and discoloured eye the better. 'It's a wonder there are any doors left standing in the place judging by the number of you who have collided with them. Didn't you have an accident, Tom?'

'I hope not!'

Tom's grin lasted until he was out of sight on the carrier's cart. Turning away, Josh knew he was going to miss the cheery Cockney.

Chapter Eleven

Josh found little time to mope about the departure of his friend. It seemed that the more he learned, the more he found to learn. It was an accumulative process.

When his first year ended Josh spent a short Christmas interlude with his family and Miriam at Sharptor. He enjoyed being with them, but with so much to talk about the time passed all too quickly. Even so, his mind was constantly slipping away to tackle an engineering problem, real or theoretical. He told Miriam about it when she commented on his preoccupied air. She accepted it proudly. She believed that Josh would one day be a brilliant mine-engineer.

It was the summer of 1840 when a disaster occurred at Sharptor which might well have altered Josh's planned career. It brought home to him, as nothing else could have done, the dangers which exist in even the best-run mine.

Josh was in Harvey's foundry yard, helping to repair a huge ninety-inch boiler, when a horseman came clattering through the works gates. The rider was in as much of a lather as the horse he was riding. As he slipped to the ground it was with a sense of foreboding that Josh recognised him as Nehemeziah Lancellis.

The gnarled little hostler saw Josh hurrying towards him and started to gasp out his story.

'Josh! Josh, boy. I've brought bad news for 'ee. Best get home. Be quick 'bout it.'

'What is it? What's happened?'

A crowd was beginning to gather about them now.

'Stand back and give him some room,' ordered William Carlyon, arriving on the scene. 'And bring something for him to sit on,' he added as Nehemeziah staggered and Josh put a supporting arm about him.

'Don't bide for me, Josh. 'Tis Ben. . . . He was working on a new adit . . . off the main shaft. New man on the black powder. Set off a bad explosion. . . . Roof's down with Ben and three more 'neath it. Schmidt won't have rescue work. He's back on the drink. . . . No sense in 'im. Best get there . . . sort it out, Josh. Hurry, or they'll be none of 'em out alive.'

'I'll go now, Mr Carlyon. I'll take Nehemeziah's horse.'

'No!' Nehemeziah waved a hand to emphasise the word as Josh lowered him on to a stool that had been produced. 'He'm clapped, Josh! Wouldn't last half a mile. 'Tis one of Strike's too. I took'n from stables. Borrowed him, like. I'll be taken in for horse-stealing if'n he dies.'

'Josh.' It was Sarah. She had run from the house in time to hear most of what had been said. 'Take Hector. He's the fastest horse you'll find.'

'Can I?' Josh turned to William Carlyon.

'Of course! It's Sarah's horse to do with as she wishes. I can think of no more important work he'll ever be called on to do. Take Theophilus Strike's horse to the stables when you go. Tell the stable boy to walk him around for a while. He's had a hard ride.'

'I'll take 'en and do it meself, if it's all the same to 'ee,' said Nehemeziah, rising stiffly to his feet. 'Then I won't worry none 'bout the way 'tis done. Don't wait for me, Josh. Get off now.'

Josh hurried away to throw off his working clothes and put on the riding trousers and boots given to him by the Carlyons. He would never manage Hector wearing his heavy mining boots.

Quick as he was changing, Sarah was leading the big

horse fully saddled from the stable by the time he arrived there.

He was now a competent rider with no fear of the stallion. As he mounted, Sarah whispered to the horse, 'Run fast and take care of him, Hector.'

As Josh wheeled the stallion about, William Carlyon handed a number of small coins up to him.

'For the turnpikes,' he explained.

Then, to a chorus of good wishes, Josh clattered out of Harvey's. He waited only until he was clear of Hayle town before shaking out the reins and allowing the big horse to stretch out into a mile-consuming gallop.

While Josh was on the road between Hayle and Sharptor things were happening at the mine.

Herman Schmidt, red-faced and angry, stood at the entrance to the collapsed adit facing a sullen crowd of copper-miners.

'Go back to work, all of you.' His words were made harsher by the gutteral German accent. 'It is doing no good to stand around here. The roof has collapsed. The men inside are dead. There is nothing else to be done. We'll start another adit somewhere else.'

The angry murmurings of the crowd grew louder and Schmidt glared at them. 'You are doubting my word? The word of a German mine captain? You are as nothing compared with me. You know nothing but the pick and shovel. I, Herman Schmidt, am in charge here. I say the men are dead. So? I am sorry. Now we go back to work.'

Thomas Shovell stepped from the crowd. 'With all due respects to you, Captain Schmidt, that isn't our way. Ben Retallick and the others might well be dead, but we'll see that they have a decent burial. We owe them that.'

'Them you owe nothing! Me you owe everything!' Schmidt shouted. 'And I say you work – you hear? Work! Work! Work! If anyone tries to go into this adit, he is no longer employed at the Sharptor mine. I will make damn sure he works in no other mine anywhere in Cornwall. The men in there are as buried as they will ever be.'

Tom Shovell's face had paled but he had no intention of retreating. 'No, Captain Schmidt. We will dig out the adit until we find those men. Dead or alive.'

There was a sudden commotion in the crowd and men were pushed out of the way as Wrightwick Roberts came to the front.

'What is this, a meeting? Hold your meetings later. What we need now are men with picks and strong arms. Come on. Give me something to dig with and follow me into that adit.'

'Nobody goes in there. I have said so,' Schmidt repeated. 'They must go back to work.'

The angry preacher looked from the mine captain to the miners and the reason for the inactivity became clear.

'They'll go back to work when they've brought out Ben Retallick and the others,' said Wrightwick Roberts. 'Come on, Tom. In we go.'

With a nod the shift captain fell in behind the preacher. Schmidt moved to block their path and was sent reeling from the entrance by a push from Wrightwick Roberts. Before he had recovered his balance the entrance to the adit was crowded with miners. Soon candles were being lit and passed forward for the preacher and the shift captain as they advanced further into the adit.

'Schmidt is going to stir up big trouble in the Wheal Sharptor over this,' said Tom Shovell.

'He's lucky I was able to get enough women together to keep Jesse Retallick at home,' retorted the preacher. 'Had she come up here, she'd have torn Schmidt to pieces.'

A hundred feet into the hillside they came to a tumbled barrier of rock that completely blocked the tunnel. It spilled down from the broken roof, carpeting the floor with boulders at a distance of twenty yards from the fall itself.

'This doesn't look good,' said Wrightwick Roberts, indicating the rock-fall ahead of them. 'What do you know about this adit, Tom? Is it loose rock right through?'

Tom Shovell looked crestfallen. 'I don't know as much as I should, Wrightwick,' he confessed. 'The men have been digging the adit as the opportunity arose while I've been kept busy with a drainage problem at the bottom of the main shaft. When they came across a seam of copper I sent Ben along to check on whether it was worth working. He must have wanted to get at a bit more of it than he could see. The man on the powder was a new man from the Kit Hill workings. He told me he was used to black-powder blasting.'

He nodded, indicating the fallen rock, sending a shower of wax to the floor from the candle attached to his helmet. 'But this isn't the work of an experienced man.' He looked thoughtful. 'I can remember them saying a few days ago that they had a tricky patch of loose rock to get through. How far it went I just don't know.'

'Then we'd better get at it and find out,' said the preacher. Lighting other candles from the one held in his hand, he placed them on rough ledges hacked into the adit walls. 'There'll not be room for more than one man to work a way through here, Tom. I'll have first turn and you pass back the rocks I get out.'

'We'll need a bit of shoring-up here and there,' said the shift captain, turning a professional eye to the job in hand. 'Pass the word back along the tunnel,' he called over his shoulder. 'Fetch in some timber for shoring-up, and saws for cutting it down to size.'

Wrightwick Roberts strained at a large block of granite that, like an iceberg, had most of its bulk hidden from view. When it was reluctantly prised free a trickle of smaller rocks showered into the place it had occupied. These were soon cleared, and the preacher climbed into the hole. He worked loose another boulder that, like the first, would require two miners to carry it back along the adit to the entrance.

Gradually, slowly, Wrightwick Roberts disappeared from view into the hole he was making. The shift captain moved candles forward with him.

As the preacher advanced, his progress slowed considerably. With his great strength he was able to work loose large chunks of rock, but then he had to manhandle them back to the beginning of the fall himself. There was room for only one man inside the tunnel he was clearing and no other Sharptor miner possessed his strength. However, the answer to this problem presented itself in the form of the three male members of the Trago family – Moses, his brother John and young Morwen, who was already beginning to outstrip his father in size and uncertain temper.

Wrightwick Roberts had advanced only some eight yards when Moses called in to him.

'Come out here and give these weaklings a hand, Preacher. I'll take a spell in there.'

Wrightwick Roberts, his fingers torn and bleeding from clawing for a grip on the rough granite, submitted gratefully. Backing out into the comparative spaciousness of the two-man-width adit he straightened up painfully. But there was little time for relaxation. Moses scrambled inside the narrow tunnel dug by the preacher's hands and continued the work as though his own life depended upon it.

With such giants of men spearheading the rescue the rate of advance increased rapidly. By the time Josh slithered the frothing, sweat-darkened Hector to a halt at the mouth of the adit, the amount of rock being brought out from inside was more than during a normal working day.

One of the boys from the Sharptor mine took the horse from him eagerly and led it away towards the mine stables. Sarah's horse had galloped its great heart out on the road from Hayle. Now with hanging head and stiff-legged gait it allowed itself to be led away as meekly as though it were an old mine hack.

Josh hurried along the adit-tunnel, impatient with the many delays he encountered as the miners brought the results of the rescuers' efforts to the surface. When he reached the place where the fall began he came face to face with Morwen Trago who, sweating and covered in dirt, had just heaved himself out of the rescue-tunnel. The two were much of a build now.

'Have you found anything . . . ?' Josh began the question, but Morwen shook his head.

'There's no sign of the end of the fall yet. That's if there is any end. It's beginning to look as though the whole length of roof has come down.'

He looked at Josh's riding habit and a trace of a sneer raised the edge of his mouth. 'You'd better wait out on grass. This is no place for gentry down here.'

Josh's reply was to strip off his jacket and shirt. Bare to the waist, he crawled into the hole, working his way forward to where Tom Shovell, Wrightwick Roberts and John Trago were backing up Moses.

The shift captain was scarcely recognisable beneath a layer of dust. 'There's nothing hopeful to be said, I'm afraid, Josh. Things are looking bad. Unless we get to the end of this fall very soon there'll be no hope at all of finding anyone alive.'

'So they said outside. I'd rather dig than think about it. I'm going up to take over from Moses for a while.'

'There'll be nobody giving up,' said Wrightwick Roberts. 'But there's no sense in raising false hopes.'

'Is Schmidt still outside?' asked Tom Shovell.

'No. They said he was off to Launceston to find Theophilus Strike.'

'What are you doing back there? Having a bloody tea-party? Take this rock from me before I lose it.' It was Moses Trago.

'Josh Retallick has just arrived,' called Tom Shovell, as the preacher wrestled with a two-hundred-pound rock. 'He's coming up to take over for a while.'

'Tell him to stay back there and save his breath for heaving stones. There's more than enough of them here. Whoever cut out this adit should be gibbeted. The shoring-up would have been better had they used hazel-twigs.'

'The team who did it are somewhere up ahead, with Ben,' said Tom Shovell, as he took the rock from Josh.

The voices of the men were hoarse as a result of the dust-laden air in the cramped tunnel.

The man at the front would often be forced to stop, coughing and choking in the cloud of dust he had raised. This in itself was unusual. Most of the mine-tunnels on this slope were excessively wet. It was quite likely that this peculiarity had contributed to the extent of the adit-collapse, the rock being more inclined to crumble.

The tunnel had progressed another twenty yards, and John

Trago was in the lead when he stopped digging and called on the men to listen. The call went back along the adit until all was quiet except for the rattle of a wheelbarrow somewhere far behind.

Then the waiting and listening men heard the sound of metal upon rock, as though a pick-axe were being used – ahead of them!

'It might be the knockers,' John Trago whispered fearfully, referring to the unseen little men of miners' folklore.

'Knockers be damned,' growled Moses Trago. 'I bet it's Ben Retallick. Here! Let me come up there.' Pushing past his brother and Josh he began attacking the fallen rock with renewed vigour. As the rocks were handed back along the tunnel at an increased rate the sound of metal against stone became clearer. Soon it was close enough for Moses Trago to stop digging and try a booming, 'Hello!'

There was a muffled shout of reply, and Moses renewed his efforts. Ten minutes later, after a struggle with a large slab of rock, there was a cascade of shale and stones away from them. When the dust cleared the excited rescuers saw the drawn face of a man who has come too close to death peering at them from the underground tomb.

'Thank God! Thank God!' The face began to contort and it looked as though the man would burst into tears.

'Thank him later, if you must.' Moses Trago slithered into the open tunnel beside the man. 'Where are the others?'

The rescued miner pointed behind him into the adit, and Moses Trago groped his way past. Josh slid down the pile of loose rubble behind Moses and followed, a flickering candle held in his hand.

Thirty feet on they came upon a second roof-fall. Protruding from beneath this pile of rock a man lay face downwards, the lower part of his body hidden by rocks. It was Ben Retallick.

He looked dead, but as Josh dropped to his knees beside him he stirred and pushed his head and shoulders up from the ground with a groan of pain.

'Aaagh! Who's that?'

The light from Josh's candle bothered him and he tried to ward it off with his hand.

'It's all right, Dad. Don't try to move. We'll soon have you out of there.'

'Josh! What are you doing here? Aaagh!'

The cry of pain came with a shifting of stones amidst the roof-fall.

'Bear with it a while longer, Ben. We'll have you out of there in a few minutes. Where does it hurt most?'

Wrightwick Roberts crouched alongside Josh.

'It's the weight on my legs.' Ben Retallick gritted his teeth. 'I think my right leg is broken. But you get on with what you have to do. The pain isn't that bad. John Maddiver took the full force of the fall, with his brother. I think one of them is lying across my feet.'

There was another slide of stones as the Tragos eased a huge slab of rock from the pile. Ben Retallick winced again, and Josh took his hand.

'Pity they can't teach you down at Harvey's how to stop such happenings,' said his father.

'It doesn't need an engineer to see that the timber work in here isn't as it should be,' said Josh.

'The boy is right,' said Wrightwick Roberts, who was standing by to wedge a fair-sized rock beneath the stone slab when the Tragos had it high enough. 'I'm surprised you didn't go straight up top and report it unsafe when you first saw it.'

Ben Retallick coughed out a harsh laugh. 'Have you tried to have a conversation with Herman Schmidt lately? That man gets rid of a miner if he so much as looks at him. There's no point in telling him about something he doesn't want to know.'

There was the sound of voices from the rescue-tunnel and Tom Shovell came into the light, followed by a tall thin man whom Josh recognised as the Wheal Phoenix mine doctor.

'It's a great relief to see you alive, Ben,' said the shift captain. 'You nearly had more company in here. Jesse's outside. She wouldn't stay home after someone went and told her Josh had arrived and was in here too.'

'We'll have him out in a few seconds,' called Moses Trago. 'Preacher, give us some of your strength on this rock. You'd best call on your Lord to help us too. Josh, pull out your father as soon as he's free. Make sure of it the first time. There's no telling what might happen once we let go of this again.'

The first attempt was abortive. Nothing moved. At the second attempt Moses and John Trago stood shoulder to shoulder with Morwen and Wrightwick Roberts. They strained together, muscles cracking until slowly the thick slab of granite began to rise, inch by agonising inch. At last, assisted by Tom Shovell and the doctor, Josh was able to pull his father clear.

As the slab of rock was lowered again Josh saw the fingers of a man protruding from beneath it, at the place where his father's legs had been.

The doctor had to do little ripping to get at Ben Retallick's leg. The trousers were already torn from ankle to thigh. As the doctor examined the swollen and discoloured leg, Josh began to thank Moses Trago. 'I don't need your thanks,' said the big miner churlishly. 'And you are not beholden to me. I owed the Retallicks a debt for what you once did for my Miriam. That debt is now paid. The Trago family owe nothing to anybody.'

After hearing the doctor's opinion that the fracture was a simple one with no visible complications, Josh left his father with Tom Shovell and Wrightwick Roberts helping to splint the leg. He made his way to the surface. Arriving there he was blinded by the sunlight and almost bowled over by his mother as she flung herself at him.

'Josh, what's going on in there? Have they found him yet – and how did you get here?'

His eyes were more accustomed to the light now, and Josh saw that it was Miriam who was gripping his arm while Jenny stood on his other side. Disentangling himself from his mother, Josh said, 'The man they brought out. Didn't he tell you?'

'Tell me what? The man was a blubbering wreck. Not able to speak a single intelligent word.'

'Dad's all right.' His mother sagged in his arms with relief.

'He's got a broken leg. But he's cheerful and the doctor is with him now.'

'A broken leg? How bad . . . ?'

'Now, Mum! I've said he's all right. I've been speaking to him. The doctor says it's a simple break that will soon mend.'

'How about the other two who were with your father?' asked one of the miners in the crowd.

'There's little chance of them still being alive,' replied Josh, remembering the fingers beneath the pile of rock. 'They were closer to the blast. It looks as though the roof came down on top of them. But Moses and the others are still digging.'

A woman in the crowd began to cry loudly.

'The price of being a miner's wife,' said Miriam bitterly as she watched the woman being led away. 'Her husband gone, a family to support, and within the month she'll have to be out of her mine cottage. If she's lucky, the poor-house will take her. If not, she'll sell herself to drunken miners to get food for her children. That's the system her husband gave his life for.'

Josh looked at her in quick surprise. She was learning more than mathematics and English at the St Cleer Chapel school. It could have been the Reverend William Thackeray himself talking.

'Hush, Miriam! Such talk will do nobody any good,' said Jenny Pearn. But Josh had heard the growls of agreement from the miners at her words. They were not all Sharptor men. It was apparent that the seeds of discontent were scattered further afield than any one mine.

Twenty minutes later Ben Retallick was carried from the adit and the Trago men came out with him. Moses singled out Mary Crabbe, standing on the edge of the crowd.

'There's work for you, Mary.'

'Both of them?' Her face was devoid of all emotion.

'Both of them. Dead because the Wheal Sharptor employs second-rate men to do its blasting.'

He said this deliberately loudly as Theophilus Strike came through the crowd. The mine-owner heard, but chose to ignore the remark. At least, for the moment. He made his way to where Ben Retallick lay.

'I'm pleased to see you safe, Ben. Herman Schmidt told me you were dead.'

'And so he would have been had it been left to that German,' put in Moses Trago.

'You've learned nothing about holding your tongue since you left my mine,' said Strike, looking directly at the big miner for the first time. 'What are you doing here now? The Wheal Sharptor has enough men to carry out its own rescue operations.'

'It should have,' retorted Moses Trago. 'But freeing trapped miners isn't part of a day's work anymore in the Wheal Sharptor.'

There were angry shouts of agreement from the crowd. Theophilus Strike flushed and pursed his lips. He turned to Tom Shovell. 'Captain Schmidt came to me with some garbled story of a roof-fall. Four men killed and you refusing to obey his orders, he said. What is it all about?'

'There's one of his "dead" men,' said the shift captain, pointing to Ben Retallick. 'Another of them has walked home. The other two are dead. Captain Schmidt wanted us to abandon any rescue attempt. He said it wasn't worth while. We Cornish don't do things that way, Mr Strike.'

'Thank God for that!' ejaculated Jesse Retallick, the crowd agreeing with her.

'There seems to be a few matters here that need clearing up,' said the mine-owner. He turned back to the Tragos. 'There will be a guinea for each of you at the mine office tomorrow. It comes with the thanks of the Wheal Sharptor.'

'You can give my guinea to the families of the dead men,' said Morwen Trago, and turning his back on the mine-owner he walked away.

There was a pleased look on Moses Trago's face as he watched his son go on his way.

'The boy's spoken for all of us,' he said. 'I've no doubt Norah Maddiver will have need of the money. She'll get precious little from those who should be giving.' He spat on the ground just in front of Theophilus Strike's riding boots. Then he and his brother swaggered away through a crowd that parted respectfully for them.

'And what are you doing here? Why aren't you at Hayle?' Strike snapped at Josh.

'I was brought word of what had happened and came straightway.'

Strike took in the filthy trousers, scuffed boots and remainder of his riding habit. 'Then you had better get back there again and not waste good learning-time.'

'My horse will be ready to ride in the morning. I'll go then.'

Strike raised his eyebrows. '*Your* horse, eh? I'm paying for you to become an engineer, Retallick. Not to learn how to be a gentleman and own horses.'

'It's not my own horse and I've learned to ride on Sundays, when there are no lessons,' said Josh defiantly. He was angrier than he should have been, but he did not like being spoken down to in front of Miriam. But the conversation had moved away from any discussion on how word had reached Josh. He would not have given much for Nehemeziah Lancellis' prospects of continued employment had the mine-owner learned the facts in his present mood.

'You are a young man, Retallick, and young men are not renowned for good manners. I will allow your insolence to pass on this occasion. But I suggest you learn how to address your employer before you return to work here or you may well find life very very difficult. Now go home and take your mother with you. I want to speak to your father before he is taken home. You too, Captain Shovell.'

Next he turned his attention to the crowd. 'The rest of you can go about your business. Anyone who is here without due cause in ten minutes' time will be prosecuted for trespass.'

'Pig!' hissed Miriam as she went off with Josh, Jenny and Jesse Retallick.

'Shh!' said Jesse. 'Theophilus Strike could have been far harsher than he was.'

'He could also have expressed some sympathy for those

who had been killed,' said Jenny bitterly. 'I don't think he even cares.'

Jesse Retallick knew the thoughts that must be going through Jenny's mind and she put a motherly arm about her 'I'm sure he cares, Jenny. It's just that Theophilus Strike doesn't know how to express kind thoughts. He feels more comfortable showing people the hard side of his character. Some men are like that.'

Miriam sniffed loudly and then grinned at Josh when Jesse went on to say, 'And you two are a fine pair of rebels to take to meet the mine-owner!' But Jesse's heart was light inside her. She had gone to the mine expecting the worst. But Ben was alive, his injury far less serious than she had dared hope. Then her son was home for a night. She missed him far more than she would admit to anyone and would be overjoyed when his course had ended, though it was apparent to all who saw Josh and Miriam together that he would not remain at home with his mother for long.

Ben came home carried between Tom Shovell and Wrightwick Roberts and escorted as far as the gate by a crowd of off-duty miners. 'Every one of them grinning like a sheep,' commented Jesse Retallick. It was with very good reason.

'Come along, Jesse,' said Ben, his face all smiles despite his injury. 'Don't be slow opening the door when your husband is carried home by the new mine captain.'

'You, Tom?' His face betrayed the answer and Jesse hugged him impulsively. 'Oh, I'm so glad for you! And for the mine. But what has happened to Herman Schmidt?'

'Theophilus Strike says he won't be back. It seems he reeked of alcohol when he barged in on a meeting Theophilus Strike was having with some business friends. He said a few things that one doesn't say to a mine-owner. Josh, take note!'

'That's wonderful news,' said Josh. 'Sharptor will be a happier mine now.'

'But that's not all the news, lad,' said Wrightwick Roberts. 'Ask your father who is to take Tom's place as shift captain – when his leg has mended.'

'Ben! You've not been made shift captain after all these years?' cried Jesse.

Ben Retallick nodded, then had to ward off his wife as she hugged him too. 'Steady now, Jesse. Remember my leg.'

'It's a pity it took two deaths to make Theophilus Strike see sense,' said Miriam.

Wrightwick Roberts' face lost its smile.

'True. But God works in His own way, as I hope you will come to accept one day.'

Miriam stared at him defiantly until the preacher's glance dropped, then she threw up her chin and went into the kitchen where she began noisily to stoke up the fire, which had been allowed to burn low in the excitement of the day.

'My God!' said Ben Retallick with admiration in his voice. 'Every time I look at that girl I see Jesse as she was when she was young. There's spirit there.'

'Too much for my liking,' said the new mine captain. 'I think women should be gentler altogether.' His gaze followed Jenny Pearn as she too went into the kitchen.

There were times later that evening when Josh too wished that Miriam were a more conventional girl with a less enquiring mind. The talk around the table over the meal moved to Josh's ride home. He had to tell them about Hector, who was now safe in Sharptor stables, and how his riding lessons had begun with the acquisition of riding clothes. Miriam asked him a number of questions, but it was not until he was walking her home that she pursued the subject of Sarah Carlyon.

'Why did she pick you out for riding lessons?' she asked.

Josh shrugged into the darkness. 'I don't know. I think it might have been because I was telling them about Nehemeziah and his horses. It just sort of happened. Besides, I don't think any of the others know much about horses.'

'Is Sarah very beautiful?' asked Miriam suddenly, after a long silence.

'No.' Josh was aware he was lying. 'Well . . . she's quite pretty, I suppose.'

'More beautiful than me, Josh?'

'No.' He was able to say it with complete honesty.

'Have you ever kissed her?'

'Of course not! She means nothing to me, Miriam. She is the works manager's daughter, that's all. I expect she only taught me to ride because there was no one else to go riding with her.'

'That's all right, then.' Miriam turned to him suddenly and threw her arms about him. As Josh drew her into his arms she responded fiercely. Lips and bodies met in a passionate kiss that made Josh feel as though his whole body was on fire.

The same heat was in Miriam, and his hands made their first voyage of discovery on her body. Gently at first and then more demanding. She responded with low moans and teeth that plucked at his skin. Then, as quickly as it had begun, she was pushing him away. 'No, Josh. No! Not now. Please – Josh!'

She slipped out of his grasp and held him at arm's length as he tried to pull her to him again.

'No, Josh. Don't let it be like that with me.'

He felt both ashamed and frustrated and let his arms fall to his sides. 'I'm sorry.'

Immediately she was back again. 'No, don't feel sorry. I want you to need me like that. But please try to wait a while longer. It won't be too long, will it, Josh?'

'No, only until the year I come home and start earning.'

She kissed him again, until his hands began roving once more.

'I must go now, Josh.'

'All right.'

'Josh?'

'Yes?'

'I love you. I love you so much that I could burst with it.'

'I love you too, Miriam.' It sounded strange now that he had finally put his thoughts into words.

'Honest?'

'Honest.'

She came back to him, fiercer than before. 'Then you can. If you really want to.'

'No.' It came easier now that it was his decision. 'We'll wait until we are properly married.'

'I'm glad. Good night, Josh.'

'Good night, Miriam.'

Another embrace and she slipped away into the darkness. On the way home to the cottage Josh heard Moses and Morwen going up the path to the moorland cave-house, coming from the direction of the village. They were both singing drunkenly. He wished his apprenticeship was already over so that he could marry Miriam and take her away to be with him.

Chapter Twelve

Josh was on his way at dawn. So too was Nehemeziah
Lancellis. Hector was stiff from his long ride the previous
day and, though he soon loosened up, Josh kept him in check.
He met up with the Sharptor hostler not far from the Indian
Queen Inn.

The little hostler was overjoyed to hear of Ben Retallick's
escape from the adit. When Josh told him of the departure
of Herman Schmidt and the resulting promotions, he thought
the old man's face would split in two.

'Things'll be better now, Josh. Ar, Sharp Tor will be an
'andsome bal now.'

'No doubt about it, Nehemeziah,' grinned Josh. 'Now, you'd
better be getting that horse back or you won't be around to
enjoy the changes. Don't let Theophilus Strike know you
borrowed his horse to come and fetch me. He wasn't too
pleased to see me!'

Nehemeziah Lancellis waved his greasy old hat in acknowledgement, and with a smile Josh wheeled Hector westwards.
There was some cloud building up way out over the sea. It
heralded rain, so Josh let Hector have his head. The big horse
chose a fast mile-eating gallop that brought the tall smoking
chimneys of Harvey's foundry into view before the midday
steam-whistle sounded.

Josh eased the horse down to an easy canter to enter Hayle. Turning in at the foundry gates he rode past the works manager's house and straight on to the stables. Here he dismounted, his legs far stiffer than those of the horse.

As he pulled the saddle from Hector's sweating back he heard his name called. Turning he saw Sarah running across the stable yard towards him, holding her skirt high to clear the mud.

'Josh, what happened?' She stepped close to him, looking up into his face, trying to read his expression. 'Is your father all right?'

He nodded happily. 'And, thanks to Hector, I was home in time to help dig him free from the roof-fall.'

'Oh, Josh, I'm so pleased!'

Impulsively she stood on tiptoe with hands resting briefly on his shoulders, and kissed him quickly on the mouth. He remembered Miriam's question of scarcely more than twelve hours before. But there was little time to dwell on that. William and Molly Carlyon arrived together with most of the apprentices. All began asking their own questions.

It was William Carlyon who rescued him. 'Come to the house, Josh. You can tell us about it over a meal. I expect you could do with some solid food inside you after your ride.'

While they were eating, he told the family about the rescue and subsequent events.

'Your father must be very highly thought of,' said Mrs Carlyon speculatively. 'He might even become the mine captain himself, one day.'

'He could do the job well enough,' said Josh proudly. 'But Tom Shovell is a good man too.'

'From what I have heard, Theophilus Strike is fortunate to have a man with your father's experience working in such a small mine,' said William Carlyon. 'His promotion doesn't come before time. There are many mine adventurers who would have made him their mine captain had he a mind to move away from Sharptor.'

Josh was considerably impressed. He had not been aware that William Carlyon knew anything about Ben Retallick.

While they were eating, Sarah called attention to Josh's hands and it caused him some embarrassment. He had done his share of removing rock from the fall and his fingers were bruised and cut from tearing out the rough granite. Despite his protests Mrs Carlyon and Sarah insisted on bathing them for him and rubbing in an antiseptic ointment.

He was relieved when the 'resume work' hooter sounded. He was able to leave the house with William Carlyon and make for the apprentices' dormitory, to change into his working clothes.

'Our Sarah was very worried about you last night, Josh,' said William Carlyon as he closed the gate after them and set off across the yard. 'She is very fond of you in her own quiet way.'

'She's a fine girl,' said Josh. 'I'm very grateful to her for allowing me to go home on Hector.'

William Carlyon gave Josh a searching look. 'I started work down a tin mine when I was ten, Josh. Don't get to imagining that the Carlyons are any better – or any worse – than the Retallicks. One day you will be an outstanding engineer, unless I am mistaken. Plan your future now, while you can see it more clearly than you will once you return to Sharptor. You'll not always be engineer to Theophilus Strike. This is the time to lay the foundations for the future, while you are here. Good Cornish engineers will never be short of work, anywhere in the world. There are copper mines opening up in South America. Tin mines too. There is no reason why you should limit yourself to copper. They will have need of mine-engineers everywhere. Some of the ship's captains I speak to these days are full of the new discoveries being made abroad. More than one of them has brought me samples of ore to check on. Most of it is good quality, Josh. If you decide that your future still lies here in Cornwall, you will need to be good to keep us on top. If we ever allow our efficiency to slide, then we will lose out to these overseas producers. Mines depend on engines, but the best engines in the world are only as good as the engineers who make and maintain them – as you have heard me say many times before.'

Josh nodded. He preferred talking engines to discussing the works manager's daughter.

'But standing here chatting is not going to qualify you as an engineer. Away you go and change. I am very pleased that things at Sharptor turned out so well after all.'

The weeks and months went by at Hayle. Lost in sheer hard work summer slipped into autumn and autumn surrendered in its turn to winter. By November, Josh was considered to be sufficiently well trained to go with a team of Harvey's engineers to a local tin mine. In this way he gained practical knowledge of installing mine machinery.

It was the best possible experience for him. He found immense satisfaction in helping to solve problems that ranged from transporting a huge seventy-inch boiler across rough uneven country to the testing and acceptance of the building that was to house the engine. The main wall of the house had to be strong enough to support the weight of the thirty-ton rocking-beam that topped the column of wooden 'plungers'. It alternately drove them into the depths of the main shaft and pulled them up again, pumping out the water from the lower levels.

The work had only just been completed when the snows came. There was not a man or woman alive in Cornwall who could remember when there had been a winter like it. The snow hid the toll-roads and spread a thick blanket on the fields and tors. And still it came down.

Hayle harbour was unnaturally still and silent, jammed with ships unable to move out because of the blinding snow that whirled in from the east. Not a single ship was able to enter or leave for two weeks. Most of those unfortunate enough to be caught at sea when the blizzard started foundered on the inhospitable coast. Others vanished without trace somewhere out in the unseen storm-tossed sea.

For Josh it meant that he was unable to make the journey home to spend Christmas at Sharptor. It was a great disappointment. He and the other apprentices had enjoyed a lucrative business clearing pathways through the deep snow between the ships and the town. The money had been spent on unexpected presents for those at home.

Neither was there any way of informing them at Sharptor that he would not be coming. Ben and Jesse knew in their hearts that travel through the snow was quite impossible and they had voiced this opinion many times throughout Christmas Eve. Only Miriam continued to nurse the hope that some miracle would occur to allow Josh to come home.

'Perhaps it is only up here on the moor that the snow is so bad,' she said. 'It might be better further west.'

She was wearing a new dress of coloured gingham pinched in at the waist the better to show off her slim developing figure to advantage. The dress had been specially bought for Josh's homecoming.

'No, it's the same all over the country,' said Ben Retallick, reclining in the rocking-chair close to the roaring fire. 'Not even a seagull could get home in weather like this. Nehemeziah tried to take two mules down to Liskeard for some mine stores. He hadn't got as far as the lower path before one of the mules slipped and went into a snowdrift. It swallowed up the animal completely. Even when Nehemeziah and the other mule had dragged it clear and turned round it was as much as they could do to follow their tracks back to the mine. I don't suppose there is anyone in the county stirring beyond his doorstep this Christmas.'

'Poor Josh,' said Miriam miserably. 'He was so looking forward to coming home. His last letter was full of it.'

'I wonder what sort of Christmas he will have at Hayle?' put in Jenny as she lifted a large steaming kettle from the fire.

'Oh, he'll do well enough,' said Ben Retallick. 'William Carlyon and his family will see to that. I think they've taken quite a fancy to our Josh. Theophilus Strike was talking to me about it the other day. He met Carlyon at some mining meeting in Camborne. Strike also said that Josh was regarded as one of the most promising young engineers they've ever had at Hayle. He sounded well pleased about it.'

'And so he should be,' said Miriam, grasping at an outlet for her unhappiness. 'He will be paying near-starvation wages for a skilled man who could go anywhere and earn good money.'

'That's as may be,' frowned Ben Retallick, 'but don't lose sight of the fact that without Theophilus Strike's money to pay for his training Josh would be slogging his life away down a mine, just like your brother.'

Jenny came across the room and put a comforting arm about Miriam. 'Never mind. Josh will be just as upset at not being able to be with you. I'm quite sure he will be home as soon as he can.'

'It's all right for you,' said Miriam. 'Tom Shovell will be here for his Christmas meal.' But the edge had gone from her voice and she managed a smile. Jenny was a very gentle loving girl. Nobody was happier than Miriam at the romance that had sprung up between the middle-aged mine captain and the young widow. While neither of them had yet broached the subject of marriage, gossip in the village had it that this would be the last Christmas that Jenny and baby Gwen would spend in someone else's house.

All the same, Miriam did not enjoy her Christmas. Not only was there the disappointment of not having Josh, there was also the misery of jealousy eating at her insides. Josh was spending Christmas with a girl Miriam instinctively knew was in love with him. Josh might not be aware of it but he could not fail to compare what Sarah had to offer with Miriam's lack of family background and possessions.

It was a continuation of this feeling that spoiled the New Year weekend for both of them. The weather broke mid-week and within forty-eight hours the snow had gone from all but the highest and most sheltered hedges of the tors. A blustery south wind helped to dry out the saturated land.

Once again Josh arrived home on Hector. Sarah had offered the horse almost casually, commenting that it would give the big horse some much needed exercise after being confined to the stable during the snows. Josh wore the new complete riding outfit that had been a Christmas present from the Carlyon family. It was actually a present from Sarah alone, but Mrs Carlyon had wisely persuaded Sarah to offer it as coming from the whole family, thus avoiding any embarrassment. As she carefully explained to Sarah, Josh was at the very beginning of his career and had little money of his own. His Cornish pride might cause him to reject an expensive present from a girl for whom he could not buy a gift of equal value.

This ploy might have fooled Josh, but Miriam immediately guessed the true source of the gift. It overshadowed her modest gift to him, and nothing seemed right from then on. It was a miserable weekend, without sufficient time for them to overcome this initial misunderstanding.

It was two very unhappy young people who said goodbye to each other on the Sunday evening, Josh to make the long lonely ride to Hayle and Miriam to spend an hour crying in the hideout on the moor before going home to face yet another violent quarrel between her long-suffering mother and drunken father.

For the next two months the letters between Hayle and Sharptor were full of self-recrimination for a wasted weekend that could never be recalled.

The year 1841 sped along as though it was in a hurry to get somewhere, and the Sharptor engine became an exciting reality for Josh. By late summer it was being assembled. It was rare for a mine-engineer to be involved in the manufacture of his own engine. In this Josh was lucky. His involvement began with a personal selection of the firestores for crushing and smelting. Then followed the careful mixing and pouring of the liquid metal into the cast which Josh had given a minute inspection. In this way was born the boiler, flawless and of the finest metal. Not for Josh the constant gnawing fear of a boiler-burst; or of working with a boiler in which there was a known flaw, unable to close down and renew it because of the loss of work for the mine. Not that every mine captain would even contemplate such a course of action.

It was often far easier to dismiss an engineer and employ another, less skilled and less aware. One who relied on a bottle or two of gin a day to help him ignore the probability of an explosion.

There were many such 'engineers' working in the mines of Cornwall. Explosions were all too frequent.

But the boiler was only part of the engine; there was also the massive beam and numerous pipes, gears and wheels associated with a shaft-head working. It was now that Josh found William Carlyon to be a tremendous help. The works manager had a background of practical mining experience. By applying this experience to the task of engine-building he was able to eliminate years of trial and error. Josh realised that the works manager was taking special pains over this engine as a particular favour to him. Harvey's was riding the crest of a great business wave, and William Carlyon had more than enough administrative work to occupy his days.

Finally, all that could be done at Hayle was completed and the equipment loaded on to a ship to be carried around the coast to Looe. There Josh would meet it and accompany the engine on the difficult overland journey to Sharptor.

Suddenly all the years of studying at Hayle were over. He was an engineer going out into the world of working men, his off-duty time his own and no necessity to spend his evenings studying. It was a strange feeling. Even leaving Hayle would be something of a wrench. For almost three years it had been everything to him – home, work and occasional recreation. But he had long since outgrown the newer apprentices. They were no longer such a tight-knit little group as they had seemed on his arrival at Hayle. Consequently, his farewell party was a quiet affair compared with that of Tom Fiddler, and he had hardly a trace of a hangover when he went to the Carlyon house to say goodbye.

This was a difficult parting. William and Molly Carlyon had treated him as though he was a son. He had become genuinely fond of the family – especially, he had to admit, of Sarah. It was not the same feeling as the one he had for Miriam. That was a tempestuous emotion, a smouldering feeling that threatened to ignite one day with an all-consuming roar of flame. His feelings for Sarah were gentler, feelings of deep affection.

When Mrs Carlyon had hugged him and given him a motherly kiss, she said, 'Surely you are not going without saying goodbye to the horses? Sarah, take Josh down to the stables. You have both had many happy hours riding together. I am quite sure the horses won't get nearly as much exercise now.'

Josh walked with Sarah in silence to the stables. He opened the door and they went inside, into the warm and familiar smell. The stables were empty except for the Carlyons' riding ponies and Hector. All the other horses were working between the foundry and the jetty.

'Goodbye, Hector, old chap,' said Josh, patting the horse's neck as the big animal nuzzled his ear. 'I'm going to miss you.'

'Will you miss me too, Josh? Just a little?' It was a very unhappy little plea.

'I'll miss you a lot, Sarah. You've been very very kind to me while I've been here.'

She turned away from him so he could not see her face. It was only when her shoulders started to heave that he knew she was crying.

'Sarah! Don't.' He touched her shoulders and she turned into him, letting the sobs come noisily.

'Please don't cry.' Her tears were wet and warm on his chest, through his shirt, and he held her close as she clung to him. Then he was kissing her, and she was responding with a hunger that made his body react as it had once before. In another place. With Miriam.

He tried to pull away, but she clung to him in fierce desperation. 'Don't go, Josh. Don't leave me.'

'I must, Sarah. My apprenticeship is over now. I have work to do. You know that.'

'I only know that I can't face life here without you,' Sarah cried.

'You mustn't talk like that,' he said gently. 'Your family have been very good to me, Sarah. If I thought I was repaying them by making you unhappy I would be very upset.'

Sarah pulled away from him and looked down at the ground. 'I'm making a fool of myself, aren't I, Josh?'

'No, of course you're not.'

She nodded her head violently. 'Yes. Yes, I am. I'm sorry.'

She fumbled in her sleeve for a handkerchief, and he handed her his own. After dabbing her eyes she blew her nose violently. 'I'm all right now,' she said thickly.

'That's good. Come on. . . .' He put out a hand to take her arm, but she stepped back.

'No, don't touch me, Josh. I shall only do something foolish again, if you do.'

'We'd better go now,' he said. 'The men will be waiting for me.'

'You go. I want to stay here for a while.'

'Sarah, I can't leave you like this.'

'It's better, Josh. Really it is.'

He hesitated. This was harder than he had ever imagined it would be. 'All right. Goodbye, Sarah.'

'Goodbye . . . Josh!'

He stopped and turned at the door.

'Will you write to me? Tell me how you are getting on?' Sarah asked.

'Of course I will. Not only that; I might even be coming back here for a while. Your father thinks we ought to have a steam-whim at Sharptor for raising the ore. If I can persuade Theophilus Strike, I'll come here myself and arrange it.'

'I would like that. Goodbye, Josh. Think of me sometimes.'

He went outside and the sunshine burned his eyes.

The men were in the wagon. As soon as he climbed on board the driver whipped up the horses and they trundled off. Harvey's was supplying a team of four men to install the engine and they were travelling with all the tools they would need for the job.

They arrived at Sharptor the following day. After a brief reunion with his family – Miriam was at work at the Wheal Phoenix – Josh hurried away to Looe. He meant to ensure that sufficient care was taken with the engine on its way up the canal to Moorswater. He left the Harvey team to inspect the newly constructed engine-house and prepare for his arrival with the machinery.

The boiler looked huge sitting on the jetty alongside the

ship that had carried it. But it was the massive beam that was the most difficult item to handle. It's thirty-ton bulk was formidable. Special equipment would have to be used throughout the whole of its journey. Josh had expressed doubts about carrying it up the canal, but the canal company had a barge which had been built for this very purpose. The Wheal Caradon had used it two years before when they had expanded their workings.

Josh thought that, if the Wheal Caradon had needed a special barge for their beam, they would probably have a wagon too. When the beam had been secured aboard the barge, Josh rode off to enquire.

'The Wheal Sharptor, eh?'

The pinch-faced Captain Frisby had responsibility for the largest copper-mining complex in east Cornwall.

'How far are you expanding? I'm not lending mine equipment to another mine that might very well put us out of business.'

Josh looked around at the highly industrialised Caradon complex, its numerous tall black-smoked chimneys and general air of bustle and industry. It was more like a small town than a mine. He could count at least a half-dozen engines of different types and sizes. The Caradon mines employed more than a thousand men. Wheal Sharptor was not in the same class, and Josh said as much.

'We'll never be able to compete with the Caradon,' he added. 'We don't have to pay shareholders, and Theophilus Strike has too many other interests to want to make us very much bigger.'

'That may be the way it is now,' said the Caradon captain, 'but who knows what may happen next year? Or the year after?' For the first time Josh recognised the fact that he might be refused the loan of the special wagon.

'From what I heard during the time I was at Hayle there just isn't enough copper being produced to meet the demand for it,' he said, choosing his words carefully and keeping a tight grip on the anger boiling up within him. Many mines were rivals, but it was unheard of for one mine to refuse to help another when it would cost nothing and was within its power to do so. But this man was not Cornish and that made a difference.

'I don't think Sharptor will ever be a big mine,' Josh repeated. 'We are too crowded. With the Phoenix to the south and east of us and Darley to the north we have only two alternatives: work to the west or sink deeper shafts. The west side has been checked out pretty thoroughly and there is not much there. So we must go down. With the money that will cost him Theophilus Strike is not going to make a fortune from it.'

This statement repeated almost word for word a conversation he had overheard between his father and Tom Shovell during Josh's last weekend at home.

'Apart from anything else,' Josh went on, 'even the biggest mines sometimes need help. One day you might need another engineer. You'll always be able to call on me.'

'If ever I need another engineer I won't send for a boy to do the job,' retorted the Caradon captain. All the same, he looked at Josh with a new interest. 'Where did you pick up engineering? Loafing about in some boiler-house and watching the fireman?'

'No, I learned it properly at Harvey's of Hayle,' replied Josh. 'The engine on its way up the canal from Looe is one that I helped to build. That's why I am here asking for your help and not the Sharptor captain.'

'Is that offer of yours a firm promise?' asked the captain. 'If ever we have need of you, we can call on you?'

'If you ever need help, I'm quite sure Tom Shovell will be happy for me to come, whether we owe you a favour or not.'

'H'm! Well, it's my experience that you get nothing given to you in this life,' said the Caradon captain. 'So if ever we are stuck for an engineer I will hold you to your promise. You can take the wagon. But you'll have to provide your own horses. I'm not wearing out my mine's horses for the Wheal Sharptor.'

Josh was quite happy with the arrangement. The Sharptor

mine had no shortage of good horses. When he inspected the wagon he knew he would need all of them. It was a very heavy low-slung construction of iron and huge wood beams. The iron wheels had rims on them as wide as a man, to prevent the wagon from sinking into the ground. Even so, Josh knew that careful thought would have to be given to mapping out a safe route for the wagon when it was fully laden.

Captain Tom Shovell could not hide his amazement when Josh told him that he was borrowing the Wheal Caradon's wagon and of the deal that had been made.

'He'll call on your services one day, you can depend on that,' he said. 'But it's a rare thing to have got something from Captain Frisby. He's the meanest man you'll find in Cornwall. You'd better go and tell Nehemeziah to give you the horses before Frisby changes his mind.'

The hostler was happy for the opportunity to do something out of the ordinary and show off all his horses. He was always bragging that they were the best in east Cornwall. Now he would prove it. In fact, Sharptor had been the first mine in the area to use horses and wagons to carry ore. The mines had always made do with a varied collection of ponies and mules to carry it. Balancing a pair of open-mouthed bags, one each side, they had picked their way from mine to port for many years. Trudging out deep narrow trails across moor and heath that would remain for more than a hundred years.

Leaving only enough horses to work the winding-whims that brought the ore to the surface, Nehemeziah and his stable-boys were able to muster seventeen pairs of horses. They were an impressive sight. Theophilus Strike had started his stable with three mares and a stallion from the shires. By careful selection and breeding Nehemeziah had expanded his working stock to its present proportions. There was not a mine hostler in Cornwall who did not know of Nehemeziah and his great shire-horses.

As the double line of horses jangled their brass-embellished harness along the track into the Caradon mine all surface work came to a halt, the women, boys and old men stopping to watch them. Nehemeziah, riding on the back of the leading

pair, was fully aware of the impression he was creating. He
shouted his orders to the horses with the authority of a cavalry
officer. The beasts did not let him down. They halted, wheeled
and backed as though each one carried a rider.

With four pairs of horses pulling and the remainder bringing
up the rear the heavy wagon was hauled away from the mine
with such ease that it might have been a pony-cart.

Captain Frisby watched the performance with great interest.
While Josh was checking and greasing the thick axles he got
into earnest conversation with the Sharptor hostler.

As they left the Caradon mine behind them Josh rode up
alongside the old man. Nehemeziah was wearing a grin that
showed off his shortage of teeth.

'You've got plenty to smile about,' said Josh. 'They've never
seen horses like these at the Caradon before.'

'Reckon that's so,' agreed the old man. 'And they won't see
the likes again – even though Cap'n Frisby said as how he'd
match 'em if I went to work for the Caradon. Give me a sight
more money too, so he would.'

'Well?'

Nehemeziah chuckled but said nothing.

'What was your reply? Are you going to accept his offer?'

'An' leave these beauties? 'Sides, I told 'en what 'twould
cost. Came damn near to choking of 'en.'

'Captain Shovell said he doesn't like to spend money. It
might put him off calling on me to do any odd jobs that he
thinks of. I'll tell him you're thinking of taking up his offer,
say you mentioned the hundred pair of shires he'll be buying
for you. He'll have nightmares about it and won't want to see
or hear anyone from Sharptor for fear they have a message
from you.'

'Cap'n Frisby'd get his money back from more than they,'
said Nehemeziah. 'His pack-'orses don't carry more'n a spoonful apiece. Two o' these pullin' a wagon do the work of twenty
o' they.'

'Don't tell Frisby that.' Josh kneed his horse forward. 'The
day might come when I'll need something to frighten him
off with. I'm going on ahead now to see that barge in.

Use the brakes down the hill to Moorswater; that's a heavy wagon.'

'Engine's your'n. 'Orses is mine,' the old man growled.

Josh grinned and waved cheerfully.

The beam was as difficult to transfer from barge to wagon as Josh had feared. He used hoists and the only available crane, but the ropes parted. The beam crashed down, smashing a line of stone paving-slabs as though they were biscuits. Then some heavy chains were produced and the work was quickly completed. With the beam on the special wagon and the boiler on one of the three long carts they began the slow return to Sharptor.

Darkness travelled faster than the wagon, as it was forced to take a long route in order to keep firm ground beneath the wheels. Nehemeziah announced his intention of spending the night where he was, with the horses. Two of the stable-lads stayed with him.

Josh rode home with one of the wagon-drivers up behind him and it was midnight before they were back at Sharptor.

The family was waiting up for him but, despite the late hour, he was surprised that Miriam was not with them. He commented on it while he was eating.

His mother was unusually evasive. 'I don't suppose she knows you're home,' she said.

'I can't believe that. There isn't one person in Sharptor or Henwood who doesn't know the engine's here. Half the county turned out to see Nehemeziah's horses. Besides, Miriam used to spend more time here than she did at her own home. What's happened?'

'Miriam doesn't spend much time at Sharptor these days,' explained his mother. 'She puts in a full day's work down at the Wheal Phoenix, then she goes to St Cleer to do her schooling, as you once did. We've seen very little of her these last two months.'

'No, it isn't Miriam's fault, Josh,' said Ben Retallick. 'She's staying away in order to save us from any unpleasantness, that's all.'

'I don't understand. What unpleasantness? I thought you

enjoyed having her here. She's almost family, and once we're married. . . .'

'Well, bless my soul!' exclaimed Jesse Retallick. 'I thought the boy was never going to say he'd marry her. It's not before time.'

'Miriam knows,' said Josh. 'But that doesn't explain what is happening.'

'It's all my fault, Josh.' Jenny Pearn rose from her seat in the corner.

Now Jenny . . .,' Jesse Retallick began, but the young widow waved her into silence.

'Yes, it is, in a way. You've been away a long time, Josh. You don't know what Moses Trago is like now.'

'He's an animal!' exclaimed Jesse Retallick.

'That's as good a description of him as any,' agreed Jenny. 'You remember how he used to be when he had been drinking?'

Josh nodded.

'Now he's far worse. It's as though the drink has drowned the normal part of his mind.'

Jenny sat down on the stool in front of the fire. 'He came to the house when your mother was in the kitchen and must have thought I was here alone. He started mauling me. Your mother had to threaten him with the meat cleaver before he would let me alone and go.' She shuddered. 'He's evil.'

'But that's not all of it,' put in Jesse. 'He began coming to the door to ask for Miriam and made more than one scene when she wasn't here. It meant nothing to him whether she was here or not. It was an excuse to leer at Jenny. It ended with another fight between him and your father. It was lucky for Moses that your father didn't know until afterwards how much of a nuisance he'd been or he would have done more than throw him out.'

'He's not a sane man anymore,' said Ben Retallick quietly. 'He's sick in his mind.'

'He has the devil in him,' said Jesse Retallick.

'And now Miriam is staying away so that he'll have no

excuse for coming here.' It was a statement rather than a question.

'Yes. I'm sorry, Josh.'

'It's none of your doing,' Josh said to Jenny. 'But I feel sorry for Miriam.'

'Then the sooner you marry her the better,' said Jesse Retallick. 'But it's way past the time to go to bed. You're home now and there will be plenty of time to talk to Miriam. Now, if you want to set off early for that engine of yours, you'd better be getting some sleep.'

Josh let himself out of the cottage into the hill mist that promised a fine day. At the gate a silent figure darted forward, and the next moment he was holding Miriam.

'I'd almost given you up for lost,' he said, holding her at arm's length in order to look at her. 'Where have you been?'

'Me?' she asked indignantly. 'I waited out here last night for so long that I almost fell asleep on my feet. I finally decided that you must be spending the night at Looe and went home. But I got up early this morning to come down here, just in case you'd come home.'

'You should have gone indoors. Mum misses you, Miriam.'

'No, I didn't want to do that. I expect she's told you what happened. I'm not going to bring trouble on them again, Josh.'

'Miriam, that's foolish. They are very fond of you and—'

Miriam silenced him with a kiss on his lips. 'We won't argue about it – especially now. Where are you going? Can I walk with you?'

'I'm going to the Sharptor stables. Then out to meet Nehemeziah. We'll have the parts for the engine back here by noon. Then I can begin to put it together. It's a fine engine, Miriam.'

'I'm quite sure it is if you've helped to build it.' She laughed happily and clung to his arm and chattered as they swung along the path in the grey morning.

They skirted the indistinct shell of the new engine-house and halted a short distance from the almost empty stables.

'Will you see me tonight, Josh?'

'I'll do my best, but it will be difficult for a couple of days. The men from Harvey's want to see the engine working by Saturday so they can return home. That means working from dawn to dusk and beyond. If it's at all possible, I'll make the time. If not, then I'll meet you on Sunday. We'll spend the day on the moor.' He smiled at her. 'I'm home now, Miriam. We have a lifetime ahead of us.'

'I know, I'm so happy I could bust. I won't wait around tonight. I'll let you get on with putting your engine together. I'll go straight on to my lessons after work. You must go to talk with William; he is always asking about you. He says you've proved to be one of his most successful pupils.'

It still sounded strange to hear her call the Reverend William Thackeray 'William'. 'Give him my regards,' he said. 'Tell him I might seek his advice on how best to convince Theophilus Strike that he needs a second engine – one that I can use to hoist men to grass at the end of a shift.'

'He'll be very happy to help. There is more than mere talk of a union of miners now, Josh. The Wheal Phoenix men are for it, and Caradon miners are talking about stopping work if the mine shop prices rise any more.'

'That's probably just what's needed.' The mist was thinning out as the sun rose over Dartmoor, well to the east, beginning to colour the sky. 'I must go now. I have a way to go.'

''Bye, Josh.'

He kissed her quickly, then strode away to the stables. He could almost imagine they were married already and that Miriam would be waiting for him at the end of a working day. But the bells that fate was planning to ring were not for a wedding.

Chapter Thirteen

As Josh had anticipated, the work of building the engine kept him working at a frenzied pace for the remainder of that week. His meetings with Miriam were brief. But the thrill of watching the engine take on working shape beneath his hands was an experience to drive away all other thoughts for much of each day.

Awkwardly, he tried to express his thoughts to the engineer in charge of the Harvey team as the engine neared completion. The engineer nodded knowingly. 'You'll never know another feeling like it, Josh. It's the nearest thing to being God that a man will ever achieve. All these parts we brought up from the foundry were just pieces of manufactured metal. Now we've put them together and given them life. You've seen the whole thing grow from nothing. For ever more this engine will have something of you in it. All engines have life and character. No one who works with them would deny that. But this engine will be something special for you. It's your creation. You'll come to know its every mood and its strength and weaknesses. I'm telling you, Josh, a man can fall in love with an engine and need not be ashamed of it.'

The engine was scheduled for completion on Saturday afternoon, although it would be another week before the long plungers would extend to the bottom of the shaft and link up with the water-pump. But on Saturday the boiler would be filled, the fire started and the shiny piston-rod would set the great beam rocking on its pivot.

During the final few hours a leak in the main steam-pipe caused some concern. A flurry of activity put it right, and by four o'clock that afternoon Theophilus Strike and some of his gentlemen friends were inside the boiler-room watching the pressure-gauge register for the first time. Outside the door, and peering in at the windows, were the families of every miner who worked on the mine, together with those miners who were off duty.

Ben Retallick and Jesse were well to the front, standing with Wrightwick Roberts. Jenny should have been with them but she had stayed at home. Young Gwen was recovering from a bad bout of measles and was not yet fit enough to leave the house.

The steam-pressure reached working level. The black smoke spewed forth from the tall stone chimney and chased the wind up the slope. The water began rattling in the pipes as the Hayle engineer tapped each one of them, checking the joints for leaks. Then, as the needle hovered halfway across the dial of the gauge, he decided it was time. 'All right, Josh. Open them now.'

Jenny Pearn filled the kettle and set it on the fire in the kitchen. She pushed it well down so that no movement of the coals would cause it to overbalance.

Behind her she thought she heard the latch on the outside door click shut.

'Is that you, Jesse? That was over quickly. How was Josh's engine? Will it . . . ? Oh my God!'

Standing swaying inside the room, his chest heaving, was Moses Trago. His face was black with underground dirt and streaked with the sweat of a long shift.

Jenny put her left hand to her throat. The other felt behind her for the door-frame. She drew support from it for a moment, then her hand felt along the wall. Slowly, very slowly, she moved along with it. She had no coherent thoughts in her mind. She only knew she had to get away from Moses, get upstairs to Gwen.

Moses followed her with his eyes, red-rimmed eyes that were as dark as fifty fathoms.

As far as the corner of the room Jenny was moving away from him, but edging along the far wall brought her closer. Moses took two lurching steps into the room, and Jenny flattened herself against the wall; arms stretched out as though she were being crucified.

Moses made a drunken unintelligible movement with his hand. 'Come here!' The words were scarcely more recognisable than the gesture.

Jenny did not move.

Moses lumbered another couple of heavy paces towards her. Now he was close enough for her to know the strong animal smell that reached out from his body and the stale gin on his breath. But it was his eyes that made her shudder with horror. There was no light in them, only a blackness as deep as the grave.

'Please, Moses, no,' Jenny begged. 'My babe. Don't . . . !' He grabbed at her as she tried desperately to slip past and he caught her dress at the shoulder.

She struggled to break free, but his grip held and the fabric parted, baring half her upper body to the waist.

Moses held her like a dog on a ragged lead, and pulling her roughly towards him, reached out with his other hand and it closed bruisingly around her flesh.

Jenny screamed, and Moses released her torn dress to strike her across the face with the back of his hand.

She screamed again, and this time his fist cut it short. The sight of blood on her lips turned Moses into a mad thing. Again and again he struck her until she slumped to the floor. Moses went down with her, his knees straddling hers while his hands ripped the remnants of her dress from her body.

Josh twisted the steam-valve, and with oiled precision the piston rose slowly from its casing, pushing the end of the thirty-ton beam with it. At the end of its stroke it returned equally slowly, with a faint sigh of escaping steam.

There were shouts and cheers from outside, and Theophilus Strike looked surprised as the engine repeated its action.

'It's incredibly silent,' he said. 'I thought it would make a din you could hear for miles.'

'You'll hear enough from it when it's driving the pumping-rods into the shaft,' answered the Hayle engineer. 'But she'll never be a noisy engine. You can thank your own engineer for that. He supervised the building of it well, Mr Strike.'

Theophilus Strike gave Josh a hard look. 'I'm pleased to hear it. Do you feel confident that you can keep it running as well?'

'If I can't, you've wasted a lot of money and I've wasted a lot of time, Mr Strike.' He held the mine-owner's gaze for a long moment before adding, 'There will be no trouble with this engine.'

Theophilus Strike nodded, expressionless, and turned back to the Hayle engineer. 'I thank you. You and your men are free to go whenever you wish. I am well pleased.' There was a dull jingle of coins from the bag he dropped into the engineer's hand.

'Now,' he turned to his friends, 'shall we go and leave things in the hands of those whose job it is to keep the mine running?'

He filed out with the others without another look at the Wheal Sharptor's engine.

When the mine-owner had gone the miners and their families crowded into the building to have a closer inspection of the working engine. Josh allowed them in but made sure they stayed away from the moving parts.

Jesse Retallick looked from the engine to her son with undisguised pride. 'It's a wonderful thing,' she said loudly. 'And to think that Josh built it. It's a proud day, Ben.'

Ben Retallick smiled understandingly and rested a hand on Jesse's shoulder. 'It is. When the engine starts pumping it's going to make life much more comfortable for the men working down below. We're getting down too deep for the horse-pumps to keep up with us. You'll be everyone's favourite then, Josh.'

'We'll have that part completed and working by the end of next week,' said Josh. 'Two of Harvey's men who specialise in pumps are coming on Monday when they've finished a repair job at Kit Hill.'

More and more miners and their families crowded into the boiler-room and engine-room. Before long the heat had become oppressive. Jesse Retallick announced her intention of going home. She had seen the engine, heard the admiring remarks about Josh's skill; now it was time to go.

'I'll come with you,' said Ben. 'I see enough of this place all week. Will you be coming soon, Josh?'

'Not for a while. As soon as everyone has left I'll douse the fire and empty the boiler. We won't be firing it again until the rods are in place.'

When his mother and father had left Josh was kept busy answering the questions put to him by the miners. Some of the questions were put from politeness but others went beyond mere curiosity. The miners realised the considerable effect the engine would have upon their lives and the future of the mine. Those miners who had worked in other mines where there had been an engine were surprisingly knowledgeable about them. Josh enjoyed pointing out all the refinements of the Sharptor engine which he knew the earlier engines had not possessed.

Tom Shovell had remained in the engine-house chatting with the miners and their families and was close to the engine when one of the Henwood boys came panting up to the door.

'Captain Shovell! Captain Shovell!' The urgency in the boy's voice killed the laughter at a joke someone had just told.

'Yes, what is it?' Captain Shovell pushed his way to the door.

'Ben Retallick says will you get down to his place. Quick as you can.'

'Why, what's happened?'

'I don't know, but he looked terrible fierce. I could hear someone crying inside the house.'

Tom Shovell set off at a run as Josh grabbed a shovel and began pulling out the coals from beneath the boiler. 'I'll be down as soon as I've cleared this,' he called.

The water from the boiler was tantalisingly slow in draining through the pipes, but as soon as he felt it was safe to leave Josh ran along the path to the cottage.

There were half a dozen or so men inside, amongst them Wrightwick Roberts and Tom Shovell. The remainder were some of the mature miners who frequently shared an evening with the Retallick family.

But this was no social gathering. When Josh entered the room they stopped talking. In the silence he heard a sound like the moaning of the wind on an autumn night. It came from the bedroom.

'Who's upstairs? What's happened?' Nobody answered him, and Josh started for the stairs. His father's arm barred his way.

'No, Josh.'

'But why? Will someone tell me what's going on? Is it Mum?'

'No, it's not your mother,' said Ben Retallick. 'It's Jenny.' His eyes were on Tom Shovell as he spoke. 'Moses Trago was here while we were all up at the Wheal Sharptor.'

The mine captain's hands closed into fists that trembled with the ferocity of his grip and he fought for control of his face.

'Evil!' he muttered. 'Evil follows Moses Trago like an evening shadow.'

'We've got to find him,' said another man. 'The Lord only knows what he might do if we don't get him quickly.'

'Is Jenny hurt bad?' Josh's throat felt dry and pinched.

'That's something only your mother and Jenny will know,' answered his father. 'It looks bad. We found her lying unconscious on the floor with most of her clothes ripped from her. She'd taken as bad a beating as I've seen for a long time.'

Tom Shovell's fists twitched again.

'We're wasting time,' said a gruff voice. 'Let's get out and find him.'

'Yes.' It was a reluctant Ben Retallick who moved away from the stairs. 'It's something that must be done.'

'There can be no other way,' said Wrightwick Roberts softly.

'I'll come with you,' Josh cried. There was a disaster looming here; he could feel it.

'No. You'll stay home.'

'Your father's right.' It was the miner with the gruff voice again. 'The fewer who know of this day's work the better. For everyone.'

'You'll need all the help you can get to bring Moses back,' insisted Josh.

'There will be no bringing him back . . .,' began one of the men, but Ben Retallick silenced him with a look.

'I want you to stay here, Josh. Moses Trago is no longer normal. He might come back. If we're not back before dark, you're to lock the doors and not open up unless you're quite sure it's one of us. You'd best get the axe from the shed. Don't hesitate to use it if you have to. Do you understand?'

'But. . . .' Josh felt as though he were teetering on the edge of a yawning crevasse with the earth crumbling beneath his feet, not sure whether to jump or go back.

'There are no "buts". This is a thing I ought to have done something about long ago and you're needed here.'

He swung away and left the house, the other men following. Tom Shovell walked like a man in a bad dream, hoping that he might wake up with the next step.

'Ben!' It was Jesse Retallick calling from the bedroom.

'He's gone out with the others.'

'To find Moses? Oh my God! Hasn't there been tragedy enough for one day? Josh, go and find them and stop them.'

'Dad said I was to stop here.' Josh looked at his mother. 'And he's right.'

'Right? There will be no right done this day. What do you think is going to happen when they find Moses? Do you believe he is going to say, "I'm sorry. I'll come back and let the judge put me in prison for the rest of my days"? Do you think your father and those other men will even try to speak to him? And I hope you looked at Wrightwick Roberts' face. If a godly man is capable of such an expression as I saw there, who's going to stand up for what's right?'

She stood in front of him, looking up into his face, pleading. 'Josh, don't think I am worried for Moses Trago's safety. He's forfeited all claim to human sympathy by his actions today. But if your father and the others do what they have in mind they'll spill his evil on to all of us. It should be locked away, Josh. Please go and stop them. I beg you!'

His mother's passionate outburst conjured up a series of confused and disjointed pictures in his mind. But his father's words had left no room for argument. 'I want you to stay here,' he had said. If he left the house now, and Moses did return, Josh could only blame himself. He could not go and he said so once more.

Jesse Retallick started to say something but she stopped abruptly, her hands falling helplessly to her sides. She knew her two men well enough to realise when they could be persuaded and when they could not. Then all other thoughts were forgotten as a drawn-out moan came from the bedroom accompanied by a loud thud. Jesse Retallick ran up the stairs followed by Josh.

Jenny Pearn lay on the floor by the open door. Josh bent down beside his mother and drew back in revulsion. Her face was puffed and bruised to such an extent as to be unrecognisable. Josh was appalled. He had forgotten what Moses Trago's handiwork could look like.

'Here. Help me lift her back into bed.' Jesse Retallick had an arm about Jenny's shoulders.

'Leave her. I'll do it.' Bending down, Josh lifted the beaten girl and carried her to the bed. As he laid her down she struggled to sit up.

'No! No, Moses! Please don't. You're hurting me!' Her voice rose to a scream, and Jesse held her down to prevent her from falling from the bed again, talking soothingly to her all the while. 'Hush! It's all right, Jenny. It's all right, my love. It's me, Jesse. You're all right. Hush now!'

Jenny stopped struggling, and the cries became sobs as she clung to the other woman. 'I couldn't stop him. He was too strong, Jesse. He did it to me. I couldn't stop him. Oh, Jesse what am I going to do? What will happen to me now?'

'Shh! Everything will be all right.' As she was talking, Jesse dismissed Josh with a movement of her head. 'We'll have you better in no time. All of this will be behind you like a bad dream.'

Even downstairs Josh could hear Jenny's crying and he went outside for the axe. Out here the thick walls and the distance muffled the sounds.

He looked up the hillside, expecting to see some of the men, but there was nothing. Nothing except for the slow-moving train of pack mules moving southwards along the slope, coming down from a new mining venture high on the moor itself.

Beyond the rocky heights of Sharptor there was a build-up of dark-grey cloud and the distant shimmer of a lightning-flash. Josh collected the axe and returned to the cottage.

By dusk there was no sign of Ben Retallick or the other men and the storm had moved closer. There was little conversation in the Retallick cottage. As the thunder rumbled outside, Jesse busied herself in the kitchen. Josh paced from window to door to hearth and back again. Growing more restless with every minute that passed.

It had been dark an hour before there was the scraping of boots on stone outside and the soft voices of men talking in whispers. Josh hurriedly unlocked the door, and Jesse came from the kitchen, drying her hands upon her apron.

The men entered the cottage grim-faced and silent, except for the miner with the hoarse voice. 'There'll be no need to lock the door against Moses Trago again,' he said triumphantly.

'He's dead?' Jesse Retallick's question was an accusation.

'Yes, he's dead,' replied Tom Shovell. 'His body is lying at the bottom of the old diggings up on Cheesewring Hill.'

'So you found him,' said Jesse Retallick, flatly. 'You found him and you were judge and jury – and God himself.'

'It wasn't like that.' Ben Retallick looked an old man. 'He fell. It was an accident.'

'An accident? Ben Retallick, I've known you for a lifetime and I don't believe you. Do you expect a jury of strangers will think differently?'

'It was an accident, Jesse.' Wrightwick Roberts' big fingers tangled and untangled themselves jerkily. 'We had him cornered at the top of the old shaft and called on him to give himself up to us. He was throwing rocks to keep us back. As he stooped to pick up one from the edge of the shaft he slipped and fell down it.'

'Are you telling me you actually saw this with your own eyes, Wrightwick Roberts? Or did one of you who was closer to Moses say that's what happened and you all agreed it must be so?'

There was an uncomfortable silence during which Jesse Retallick looked at each of the men in turn, hoping that one of them would meet her gaze.

'Tom, you'd better go upstairs to that poor girl. If she's awake she'll have need of your kindness. Say nothing of what's happened to Moses. I only hope there were no witnesses to this night's work.'

Again the men looked uncomfortable, and Jesse gasped, 'For God's sake! Someone did see you! Who was it?'

'There was no other to see what happened.' This from Wrightwick Roberts. 'Although the Trago girl was following us shortly before. But it really was an accident, Jesse.'

Josh never waited to hear the last part of the sentence. He could imagine Miriam following the men who were hunting her father, hoping to find him first and warn him. Then to witness his death – however it occurred. He had no doubt that she had seen it. He reached for his coat and bolted through the door before anyone was able to say anything to him.

The storm was almost overhead now. Between the rumbling thunder the lightning picked out the bushes and rocks of the moor, enlarging them and giving them long trembling shadows.

As he stumbled through the undergrowth, Josh reproached himself bitterly. If he had not been so completely wrapped up in the Sharptor engine he might have heard something from Miriam of her father's state of mind. There might even have been a way of averting today's series of tragedies.

He heard a movement in the undergrowth ahead of him and stopped, suddenly fearful of what else might be abroad on this wild night. It was one of the shaggy moorland cattle, stunted like a tree on the high moor and equally as wild.

The cottage had been sheltered by the bulk of the tor from the north-easterly wind. Up here it was much more exposed. The uneven gusts of wind ripped through the green undergrowth like a prophet spreading the gospel of the storm to come.

Finally Josh reached his destination. On hands and knees he crawled through the gorse-tunnel into the rock hideout. It was silent inside and he thought he had guessed wrong. Perhaps Miriam no longer used her old hideaway. Then a sustained web of lightning broke up the sky and he saw her. She was crouching in the corner where he had once found her with a face as badly battered as the one he had seen today.

'Miriam! I thought you would be here.' He dropped down beside her. 'I'm sorry. I really am.'

He had hoped – expected – that she would fall into his arms and cling to him, that he would comfort her and wipe away her tears; but she was showing no emotion. Her body was stiff and rigid. Only her lips moved.

'They killed him. They cornered him like a dog in a sheep-pen. Then they killed him.'

'Try not to think about it, Miriam.' His hands went out to her shoulders. 'They didn't mean to do it. He slipped.'

'No!' She spat the word out. 'They killed him. I saw it.'

'They wanted to take him back. He had to be caught after what he did to Jenny today. Nobody wanted it to end that way.'

'Yes, they did. That was exactly how they wanted it to end.'

His arms were about her now. He tried to draw her to him, but she did not unbend.

'Miriam, don't hold the pain in like this. Cry, scream, shout, do anything, but don't just shut yourself off from me.'

She remained stiff for another minute, and in the light from another flickering lightning-flash he saw her face turn to him, her eyes dark hidden shadows. Then suddenly, without any warning at all, she brought her mouth up to his. Her arms went about him, fierce and demanding.

It took him by surprise, but he responded immediately and eagerly. He had known that she would listen to him. Her mouth moved wildly beneath his before her teeth sank into his lower lip. He tasted blood. She slipped sideways to lie on the grass of the hideout, and he went down with her. Side by side their bodies strained to each other. Her hands slipped inside his jacket and began plucking his shirt loose from his trousers. Then her hands were clutching, clawing at the skin of his back.

His hand pushed clumsily inside her dress and closed about the firmness of one of her breasts. She moaned. The sound grew louder as, button by undone button, his hand worked down her dress. Her body writhed. Throbbed warm beneath him.

Then he was fumbling at his trousers, inexpertly and hurriedly. When he rolled on to her she strained to receive him. Thunder and lightning was all about them, their bodies the hub of the storm, everything radiating outwards from them. The storm grew fiercer and more violent, reaching its climax in a vibrating roll of thunder that left the earth trembling. Josh shuddered with it, gasping for breath.

When it died away he lay still for a long time, moving only when he felt the rain pounding against his near-naked body.

He stood up slowly, reluctant to leave her. Self-consciously he pulled his clothes together.

Miriam lay where he had left her, not moving, her white skin glistening with rain in the light of the now passing lightning.

Josh was uneasy. Something was not right.

'Here. Take my jacket. You're getting soaked.' It was a stupid meaningless thing to say. But he took off his jacket and laid it over her. She ignored it and rose to her knees. The jacket slid to the ground. Then slowly she got to her feet.

'Miriam, are you all right?'

He reached out a hand to her, but she flinched back as though he had tried to strike her.

'Don't touch me!'

'What's the matter? Did I hurt you? I'm sorry, but you wanted it to happen as much as I did, didn't you?'

She moved back from him. 'Did I, Josh? Are you quite sure? When I tell Morwen and Uncle John what happened up here will they believe you – or me? You can't deny it happened. There's blood to prove it because I've never been with another man, Josh. What do you think they will do when I tell them you forced me? Held me down and took me. Will they get the Wheal Phoenix men out to hunt you? Carrying sticks and shouting like huntsmen when they see you? Perhaps they'll drive you backwards and surround you at the top of some mine shaft. They'll give you a choice, Josh. Face their stones and flailing sticks – or back to the hole in the ground. The hole with crumbling edges. Tell them they've made a mistake, Josh. Tell them we both wanted to do it. Do you think they'll believe you? Do you think they'll even listen?'

'Miriam, you don't know what you're saying. We're going to be married—'

'No!'

The thunder rumbled away in the background. Miriam's hair lay long and wet down her face and over her shoulders as she shrugged herself back into her limp dress. 'How can I marry you? Your father killed mine.'

Josh attempted to deny it, but her voice was a scream that cut him short.

'He did! He did! He murdered him. I can't marry you now.' Her voice broke. 'It's over between us, Josh. Finished. I told you once that you would be the first man to have me, and I've kept my promise.' She tried to swallow the sob that rose into her throat, but it escaped.

Josh took hold of her, but she broke free, slipping beneath his arms. Before he could stop her she had gone, into the gorse-tunnel.

'Miriam, come back!' A flash of lightning ripped the sky, blinding him, and the thunder laughed as he stumbled into the pin-sharp gorse.

Beyond the tunnel, away from the hideaway, he called again. The wind threw the words back in his teeth.

He wandered the moors searching and calling until the storm tired of playing with him and, drawing its cloak of rain about itself, moved on. Later still the moon showed itself, pale and weak, but it was almost dawn before Josh went home to the cottage, thankful for the grey darkness. He sat in his father's rocking-chair in the kitchen and watched the dawn come in through the window. When he heard stirring upstairs he let himself out and made his way to the Sharptor mine and the Harvey engine.

Chapter Fourteen

Moses Trago was buried at St Cleer with only his family and a couple of inquisitive miners present. The Reverend William Thackeray took the service and he spoke of the 'tragic accident' that had taken Moses from them. Morwen scowled angrily and was about to dispute the preacher's statement when his mother put a restraining hand on his arm. She did not relax it until the uncomfortable eulogy came to an end and the first spadeful of earth rained down upon the rough-planed coffin lid.

Miriam, looking ill and strained, continued to stand gazing unseeingly into the narrow trench until William Thackeray put a comforting arm about her shoulders and led her from the graveside.

'We'll all go back to my cottage for some refreshment,' he said to Kate Trago. 'There's something I wish to say. It may not be altogether proper at this sad time, but there is little sense in delaying it.'

Miriam's shoulders heaved beneath William Thackery's arm as she noisily fought back a sob, and Kate Trago moved forward to comfort her with soft words. John Trago followed in her wake, but the scowling Morwen turned and walked away with neither a word nor a backward glance.

Josh knew about the funeral and that Miriam would be

there; but, though he desperately wanted to speak to her, he knew better than to attempt it.

He was still bewildered and unable to think straight about Miriam and himself. For a couple of days after the night of the storm his unhappiness had been mingled with fear. But there had been no knock at the door, no crowd of angry miners eager to avenge the seduction of a young girl. Now only the uncertainty remained.

He tried to intercept Miriam on her way home from her work at the Wheal Phoenix, but she never came. When he enquired he found she had not been to work since the death of her father.

He made various attempts to see her again after the funeral but never caught so much as a glimpse of her. Then he changed his tactics and waited near the Tragos' rock home. Here he came into violent contact with another member of the Trago family.

Josh was watching the path from the cover of an ivy-clad rock when he heard the faintest of sounds from the undergrowth to one side of him. He turned to see Morwen Trago coming at him.

Declining to give ground, Josh waited as Morwen crashed through the last few yards of fern to face him.

'What are you spying on us for, Josh Retallick? Haven't you and your lot done enough? What are you after now?'

'I came up here to see Miriam,' said Josh.

'Did you, now?' Morwen Trago mocked. 'Then you'll have a very long wait because Miriam isn't here. I don't suppose you'll ever see her here again.'

'What do you mean? Where is she? I must see her.'

'Must? Who do you think you are? Just because you've been away to learn about engines and come home wearing fancy clothes and riding a horse with a saddle, you needn't think that everyone is going to jump to do your bidding. The Trago family has suffered enough at the hands of the Retallicks and their friends. Go away and leave Miriam alone. She's showing some sense at last. She doesn't want to see you again.'

He turned to go, but Josh caught his sleeve. 'You're lying, Morwen. She'd never say that. Where is she?'

The expression on Morwen's face was as venomous as his father's had ever been and he knocked Josh's hand from his sleeve. 'No Retallick calls me a liar. I've told you to leave Miriam alone. This should help you remember it.'

Josh was expecting a blow from Morwen's fist, but it was his booted foot that lashed out first. Josh managed to twist his body enough to prevent the steel-rimmed heel from sinking into his groin, but it raked painfully across the front of his thigh.

Josh grabbed at the boot and twisted, bringing Morwen to the ground. As he tried to rise Josh hit him in the face before closing in and grappling with him. Wrestling and gouging, they rolled crashing down the slope to land with a breath-shaking thud on the hard-packed earth of the path.

Morwen was a stone heavier than Josh, but there was little to choose between them when it came to actual strength. Few blows were struck on either side. Instead, it was a mauling, wrestling fight. Neither of the participants had been more than bruised when the hands of a man stronger than either of them reached down and prised them apart with a stranglehold on their collars.

'Hasn't there been enough fighting between our two families? Is it going to be carried on by the sons now?'

It was John Trago, the brother of Moses.

Morwen began to struggle as John lifted them both to their feet, but John shook his nephew until his teeth rattled.

'Stop it, I say!'

Morwen ceased his struggles, and John Trago released them both.

'Now, what's this all about?' The big man's voice was surprisingly soft. Perhaps it was because Josh had never really listened to him before today. John Trago had always walked in the shadow of his elder brother. Moses had made the decisions and said all that was necessary. John had usually stood silently by, with no evident thoughts or opinions of his own.

'I caught him snooping around, spying on us,' said a surly Morwen.

'I was trying to see Miriam.'

'You won't find her here anymore,' said John Trago.

'I told him that,' put in Morwen.

'Then where is she? I must see her.'

'She's at St Cleer, staying at Preacher Thackeray's house.'

'Thank you. That's all I wanted to know.'

'Josh!'

He had turned to go when the call stopped him.

'You must leave her be, now.'

'Why? We have something that needs talking about.'

'She's getting married this coming week.'

Shock and disbelief hit Josh with a near-physical blow, and he reeled under the impact.

'Married? It isn't possible! Who . . . ?'

'The preacher. She's marrying Preacher Thackeray.'

Josh's mouth hung open like an idiot's. William Thackeray had been his friend and tutor. He had taught Josh not only how to read and write, but even how to think.

It had been his guide-lines that Josh had followed through recent years. Furthermore, the preacher had known of Josh's love for Miriam. He could not be marrying her. It would be a complete and utter betrayal. He hardly heard the rest of John Trago's words.

'Don't try to see her there, Josh. It would only distress her. This is a good marriage for Miriam, a chance to get away from the past and lead a normal happy life. If you think anything at all of her, don't take that chance away.'

Josh stumbled away along the path, followed by Morwen's derision. His mind was in a turmoil. He did not choose his direction and walked unknowingly, aimlessly. When he did become aware of things around him he looked up to see the rock hideout just ahead. He crawled gratefully into its shelter.

He needed to think, to find some way out of this incredible nightmare. Engineering problems he had been taught to deal with. Human ones were something new.

He sat looking at the spot where he had lain with Miriam on that stormy night less than a week before. He had believed that the act of making love would bind them closer together. Even her outburst afterwards could be explained away. She was so terribly grieved and upset by the events of the day; but he had always believed she would come back to him, that he would be allowed to make up for all the bad things that had happened in the past. But to marry William Thackeray – it was unthinkable.

He raised his head and saw something metallic gleaming in a crevice between the rocks. It was a tin box. Lifting it down, he prised off the lid and saw it was full of papers. He pulled them out and looked at them and found that he held in his hands a full record of the relationship between himself and Miriam. Not only were there all the letters he had sent to her while he was at Hayle but also the pages of arithmetic he had taught her, the names of towns and countries he had written for her. Finally, on a scrap of paper he found a faded word that had once brought such pleasure to Miriam. It was her name. 'Miriam.' She had been happy that day, delighted at seeing her name in writing for the first time. 'I'll keep it for ever,' she had said. It seemed that the 'for ever' had come to an end.

For the next few days Josh drove himself hard at the mine, helping to get the pump working. He drove others too, and after two days during which he rounded on any-one at the slightest provocation he was called to the mine captain's office.

Tom Shovell came immediately to the point. 'I've called you in here because you are upsetting the men who are working with you. They haven't complained to me, but I've got eyes and ears to find out things for myself. All right, so you've got problems. I know about them and so does every other man on the mine. I suspect that's the only reason someone has not tried to knock your angry young head off. I've known you a very long time, Josh. My friendship with your father is something I value highly. But I'm not having your personal problems interfering with the efficient running of the Wheal

Sharptor. Nobody here is in any way to blame for them. I
suggest you do something about sorting it out at source. If
it means taking a day off, then do it. It will save me more
hours in the long run.'

Walking away from the office, Josh had to admit that the
mine captain was right. When he returned to the shaft he
apologised to the men working with him. Because he was
liked, his apologies were waved aside. But the men were
relieved to see him behaving normally again.

Josh did not go straight home that evening. When work was
over he set off in the opposite direction – to St Cleer. Tom
Shovell had mentioned the source of the trouble, and Josh
was on his way to see the Reverend William Thackeray.

At the gate to the preacher's small stone cottage, situated
behind the chapel, Josh hesitated. Coming across the moor
he had rehearsed what he would say to the preacher. He
would tell him that for Miriam to marry anyone but himself
would be a dreadful mistake. They, Miriam and Josh, loved
each other and always had. They had promised themselves to
each other. He had thought of saying that they had already
given themselves to each other but decided to keep that as a
last desperate bid to prevent the marriage.

Then, as he squared his shoulders for the coming confrontation, a sudden thought made a coward of him. What if
Miriam opened the door? He had no speech rehearsed for
that eventuality. The wrong words could ruin the future for
both of them.

While he hesitated, the problem was solved for him. William
Thackeray came out of the cottage. Closing the door behind
him, he walked down the path towards his former pupil.

'Josh! How wonderful to see you. How are you?'

Josh ignored the preacher's outstretched hand. William
Thackeray dropped it to his side without changing his
expression. 'I knew you were home and was hoping you
would find time to come and see me. I have also heard how
busy you are working.'

'Is there some place where we can talk?'

The preacher indicated the books beneath his arm. 'I am on

my way into the chapel to do some teaching. It's something I
do every evening at this time. Surely you hadn't forgotten?'

'No. That is – I hadn't thought about it.' In fact he had
forgotten, but it was not this which disconcerted him. It was
the aura of complete confidence which always surrounded
William Thackeray. For Josh this was a violently emotional
problem. He could not understand how the preacher was able
to maintain such a calm composure.

'I want to speak to you about Miriam,' he blurted out,
feeling awkward and adolescent, a pupil with the master.

'Yes, I know.' Preacher Thackeray stopped and looked at
Josh. 'But talking will not change anything. Miriam and I are
to be married.'

Josh drew in a great gulp of air. It was out in the open
now. William Thackeray had set the fact out in front of him
as though it were a mathematical problem to which he already
knew the answer but wanted to see what sort of a hash Josh
would make of it.

'She was going to marry me,' he said, totally inadequately.

'Yes, I know. That is why I am glad you have come to see
me, Josh. We have been friends for a very long time. I would
have been unhappy in the knowledge that someone we both
care so much for had come between us. I know Miriam feels
the same way.'

'She said so?'

'Not in so many words, but the feeling is there nevertheless.'

'Where is she now?'

'I'm sorry, Josh. That is something I am not willing to
tell you.'

'I want to see her. I want her to tell me herself that everything is over between us. I'll believe it then.'

'No. It would serve no useful purpose, and she has suffered
quite enough recently. Don't you agree?'

'I only want to hear her say the words. I'll accept it then.'

'You will have to accept it from me, Josh. Miriam is going
to be my wife.'

Josh towered over the preacher, but William Thackeray was

well experienced in facing angry men. They held no terror for him.

'I don't believe this has just happened,' Josh said angrily. 'You've been working towards this all the time I've been away. Miriam was desperate to learn things and to get an education. You've taken advantage of it.'

'You just told me yourself that she was going to marry you. Circumstances have changed only in the last couple of weeks, Josh. I can hardly be blamed for the reasons behind that change.'

The preacher's quiet reasonable tone only served to make Josh angrier. 'She can't marry you! She can't! Ask her about—' Josh was going to tell him about the events of the night of the storm, but the words stuck in his throat.

'She has told me all I want to hear and we will be married on Sunday. I think—'

'I don't give a damn what you think!' Josh blurted angrily.

'We really won't achieve anything pursuing this conversation.' William Thackeray turned in towards the chapel. 'I would like you to come into the chapel with me, Josh.'

Josh stopped and the preacher looked back at him sorrowfully.

'I'm sorry, Josh. I'll pray for your peace of mind.'

Josh turned away, angry and ashamed at the tears that stung his eyes. William Thackeray had won. Josh was not proud of himself for having even contemplated mentioning that night in the hideout with Miriam, but he would not allow this man who had once been his friend to witness his humiliation.

But someone else witnessed his defeat. Miriam saw it in his step and the abject droop to his shoulders as he walked away from the chapel. Her eyes burned for him.

From her room upstairs in the preacher's home she had watched him approach the house, until suddenly her knees had become so weak she had to cling to the brass upright of the bed for support.

At the same time she heard William rushing to gather books from the study and leave the house, heading off Josh before he reached the door.

While the two men were talking at the gate she felt physically sick, not wanting to look at them standing together, yet unable to turn away.

Then, as they moved off, she almost screamed at them to come back, to remain where she could see them.

Now, as Josh walked away hunched in his unhappiness, it was his misery she shared, not William Thackeray's victory.

When he passed from her view she laid her forehead against the cold metal of the bed. Closing her eyes she wept as she never had before. Now there could be no turning back. Her tears were for Josh's today and both their tomorrows.

There were two weddings that month. In the chapel at St Cleer, William Thackeray was married to Miriam Trago; while, in the little whitewashed chapel at Henwood, Jenny Pearn became Mrs Shovell.

Josh went to neither wedding. He made the weak excuse to Jenny that there were last-minute adjustments to be made to the pumps in the Wheal Sharptor. He could not have sat through the service without torturing himself with thoughts of the other wedding taking place only a few miles away.

Although his absence was for emotional reasons, there *was* something he was working on in the mine – and it was being done without the knowledge of Theophilus Strike.

The pump was worked by a series of huge wooden rods, alternately pushed down and drawn up by the movement of a rocking-beam. They extended from the grass to the bottom of the shaft and rose and fell extremely slowly, at a rate of scarcely more than five strokes a minute.

Inspired by the plans given to him by Francis Trevithick, Josh was using this slow speed to provide a simple means of raising men to the surface.

The idea was starkly simple: The length of the engine's stroke was some twelve feet, and Josh had bolted blocks of wood to the rods at a distance of twelve feet apart. At the same intervals up the shaft he had built tiny platforms into the wooden framework. It would be a simple matter for a man to step on to a block and ride up for twelve feet. Then he would step off and wait for the next stroke of the pump to ride up the next twelve feet in the same manner.

The experiment had Tom Shovell's blessing, even though he lacked Josh's conviction that the mine-owner would appreciate the advantages to be gained from the experiment.

As it happened, he did not have to wait long to discover the mine-owner's reaction. Theophilus Strike arrived to see the inauguration of the pumping operation, this time without his retinue of friends.

The engine-men who would be operating the engine on a shift basis were all experienced. Josh had satisfied himself that they knew what they were doing before he allowed them to operate his engine.

The fire had been stoked up from early morning and the hissing of steam from the escape-valve was a new sound in the Sharptor air. When Strike, Tom Shovell and the shift captains were assembled, Josh signalled for the engine-man to set the pumping-engine in motion. With a gentle hiss of steam and protesting creaks from the wooden rods, each one a foot in diameter, the horse-operated water-pump became a piece of history and steam took over. Without ceremony and with no fuss it had all the ingredients of an anti-climax.

'So now we have become a modern mine,' said Theophilus Strike to Tom Shovell. 'How is it looking down below?'

'Why not go down and see for yourself, Mr Strike?'

Theophilus Strike looked at Josh, who had made the suggestion, not quite certain whether it smacked of insolence.

'I've built a new idea into the pumping system,' Josh went on. 'It means that the men will be able to come up from the levels without using the ladders.'

'What the devil do you mean?' Strike blazed. 'Your job was to put in the engine and pumping system and see that they keep working. Not install some fool idea of your own.'

'It's not exactly my own idea,' said Josh, realising that Theophilus Strike was capable of dismissing him on the spot. 'It was Richard Trevithick's idea. His son gave me the drawings.'

'Francis Trevithick?' There was an immediate change of

attitude. The Cornish engineering family was highly respected in the county. 'When did he come to Sharptor?'

'He didn't. I met him at Hayle and we discussed means of lifting men to surface. He told me that when I installed the engine into Sharptor I was to be sure to build a man-lift into it. He even sent me a completely detailed set of plans his father had drawn up.'

The mine-owner's look searched Josh's face. 'And how much did this idea cost?'

'It cost virtually nothing,' Tom Shovell broke into the conversation. 'We made use of materials that were already to hand.'

'So you knew about it too? Your job is to keep me informed about Wheal Sharptor, Shovell, not to do things behind my back. Now, you!' He pointed a finger at Josh. 'How is this new idea supposed to work?'

Josh explained, and Theophilus Strike listened intently. 'And how many mines are using this method to bring their men to the surface?'

'Wheal Sharptor will be the first in Cornwall,' Josh said proudly.

'All right, take me down to the fifty-fathom level and I'll see for myself how it works. Give me a hard hat, someone.'

Hurriedly Tom Shovell sent one man to find a hard hat and another to take candles to place by each platform in the shaft down to the fifty-fathom level.

Josh explained the workings once again at the edge of the shaft where the objects of his labours could be seen. He pointed out the huge iron staples driven into the rods at shoulder level to provide a hand-grip.

The primitive man-lift was totally lacking in safety measures, but it was less dangerous than a narrow wet ladder to a tired man.

There was a certain reluctance to be the first man to use the man-lift and so Josh led the way, stepping on to the block as it came up to its maximum height. It was easier than even he had thought it would be. The platform were sufficiently large and the low speed of the engine eliminated much of the danger.

Theophilus Strike followed him, and his appearance in the fifty-fathom working tunnel startled the miners. It was the first time the mine-owner had visited a working area that was not directly accessible via a horizontal adit.

When his tour of inspection was over Theophilus Strike returned above ground. The minute he stepped on to grass once again it was obvious to everyone he had enjoyed the novel experience.

'I approve of your work, Josh. You have done well. Thanks, I have no doubt, to Trevithick's plans. It pleases me that the Wheal Sharptor is able to show the way to other mines. I only hope your lift is not going to make my miners soft.'

'At the end of a shift a man is already tired,' said Josh quietly but intensely. 'Anyone who has ever seen a man lying gasping for breath after climbing the ladders would never think it soft to find another way to get them up. Why, when they had an expert look at the new treadmill in Bodmin Jail he said that no prisoner should have to tread more than twelve hundred rungs in one day's work, yet a miner working at three hundred fathoms climbs eighteen hundred – *after* he's finished his day's work. Doing away with that can do nothing but great good.'

'Joshua Retallick, I like your initiative, and I'm satisfied with your skill as an engineer, but you will keep your radical thinking to yourself. I will agree to allow the men to use this "man lift" as you call it, but I do not need to be lectured on the lot of the miner. On the Wheal Sharptor a man is paid a fair wage for a fair day's work. No one is forcing him to stay. I've heard all about these people who mutter about a "union of miners" and try to tell mine-owners what their men can and can not do. I'll have none of that talk here. Anyone who thinks differently would be well advised to leave now. Do I make myself quite clear?'

'I think Josh was only trying to explain that we'll be able to use our more experienced men at the deeper levels now we have the man-lift,' put in Tom Shovell. 'We haven't been able to use them before because the climb back up was too much.'

'I'm fully aware of what he was saying,' replied the mine-owner. 'I hope he is equally certain of my meaning. There is quite enough discontent in this area. I'll have none of it at the Wheal Sharptor. Now we'll go to the office. I have some business to discuss with you.'

'You'll have to watch that tongue of yours,' said Ben Retallick when the mine-owner and his captain had gone beyond hearing. 'Wag it if you must, but not when Theophilus Strike is about.'

'What did I say?' protested Josh. 'I only spoke the truth. I've seen you on the ground by the shaft gasping for air like a drowning man. And a hundred others beside.'

'Strike doesn't want to know about that,' Ben Retallick said. 'While you've been away your friend the preacher at St Cleer has been out and about complaining of the miners' conditions. Wherever he goes there is trouble. Strike knows you were schooled by him and it bothers him. Learn to choose your words when he's near. He may be a bit touchy but he's a good man to work for.'

'He needn't worry about my association with Preacher Thackeray,' said Josh bitterly. 'He's no friend of mine.'

Josh may have considered his friendship with William Thackeray to be at an end, but every evening a prayer for him went up from the preacher's house.

Kneeling by the bed she shared with her husband, Miriam first prayed to be given the strength to make William Thackeray a good wife although she did not love him, accepting that she needed to work hard at it because of her hunger for Josh. It was a Trago curse passed on from her father. As he had craved after Jenny, so she wanted Josh. But Josh must never know of her feelings, and because of this she also prayed for forgiveness for the hurt she had inflicted on him.

This private evening ritual was a penance she accepted. It continued even when kneeling was a feat of will-power made daily more difficult by the new life swelling inside her – the child of the moor with no birthright in this house.

Chapter Fifteen

As close as the weddings of Miriam and Jenny had been, the births of their respective babies in the middle of 1842 were closer. Both children chose to enter the world in the dark of the same night – hoping, some said, that the absence of light might hide their secrets.

Miriam's son was born after twelve hours of painful labour. She writhed on the bed in the cottage behind the chapel, arching her back as she gripped the head-posts, fighting to bite back the screams that each labour-pain drew from her and the name that was on her tongue.

Not until the pain had almost sapped the last of her strength and caused the women attending her to send out an urgent call for a doctor did the baby finally make his way into the world, adding his cries to the gasps of his mother.

Jenny had an easier time, if such events are measured only in terms of physical pain. It began not long before midnight. By the time Mary Crabbe arrived to perform the duties of midwife, the birth was well under way.

The old crone took complete charge of the proceedings. Hustling the women neighbours from the room, she opened the door only in order to receive the boiling water that was passed through in bucket and kettle. By two o'clock in the morning it was all over. But there were no baby sounds heard in Tom Shovell's house, no admiring women to cluster about the bed. The baby, also a boy, was still-born. Its death brought about by an umbilical cord wrapped about its neck.

There was sympathy for Jenny, but little sorrow at the loss of the innocent child. Those who saw it said it had the scowl of Moses Trago on its screwed-up face. Others described the expression as more evil than a scowl. But a strangled child is never a pretty sight.

All the women agreed about one thing. The baby's death had been no more natural than Moses Trago's. It was no secret that Mary Crabbe had hated Moses. But the women kept their thoughts about the death of the child to low whispers, passed on only behind closed doors. Mary Crabbe could cure a coughing cow with the breath from her own mouth. She could touch a wart with her fingertips and it would shrivel and fall off. There were few who had not drunk one of her potions when they were sick. But after Nehemeziah's old dog had got among her chickens, killing half of them, it had begun to waste away for no apparent reason. Within a month it was dead. So there was not a woman who would willingly risk her displeasure.

Less discreet was the talk about Miriam's child. That it was conceived out of wedlock was unanimously agreed. The only point at issue was whether or not the Reverend William Thackeray was the child's father. Most of the gossips had it that he was, but there were others who gave knowing looks in Josh's direction. For his part he gave no sign that he knew of their opinions. Or cared, if he did.

The engine at the mine was running well, carrying out both its primary and secondary tasks. Although many of the older miners had scoffed at the idea at first, more and more of them were now using Josh's man-lift to ride to grass. The womenfolk of those who worked in the lowest levels no longer had to delay a meal until their men regained enough energy to eat. They blessed Josh for his innovation.

As word of Josh's man-lift spread around the area it became commonplace to see off-duty miners from the Wheal Phoenix and Caradon mines crowding around the top of the main

Sharptor shaft, watching the lights from the candles on the hats of the ascending miners come slowly to the surface. They would gasp in disbelief when, in answer to their questioning, a comparatively fresh man would state he had come up from the two-hundred-fathom level.

It was not long before Captain Frisby from the Wheal Caradon sent a messenger asking Josh if he would call to see him.

Josh went after work that same day. The Caradon captain came immediately to the point.

'Tell me about this man-lift idea of yours,' he said. 'How much would it cost to put one into the Caradon for me?'

Josh grinned. 'It would cost next to nothing. But since when has the Wheal Caradon been so concerned about its men?'

'You don't want to believe everything you hear, young man,' snapped the captain. 'I can't help it if the Wheal Caradon has more than its share of trouble-makers. We are a big mine, not a little family concern like the Sharptor. We can't be so fussy about who we take on.'

'You get what you pay for,' retorted Josh. It was well known that, for all its great size and high production, the men working for the Wheal Caradon were amongst the worst-paid miners in the country. And it showed in the amount of ore brought out per man.

'You sound like a union man,' said Captain Frisby angrily. 'I get enough of that every day. But I didn't bring you here to quarrel. I'm asking you to do this job for me. Convert the main pump into a man-lift – if it doesn't cost too much. Perhaps that might stop some of the grumbling. I do my best for them and that's what I want to do now.'

Josh looked at the mine captain suspiciously. His words did not fit in with the stories that Josh had heard about him.

'Let's go and have a look at the pump-rods,' said Josh. 'A lot depends on their type and the way they've been fitted.'

On the way Josh questioned the mine captain about the main shaft. Unlike the Wheal Sharptor, the Caradon shaft was not entirely perpendicular. In places the pump-rods worked along an incline, resting on rollers. The men would have to use ladders for these parts of the climb. For the remainder of the way it would present no problems. The pumping-engine could be adapted in the same way as at the Wheal Sharptor.

He said as much to Frisby and the mine captain was well pleased. 'Good! Good! When can you make a start on it?'

'I can't,' said Josh. 'But send a couple of your carpenters and fitters across to the Sharptor tomorrow and I'll show them what to do. Then they can come back here and do it themselves.'

Frisby frowned. 'I suppose that will have to do. Will you inspect it when it's done? I don't want any mistakes caused by shoddy workmanship or by men not knowing exactly what they are about.'

'Yes, I'll do that,' agreed Josh. 'But what's wrong with your own engineer? He'll be able to tell whether it's a good job or not.'

'Caradon hasn't got a proper engineer at the moment,' said Frisby. 'You could have the job if you wanted it. I'll pay you half as much again as you are getting now. There would be no shortage of work. We have plenty of equipment here and more engines than you'll ever see at Sharptor.'

'I don't doubt there would be the work. How many *new* engines do you have?'

This was a blow in a sensitive spot and Josh knew it. The two most recent engines acquired by the Caradon mine had been bought from a tin mine near Truro. There they had already performed many years' service.

'You want me to buy all new equipment as well as pay you a good wage? Young man, if I bought new engines I wouldn't *need* an engineer!'

Josh smiled. 'Sorry, Captain Frisby. I appreciate your offer but Sharptor suits me for now. I wouldn't fancy working on an unhappy mine. Pay half as much again to all your men and you wouldn't have to look for engineers. They'd be banging on your door.'

'Yes, and so would the shareholders. Thank you for nothing. Perhaps it is just as well you won't come to work for me. I have no shortage of men to preach about fair pay for the miner and about their union. Bah! It's just another way of getting more for doing less.'

He was still grumbling about the union when Josh left him.

But Captain Frisby was not the only one to become increasingly aware of union talk. It was something that had been discussed in a half-hearted way wherever miners gathered for years, yet there had been no positive moves to unite the miners until Preacher Thackeray came to St Cleer. It was his dedication to unionism as much as to religion which had made the talk reality. He was an eloquent speaker, yet down to earth enough to get through to the uneducated miner. Neither was poverty any stranger to him. It had been a persistent foe throughout his childhood days in the East End of London. But, always bright, he had been singled out for special education by the City Road Mission, later being sent to work and preach in the black coal valleys and iron hills of Wales. There he had seen the violence that erupted when men sought to better themselves. He came to recognise the power that ordinary men wielded when they united in common purpose. Unity. Union. It was the same thing.

William Thackeray had become a keen convert to their cause, travelling many miles to address meetings. Then he had been abruptly transferred to Cornwall. He had been told that the Cornish system of mining, with each man seemingly his own master, made the Cornish miner less likely to be interested in the ideals he preached. William Thackeray was proving them wrong. At least in east Cornwall. When he spoke of unionism men listened. When they returned for the next meeting they brought friends with them. They came to him with their problems, asked his advice.

During the years he had been taught by him, Josh had assimilated many of Preacher Thackeray's beliefs. He was never reluctant to argue the cause of a miners' union with anyone who had a point of view to put forward.

He had even recently attended one of William Thackeray's open-air meetings. In a crowd of almost a thousand his anonymity was assured, but there were many times during

the preacher's speech when he felt he had been singled out
as the target for a particular phrase or remark. It was this, he
realised, that was the secret of Thackeray's power of oratory.
Every man there left the meeting believing that the preacher
had been speaking personally to him.

The reason that Josh had not attended any more meetings
was because Miriam now occasionally delivered a speech with
her husband. Josh did not feel able to face her, although it had
been more than a year since her marriage.

The time had brought changes for the whole of the Trago
family. Soon after Miriam's wedding John Trago had come
down the hill to the Retallick cottage. He stood in the doorway,
changing his considerable weight from foot to foot, big and
awkward. Although every broad inch of him was a Trago, he
lacked the ambient menace that had always travelled with his
older brother.

'Well, come on in, man,' said Jesse Retallick. 'Though I can't
think of a Trago who's crossed this doorstep without bringing
trouble into the house.'

'I hope all that is past, Jesse,' said the big miner. 'That's
what I've come to speak to you and Ben about.'

'Then take a seat,' said Ben. 'You're so big you're blocking
out the light.'

'I'm sorry.' John Trago obligingly moved across the room
to place his back against a blank wall. 'But I won't sit down.
I'm not stopping.'

He cleared his throat noisily. 'I wanted to tell you that I hold
no grudge against you, Ben, or against any of your family. No
more does Kate. We neither of us believe that the death of
Moses was deliberate.'

It was Ben Retallick's turn to look ill at ease.

'Not that anyone could have blamed you had it been
otherwise. He did a terrible thing to Jenny in your house.
There's nothing can be said on his part for that. The drink had
got him so bad he wasn't living his own life, Ben. How any of
us put up with him I don't know – especially Kate. He would
hit her around cruelly if we weren't there to stop him.'

John Trago cleared his throat nervously once more. 'I'm

going to marry Kate and look after her and the children. I'll try to give them a bit more of life than they've been used to up to now.'

'That's a fine thing, John,' said Jesse. 'And I'm sure that you'll make a job of it.'

'Thank you, Jesse. I'll do my best.' His face was red and he was perspiring. Talking came harder to him than physical labour.

'You have my good wishes too,' said Ben. 'But you haven't come here today because you want us to be the first to congratulate you. What else is on your mind?'

'There is something else, Ben. You see, I think the children should be brought up to feel they are just like everyone else. Not some strange beings who live in a cave on the moor. There's a house to rent in Henwood that I've been promised. That's a start. But I want it to be a real beginning, Ben. I want Kate and the children to make friends and live without people pointing a finger at them, whispering that they're the family of Moses Trago, the man who raped Jenny and ended his days in a mine-shaft, hunted by the men of Wheal Sharptor.'

Ben nodded seriously. 'That makes good sense. How can I help?'

'You're a respected man in the village. If you put it about that you have no argument with us, everyone else will do the same.'

'We'll do that willingly,' Jesse Retallick said firmly. 'And tell Kate I'll help her to move in. It will be Tillie Coryton's old cottage you are talking about?'

John Trago nodded. 'Yes. It'll need a bit of work doing to it, but I'll see to that.'

'You'll need some bits of furniture to put in there too,' said Jesse. 'We've got a few things to spare now that Jenny has gone. You can have them. I'll get Ben and Josh to take them down for you.'

'I'm grateful to you,' said John Trago. 'Kate will be too. She thought . . . well, that you probably wouldn't want anything more to do with us, what with Moses, then Miriam marrying that preacher from St Cleer.'

'We won't talk about that,' said Jesse Retallick firmly, her lips narrowing into a tight line, 'or I might forget all my good intentions. She did something that has hit our Josh hard. It hurts me to see how he looks sometimes.'

'It came as just as much of a shock to us,' said John Trago. 'It didn't make any sense. Miriam had always been keen for Josh and she isn't the sort of girl to change her mind overnight. Kate went over to stay with her the night before the wedding. She woke up in the night and heard Miriam crying fit to bust, but the girl had locked her door and wouldn't let her mother in.'

'What does Morwen think about this new arrangement of yours?' Ben Retallick made an effort to change the subject.

John Trago shook his head. 'I don't think he's too happy about it. He has some idea in his head that it's breaking faith with his father. I am afraid there is a lot of Moses in that boy, Ben. But it doesn't much matter now; Morwen's gone. He left yesterday for Bodmin to take the Queen's shilling. He thinks a soldier's life has more to offer him than being down a mine. I can't say that he's wrong. We parted on good terms. I doubt if we'd have done that had he stayed any longer. He has his father's weakness for drink. But I'll say no more about him. He's left. I wish him well in the service of the Queen.'

He edged his way to the door. 'I'm very obliged to you both for listening, and for your kind offer, Jesse. I know it will make Kate very happy.'

'She'll be happy enough already in knowing she'll have a good man to look after her,' said Jesse. 'Tell her to come down and see me tomorrow. I expect we'll find a few more things to come in handy in that new cottage of yours.'

Chapter Sixteen

By the year 1843 the copper mines were going through a boom such as they had never known. Demand for copper ore far exceeded supply, keeping prices up. Expansion was the order of the day. But the boom was not indicative of the country – or even Cornwall – as a whole.

Corn was once again short. Why, nobody knew. The market was there but there was little corn to be harvested and many farm-workers were on the parish, out of work with families to support. In Cornwall the situation was aggravated by a slump in the market for tin. The tin-miners wandered the county in search of work and food. Many of them found temporary lodgings with relatives and friends who earned a living digging copper. Some of them were given work on the copper mines – not the regular underground work to which they were accustomed, but part-time work on the surface, grading and sorting the ore. Women's work. Children's work. But for those tin-miners prepared to swallow their pride it meant they could afford a meal and a drink. The Wheal Sharptor had a dozen of them digging a new shaft, more to give them employment than because the need was there.

A few mines – and the Caradon was one – saw the plight of the tinners as something from which to gain advantage. In an effort to increase their profits they took them on at low wages and then cut back the pay of their own men. It aroused great anger among the established miners, but they dared do little but talk. For every copper-miner who left there were fifty out-of-work tinners clamouring to take his place, however low the wage. It took a man like Captain Frisby to wring the full advantage from the situation.

The tinners were in the habit of crowding around outside a mine, waiting for someone to be dismissed or for an accident to occur. Twice fights broke out between the Caradon miners and the waiting tinners. It did nothing for an injured man's peace of mind to see men scrambling for his job as he was carried homewards. It made the miners jittery. They felt the tinners were putting an evil influence on them, wishing them ill.

When Captain Frisby first began to take on the tin-miners at a lower wage some of the Caradon men asked Josh to intercede with the mine captain on their behalf. He refused. He realised that it would merely have given Frisby an excuse for widespread sackings. There was nothing for the miners to do but to grit their teeth and sweat it out. It set out a strong case for a union of miners. Had one been in existence such a situation would never have arisen.

When Josh would not help, the men went to Preacher Thackeray. He gave them the same advice. Thackeray had already held fruitless meetings with the tin-miners. They had been well attended. The tinners had little else to do with their time.

They listened to what he had to say, agreed there was a need for all miners to show a solid front if they were to better themselves; then, if an hour later they were offered a job of work at half-pay, they jumped at it without a twinge of conscience. Principles do not sit well in the stomach of a hungry man.

Another result of the slump in tin-mining was that the demand for mine-engines dropped and the Cornish engine works had to search out new customers.

Josh was in the engine-house of the Sharptor mine, reassembling a steam-valve he had stripped down, when a voice from the doorway said, 'I'm pleased to see you haven't forgotten everything you learned at Harvey's, Josh.'

Swinging around, Josh saw William Carlyon standing in the doorway. Then Sarah pushed past her father. Rushing across the engine-room she flung her arms about Josh's neck and kissed him. The engine-man and two of the Sharptor miners looked on with great interest. Rumours would not be slow in going around Henwood tonight.

Josh was unable to ward Sarah off because his hands were black with grease. He had to stand with arms extended to his sides to avoid spoiling her clothes. There was nothing to do but enjoy her embrace.

'A little grease never hurt anyone,' said William Carlyon and he grasped Josh's hand when Sarah finally released him.

'What are you doing here?' Josh spoke to the Harvey manager, but his eyes were on Sarah. She had grown taller since he last saw her. With her long blonde ringlets tied behind her neck she was a strikingly beautiful girl. Her clothes too were of a quality seldom seen in this area.

'We came here especially to see you,' teased Sarah happily. 'You hadn't written to me for so long I became worried about you. So here we are!'

Josh looked at her father for confirmation and William Carlyon smiled. 'It's all right, Josh. That isn't true. I have to go to Bristol on business. We want to make the boilers for a new ship they are planning. I thought it a good opportunity to give the family a holiday. Mary and Mrs Carlyon are with your mother at the cottage.'

As they talked Josh rubbed the grease from his hands with a piece of rag.

'I rode all the way here on Hector,' said Sarah. 'And Mary rode part of the way on the pony you used to ride when you were at Hayle. The rest of the time she rode in the coach with Mother.'

'You rode Hector wearing that dress?'

'No. I changed when we reached your cottage. It's a new dress. Brought specially from London for me by one of the ship's captains. Do you like it?' She struck a pose, holding the full skirt out to her sides.

'It's a beautiful dress,' he said truthfully. 'Far too good to wear in an engine-house.'

'That's what I told her,' said William Carlyon, 'but she would take no notice of me.'

He nodded towards the engine, its exposed metalwork bright beneath a sheen of grease. 'I can see you are keeping it in good order. If every one of our engines was looked after as well there would be little go wrong with them.'

Josh was pleased at his words. They too would be repeated many times by the listening Sharptor men. William Carlyon's name was well known in the mining fraternity, his opinion respected. If he praised Josh there could be no doubt that the Wheal Sharptor had an engineer to be reckoned with.

'I would like to meet your father and Captain Shovell,' said the Harvey manager. 'One of the men outside told me they were together at the explosives store. Where will I find that?'

Josh started to lead the way but William Carlyon stopped him with a gesture. 'No, just point me in the right direction. I'll find it. You see that Sarah gets back to the cottage. It's all right. We spent last evening dining with Theophilus Strike. I told him we should be robbing him of his engineer for as long as we were here. He made no objection.'

Josh sent one of the miners to guide William Carlyon to the explosives store. It stood some distance away from the mine buildings. Then, after giving instructions to his engine-man, he washed his hands and set off down the track with Sarah.

'Are you pleased to see me, Josh?' Sarah looked up at him provocatively.

'If you are fishing for compliments, then the answer is "Yes". I am pleased to see you. You are even more beautiful than I remembered.'

The Josh she had known at Hayle would not have had the nerve to pay her such a compliment and for a moment Sarah was taken aback, not at all sure that she enjoyed such blatant flattery. Then she looked again at Josh and saw the new confidence in him. He was a young man with the knowledge of his own ability as an engineer, and a man to whom others looked for leadership, respecting his learning. Josh would be a leader in whatever he set out to do. Some men develop in that way without being able to help themselves.

Because of this Sarah accepted the compliment and was stirred by the strength in him.

'You have changed, Josh.'

'Is that good? Or bad?' His smile was a challenge.

'I'm not sure. For you it is probably good. For me . . . ?' She shrugged and there was a moment of silence between them. Then she smiled, removing all tension between them. 'Come on, Josh. If I don't get you home soon Mary will come looking for you. She has talked of nothing but coming to see you for days.'

For the remainder of the way they spoke of people they had both known at Hayle, of the foundry staff, apprentices long gone, and newer ones of whom Sarah despaired. 'They are all so young and terribly serious about their work.'

When they arrived at the cottage Mary ran out and flung herself at him. She seemed hardly to have grown at all.

Mrs Carlyon made the right noises about Josh having 'filled out', and she had a speculative look in her eyes when she watched Sarah and Josh together. Jesse too showed more than a passing interest in the lovely young girl from Hayle. It was a relief when Sarah asked Josh if he would like to go for a ride to show her something of the moor. Josh protested that he would have forgotten how to ride, but he allowed himself to be persuaded and soon he was riding Mary's pony along the path to the high moor, while Sarah followed on Hector.

Once above the ridge, they rode knee to knee through the bracken. 'This is heaven!' Sarah took a deep breath and closed her eyes. 'There is no smell quite like that of fern and heather.'

She gave Josh a warm smile. 'This is just like old times. You don't know how much I have missed riding with you. Have you done much riding since you left Hayle, Josh?'

He looked at her sharply. Did she really understand so little about life in a mining community? Or was she joking?

He saw that she was quite serious.

'No. I haven't ridden since the day I brought the boiler and beam up from Looe. I'm a working man now, Sarah. I have little time to ride and no horse to use if I wanted to.'

'You could ask Mr Strike,' Sarah said seriously. 'I am quite sure he would loan you one of his horses. He is a very nice man.'

'He's a mine-owner. What is more, he owns the mine where I work. He pays me a wage for doing a job of work. I don't think he would take kindly to a request from me to borrow one of his horses for my pleasure.'

'I am sure he would,' replied Sarah. 'But it is far too lovely a day to have an argument. I'll race you to that circle of stones over there.'

The circle of stones was a mile away, and Sarah and Hector arrived a hundred yards ahead of Josh.

'Phew! I'd forgotten a lot of things about riding. One of them was that unless you are in practice it leaves you as blown as the horse.' He dismounted, throwing the reins over the horse's head before helping Sarah to the ground.

She rested her hands on his shoulders and jumped down lightly. But when she landed on the springy turf she did not remove her hands immediately.

Josh looked down at her and she came to him, arms meeting about his neck. For a few minutes, as they kissed, her ardour matched his own. Then he slid one hand up to enclose her breast through her dress. She breathed heavily against it for perhaps ten seconds. Then a tremor went through her body and gently but firmly she took his hand away and placed it behind her back.

'Don't do that, Josh.'

He put the arm back around her and she kissed him wildly. Finally, breasts heaving, she rested her head on his chest, still holding him tightly.

'Oh, Josh! I have missed you terribly.'

'I think you really mean it.'

'You know very well I do. I told you so in every one of my letters. Didn't you read them?'

He had received a letter from her every week and had written perhaps five or six in reply.

'Yes, of course. I wish I could write letters as well as you.'

She pushed away from him and smiled. 'Oh well! A girl can't have everything. At least you had not forgotten me.'

She took his hand and began to lead him towards the stones.

'What are they?'

'Just some stones that the "old men" put up. Legend has it they were people who played football on a Sunday and were turned to stone for their sins.'

'Poor people,' said Sarah. She stooped and picked up a raven's feather from the ground, twiddling it, black and glossy, between her fingers.

'Are you really pleased to see me, Josh?'

'Very pleased.'

He was.

'What about that girl you used to write to when you were at Hayle? The one you told me about. Miriam? Do you still see her?'

'No.'

It was too positive. Too sharp an answer. Sarah looked up quickly.

'She married a preacher. Preacher Thackeray. They live in a village not far from here.'

'Preacher Thackeray!' She was happy again. 'Mr Strike was telling Daddy about him last night. He preaches for a union of all the miners, doesn't he?'

'He says that miners and their families should have fair wages and reasonable working conditions,' said Josh.

'Well, it was something like that,' said Sarah. 'Mr Strike said that Preacher Thackeray is a pain in the neck and ought to be moved to one of the cities. Well away from Cornwall.'

'I told you, Theophilus Strike is an employer. He's bound to oppose Thackeray.'

'Don't tell me you agree with this preacher?' Sarah was only half bantering.

Josh stopped and pulled her gently round to face him.

'Sarah, I don't think you understand. Of course I agree with him. I'm bound to agree with him. He's trying to help men like me. I'm a miner. My father is a miner. All my friends are miners!'

'No. You are not like those creatures we saw coming out of a shaft on our way here. They were filthy dirty, horribly coarse men. You are an engineer, Josh, and your father is a captain.'

Josh was about to argue further. Instead he looked at Sarah and shrugged his shoulders. 'It doesn't matter. We agreed not to argue.'

'Silly! There is nothing to argue about. I think it is a splendid thing for you to care about the miners. I am sure they need someone like you to take an interest in them. It is a pity, though, that they do not have a bit more pride in themselves. Try to keep themselves clean and tidy.'

Sarah had absolutely no conception of conditions below ground in dark, wet, dirty tunnels. Life for her was quite straightforward. When she got dirt on her hands she washed. When she was hungry she ate. Josh doubted whether she was aware that miners' children frequently died from malnutrition, but he had no wish to spoil her day by explaining the facts of mining life to her. She was far too happy. She was also very lovely.

'One day I'll take you down a mine,' he promised. 'Then you'll see for yourself how difficult it is for a man to keep clean when he's working.'

'I will keep you to that, Josh Retallick. But right now I want you to show me Dozmary Pool. That is where King Arthur's sword is supposed to have been thrown when he was dying. Did you know that?'

'No.'

'I read about it recently. That reminds me. I have had a beautiful book of poems given to me. I will send it to you with my next letter.'

'Thank you.' Josh would be pleased to have something fresh to read. Because of his rift with Preacher Thackeray he had not been able to obtain any new books. He missed them. At Hayle he had been able to help himself to whatever books he fancied from William Carlyon's house.

He helped Sarah into her saddle and they rode together to Dozmary Pool and looked down at it from the top of a low hill. To Josh there was nothing mysterious about it. It was simply a small lake with low muddy edges.

'It isn't much to look at,' he said aloud.

'No, but it has an incredible atmosphere.' Sarah shivered. 'It is such a dark brooding place. Don't you feel it, Josh?'

He felt nothing but wisely kept quiet.

'I have heard that it is so deep that no one will ever be able to find the bottom of it. Any animal that strays into it is lost for ever.'

'You could say the same about a lot of the marshes on the moor. If an animal starts sinking into them it's not safe for a man to go in after it. One of the moor farmers was lost that way when I was a boy. He sank so fast that he was gone before his friends could get a rope to him.'

'Ugh! How horrible. I think your moor is a cruel place, Josh.'

'It's a hard place,' he admitted. 'But I wouldn't live any-where else.'

'Then what do you intend doing, Josh? Surely you aren't going to stay as the engineer on the Sharptor mine? You would be wasting your training and your ability if you did that. The Sharptor isn't even a big mine.'

'I don't know.' They had turned their horses now and were riding slowly back across the moor. 'I enjoy working here.'

'We had a letter from Tom Fiddler a couple of months ago.'

Josh grinned, remembering Tom's hectic farewell party. He had heard nothing of the Cockney since then.

'He is doing very well in South America. He has made a lot of money and bought a half-share in a gold mine. He hopes to be coming home for a holiday in two years' time. He says he will probably be a rich man by then.'

'I'm sure he will be,' said Josh. 'Tom has both the nerve and the luck to become rich. I'd like to see him again if he ever came to this part of the country.'

'Wouldn't you like to work in a place like South America, Josh?'

'I don't think so.'

'I would love to travel and see the world. That's where men are so much luckier. Unless a girl has a husband to take her with him on his travels she can never go anywhere.'

What Josh's reply might have been was never known. At that moment a fox broke from the cover of a gorse-thicket not twenty yards ahead of them. With a yell Josh kicked his heels into the ribs of his startled pony and gave chase. Sarah was slower off the mark, but Hector quickly overtook Josh's mount. The fox dodged first one way and then the other, leaping through spaces between granite boulders that they had to circle around. It was a hot hectic chase that ended in the gully where Josh had once watched badgers. The fox scrambled up the bank into an area of jumbled broken rock where the horses could not follow and was quickly lost to sight.

Sarah thoroughly enjoyed the gallop and they arrived back at the cottage hot and pink. Sarah gave the two families a dramatic version of the pursuit of the fox, and Mary pouted with envy.

'If I had been there I'd have caught it.'

'I'm quite sure you would,' agreed Josh.

'I can ride as well as Sarah,' said Mary, determined to impress him. 'You come and watch me when I go out riding at home.'

'I wish I could,' replied Josh.

'You'll get that chance sooner than you expect,' said William Carlyon. 'That's the reason I wanted to see Captain Shovell today. I had a long discussion with Theophilus Strike last night. I managed to pick up some business from him. He said that, if Tom Shovell thought it a good idea, the Wheal Sharptor should have a whim-engine. Tom thought it an excellent suggestion. He is to hasten the digging of the new shaft, and when it's finished it will be used exclusively for hoisting ore to the surface. It will speed things up enormously.'

Josh felt he should have been consulted on the matter of the engine. But any resentment he might have felt was dispelled by William Carlyon's next words.

'It was entirely my idea, Josh. I persuaded Theophilus that it would make sense to have another engine. He said that if Captain Shovell thought we needed another engine, then he would leave the choosing of it to you. He wants you to come to Hayle to supervise the making of it – just as you did for your present engine. He is very pleased with the way that one has done its work. He feels its success is due entirely to the personal interest you had in its manufacture.'

While William Carlyon was talking, Jesse Retallick had been watching Sarah. She saw her face light up when her father said that Josh would be going to Hayle. Jesse was both pleased and saddened. Josh might not be aware of it yet, but she knew she was going to lose her son to this girl one day. She successfully shrugged off the vague feeling of uneasiness it gave her.

Chapter Seventeen

Josh travelled to Hayle early the following month, riding a horse from Theophilus Strike's stable. As William Carlyon had told him, he had a completely free choice in engines. More, there was a promise of a rise in salary upon his return – for 'increased responsibility'.

What Josh did not know was that when the tin mines had crashed many of their engineers had taken posts abroad. Most of them in various South American countries where mining was on the increase. Now there was a slight upsurge in the demand for tin, and some tin mines had begun working on a small scale once again. Unfortunately, the lay-off had not improved the condition of the engines. Engineers were at a premium. Furthermore, Josh's ideas on man-engines to bring the miners to the surface had captured the imagination of both miners and mine-owners. His reputation had spread far beyond his experience. Theophilus Strike had no intention of losing his engineer because he was not paid enough.

Although Harvey's foundry had not changed, Josh was no longer an apprentice and life was very different for him. Now he was a guest in the works manager's home with ample spare time on his hands. He discussed engines and the latest modifications with William Carlyon and Harvey's designers, and although he lacked years his ideas were taken seriously by the Harvey men.

It was not merely that Josh represented a customer. William Carlyon had once said that the Sharptor engineer was a particularly gifted apprentice. It was true. Engineering came as naturally to him as did singing to some other men. Training had been necessary, but the gift was there to begin with. Harvey's top men realised that Josh was cast in the Richard Trevithick mould, lacking only that great man's burning ambition to make his mark on the world.

But the time Josh spent at Hayle was not devoted entirely to work. One evening he accompanied Sarah and Mary to a concert, given in the large chapel by a touring orchestra.

Sarah pouted and threw a tantrum when her mother insisted that Mary accompany them. 'Why does she have to come? She is too young to appreciate the music. We manage very well without her when we go riding. We don't need a chaperon.'

'Not when you're riding, although many parents would insist upon that. But riding is a family matter; this is not. All the people we know will be there. If you were to be seen accompanied only by Josh there would be gossip. You would be regarded as . . . well, as not a nice girl. I'm quite sure you don't want that. Neither does Josh.'

So Mary went with them. But Josh had other problems to cope with at the concert. He was wearing his Sunday clothes, bought since he had begun to earn. He was, he felt, a well-dressed man of the world, proudly escorting an attractive girl to a concert. But when they entered the chapel he was brought sharply down to earth. William Carlyon had obtained the tickets for them and they were in the most expensive seats.

It was a mistake.

The men around them here were not just well dressed. They were elegant! Amongst them Josh felt a shoddily dressed lout, his Sunday suit of good stout dark-blue serge shown up for what it was – an ill-fitting outfit of cheap cloth and poor workmanship. He could see it for himself. He did not need the thinly disguised contempt on the faces of numerous well-dressed young men to tell him. They called their greetings to the Carlyon girls, ignoring him.

It was a relief when the music began and he had something else to think about. It helped too when Sarah's hand found his own. After squeezing it reassuringly she kept tight hold of it as the music swelled and filled the building.

It was a Beethoven programme, and as the strains of his great Eroica Symphony rose and fell Josh found himself in a new land, his cheap suit forgotten. He had discovered music.

'Isn't it beautiful?' Sarah whispered, and he could only nod in agreement, not daring to speak. When the music ended Josh applauded in numbed amazement. He returned to earth only when they left the chapel and went outside – to the world of belching chimneys, clattering hoofs and the smell of the mud of a falling tide.

The return was made harder because with it came the knowledge that he would probably never attend another concert. Such an event had nothing in common with his life at Sharptor. No, it had been a once-in-a-lifetime experience, and he felt richer for it.

'What is the matter, Josh? Didn't you enjoy the concert? You are looking very unhappy.'

'I enjoyed it very much. If I was looking sad it must have been because I was thinking that I might never attend another.'

'Why not? We have a concert at Hayle a couple of times every year.'

'But I'm not working at Hayle,' he reminded her.

'You could be,' Sarah declared pointedly. 'Daddy would be very happy for you to join the engineering staff at Harvey's. He has said so more than once.'

'Yes, Josh, come and work here,' said Mary excitedly. 'Then we would be able to see lots more of you. If you don't we will have to come all the way to Sharptor to see you and Sarah if you get—'

'*Mary!*'

The young girl bit back her words and looked fearfully at Josh, as though expecting him to flee from their company.

To Mary's relief and Sarah's embarrassment he laughed. The thought of marriage to Sarah had been with him as a vague shapeless thought ever since her visit to Sharptor. He did not love her – certainly not in the tempestuous way he had loved Miriam. But he was fond of her. Very fond. And he was desperately lonely, deep inside. He had his work, his engine and his inventive ideas, but they were all at the Wheal Sharptor. Outside of the mine he led a solitary life. The cottage seemed empty without Jenny and baby Gwen. And he met too many memories walking alone on the moor.

Marriage was one way out of the cocoon of loneliness Fate had weaved about him, and Sarah was a very lovely girl. . . .

'That's all right, Mary. I think you might have done me a very big favour.'

Looking back on it later, Josh knew that if it had not been for Mary's words he would never have made his decision. He would have been unable to summon up the courage had he not been aware that Sarah had herself discussed it – if only with her young sister.

'I want you to go home by yourself, Mary. I'm taking Sarah for a walk by the river.'

'Mummy said I was to come with you or people would talk.'

'That was at the concert, stupid! Go on home.'

'It's all right, Mary. I'll explain it to your mother when we get home.'

Mary watched as Josh and Sarah turned off into a lane that led to the river, then she ran home as fast as she could go.

'Why did you insist that Mary went home?' Sarah released his arm and took his hand.

'I only asked her. You insisted.'

Sarah's face reflected the pink of the sky above the distant sea. 'You know very well what I mean,' she said.

'And I think you know why I wanted her to leave us,' replied Josh.

Sarah said nothing.

'But there are a few things that must be made clear before I can say what's on my mind, Sarah.'

She looked up at him, but he avoided her eyes as they walked slowly on, hand in hand.

'We come from very different backgrounds, you and I,' he began.

'Wrong, Josh! You know yourself that Daddy is always talking of his mining background. He is very proud of it.'

'Yes, but you've never had to live on a miner's pay. You've been brought up to expect things like a large house, nice furniture and a horse. A miner could never give you all that.'

'Daddy never had all that when he married. The first home he took Mummy to was a one-up-and-one-down house in a terrace. But you keep talking of miners, Josh. You are an engineer.'

'True.' He remembered the rise in pay that Theophilus Strike had promised him on his return to Sharptor. It would place him almost on a par with his own father. 'But I live and work in a mining community. I'm one of them and there is no getting away from that. There would be no horse, no concerts like tonight.'

'Concerts are nice but they are not essential. I disagree about a horse. It would cost little to feed Hector if there were some grazing available. There is no shortage of that about Sharptor.'

'There are other things too. I spend hours at the mine, and you would have no one to talk to – at least, no one of your own intelligence. You would probably become bored and unhappy. I wouldn't like to see that happen.'

They stopped at the water's edge. The sun had gone and the curved slice of pale moon had the sky to itself.

'Josh!' Sarah turned to face him, the moon at her back hiding her face in shadow. Only her voice, low and husky, gave away her deep emotions. 'Josh, you are taking a great many things for granted, whatever it is you are trying to say. Either you don't know me as well as I thought – as I hoped – or you are trying to argue yourself out of something. Either way I don't think you should say any more. When you have made up your mind you will know what to do, and how to find the answers to your questions. Right now I think we had better be getting home. I am sorry if Mary made you feel that you had to say something. You don't, and I promise I will try not to embarrass you in any way. Now, shall we go?'

Her voice broke a little on the last word, but she held her head high.

'No.' He believed she must be able to hear his heart pounding. 'I have already made up my mind. But it's a big step to ask you to take. I don't want you going into something that might not measure up to your expectations. What I am trying to say is . . . Sarah, will you marry me?'

'You mean it, Josh? You really mean it?'

'Yes, Sarah. I mean it.'

'Oh yes, Josh! Yes! Yes! Yes!'

She clung to him and he could feel tears running warm and wet down her cheeks.

'I thought you had decided that you didn't want to marry me, Josh. I was trying to be brave and sensible about it but I was so unhappy inside.' She clung to him as though he might run away from her. 'Josh, I love you so very very much.'

'I'll try to make you happy, Sarah. I'll try very hard.'

She kissed him hungrily. 'And I will make you a good wife. I can cook and sew and housekeep – and I will get rid of Hector.'

'No, you won't. We'll find some way to keep him. Some day we might even get another horse. I won't have anyone saying that you lowered yourself to marry me. A man has to try to better himself, not stay down at the level of the lowest.'

Sarah laughed through the tears of happiness. 'Oh, Josh, you are funny! Just now you were saying that I couldn't have a horse. That you were a miner and wouldn't have much money. Now you are reversing your argument.'

'It wasn't so much arguing as thinking aloud.'

Now the decision had been taken, the all-important question asked, Josh felt a nervous elation. He had been accepted. By

Sarah, if not by her father. But nothing was formally settled. William Carlyon might refuse to allow Sarah to marry him. She was only nineteen and there was little that could be done if the Harvey manager had other plans for the future of his elder daughter.

He voiced his thoughts to Sarah as they made their way homewards, his arm about her waist, her head resting back against his shoulder.

'Daddy won't refuse.'

'You sound very sure.'

'I am.'

She looked up at him and he saw the white gleam of her teeth. 'He has known of my feelings for you since you first came to Harvey's as a new apprentice. I have loved you for a very long time, Josh. But when you left Hayle I thought you had gone back to your girl at Sharptor. I was very unhappy. For a long time I thought I had lost you, although I realised I had no claim on you. I am glad that Miriam married someone else. That left the way clear for me, and I knew I would get you sooner or later.'

The mention of Miriam jolted Josh, and the fact that it could alarmed him. Then he thought of something else. Should he tell Sarah of that last night on the moor? Of the baby? He decided against it. Nothing good could come of it. The secret was his. And Miriam's.

'You have gone very quiet, Josh.' They had arrived at the edge of the town now, and as he took his arm from her waist she clasped her two hands about it. 'Are you worried about speaking to Daddy?'

'Yes.' It was the truth. He tried to think of what he would say, but his mind refused to function along the right lines.

At the door of the house Sarah turned to him, smoothing down the lapels of his jacket. 'He won't dare refuse. He knows if he does his whole family will never speak to him again.' She kissed him. 'That one is for luck.'

The Carlyon family were sitting in the large lounge. They all looked up when Josh walked in with Sarah and there was an air of expectancy in the room. Certainly Mrs Carlyon gave both he and Sarah a questioning look. Sarah seated herself on the sofa beside her mother and looked down at her hands clasped tightly in her lap.

Mrs Carlyon's expression changed to a deep frown.

'Sit down, Josh. There's plenty of room. Take the chair over there.' William Carlyon pointed through the smoke from his pipe to the armchair that faced his own.

'I'd rather stand, if you don't mind. There's something I would like to say – I mean, to ask.'

Relief flooded into Mrs Carlyon's face.

'That's all right, Josh. Sit down and feel free to ask.'

Josh looked around the room and licked his lips. They had become inexplicably dry.

Instantly, Mrs Carlyon was on her feet. She ushered Sarah and the vigorously protesting Mary from the room.

Josh continued to stand and cleared his throat twice before William Carlyon said, 'For goodness' sake come and sit down, Josh. If I have to keep looking at you over my shoulder I'll end up cricking my neck. All right. You want to marry Sarah. Now I've said it for you. It need choke you no more. Sit down and we'll talk about it.'

William Carlyon looked at Josh in sympathetic amusement as he moved across the room to perch on the edge of the armchair.

'That's better. Now, what do we have to discuss? I know you. I know your family. I am aware of your capabilities and I have a shrewd idea of your future. What more should a prospective father-in-law want to know? You've already asked Sarah, of course?'

Josh nodded. 'Yes.'

'There's no need to ask what she said. I'm surprised she hasn't proposed to you long before this.'

There was a silence lasting a few minutes before William Carlyon said, 'Do you have any idea where you might live?'

Josh had not.

'Good. That's what I was hoping you might say. Now, don't think I'm interfering, but Sarah is used to a little more material comfort than you are able to provide for her at the moment

– though it's far more than I would have been able to offer when I was your age.'

'I'm aware of that. I said so to Sarah.'

'Then you'll understand my thoughts on the subject. What I have to say is this. When I was at Sharptor I noticed a derelict house a couple of hundred yards up the hill from where the new shaft is to be sunk. It seemed to be quite a big place, with a couple of cleared fields behind it. Do you know where I mean?'

'Yes, that's the idle farm – at least, that's what it's called in the village. It's never been lived in during my lifetime.'

'Who owns it?'

'I couldn't be sure, but I think it belongs to Theophilus Strike. I seem to remember there being some talk about his buying it when I was a boy.'

'That couldn't be better. Josh, you and Sarah have my blessing for your marriage. And if that derelict farm and the two fields belong to Theophilus Strike I'll buy it for you and Sarah as a wedding present. We'll also give you a houseful of furniture to go with it. All I expect of you is that you will get your miners together and put the house in order.'

When Josh protested the works manager was being too generous, William Carlyon cut him short, 'I'm a reasonably wealthy man, Josh, and the house and land will be cheap. But it does mean that Sarah will be able to keep that horse of hers. There will also be room for one of your own if you feel later that you want one. The house itself is larger than a miner's cottage and will give you a status that all engineers should enjoy. As for the rebuilding of it – well, you can incorporate your own ideas in that. It will give me a great deal of pleasure to make you a gift of your first home.'

William Carlyon beamed. 'Now, that's settled. I'll write to Theophilus Strike in the morning and your wedding can take place when the house is completed. That means that the date is entirely in your own hands.'

'I can hardly believe it!' exclaimed a dazed Josh. 'Sarah will be as excited as I am.'

'Then let's tell her! Call everyone back into the room while

I bring out the brandy. I'm not a great drinking man, but I feel this occasion calls for a celebration.'

Sarah had told Josh that her father would raise no objection to their marrying, but after leaving them together it seemed a very long time before Josh came out to call her and the family back into the lounge. One look at his face told her all that she wanted to know.

'Molly! For some quite inexplicable reason this young man wants to marry our daughter. I thought it better to say yes, to humour him.'

Sarah was so happy she did not know whether to rush to Josh or her father first. She eventually hugged Josh quickly and then ran across the room to fling herself at her father. He managed to ward her off long enough to place the glasses he held on to a table, then he clasped her to him and told her how pleased he was for her.

Meanwhile Josh was receiving the excited congratulations of Mary and the less exuberant embrace of Mrs Carlyon. Afterwards the glasses were handed around and William Carlyon proposed a toast.

'To Sarah and Josh. May they share happiness, prosperity and a long life together.'

His words were echoed, the toasts were drunk and everyone began chattering at once. Josh tried to tell Sarah about the house on the slope above the mine, but it seemed that all her family wanted to talk to her at the same time.

He returned home to Sharptor earlier than he had planned to break the news to his family.

Jesse was delighted. 'She'll make you a good wife, Josh. She's a fine girl. A daughter I'll be pleased to welcome.'

It was a proud day too for Ben Retallick. Josh would be making a good marriage – far better than Ben could ever have predicted. Not only that; his son was to become a land-owner, with room for a couple of cows and any other livestock he might want. It would give Josh a degree of independence unique in a mining community.

Theophilus Strike was happy to sell the old farm to William

Carlyon at a fair price. His own contribution to the wedding present was a generous one. He undertook to supply all the building materials necessary for its renovation. He had recently bought the granite quarry on the tor, so there would be no shortage of stone. Wood too was plentiful in the mine store.

Later that weekend Josh inspected the farmhouse in company with his father.

'It's going to be a major job,' said Ben Retallick when the tour of inspection was over. 'It needs new floors, roof, doors and windows. You've got little more than a shell of a house to work on; but the walls are as stout as you'll find anywhere.'

The house was larger than Josh had expected. It had four rooms downstairs and five up. In addition, there were a number of outbuildings in better condition than the house itself.

'You'll live like a king up here, lad,' said Ben Retallick. 'When it's finished and your mother comes visiting she'll be putting on her chapel clothes.'

'As long as she doesn't expect a formal greeting when she gets here,' smiled Josh. 'But I can't see it ever being ready to live in. There is so much to do and I'll be away for a few weeks yet supervising the building of the new engine. There just won't be the time.'

He looked ruefully at the stark grey stone walls and heaps of disintegrating timbers.

'Nonsense! The first thing needed is a roof to keep the weather out. There are thousands of slates piled up at the back of the Wheal Sharptor building-store. Theophilus Strike has said we can take whatever is needed to put the place to rights. We'll have that done by the time you come home with the new engine. We might even have the floors down too.'

Ben Retallick was better than his word. When Josh brought the new engine around the edge of the hill, above the Wheal Phoenix, he saw the once idle farmhouse standing proud and tall with new roof and doors, and windows that reflected the sun. The men from the mine had completed everything but the plastering inside.

By working really hard at it Josh could have the house finished and be married to Sarah in little more than a month.

But before he was able to make a start on the house, he had to install the whim-engine. This would take longer than usual because he wanted to experiment with a new tipping arrangement. He had designed it himself to speed up work at the head of the shaft. There was another reason. Another man-lift. This one would be incorporated in the ore-hoist and, if successful, would mean the men coming to the surface in one continuous hoist. He was convinced it would work, as were the engineers at Hayle with whom he had discussed it. But there were still a few safety innovations to be perfected before he brought it to Theophilus Strike's attention.

The whim-engine and new shaft were inaugurated with more ceremony than the previous engine had enjoyed. Sarah and her family came to Sharptor for it. As Josh's future wife, Sarah was generally acclaimed by the miners to be a 'fine-looking maid'.

She was thrilled with the progress on the farmhouse. 'It's just too wonderful, Josh. I can't believe it has been built up so quickly. Why, we could move in tomorrow!'

'Not quite!' But he was pleased at her enthusiasm. 'There's still a lot of work to be done inside, and I have to do that myself.'

She pouted in a very characteristic manner. 'I think you are deliberately putting off marrying me for as long as you can.'

He took her hand and led her away from the others, up the stairs to the bedroom cluttered with plasterers' tools and material. Here he took her into his arms and kissed her until she was breathing like a winded doe and pushed him away.

'Josh Retallick! This is not our bedroom yet. Stop! Someone is coming upstairs.'

She hurriedly patted her hair into place as a miner took some timber into another upstairs room.

'I thought you needed convincing that I wasn't trying to put off the wedding.'

'All right, I'm convinced. I am also very happy. This is the first room in the house where we have kissed. I want it to be our own bedroom.'

Josh nodded. 'So be it. I'll decorate it accordingly.'

'We will have the bed here,' said Sarah, pointing to the back of the room. 'Then we can wake up in the morning and see to Kit Hill and the Devon hills.'

'I envy you both,' said Mrs Carlyon, who had entered the room quietly while Sarah was talking. 'You have a house in a beautiful setting and are beginning a new future together.' There was a wistful note in her voice as she added, 'There is so much to be got out of life.'

She went to the window as her husband came upstairs. 'Look out there, William. Will you ever be content to gaze out at grimy foundry walls after seeing this view?'

William Carlyon smiled happily. 'I fell in love with this place the first time I saw it. I thought then how wonderful it would be to live here. I toyed with the idea of buying it, but there are many years to go before I retire. It would be a crime to leave such a house derelict and unloved for so long. Now we've found the perfect answer. I shall be happy knowing that Sarah and Josh are living here.'

'Oh, Daddy! It's a marvellous present. It really is.' Sarah hugged her father. 'And I am so happy.'

He squeezed her close for a few seconds. 'That's how it should be. Now, let's have a look at the bedroom your mother and I will have when we visit you. I want a room with a view that includes Sharptor. I haven't seen a rocky peak like that anywhere else.'

That evening the wedding arrangements were finalised. The ceremony would take place at Hayle at Easter-time. In the meantime Josh would complete the inside of the house. Sarah would be sending furniture to the house as it was purchased. They had discussed what they wanted and Sarah was to organise the buying of it. Between now and the wedding day Josh would make the journey to Hayle on at least two occasions. Sarah would visit Sharptor once more, when the house was quite ready.

There was plenty to keep Josh busy. He now had two

engines and was responsible for training two young lads in the rudiments of engineering. As if this were not enough, an unforeseen incident occurred at the Caradon and Josh became involved in it.

Captain Frisby had continued his policy of taking on destitute tin-miners desperate for work. Their numbers now equalled those of the thoroughly disgruntled copper-miners, who were bearing the brunt of any tasks requiring skill and knowledge in copper-mining. It was at this stage that Frisby played his joker. He declared that the wages of the copper-miners would be cut to correspond with that paid to the ex-tinners. The smouldering anger of the copper-miners exploded into action. They downed tools and a noisy crowd assembled in front of Frisby's office, demanding that the decision be reversed.

His answer was to declare that all those miners not willing to accept the new rates of pay were dismissed. He would take on tinners in their place, he said. One miner was as good as another to Frisby. If half his work-force was content to work for less pay, then the others must follow suit – or go.

Word went around quickly that there would be vacancies at the mine, but the out-of-work tinners who hurried there found the way to Captain Frisby's office blocked by a determined group of Caradon miners. They wisely decided that a hungry belly was preferable to a cracked skull.

But worse was to follow. The Reverend William Thackeray heard of the troubles and hurried to the mine. He arrived in time to catch Frisby's night shift of ex-tinners reluctant to pass the angry copper-miners.

Thackeray seized the opportunity to call a meeting of the men. They gathered within sight of Frisby yet far enough away to prevent their words from carrying to the pale-faced but determined mine captain.

William Thackeray sympathised with the copper-miners and applauded their actions. Standing on a rock so he could be seen by everyone, he also praised their courage.

'It's fallen to you, the miners of Caradon, to make a stand against greed and injustice. What you do here today will be a yard-stick for every mine captain and miner in Cornwall. If justice prevails you'll have struck a blow that will be felt throughout the county. Fail, and twenty years of fighting for better conditions will have been wasted. You've proved your determination. Now, remember that it's your very livelihood you're fighting for – the future not only of yourselves but of your families.'

'Tell that to the tinners!' called a voice from the crowd and there was loud agreement.

'While there are "tinners" and "copper-men" you'll never achieve anything,' replied Preacher Thackeray. 'When you accept that you're all miners you will have won a major battle. There are differences between you now that should never be. No man from Cornwall must keep another from working merely because he gained his experience in a different type of mine. Any more than a stranger has the right to come here and take away another man's livelihood by selling himself cheap.'

Banging palm with fist to emphasise his words, he shouted, 'Until you can greet each other simply as "Miner" you are playing the adventurer's game. Boosting his profits and ensuring that you remain poor men.'

The roar of approval was interrupted by a shout from one of the tinners.

'That's easy to say when you've got a full belly, Preacher. When you've been without food for a week and hear your kids crying night after night because hunger pains won't let them sleep, you'll work for food alone. We've seen hard times from too close.'

Now it was the copper-miners' turn to remain silent and listen to the tinners backing up their spokesman.

'But in the long term your way only helps the few. Can't you see that? If only you would all join together the mine-owners wouldn't dare to lower wages for anyone. If they tried you could down tools and hold out for a fair wage. One that might even go up as profits rose. You could start a miners' fund. The men who were in work would pay into it while those who were out of work could draw enough to buy food for their families.'

Agreement and derision were equally divided between the miners this time.

'This is all very well, Preacher Thackeray, but all this talk of union is tomorrow talk. We've had our pay cut today. What do we do?'

The words came from John Kittow, the man who had masterminded the sale of corn in Callington market some years before. He had been at the Wheal Caradon since the day they had first begun mining copper. As well as being an excellent miner and a much respected man he was pointed out to newcomers as a man who had survived three roof-falls. Perhaps it was this – being alive after three times beating the odds – that made him contemptuous of pretension. He spoke his mind and went his own way. Whether other men followed meant little to him.

The muttering in the crowd swelled loud again.

'You do what you please,' shouted one of the ex-tinners. 'We're going on shift.'

The noise that went up from the men who had downed tools was an ugly one. The main body of them surged around in a movement that took them across the line of anyone with a mind to go to the shaft.

'There'll be no work done tonight,' called a Caradon man.

'Not unless a tinner wants his head busted by a copper-man's shovel,' called another.

'No violence!' called Preacher Thackeray. 'No fighting, or Frisby will call the militia in.'

'Their heads will dent as easy as a tinner's,' called the copper-man who had just spoken. The others hooted their approval. The angry Caradon copper-men outnumbered the night shift of tinners by four to one. It would have taken a brave man to be the first to push his way through to the head of the shaft.

'Please, no fighting!' pleaded Preacher Thackeray. 'You need to show a united front to beat Captain Frisby.'

He turned his attention to the incoming shift. 'This is your chance to show Frisby he can't set miner against miner. Call off your shift tonight.'

'They can't do anything else,' called one of the copper-men. 'They won't get past us.'

There was uncertainty amongst the tinners, and Thackeray seized eagerly upon it. 'Turn around and go home,' he said. 'You can't be blamed for not working tonight.'

'That's all very well,' growled one of the night shift. 'But Captain Frisby won't pay us for what we don't do. We've got to live.'

'I'm pleading with you not to try to work below ground tonight,' Thackeray repeated. 'Turn around and I'll speak to Captain Frisby. I'll tell him I've suggested there be no work done tonight.'

There was an earnest conversation among the night shift, a few lifted shoulders and general nodding of heads.

'All right,' said their spokesman grudgingly. 'But we'll be back for work tomorrow.'

'Bless you!' said Thackeray. 'You've avoided violence and struck a blow against those who want to see the miner stay poor.'

'We'll never get rich if we can't work,' retorted the miner, but he and the remainder of the night shift of miners turned away and slowly made their way from the mine.

From his office Captain Frisby watched them leave and anger boiled up inside him. Most of it directed at Preacher Thackeray. He had been unable to hear what was being said but he put his own interpretation on what he was able to see. He was in no doubt that the preacher had turned back the men who wanted to work. Thackeray's sympathies were well known to lie with the others – the trouble-makers.

With Captain Frisby in this frame of mind there was no chance of Preacher Thackeray negotiating with him on the men's behalf. When the object of his anger came to the office in an attempt to speak to him Frisby turned the key in the lock and refused to open the door, ignoring all the preacher's pleas.

'You can say what you've got to say from there, Preacher Thackeray. You'll not come in here with your seditious talk.

I've heard all about you and tonight I've seen it for myself. Preventing honest men from working, and stirring up trouble. That's what your talk is all about.'

'I stopped the night shift from working to prevent trouble,' said William Thackeray. 'The men were so incensed they would have fought a bitter and bloody battle.'

'If they were it was because of what you had been telling them. Go away. Go to your chapel and do some praying for your soul. Leave the running of a mine to someone who knows something about it.'

'It was your way of running the Caradon that caused them to stop work in the first place. But I've not come here to quarrel with you, Captain Frisby. I'm here to discuss the men's grievances. It would be far easier if you opened this door and let me in.'

'I've nothing to say to you, or to those men out there. As far as I'm concerned they no longer work at the Wheal Caradon. Tomorrow I'll take on new men to fill their places. There's no shortage of good miners.'

'Captain Frisby, let me in and we'll talk this matter over sensibly—'

'There's nothing more to be said. I've done talking. Go away!'

For a few minutes more William Thackeray tried to persuade the mine captain to change his mind, but Captain Frisby refused to acknowledge his presence, and eventually the preacher went back to the miners.

'He's angry tonight,' he said. 'Give him time to cool off and he'll talk. If you can be here to stop the morning shift from starting work he'll know you mean business. I'll come back to see him later in the day. If he realises that the mine is going to lose production he'll agree to whatever demands you care to make.'

'Preacher Thackeray!' John Kittow spat on the ground. 'I don't like all this talk of "demands" and scoring victories. All we want to do is to go back to work for the pay we were getting before today. None of your long words is going to do that for us.'

'Aren't you forgetting the tinners, John?' demanded Thackeray. 'Were they getting a fair wage?'

'I care as much about the tinners as they care about me,' stated Kittow, meeting the preacher's eyes. 'They would have come in and taken our jobs for half the pay and not cared what happened to us. If that's the way they feel I don't give a damn about them. If you have their interests at heart I suggest you go and see them. Warn them not to try to come into work until our pay is back to what it was. If they don't listen they'll be walking straight into big trouble.'

'And that's your answer to Frisby? To cause trouble? To give him an excuse to bring the magistrates out here and call in the militia?'

'No, Preacher Thackeray, I'm on my way now to ask some-one to come to talk to Captain Frisby for us.'

'I don't think Captain Frisby is in the mood to talk to anyone,' said William Thackeray. 'He went so far as to say he no longer considers any of you to be employed at the Wheal Caradon.'

'Then we've nothing to lose,' said John Kittow matter-of-factly. 'But if Joshua Retallick will agree to talk for us I think Captain Frisby might listen. He's a great deal of respect for him.'

Thackeray's surprise at the mention of Josh's name was apparent, but after a while he began nodding thoughtfully. 'Yes. Yes, I'll concede that Captain Frisby might listen to Josh. But it's a lot to ask a young man to take upon his shoulders.'

'You may be right. But his shoulders are broad and he's nobody's fool. I can't think of anyone else who can help us.'

He turned to the other miners. 'You stay here. I'll go and find Josh and try to get him over here tonight. The longer this drags on, the harder it will be for any of us to give way to the other. Just make sure Captain Frisby stays in his office until I get back.'

'There seems to be little I can do here at the moment,' said William Thackeray. 'If you need me I'll be at my home. I wish you luck in your efforts. But I had hoped you might see the wider issues involved. You in particular, John.'

''Tis hard to see past the next pay-day these days,' said one of the men. 'Especially when there's little 'uns at home depending on you. But you've done your best for us and we're grateful for it. If you've a mind to offer up a prayer for us when you get back to the chapel we'd take it kindly.'

The gratitude of the miners was genuine enough. But as William Thackeray rode home he felt he had suffered a personal defeat. It was a bitter and unusual taste in his mouth. The formation of a powerful union was a personal crusade, something too great to be entrusted to any other man. Yet at a crucial moment the power in him had failed. Nothing he could say or do would make any difference. He had allowed the initiative to slip from his hands and pass to someone else.

The truth was that the foundations of Thackeray's dream had been built on unsafe ground. Men, unlike bricks, are not of a uniform size, to be laid one upon the other in order to build a solid structure. They have to be shaped by time and cemented together by circumstance. The time was not yet and circumstances were against Thackeray's ideas of unity. Miners are slow to accept new ideas, Cornish miners more than most. Preacher Thackeray still had much to learn about them.

Miriam tried to tell him something of this when he reached home. But William Thackeray was tired and short of patience.

'They'll have to learn to accept new ideas if they want to improve conditions. I doubt whether Josh will have any more success with them.'

William Thackeray's back was turned to his wife and he missed her expression.

'Josh was there? You saw him?'

He turned quickly but she had bent low over the bread she was slicing.

'No, he wasn't there, but the miners are going to call him in to speak for them. I wish him well.'

'We both wish him well, William,' Miriam said quietly.

*   *   *

Josh was in the kitchen of the Retallick cottage talking to his father when John Kittow arrived. To the best of his knowledge Josh had never spoken to the man and he was puzzled when Kittow said he would like to speak to him.

'It's to ask a favour of you,' the miner added.

'A favour? Something to do with engineering? I'll be happy to help if I can.'

'No, it's not to do with engineering.' The miner looked at Jesse Retallick, unhappy that she was listening.

'Is it something that you'd like to say to me in private? We can go outside . . .'

'No. No, it doesn't matter. Word will be about soon enough. There's trouble at the Wheal Caradon. Bad trouble. I think – and the other miners agree with me – you are the only man likely to be able to help us.'

Josh was no wiser, but, gaining confidence, John Kittow went on to tell him about the events that had followed Captain Frisby's announcement of the wages-cut.

'Why, the mean old skinflint!' Jesse Retallick was unable to contain her anger. 'It's hard enough for a man's family to manage on a full week's pay these days, without having it cut down.'

Ben Retallick waved his wife into silence. 'The man's a fool,' he said. 'There's more to running a mine than getting copper above ground. But Theophilus Strike won't be happy about you getting mixed up in the Caradon's troubles, Josh.'

'It isn't in Strike's time,' retorted Josh. To John Kittow he said, 'How do you think I can help? Preacher Thackeray is a more persuasive talker than I am. If he failed . . . !' He shrugged his shoulders.

'The preacher might be more used to talking,' agreed John Kittow, 'but Captain Frisby knows you. He'll listen to anything you have to say. You know our problems. You've been brought up in mining and you've done a great deal of learning. There's none of us is good enough to state our case to Captain Frisby. There might be something we don't know about, something he won't tell us. The other men agree that whatever you decide is best we'll go along with. We're in need of help and there's no one else we can turn to. We've got to work because we've families to keep, but that doesn't mean we have to be trodden into the ground. If we don't work, then the Caradon doesn't work. Even if it means cracking a few heads along the way.'

There was a long silence when he stopped talking. It lasted until Josh said, 'All right, I'll come up to the mine with you.'

'Good boy!' said Jesse Retallick, and John Kittow looked greatly relieved.

'Don't get too involved,' warned Ben Retallick as his son prepared to leave the cottage with the Caradon miner. 'You'll make more enemies than friends by taking up other men's disputes. Having said that, I wish you luck.'

'Take no notice of your father,' whispered Jesse as she stepped outside the door with Josh. 'He'll be the proudest man on this side of the moor if you can get those men back to work again.'

On the way to the Wheal Caradon, Josh kept John Kittow talking. By the time they arrived he had built up a sound background of the way the mine had been changing in recent months. It was not a happy picture and reminded Josh of the Sharptor mine during the last period of Herman Schmidt's reign.

It was quite dark now, but few miners had gone home. They sat around bonfires near to the main shaft. The earlier excitement had worn off, and the shadowy faces in the firelight were those of worried but determined men. Behind them the beam of the big pumping engine rocked slowly on its axle. Irrelevantly, Josh's engineer's mind noted that behind the steady thump of the engine there was another, less usual, noise. The packing on the huge piston was disintegrating.

'I'll go over to see Frisby on my own,' he said to John Kittow. Waiting until the self-appointed spokesman had joined the others around the top of the shaft, he headed towards the mine captain's office.

There was a light inside but it had been turned down too low for anyone to be visible.

Josh knocked heavily on the door. When he received no immediate reply he knocked again.

'Who is it?' Captain Frisby's voice was thick and surprised. The voice of a man who had either been dozing or very deep in thought.

'It's Josh Retallick. Can I come and speak to you?'

'What for? If you come from that preacher you're wasting your time. I've nothing to say.'

'Preacher Thackeray is quite capable of talking for himself,' Josh said sharply. 'I'm not running his errands. Your miners asked me to speak to you. Out of regard for both yourself and them I agreed.'

'Those men out there are not my miners,' shouted Captain Frisby. 'They ceased to be employed here when they stopped work.'

'And the Caradon mine will cease to exist if you don't do something to save it,' retorted Josh. 'But I'm not standing out here trying to hold a conversation with you through a closed door. Will you let me in, Captain Frisby? Or shall I go home and attend to my own business and forget about your troubles?'

There was no reply, and Josh was about to turn away when a key grated in the lock and the door swung open. Two steps inside and the door was slammed shut and locked behind him. Josh waited in the gloom until Captain Frisby had turned the wick of the lamp up. Then he took a seat to face the weary Caradon mine captain across the breadth of the large desk.

Captain Frisby's first words were defiant.

'I'm prepared to talk to you, but I've no intention of going back on my decision. I'll not be dictated to by the rabble outside.'

'Captain, that "rabble" has built the Wheal Caradon up into one of the largest copper mines in Cornwall. They can just as easily destroy it again. With a little help from you.'

'What do you mean, "destroy it"? I'll get the militia in. They won't get away with smashing equipment on this mine.'

'Nobody will have to touch a thing,' said Josh. His quiet confidence made the mine captain listen. 'The piston-packing is going on the pumping engine. I give it twenty-four hours before it breaks down completely. You haven't an engineer at the mine at the moment, have you?'

'The engine-man can carry out simple repairs like that,' said Frisby quickly. 'I don't need an engineer.'

'You've just cut the engine-man's wages with the others,' replied Josh. 'They're keeping the engines running at the moment, but I can't see them doing any repairs unless matters are settled very quickly.'

As Frisby thought about it, Josh added, 'I believe your deepest level is rich but wet, Captain. How long would it take to become flooded?'

Captain Frisby looked at him and licked his lips. It had been a very wet season. A mere forty-eight hours without pumping would be sufficient to stop the new level from being worked for a very long time. Longer than that and the workings might be under water for months. Josh knew it too.

'All right. Tell the engine-men their pay stays the same. But that only applies to the engine-men.'

'I'm sorry,' said Josh. 'But they have no alternative now. They must go along with the miners. Your action today has done more to bind the copper-men together than all the speeches Preacher Thackeray has ever made.'

'Then I hope it keeps their families fed. They won't have a job to do it for them.'

'I'm sure you're right.' Josh changed his tactics. 'And I don't suppose you'll find it easy to get another job after this.'

The mine captain's head snapped up.

'Me find another job? The shareholders won't dismiss me for doing what I'm paid for.'

'How do you see your job, Captain Frisby?'

'The same as every mine captain. To run my mine, bring up the maximum ore and make a good profit for the share-holders.'

He said it as though it was a maxim he repeated to himself every day of his life.

'That's exactly why today's events will mean your looking for work somewhere else.'

'Don't try to frighten me, Josh Retallick. I know what I'm

doing. It's those good-for-nothing miners out there who'll be looking for somewhere else to work. There are more miners than there is work. They must take what they can get and be grateful to be working at all. I'll give a job to the cheapest man and he'll work harder because he's frightened to lose it. The result is more ore, lower costs and higher profits.'

Josh looked at the mine captain with distaste. If he hadn't heard it for himself he would have scoffed at anyone else repeating such a statement. To Captain Frisby miners were not men with thoughts, ambitions and problems. They were units on a balance-sheet. Even so, the mine captain's mathematics were wrong. Josh lost no time in telling him so.

'How much have your profits risen since last year?' he asked.

'They haven't,' admitted Captain Frisby. 'But they've not fallen, and a lot of man-hours have gone into opening up the new deep level. With this cut in the men's wages there might even be a slight increase by the end of the year.'

'Not if the engine breaks down and the deep level is flooded.'

'That's something that no mine captain can anticipate. Look, Josh, you know the engine-men. Get them to put that piston right and I'll give them an extra two days' pay as well as keeping them on at the old rate.'

Josh ignored this plea. 'The Wheal Sharptor has gone deeper to open a new level. Yet the profit for this year is running fifty per cent above last.'

'The Sharptor's a small mine. You can't compare it with the Caradon.'

'Then take the Wheal Phoenix. Their profit is up a hundred per cent.'

'Sheer luck!' argued Frisby. 'They drove into a rich lode.'

'No, Captain. There's never been such a boom in copper. Every mine in the county is riding high. When your share-holders see their dividends at the end of this year they're going to start asking questions. I don't think you have any of the answers.'

Josh had put his finger on the root of the trouble at the

Wheal Caradon, Frisby's real reason for cutting the miners' pay. It was a last desperate attempt by him to bring the mine profits up.

'It's the men,' Captain Frisby mumbled desperately. 'They're lazy. I should have cut their pay months ago. If I paid them what they're worth their families would all go hungry.'

'No, you're wrong.' Josh stood up and paced restlessly back and forth across the office. 'You have good men here, Captain. They're as good as miners anywhere in Cornwall, a great deal better than most.'

He stopped to look down at the mine captain. 'Why don't you bring back the tribute system? That way you couldn't lose, and the men would be happy.'

'Tributing' was a traditionally Cornish method of mining. The miners, working in small teams, would bid for a particular section of the mine. They would be paid a percentage of what the ore they brought to the surface fetched. If it were a particularly good section and they were exceptionally hard workers the team would make good money. If they had chosen badly they had a lean time of it. Either way the mine was never the loser. It was a system with an element of chance that satisfied the fierce independence of the Cornishman. Working as a tributer he felt he was his own master.

'The shareholders are against tributing,' said Frisby. 'They said that everyone was fighting for the best levels and the mine wasn't expanding as it should.'

Josh could hardly point out that a good mine captain would have been exploring and tunnelling, seeking new and profitable lodes, using his experience to read the signs and follow the copper.

'Then you need to keep good miners,' he said. 'And you must face the fact that your methods have failed. Pay low wages and you get a second-rate man. The good miner will go where he's paid for his experience. You still have a few of them left. Pay them well and let them set the standard. When other men become experienced enough, then raise their money too. Give them a few shillings extra when the tonnage is up and they'll have something to work hard for.'

Josh expected Frisby to argue, but he stayed silent. Encouraged, Josh went on.

'There are still a few months to go before the dividend is called. Give your miners some encouragement. There's a good chance that your profit will be up enough to satisfy all but the greediest shareholder.'

He paused.

'Stay stubborn, put down the pay of your best men and there can be only one possible result. The Wheal Caradon will be the only established copper mine to lose money this year. You'll be dismissed and you'll leave with a reputation to keep you out of mining for the remainder of your life.'

Josh could see the uncertainty on Captain Frisby's face. He had almost won. It was time to take his greatest gamble.

'Well, I've said all I have to say. I'll be going now. I have my own job to get up for in the morning. Good night, Captain Frisby.'

'Wait!'

The cry was one of sheer desperation.

'Don't go just yet.' Captain Frisby was on his feet. He moved across the office to stand between Josh and the door. 'Josh, you must see how it is with me. If I agree to do the things you've mentioned, the men will think they've beaten me. I wouldn't be able to hold my head up on the Wheal Caradon. I'd see the scorn in their eyes every time I gave one of them an order.'

Josh shook his head. 'That won't happen if you take the men into your confidence. Tell them you made the decision to cut their wages because the Wheal Caradon is the only mine not to have a rise in profits. Tell them if they are prepared to raise production you will keep their wages at the present level – and might even throw in a small bonus. Try to get them working with you instead of against you.' He had a sudden thought. 'Who are your shift captains?'

Captain Frisby avoided Josh's gaze again. 'I haven't any just at the moment. They've all left. I don't have men with enough experience to replace them.'

Josh shook his head incredulously. 'Captain, I'm surprised

you've managed to keep the Caradon running at all. Do you know John Kittow?'

'Yes. He's one of the men out there, isn't he?'

'He's the man who came to ask me to help,' said Josh. 'He realises that there are two sides to every dispute. He even suggested there might be some reason why you cut the miners' money. What better opening could you want to explain your point of view? Tell John Kittow you've reconsidered the situation. He's a good sound miner. I've heard others say so. Make him your senior shift captain. Explain things to him. He'll do the rest. Well, Captain, what's it to be?'

It took the captain a full minute to make up his mind. He nodded. 'All right. If Kittow will guarantee to raise the tonnage I'll agree to try things your way. But I want it known that I've not given in to any threats. I've reconsidered my position, that's all.'

'The men will be too grateful to think about anyone giving in, or winning. You've made a wise decision, Captain Frisby. I'm sure you won't regret it.'

'I hope not,' growled Captain Frisby. 'Tell Kittow to come and see me now. We might as well get things sorted out tonight. Then I can go home to bed.'

The men seated about the fires rose to their feet as Josh came into the light of the flickering yellow flames. There was little optimism on their faces. He sought out John Kittow. 'Can I have a word with you, John?'

'Have we still got a job here, Mr Retallick?' The question was asked by an anxious fifteen-year-old, the sole wage-earner for his mother, two younger sisters and a mine-crippled father.

'You'll be back at work tomorrow,' said Josh, and as he and John Kittow left the firelight there was a buzz of excitement behind them.

'Is that true? Has Captain Frisby agreed to take us back on full pay?'

'He's done more than that. . . .' Josh told the miner of his conversation with Captain Frisby. 'So take things easy with him. Don't let him feel he's given in to anyone. He has his pride, for all he has some peculiar ways.'

'Josh, we owe you a very big debt for tonight's work. I'll make sure the Caradon men never forget it.' The miner shook Josh's hand gratefully.

'Never mind about that. Get in there to see Frisby before he changes his mind.'

As John Kittow headed for the mine office Josh walked away from the Caradon feeling elated at having been able to solve the miners' problem.

Jesse Retallick was overjoyed. 'There! And you succeeded where Preacher Thackeray failed, in spite of all his learning.' She looked at Josh with pride. 'They won't be talking of anything else in Henwood or St Cleer for days.'

'You did well for the men, Josh,' said his father more soberly. 'It was time someone put Captain Frisby right. But I doubt if that's the end of it for you. Now you'll be called into every dispute that breaks out around here. Getting yourself known as the men's spokesman isn't going to help further your career as an engineer. It won't put you into favour with everyone.'

There was a prophetic ring to his words, but on this night Josh was too pleased at having achieved something worth while to give it any thought.

Chapter Eighteen

As the wedding date neared, the house on the hill occupied most of Josh's spare time. The plastering was almost finished, but there were still fire-grates to be built, doors to be hung and a hundred other improvements to be carried out. All of these Josh was doing himself, now that the major building work had been completed.

Sometimes he would go up to the house when there was not enough light left by which to work and just sit at the window. Watching the darkness advance over the land, he tried to identify the pin-points of light that loosely speckled the countryside. On the distant horizon a rash of lights marked the great city of Plymouth. Josh had never been there, but he had built up a mental picture from the tales he had heard and the lights that could be seen.

He wondered what it would be like living in this house and looking out on all this with Sarah. More, sharing his whole life with her. There were times when he had grave doubts about their future together, but he had heard this was a natural premarital state.

One day, early in March, he was called from his bed at four o'clock in the morning because a rod had broken in the whim-engine. It took him until midday to complete the repair. Then he carried on with routine work until four o'clock in the afternoon, when he stopped work for the day. Instead of going back to the cottage, he cut across the moor to the farmhouse. A cartload of furniture had arrived from Hayle the day before. After carrying it upstairs he began to paint one of the bedroom doors.

He had almost finished when he heard the kitchen door open downstairs. It did not surprise him. His mother was a frequent visitor and always used that door. He waited for her to come upstairs or call out to him. Instead, he heard a sound he could not place. It was a low gurgling noise. He waited and it was repeated, but this time from a different room.

He was about to investigate when he heard the stairs creak. Moving quietly back into the shadows, he waited as the complaining stairs reported the progress of the mysterious visitor.

Then a head appeared above the hand-rail, and seconds later Miriam was standing at the top of the stairs, her young son in her arms.

She was the last person he had expected to see. The surprise was so complete he dropped the paint-brush to the floor.

The sound brought Miriam to an abrupt halt. Even in the poor light at the head of the stairs he could see changes in her face as the blood first drained away and then came rushing back to her cheeks.

'Josh?'

'Wh-what are you doing here?'

'I'm sorry. I came to Henwood to visit my mother. I thought – I'd heard about your house. I wanted to see it. I shouldn't have come. But I didn't think you'd be here at this time of day.'

The words came tumbling out, tripping over each other. In her arms the baby gurgled away completely unconcerned.

Miriam turned quickly as though to run down the stairs.

'No, don't go! I mean. . . . You can look around if you want to.'

He did not know why he said it, why he never remained silent and allowed her to go, but his heart was pounding so hard inside him he would not have heard the voice of reason had it shouted at him.

'I would rather not, Josh. Not with you here.'

'I'll go if it makes you feel any easier.'

'Don't be silly!' Her laugh was softer, less uninhibited than he remembered. 'It's your house, not mine.'

'Yes.'

She looked at him as he moved forward to stand by the open bedroom doorway, the light shining in upon his face.

'You're looking well.'

'Am I?'

He felt awkward, tongue-tied, not able to think of anything to say, yet not wanting her to leave.

She slowly walked down the stairs and he followed. Stopping in the kitchen, she ran her finger over the dust on top of the range that had been cast in the Harvery foundry.

'This is a fine stove, Josh. Sarah will be able to cook some grand meals on it for you.'

'It was specially made at Hayle. But who told you her name?'

'You did, a long time ago. I always wondered whether you might marry her one day.'

'That's funny.' His expression belied the statement. 'She always thought I would marry you. . . .'

Her finger stopped tracing in the dust.

'. . . and so did I.'

She turned to face him, and he thought she was angry. Then he saw the expression on her face was anguish. 'I couldn't have married you, not after everything. Couldn't you see that?'

'No. I would have accepted that you couldn't marry me right away. But to marry Preacher Thackeray within a few weeks of. . . .'

His voice trailed off as she turned away from him.

'Josh, don't talk about it now. Please! We shouldn't be saying such things at all. Not in this house. This is where you and Sarah will live. Oh! I shouldn't have come. I'm sorry, Josh.'

The baby tugged at the white woollen bonnet he was wearing, pulling it off and dropping it to the floor.

Josh stepped across the room and retrieved it. Tiny fingers reached for it and he handed it over. The baby was chubby and contented, his eyes as blue as Josh's own.

'What do you call him?' The baby had his finger in his grasp now.

'Daniel.'

'Hello, Daniel.' He jigged his finger up and down and the child chuckled.

Miriam pulled the baby away from him.

'Don't, Josh. Don't!'

He beat her to the door and put his back against it. 'Why not, Miriam? Why mustn't I play with him?'

Tears stood out from her eyes as she shook her head. 'Don't make me say it, Josh. Please don't make me say it.'

The tears broke free from her eyes and she crumbled. 'Oh God! Why did I come here? I must be mad!' She sank down on to the wide window-seat.

Josh moved away from the door and stood over her, his face working. He had wanted to hurt her, wanted to get some reaction from her, some recognition of what had once been between them. But seeing her cry like this threatened to tear him apart.

'I'm sorry, Miriam. I shouldn't have pushed you into that.'

She was shaking now and it alarmed the baby.

'Here. Let me take him.' Dropping to one knee, he took Daniel from her, holding him as though he was made of delicate china. He laid him on the floor on a pile of cloth that had been used to protect the newly delivered furniture.

Miriam fumbled in her sleeve for a handkerchief. When she found it she crumpled it in her hand, crying and talking and occasionally drawing in great shivering gulps of air.

'William has been very good to me – to us, Josh. He's a kind man who still talks well of you. He was so proud of what you did at the Wheal Caradon. He thought their cause had been lost. But you saved it, he says. He has wanted to invite you to our meetings, but I dreaded seeing you again. I didn't know what I might do if we ever came face to face. I was frightened. I didn't know what you would say or do.'

She bit at her lip in an effort at self-control, and Josh desperately wanted to help, wanted to stop her baring her heart.

'Don't say any more, Miriam.' He put a hand on her shoulder.

She raised her eyes to meet his and he tried to read what was in them, but all the emotions he thought he could see there were his own. Yet her eyes drew him on like magnets. It was madness! He knew it – and disregarded it. He swayed towards her and suddenly he was holding her. His mouth crushed hers and her arms were about him, pulling him to her.

It stopped as suddenly at it had begun and they drew apart, both shocked with the force of the impact.

'I'm sorry,' he said lamely.

'It was as much my fault as yours.' A strange calmness fell between them as the emotion drained away.

'Now I don't need to ask myself what I might do if I were to meet you,' she said. 'I have my answer.'

She picked up the baby and gave Josh a warm gentle look.

'Don't go yet,' he said. 'Stay for a while longer.'

She shook her head. 'No, Josh. I'm married now. You too have your future to think of.'

'What future? I can't marry Sarah. Not now I know how I feel. . . .'

'Shh!' She silenced him. 'You felt sorry for me, that's all. Of course you'll marry Sarah and both be very happy in this lovely house. But I'm glad you've seen Daniel. It has worried me – trying to decide whether you should see him or not.'

She smiled at him. 'I'm glad I came here after all, Josh. There's been a lot of pain and bad thoughts inside me. They've gone now.'

'You just can't walk out of my life, Miriam – not again.'

She was in complete control of herself now. 'You know I must, for everyone's sake. Be happy, Josh. I'll pray for that. Be happy.' She opened the door and was gone. He called after her, but she never turned. He knew if he ran after her there would be a scene that could only end in complete humiliation for him. Miriam had made up her mind.

He watched her until she was out of sight, lost in the shadows of the tall bracken of the moor.

Miriam knew he was watching and she willed herself not to turn around for one last glimpse of him. Nobody else would ever know what it had cost her to push Josh away when every part of her being was screaming out for him. She had wanted him physically and emotionally. But she had been the cause of great unhappiness to him once. She was determined not to repeat it. Miriam had paid for her treatment of him, paid in the agony of childbirth, bringing his baby into the world to take another man's name. She paid every day when she looked into Daniel's eyes and saw Josh in them. And she paid by being married to a man she had never really loved and never would.

Josh did not go near the house for a week after the meeting with Miriam. Then more furniture arrived from Hayle and he was forced to help place it. The house was almost ready when, with the wedding less than a month away, Sarah came to inspect it.

She was delighted with what she saw – and promptly ordered a major change-around of the furniture. Sarah had very decided views on where everything was to be positioned.

'I've planned it out very carefully,' she said when Josh was taking a breather after moving almost every single piece of upstairs furniture into different rooms. 'As each piece was sent on its way I made a note of where it would go.' She paused. 'I am not very sure about that wash-stand, though. I feel it might look better against the wall over there.'

Josh groaned and she squeezed his arm sympathetically. 'Poor darling. You are having to do so much. But it will be worth it when it is all finished. It is very exciting, isn't it?'

'Yes.' It came out a lie.

'Well, try to sound a tiny bit enthusiastic about it!'

'I think you have enough enthusiasm for both of us.'

'I suppose that is true. But marriage is such a great event in a girl's life. She gets her own home, a place where she makes the decisions about what goes where, what she will cook for every meal – even how she does the housework! I suppose it is different for a man. When he gets married he gives up the right to do whatever he pleases.'

She looked up at him. 'I will work hard for you, Josh. I will try to make you a good wife.'

'I'm sure you will.' Her sincerity touched him. Then he looked past her, through the window and across the moor. 'I only hope I prove to be as good a husband. . . .'

The wedding was proclaimed the event of the year in Hayle. The chapel, decorated with hundreds of flowers for the event, was packed with guests. Included in their ranks were Theophilus Strike, Tom Shovell and Jenny from Sharptor, and Wrightwick Roberts was there to help the Hayle preacher with the service.

As a mark of respect to William Carlyon, most of the Harvey family were present, looking well dressed and well bred. But Ben Retallick would not allow Jesse to be over-awed by them. 'We're God-fearing folks who owe nothing to anyone and we have a son any of them would be proud to own today.'

The ceremony was simple and moving. When it was over Josh and Sarah returned to the Carlyon house in a gaily decorated pony-trap.

In the house the presents were on view, among them a silver dish from Francis Trevithick. During the reception Josh discovered that the mine-owners and engineers in this part of Cornwall had heard of his man-lift innovations. He was asked many questions about it by men who were complete strangers to him.

'It is wonderful to have a famous husband,' teased Sarah, rescuing him from a small group of ex-Harvey apprentices who were asking technical details about Josh's latest lift. 'But I am quite sure that it will keep until after our wedding day.'

'I don't mind,' said Josh. 'If even one of those engineers goes back to his own mine and puts in a man-lift, it will save many men who otherwise would not be at the wedding of their sons.'

'Josh, I am sure that my whole life will soon be tied up with mine-engines, boilers and all the other things that are important to a very clever engineer. But this is my wedding day and I want to enjoy every minute of it.'

Josh gave in without further argument. He was soon shaking hands and making smalltalk with young men who all looked alike and young women who gave him and Sarah shy knowing glances.

Eventually the guests began to drift away. Soon only family were left standing between mounds of dirty crockery and dejected foodstuffs. Then they adjourned into another room and everyone talked until well after their usual bedtimes. Finally, in an agony of embarrassment, the newly-weds were ushered upstairs to the room they were to occupy for that night.

Spending the first night of their married life beneath the Carlyon roof was a mistake. Sarah's initial shyness was so acute it only just fell short of terror. Although she snuggled up to Josh in the luxurious bed which was usually occupied by her parents, she would not allow Josh to consummate their marriage that night.

'I just couldn't!' she whispered. 'Not here in their bed. In this house. It – it just wouldn't seem right somehow. You do understand, don't you, Josh?'

He managed to convey the fact that he was offended in a single grunt.

'I am sorry. But tomorrow night we will be in our own house. Just you and me. It will be different then.'

They travelled to Sharptor by coach the following day. Alone. Jesse Retallick protested that it was unnecessary extravagance to use two coaches when they were all going to the same place; but William Carlyon stayed firm, and Sarah and Josh went ahead of the others in a light fast carriage.

The newly-weds arrived at their future home to discover it had been cleaned that very morning. A fire was burning in the lounge and there were fresh spring flowers everywhere, all provided by the wives of the Sharptor miners. This was a traditional homecoming, the wives' way of welcoming Sarah to their midst.

There was something else too and it pleased Josh out of all proportion to its value. It was a grandmother clock, standing conspicuously on the table in the lounge – a present from the miners at the Wheal Caradon.

Much later that night Josh lay in bed, thinking about the future. Beside him Sarah was curled up, asleep, the tears on her cheeks now dry. They had made love for the first time together. Sarah had given her all to him but it was not a wildly passionate union. Even the tears she had shed were more of relief because the act had not caused her as much pain as she was expecting. In a whisper Sarah had told her new husband that it had been wonderful, all she had hoped it would be. But Josh realised then that love-making for Sarah would be more a wifely duty than an abandoned pouring out of her love for him.

But lack of enthusiasm in bed was the only criticism he could possibly have levelled against Sarah. She was a promising cook, a good housekeeper, and she genuinely loved Josh.

'You've got a good wife there, Josh,' said Ben Retallick one evening as he and Josh walked down the hill in the dark after Ben had called in on his way home from the mine. 'Mind you take good care of her.'

Josh confirmed that he would.

'Have you seen anything of Miriam since you've been wed?'

Josh answered quite truthfully that he had not.

'Good! From all accounts she's leading her husband a merry dance. You were wise to break with her when you did.'

Josh did not correct him. Instead he asked, 'In what way is she leading Preacher Thackeray a dance?'

'By making him look a fool in front of his own parishioners, taking meetings of miners, trying to tell grown men about the benefits of this "union". Some folk seem to think it would cure all the ills of the miner, change him from what he is into something he can never be. Telling him he is as good as the men who give him his living.'

'You surprise me, Dad. I always thought you were on the side of the miner.'

'So I am,' retorted Ben. 'Which is more than I can say for anyone who fills his head with a lot of dangerous nonsense. Not that many of them take in what she's saying. All they go to her meetings for is to see her getting excited about something that's none of her business.'

Josh laughed. 'Have you heard Preacher Thackeray complaining about it?'

'No. I wouldn't expect to. But I can imagine what he says to her in private.'

'I think he's well pleased with her. Preacher Thackeray believes not only in the equality of all men – but women as well.'

'Then he's more of a fool than I would have taken him for. It's not a woman's place to be talking to a crowd of men. It's not decent.'

'Preacher Thackeray is a man who will use all the means at his disposal to put his beliefs across to the miners. And what he preaches is perfectly right.'

'I'd rather not hear that talk from you, Josh. Especially now. You've moved up in the world. You have a good skill at your fingertips and a wife from a good family. Be thankful for it. Don't go getting mixed up in any of Preacher Thackeray's doings.'

'But that's just it, Dad. Don't you see? What you've said proves how right Preacher Thackeray is. He taught me to read and write and do sums. He also taught me to think for myself. That's a right that every miner's son should have. But if it hadn't been for him I would never have been able to go to Hayle and learn how to be an engineer. His arguments are sound. Do you think Theophilus Strike is a better man than you? I don't. Neither should you.'

'Theophilus Strike is the mine-owner. As such we owe him our respect. I for one am indebted to him, for making me shift captain.'

'Dad! That argument won't hold water. I respect Theophilus Strike as I respect any other man. But he gave you the shift captain's job because you're the best man for it. Any Sharptor miner would tell you that. By appointing you shift captain he was doing what's best for the mine, and for himself. I'm grateful to him for giving me the opportunity to become a mine-engineer, but I'll repay his investment by keeping his engines trouble-free. Theophilus Strike is in a position to do what he has for you and me because of money he never had to work for. We're proving that we can do things without having that sort of money to help us. How does that make him better than us?'

'I don't like to hear you talk like this, Josh. When you settled the trouble at the Caradon mine I was pleased. It saved a great many jobs. But I've heard since that Preacher Thackeray uses it to prove to miners what they can get if they stand up to those who give the orders. It's dangerous talk, Josh, and I'd be pleased to hear you speak against it.'

'I'm sorry, Dad. I can't speak against something I believe in. Preacher Thackeray is telling the truth. If the Sharptor miners hadn't defied Captain Schmidt you wouldn't be here today talking to me.'

'Things have a habit of sorting themselves out, given time,' said Ben stubbornly, determined not to be convinced. 'All I ask is that you don't concern yourself with Preacher Thackeray's doings. You've got a wife and position to think of.'

'I'll remember that,' said Josh. 'But I'll still speak up for things I believe in.'

There was a resigned sigh from Ben Retallick. 'That's just what I said your reply would be.'

'"Said" . . . ? To who?'

'To Theophilus Strike, Josh. I was hoping to get you to see sense without bringing his name into it. Since my arguments don't move you I'd better tell you his words. He inspected the mine this morning. He tried out your new man-lift and thought it could prove useful, though he seemed to prefer the first one. He had a good deal to say about your engineering and said he was well satisfied with your work.'

Ben Retallick paused and crossed himself quickly as a star dropped diagonally across the sky to be swallowed up in the vastness of time and space.

'He also said he was disturbed – no, "concerned" was the word he used – concerned at some of the talk he'd heard about men coming to you with their problems. He said he'd even heard it rumoured you were for a miners' union. He was mightily relieved when I told him that, while I couldn't know who might have sought your advice, I could say there was no truth in the talk of you preaching for a union.'

'Dad, I haven't preached for a union – yet! If I was asked to I'd think seriously about it. As for giving men advice – yes, I have. Whenever I've been asked for it. I don't have to ask Theophilus Strike for his permission. He pays me a wage for a day's work. Whatever else I do is none of his business!'

'All right, Josh. Don't get angry with me. I've only told you what has been said. All I ask is you give it some thought. There's no sense in stirring up Strike. He's a good man; but he likes to think he's getting his own way – whether he is, or not. Now, I've kept you away from Sarah for long enough. I'll bid you good night. Don't forget you're both eating with us this Sunday.'

He walked away down the hill to the Retallick cottage, leaving Josh struggling to shrug off his anger. He considered the mine-owner's comments to be undue interference in his private life. He could not believe it was coincidence that it came at a time when the union of the miners was becoming more than a preacher's dream.

The movement was a long way from having the unanimous approval of every miner, but it was gaining ground. Each mine now had a small nucleus of men who met regularly and exchanged ideas with men from other mines. They elected members to attend meetings presided over by Preacher Thackeray and report back to their own committees. These were not the open 'conversation' meetings that Preacher Thackeray held to gain recruits, but a gathering of dedicated 'unionists' – men who gave their time and application to bringing about a revolution in the miner's way of life.

Josh was interested in the movement but he had taken no active part in the affairs of the miners since the trouble at the Wheal Caradon. It was for this reason as much as anything that he considered Theophilus Strike's words to be particularly unfair. He smarted under them all the way back to the house.

Chapter Nineteen

'What are you thinking about?'

It was a sultry late-summer night and the bedroom was filled with soft silver moonlight. Sarah turned on to her side to face Josh and slipped her arm over his chest.

'I thought you were asleep,' Josh replied quietly. 'Did I wake you?'

'No. I have been lying here trying to read your thoughts. Is something worrying you, Josh?'

'No.' He pulled her towards him. 'I can't sleep, that's all.'

'Are you quite sure, Josh? You aren't tired of me already?'

He snorted with amusement. 'That's a fine thing to say after only four months of marriage! Ask me again after four years.'

'I'm glad.' She snuggled closer to him. 'I am very happy. But something is bothering you. Is it anything to do with that man who called to see you this evening?'

'John Kittow? Not entirely. The miners over at Kit Hill are having some sort of trouble. He wants me to go to a meeting they're holding at Kelly Bray tomorrow night.'

She rose on one elbow to look down at him. 'You are not going?'

'I told John Kittow I would.'

'But why? It has nothing to do with you. Whatever trouble

they have there concerns neither you nor the Wheal Sharptor.
Why get involved in it?'

'I'm not getting involved. I've simply been asked to go to
a meeting. I'm going because I'm interested.'

'Theophilus Strike won't like it.'

'Sarah, I don't *care* what Theophilus Strike likes. This is none
of his business.'

'And the Kit Hill miners are none of *your* business, but that
is not going to prevent you from going to their meeting.'

Josh said nothing. It was their first argument. He felt
the unhappiness knotting itself inside her. They lay side by
side in silence for a long time before Josh felt a tremor run
through Sarah's body. It was followed a few seconds later by
a strangled sob that racked her body for the second time.

'Sarah, please don't cry.'

'Oh, Josh! I'm so miserable!'

He turned and put his arms about her and she clung to him,
tears coursing down her face and soaking his shoulder.

He held her for a long time, soothing her and brushing the
hair back from her face until she stopped crying.

'I'm sorry, Josh. That was silly of me.

'No!' She stopped him as he was about to protest that it
was his fault. 'You must do what you feel you should do. I
have no right to object.'

'You're my wife, Sarah. You have every right to express
your opinion. All I wish is that you were interested enough
to want to know what it's all about, instead of condemning
my involvement out of hand.'

'I don't want to know, Josh. I probably wouldn't understand
it anyway. But you know what you are doing. I accept that.
Now, don't be angry with me anymore.'

She drew him to her and that night their love-making found
the fervour that had been missing before.

Josh rode Hector to Kelly Bray with John Kittow behind him.
The meeting was held in a clearing behind a miners' inn and
was well attended.

The men's grievance was with the mine store. Every mine

ran its own store and it invariably gained a stranglehold on the miners and their families. When a man started work on a mine he rarely had the money to see him through the first month. The only place he could obtain credit was the mine store. His tools came from there, together with the essential items of furniture to set up home. The cost was higher than elsewhere, but few men had any choice. It suited the mine-owners – who also ran the store. A man had to work hard to keep up with his indebtedness. He was fearful of losing his job. It also meant that, as soon as he was paid, the money was returned to the mine-owners via the store.

Occasionally it happened that the owners became greedy, especially if they thought some of the miners' money was escaping them. Then they simply increased the store prices.

This was the problem at Kit Hill. The men had complained of high prices to no avail. So deeply in debt were they that few of them could afford to break the vicious circle by buying elsewhere. Two men who had walked the miles to a Gunnislake mine store on pay-day had been dismissed and told they were lucky not to have been taken before the magistrate for attempting to obtain 'false' credit.

Incredible though the allegation was, had it gone before the local magistrate there would have been a conviction. Magistrates were well-to-do local men, most of them with shares in at least one mine.

It was against this background that the meeting had been called.

It got off to a slow start. When Josh and John Kittow arrived there must have been a hundred and fifty men in the wide piece of open ground. Men stood in small groups, some arguing among themselves, others looking embarrassed at being there at all.

John Kittow and Josh picked their way through the crowd, the Caradon shift captain occasionally greeting an acquaint-ance. When they reached a heap of mine waste that would serve as a platform Josh looked about them and said, 'John, this is a complete waste of time. Unless someone starts talking to the men they'll all begin to leave. I'll probably go with them. Who called the meeting?'

'A miner named Harry Reeve,' said John Kittow. 'I can't see him here.'

'Well, if he can't bother to turn up for his own meeting I see no sense in staying.'

'Give him a few minutes,' pleaded John Kittow. 'Something must have happened to keep him away. He's a reliable man, or so I'm told. I must admit I don't know him well.'

They began moving slowly back towards the place where Josh had left his horse when there was a sudden upheaval in the crowd in front of them and voices raised in anger. A red-faced man, perspiration tracking down his face, pushed past them, heading for the heap of mine waste. When he reached it he turned to the crowd, holding his hands aloft, calling for silence.

'Quiet, please! Listen! Listen to me! Shut up a minute!'

The noise died down and the hot newcomer, who seemed to have the greatest difficulty in standing still, raised his voice and shouted unnecessarily loudly.

'Harry Reeve won't be coming here to speak to us tonight . . .'

An angry buzz from the crowd drowned his words and he waved his arms wildly again until the miners fell into a near-silence.

'It's not his fault. He's been arrested.'

There was complete stunned silence.

'Not only Harry Reeve, but also Richard Crossentine, Daniel Trehane, Sam Maddiver and Wesley Barnicott along with him.'

The crowd erupted into anger as the miners took up the cry of 'Why? Why?'

'I'll tell you why,' shouted the sweating man. 'It's because the adventurers heard there was to be a meeting about the store. They thought they'd put a stop to it by having Harry Reeve and the others arrested. They are to be taken before the magistrate and charged with "incitement to riot"!'

There was another roar from the assembly and a second man

scrambled up on to the rubble. He had difficulty in maintaining his balance. Josh thought he was probably drunk.

'We'll show them what a riot is,' he shouted. 'We'll go and get Harry out.'

The crowd was for leaving on a rescue mission there and then. But the first man tried to bring some order to the meeting. 'No! We mustn't do anything just yet. Someone went from Callington to fetch Preacher Thackeray as soon as we found out they had Harry and the others in the lock-up there. He'll be here soon. He'll know what to do.'

'We already know what to do,' said the second man, intent on rousing the crowd. 'We don't need a bloody preacher to tell us. If he wants to talk he'll find us at Callington lock-up, getting Harry Reeve and the others out!'

Once again he had the crowd's approval and there were shouts of 'Come on. What are we waiting for? One and all! One and all!'

This was the age-old cry of the Cornishman and had preceded more than one bloody riot.

Josh pushed his way roughly through the miners and climbed up to join the other two on the waste-mound. He was big enough to gain the attention of the miners without using any tricks, and they fell silent as he called to them.

'Wait! If you go to Callington and break into the lock-up there's not a court in the county will find Harry Reeve and the others not guilty. You'd condemn them by your actions.'

There were catcalls and some shouts of 'Who are you?'

'This is none of your business. Leave it to those of us who are friends of Harry Reeve.' This from the man who had advocated rescuing the arrested men.

'Don't do anything you'll regret,' Josh reasoned. 'You met here to talk of union, of action to right a wrong. Don't let this panic you into doing something that will give the adventurers an excuse for taking action against unionism.'

'And what's arresting Harry Reeve if it isn't taking action against us?' The man on the mound beside Josh pushed his face towards him. His breath confirmed Josh's earlier opinion that he had been drinking. At the same time Josh heard his own name being spoken among the crowd of miners.

'Get off here and let me talk to them.'

The drunken miner pushed Josh, but in a quick move Josh took hold of the man's arm. Swinging him around to face the crowd he pushed him off instead. His action brought a cheer from the miners at the back of the clearing. When he tried to make himself heard above the hubbub someone called, 'It's Joshua Retallick. Let him speak.' Others took up the call, and when he spoke he had their full attention.

'The worst thing you could possibly do is use violence. That will solve nothing. There are other ways of achieving your ends. But you must decide here and now what it is you want. Then make sure every last man in the Kit Hill mine is with you. If you don't show complete unity you might as well walk away from here right now and forget about helping either Harry Reeve or yourselves.'

'That's the soundest advice I've heard at any meeting. You are absolutely right, Josh.'

It was the Reverend William Thackeray. During the argument he had arrived unnoticed, his neat little gig making no sound as it approached across the soft grass.

But it was not the preacher who caused Josh to become suddenly tongue-tied. It was Miriam, seated beside him.

Miriam was just as surprised to see Josh at the meeting but she managed a faint smile that gave no hint of her inner turmoil. With her long loose hair blown by the wind and her face flushed with excitement she still had all the wild beauty of the young girl Josh had explored the moor with. There was not a man at the meeting who was not stirred by her presence.

But this type of gathering was William Thackeray's natural environment. Giving the reins to a nearby miner, he handed his wife from the gig and pushed his way to the front of the crowd with Miriam following.

As the man who had brought the news of Harry Reeve's arrest reached down to help them on to the rock platform, Josh began to climb down, not wishing to be confronted by Miriam in such a confined area. It was William Thackeray who stopped him. Gripping Josh's arm, he spoke to him in an urgent whisper. 'Stay here, Josh. We have need of you.'

To the crowd he cried, 'You've heard what Josh Retallick said. I endorse his every word. Is there any man here who has other ideas?'

There were a number of dissenters but not as many as had enthusiastically supported a march on Callington lock-up.

'Then let's hear them. You! The bearded man at the front here. What do you suggest we do?'

The bearded miner was unhappy at being singled out for attention. He looked about him for some visible sign of support, but men avoided his eyes.

'I say we march on Callington and release Harry Reeve.' It was said hesitantly and without conviction but there was a degree of agreement in the crowd.

William Thackeray turned to Miriam in a routine that would have had a familiar pattern to any miner who had attended some of their previous meetings. 'He suggests this band of good men . . .' He waved his hand in a gesture that took in every miner. 'This crowd of – how many? One hundred? Two, perhaps?'

Miriam nodded seriously.

'All right, let's say that two hundred miners were to march on Callington. What do you think would happen?'

Miriam looked slowly over the crowd and nodded her head again. 'They are fine men. I doubt if you could pick better anywhere. Each one capable of holding his own in a fist fight with any man.'

Her clear voice rang out so that not one man missed her words. Josh was impressed by the self-assured manner in which she held their attention. Then he remembered an evening when as a young girl she had prevented a fight between Morwen and himself by projecting just such an authority.

Preacher Thackeray was talking again. 'Two hundred brave Cornishmen, prepared to storm the Callington lock-up and release their friends.'

Some of the miners were looking puzzled. The preacher

and his wife seemed to be contradicting William Thackeray's earlier statement, agreeing that a march on Callington would succeed after all.

'Yes. We'll do it too!' someone shouted.

Miriam stepped in front of her husband and reaching down inside the front of her dress pulled out a small linen bag attached to a long drawstring looped about her neck. The curious crowd fell silent.

'You are brave men,' agreed Miriam. 'Any man who earns his living below ground has courage. None could deny it.'

She held up the small linen bag for all to see, and her next words rang out with all the power she could put into them. 'Yet this small bag would hold enough musket-balls to kill every one of you!'

The men were looking puzzled again, but Miriam did not leave them in suspense for long.

'You wonder what this has to do with you? Then I'll tell you. At this very moment a full company of soldiers, regular disciplined troops – more than a hundred of them – are riding post-haste from Bodmin barracks to Callington. *Every single one of those soldiers carries this many musket-balls!*'

In the stunned silence that followed the miners stared at Miriam in disbelief.

'Yes, a full company of soldiers will be in Callington before nightfall.'

Pushing the bag back inside her dress, Miriam struck a pose with hands on hips. 'Do you take the Callington magistrate for a fool? He knew what the rest of you would do when he arrested the leading Kit Hill unionists. There was a horseman on his way to Bodmin for soldiers before the ink was dry on the warrant for Harry Reeve's arrest!'

Josh was as surprised as the miners. His object in preventing them from marching on Callington was so as not to prejudice the case of the men held in custody. He had never envisaged the military becoming involved.

'Then what can we do?' called one of the miners. 'We can't just stand back and do nothing.'

This was a cue William Thackeray had been waiting for.

'That must be for you to decide,' he declared. 'I can only advise you on ways to achieve the aims of all Kit Hill miners. But, first, how many of them are *not* at this meeting?'

'Not more than fifty,' replied the miner beside him.

'I suggest you make certain those fifty join with you to stop all work in the Kit Hill mine.'

This provoked noisy mutterings among the miners. 'How are we supposed to live while we're out of work?' asked one, and others echoed his question.

Miriam glared angrily at the crowd. 'Men are in prison for no other reason than that they tried to help you. They face trial – for you. I know you have families to think of. So does Harry Reeve. Who will feed his five children?'

'My wife is right,' said William Thackeray. 'Conditions won't improve without some sacrifices being made by everyone. Stopping work at the mine will hurt your pockets, yes. But it will hit the pockets of the adventurers too. They won't allow such a state of affairs to go on for long.'

'What do you say, Retallick?' one of the miners called.

Josh had been standing at the rear of the group on the mound, happy to allow the others to do the talking. Now, as they stood aside for him, he stepped forward, avoiding meeting Miriam's gaze. Instead he looked down at the anxious faces in the crowd, aware that his answer would decide the miners' actions and choosing his words carefully.

'I say do as Preacher Thackeray suggests. Get the others with you. Tell the captain you'll allow the engine-men to go in for one week only. By the end of that time the prices in the mine store must have been lowered and Harry Reeve and the others released. If they haven't, tell him the engine-men will shut off the pumps and allow the mine to flood.'

Josh's words received noisy approval.

'But you must have a leader,' declared William Thackeray. 'Someone you can trust to carry your decisions – to the adventurers, if necessary – without being cowed by them. Do you have such a man?'

A number of men called the name 'John Trehane'.

'Is John Trehane here?' asked William Thackeray.

'That's me, Preacher,' said the miner on the mound with them.

'Then the meeting is all yours, John Trehane. I wish you good luck. If you need help or advice you know where to find me.'

'Thank you, Preacher – and Mistress Thackeray. You too, Mr Retallick. You're well thought of by the men and we appreciate your coming to show support for us.'

Miriam was being helped to the ground by William Thackeray and John Trehane when John Kittow pushed his way through to them.

'I'd like to have a word with the men before you go,' he said, and Josh helped him up on to the stones before joining Miriam and William Thackeray on the ground.

John Kittow came straight to the point. 'I've brought an answer to one of your problems,' his deep voice boomed out over the assembly. 'You wanted to know how your families would manage to live if you weren't working. I'll tell you. We've been through troubles ourselves at the Wheal Caradon, as Josh Retallick could tell you. Because we know what it means to have support at a time like this we held a meeting at the Caradon last night. It was agreed by our men that they would each give a shilling a week to help during the time you're not working.'

The cheering and shouting showed what the men of the Kit Hill mine thought of the gesture. But John Kittow had not finished.

'Not only that – listen now! Not only that. The Wheal Phoenix men have told me to tell you they'll each give sixpence a week too.'

'We've done it! Miriam. Josh. We've done it!' William Thackeray was pumping Miriam's and Josh's hands and literally dancing up and down. 'A union of miners has become a reality in this part of Cornwall. There'll be no stopping us now. This is what I've been working towards for all these years.'

His elation was almost matched by that of the miners. With the threat of starvation removed they knew they could win the fight against the high mine-store prices.

Josh was still not comfortable in Miriam's presence but it was difficult not to get caught up in the infectious enthusiasm of the crowd.

'All we need now is the acquittal of those men in custody at Callington. Then it will be a victory,' he said.

'Of course, Josh. But come. We must talk about these exciting happenings over a glass of wine. No, Josh! The evening will turn sour if you don't come home with us.'

Miriam felt as apprehensive as Josh but she managed a 'Please, Josh,' and was not certain whether she wanted him to accept or refuse.

'Of course he'll come. He's been absent from our circle of friends for far too long. This evening's happenings have been brought about as much by what he did for the miners of Wheal Caradon as by my own efforts. Come, Miriam. We'll ride in the gig and Josh can accompany us on that fine horse of his.'

As John Kittow declared his intention of remaining with the Kit Hill men and finding his own way home later, Josh was unable to make an acceptable excuse for not going to St Cleer.

The preacher drove his horse along at a fast trot and it was not long before they reached St Cleer and drew up outside the preacher's house.

'Now, you two go into the house while I put the gig away. Leave your horse tied up at the gate, Josh. I'll give him some water. When I come in I'll open a very special bottle of port wine. I've been saving it for just such an occasion as this. Go on inside now.'

Dusk was not far off, and inside the house it was dark and quiet. Josh followed Miriam into the comfortable lounge and, when she had lit a lamp, seated himself in the corner furthest from it.

After a heavy silence, Miriam said, 'It's nice to see you here in this house, Josh.'

'Is it?'

'Yes, it makes me very happy. I'm quite sure William feels the same. He's missed your friendship. We both have.'

'Don't you think friendship might be difficult in the circumstances?'

'No, Josh. There are many things William doesn't know – and needn't know. But even if he did I feel sure he'd forgive both of us. As a preacher he's well aware of the weaknesses of men and women. It would distress him, but I'm sure he would find forgiveness. Especially if the interests of the union were involved. That comes before anything with William.'

Josh looked for some sign of bitterness in her face, but there was none.

'What about Daniel?'

Miriam drew in a deep breath. 'Daniel is part of William's family. He loves him very much. I don't believe anyone would be cruel enough to destroy that feeling.'

There were words in Josh's throat but they caught there. Instead he said, 'Where is Daniel now?'

'With my mother for a few days. . . .' Miriam looked at him and bit her lip. 'Josh, let's not make tonight unhappy. I really am pleased to have you here. I feel as though I am singing in here.' She put a hand to her breast. 'William is happy too – and you can't tell me that you aren't very proud of your part in what has been achieved today.'

She moved closer to him. 'Do you realise what it means? Now the miners are strong enough to stand against the mine-owners. By joining together they can improve their living standards, get a fair wage, and will not have to accept the many unfair conditions that go with their work.'

William Thackeray had entered the room quietly. He saw the look on Miriam's face as her hand rested on Josh's chair for a brief second but he said nothing. Going straight to a cupboard he took out three glasses and filled them from the bottle he carried in his hand.

Handing the glasses around he raised his in a salute.

'To the Union. To the Miners' Fund and to a better under-standing between all Christian men, whatever their lot in life. May they all be as God made them – equal!'

'I'd like to propose another toast,' said Josh gravely. 'To the freedom of the men who were arrested today for trying to exercise that equality.'

*   *   *

That very night the Kit Hill mine store was burned to the ground. It was difficult to say when the fire started because the mine was not being worked and the engine-man spent most of the night dozing. It was left to the Callington town watchman to raise the alarm when he saw the flames lighting the sky-line atop the hill, as though it was the Midsummer Night bonfire.

The fire brought the military to the mine. They stayed for a week. There were angry words exchanged between soldier and miner but, although they came close to blows on more than one occasion, the peace was kept.

There were few miners who regretted the destruction of the store and they made no secret of their feelings. But the incident sealed the fate of the five union leaders held in custody. There had been hopes that they would be brought before the magistrate on a trifling charge and be summarily dealt with once the miners' terms had been met. But the fire made the matter far more serious. They were sent in custody to Bodmin Jail to await trial at the next Assize, charged with conspiring to destroy property. It was generally recognised that they had little chance of an acquittal now.

'Whoever set fire to that store convicted them as surely as though he were the Assize judge himself,' said William Thackeray when he rode over to the Sharptor mine to tell Josh the news. Josh already knew; the store-burning had relegated all other news of the day in the area.

'Is there nothing that can be done for them?' asked Josh.

William Thackeray shook his head. 'Nothing. The miners are collecting to engage counsel for them, but it will be a token defence only. The judge will be determined to make an example of Harry Reeve and the others. The mine-owners must be rubbing their hands at such an opportunity.'

They were seated in the lounge of Josh's Sharptor house. Sarah came into the room bearing a tray with tea and cakes upon it. She was pleased at the opportunity to be a hostess. A minister was of sufficient status to warrant more formality than the friends and acquaintances from the mine who occasionally called in to see them.

'We are discussing the plight of the men from Kit Hill mine held for trial at Bodmin, Mrs Retallick,' said William Thackeray, seeking to draw her into their conversation.

'I am quite sure they will get their just deserts,' said Sarah icily. 'I wish that Josh would keep well out of it. No good can come from such goings-on.'

She was pouring tea and so was unaware of the slightly raised eyebrow as the Reverend William Thackeray looked from Sarah to her embarrassed husband.

'Sarah is the complete boss's daughter,' said Josh.

'I am not a snob, Josh,' Sarah said. 'The Cornish miner is the best in the world. I have heard my father and his friends say so many times. But he should keep to working in a mine and leave the running of it to those who are experienced in such things.'

Preacher Thackeray recognised there was a basic difference of opinion between the couple and he launched into the sort of traditional smalltalk that Sarah was used to hearing from the Hayle preachers.

William Thackeray only briefly mentioned Sarah's attitude. That was when Josh walked beside the minister's pony as far as the Sharptor mine. 'Your wife is a charming girl, Josh. She shows her breeding. I don't think you'll have an easy time convincing her of the justice of unionism.'

'Sarah will think differently about it when she understands it better. The only talk she has heard until now has been against it.'

'I ought to send Miriam on a visit to convert her,' said the preacher as he dug his heels into the pony's ribs.

Watching as pony and rider merged with the dark shadows along the path, Josh thought it might be as well if Sarah and Miriam did not meet. He knew instinctively they would strike sparks from each other.

Sarah was not the only one to be unhappy at Josh's involvement with the unionists. But Theophilus Strike had none of Sarah's charm to offset his displeasure. Josh had never seen the mine-owner in an angrier mood.

He went for Josh as soon as he arrived at the Wheal Sharptor, a few days after the Kit Hill fire.

When Josh entered the office he was standing behind the mine captain's large desk.

'Joshua!' Strike's voice was normally loud and now his words fairly thundered out. 'What's this nonsense I've heard about you being involved with the criminals who burned down the Kit Hill mine shop?'

'I know nothing about the burning-down of the Kit Hill store,' Josh replied, meeting the mine-owner's eyes and keeping his voice normal.

'Don't lie to me, Joshua. I have it from a very reliable source that you were at the meeting that preceded the burning of the shop.'

'Then your reliable source will have told you I warned the miners against taking any unlawful action.'

'So you don't deny attending this meeting of Kit Hill riff-raff?'

'I don't deny it, Mr Strike. I'm of the opinion the Kit Hill miners have a just grievance.'

Theophilus Strike looked at him in amazement. 'Do you realise what you are saying? You have the nerve to stand there and tell me quite blatantly that you support men who burn a building to the ground? Five rogues are due to stand trial for just such support. Are you quite mad, Joshua?'

'I'm not mad, Mr Strike, any more than those five miners are guilty of involvement in the burning of the mine store. They were arrested before the meeting. The only thing of which they are guilty is of speaking their minds about the prices in the Kit Hill mine store.'

Theophilus Strike leaned forward across the desk, supporting his weight on clenched fists.

'I've a good mind to dismiss you here and now. Anyone who condones violence among miners and refuses to deplore the destruction of mine property is a dangerous man to have around.'

Josh paled at the threat but he refused to be cowed by the mine-owner.

'I've never condoned violence or supported the destruction of any property. I'm in sympathy with the Kit Hill miners because they have a just grievance. I don't expect you to understand; the Wheal Sharptor has never been run along Kit Hill lines. The miners here earn a good wage and the shop prices are fair. That's why this mine is free from trouble. A fair wage for a fair day's work is all that any miner wants.'

The mine-owner continued to glare but waited for Josh to continue.

'Perhaps if I quote some prices charged at the Kit Hill store you'll begin to understand.' He began with the prices of food-stuffs – they were roughly twice the normal. Then he mentioned candles, and the tools a miner needed below ground – some were almost four times the fair price. Theophilus Strike was a merchant, aware of the wholesale prices of the items Josh mentioned.

'That's preposterous!' he declared when Josh had finished. 'I don't believe it.'

'It's easy enough to prove,' replied Josh. 'Ask any of the men who had to pay those prices. Then add the interest that the store-keeper levied on those whose payments fell behind.'

Josh had succeeded in shaking Strike, but he was an owner, not a miner.

'Even if the Kit Hill miners were being robbed, what business is it of yours? You're an engineer, not a miner. Why did you go to this meeting?'

'I was asked to go with a friend from the Wheal Caradon,' replied Josh. 'I went because I'm interested in miners. I try to make their work easier by introducing such things as the man-lift. I'll do anything within my power to help them lead safer and more comfortable lives.'

Taking a deep breath he put into words what he had hardly been able to channel into conscious thought before.

'I'm an engineer now, Mr Strike. I have you to thank for that. But long before I learned to be an engineer I was a miner's son. I would take food to him on the days when sheer exhaustion caused him to oversleep and rush off to work without anything to eat. I've crawled along tunnels scarcely high enough for me to wriggle through. If there had recently been an explosion there was more dust than air. In side-tunnels all the way along I could hear the echoes of men coughing up what was left of their lungs.

'I can remember my father crushing me against the wall of the shaft so I wouldn't be knocked off the ladder, as a man – no, a boy – one who'd been like a brother to me – fell to his death because his hands were too numb to keep a grasp on the rungs. Then I went home and spent the night listening to the heart-break of a widow only a couple of years older than myself.

'Then there were the evenings when I went to the top of the shaft to wait for my father to come up from shift. The good days were the ones when he was working on one of the upper levels. He might be able to manage a "Hello, son," after ten or fifteen minutes. The bad days were the ones when he was down at the deeper levels, when he wouldn't even see me. He'd crawl from the shaft and collapse on to his belly, sucking in air with such a noise I feared his lungs might burst. It would take him half an hour to regain the strength and breath to get to his feet and walk home with me. Sometimes I couldn't bear to stand and watch him and I'd run off on to the moor. When I got home he'd ask me why I hadn't met him. I'd lie and say I'd forgotten.

'No son should see his father in that condition, Mr Strike – defeated, crawling like a wounded animal from a hole in the ground. Those evenings when I ran away from watching him on the ground I'd walk on the moor, begging God to give me the opportunity to help him and the other men like him. Some of the older men were in an even worse condition. They would try desperately to get to their feet at the same time as the younger men, frightened that the mine captain might see them and decide they were too old to work at the bottom levels where the money could be earned.

'I worked at Hayle, Mr Strike. I was determined to master engineering. It was a way of making sure my sons would never have to see me lying on the ground at the top of a mine shaft. That's why, when Trevithick gave me the plans for a man-lift,

I built it without asking anyone – in case you tried to stop me. But it doesn't end there. Other things in a miner's life are just as wrong. If he's lucky he might live to be forty-five years old. For every one of those years he's had to put up with unbelievable hardships at work and little enough comfort at home.

'I've seen that there's more to life than that. I've ridden in a coach, galloped a horse – one with a saddle on it. I've been to a concert and heard music I never knew existed. I've seen what life is like outside a mine. I'm realistic enough to know that every miner can't become a gentleman overnight. But there must be more for him than bed, drink and work.

'Maybe that's why I went to that meeting. Perhaps I wanted to tell them something of what I've just told you.'

'It's as well you didn't, Joshua. They would probably have laughed at you. You are too young and too sensitive to take that.'

Strike was looking at Josh in a strange way. 'You're a humanitarian, Joshua. I fear you'll find it an unrewarding field of endeavour.'

His anger had completely gone.

'I respect your motives, but I question the effect they will have upon the men and upon you – especially upon you. I'll be perfectly honest with you, Joshua. I rode here with the express intention of dismissing you. I had no thought of giving you a hearing. Now I have and I can respect your sincerity. But I must doubt your cause and I feel sure I'll be called upon to defend my tolerance in the future. However, just so long as I have no trouble in the Wheal Sharptor I will accept your right to pursue your beliefs.'

Josh began to thank the mine-owner, but Theophilus Strike cut him short with an impatient gesture. 'Don't thank me, Joshua. I'm doing you no favour. In all probability I would be helping you more if I were to give you an ultimatum: forget your ideas or lose your post here. But I believe you have to work out your own destiny – and God help you!'

With that Theophilus Strike strode out of the office, leaving Josh feeling as though he had spent a long day working in the heat of the boiler-room.

Chapter Twenty

The Kit Hill miners kept the mine idle for a full week before an extraordinary meeting of the mine-adventurers was called. There it was reported that the engine-men were ready to join the miners.

The shareholders hurriedly arrived at a solution whereby the whole of the blame for the men's grievances was placed upon the mine captain. It was grossly unfair. The mine captain had done nothing more than follow the instructions of the adventurers. But this was an accepted hazard of a mine captain's job. With their scapegoat out of the way a settlement was agreed and the miners resumed work immediately. A new store went up on the site of the old one, with the promise that the prices of the goods sold would not exceed those of other mine stores.

But there was to be no happy ending for Harry Reeve and those arrested with him. When the miners demanded their release they were told the matter was out of the adventurers' hands. The miners' leaders had been arrested by the soldiers and sent for trial by the magistrate. Now the Law must pursue its ponderous relentless course. As the mine captain had been dismissed as a sop to the miners, so would their own leaders be arraigned as a reminder that there was always a price to be paid for each 'victory'.

The Law exacted a cruel price from the miners.

Preacher Thackeray attended the trial and late on the second day Josh saw him coming down from the high moor, riding direct from Bodmin.

When the preacher pulled his pony to a halt it was well lathered.

'The court found them guilty, Josh.'

It came as no surprise. The whole countryside had been expecting it.

'And the sentence?'

'Fourteen years' transportation!'

Josh winced. It was a vicious sentence. Except in very very rare cases such a punishment meant banishment for life. A man was shipped abroad, usually to Australia, to work as a convict for the duration of his sentence. Upon its expiration he was 'free' to work for his fare home – if he could find someone to pay him more than a subsistence wage and was able to keep his money safe for the years it would take him to save the fare.

'What are we going to do about it?'

'That's what I hoped you would say, Josh. Fetch your horse and we'll go to see the men at Kit Hill. I would like to see a march on Bodmin Jail. We'll show the judges that the miners will not accept this without a struggle.'

Josh saddled Hector and rode out to join William Thackeray, closing his ears to Sarah's protests. Her dislike of unionism had hardened since a weekend visit home two weeks before and she made no secret of her disapproval. Neither would she speak to Preacher Thackeray now.

But, if William Thackeray expected the Kit Hill miners to down tools and make an immediate protest at the sentence inflicted on their colleagues, he was bitterly disappointed.

The miners were sorry to hear the news. Shocked even. It was a 'shame'. But when action was suggested they looked down at the ground, up at the sky, and shuffled their feet uncomfortably.

''Tis difficult, you see,' said one of the miners, summing up the situation. 'We'd love to do something to help 'em.

But we've got to think about our families now, haven't we? I mean, we didn't have a proper week's pay when we was striking. We've got to make that up. Besides, the adventurers might not take it kindly if we stopped work again.'

'But Harry Reeve and the others have families too,' said Josh. 'And their children are receiving no money. All this because they wanted to help you!'

''Tis sad, I agree,' said the spokesman. 'But it won't help them if we lose our jobs as well. Will it, now?'

Josh bit back the retort that the imprisoned men had lost far more than their jobs on behalf of the Kit Hill miners. There was no moving them.

The most that William Thackeray could get from the miners was a half-promise to attend a prayer-meeting outside the Jail gates the next Sunday afternoon. It had to be designated a prayer-meeting. All other public meetings were banned on a Sunday.

Not surprisingly, the other mines in the area were not prepared to give Preacher Thackeray more support than the Kit Hill miners. He had to be content with the projected prayer-meeting. The Caradon miners promising him a hundred-per-cent turn-out.

As the horses' heads were turned towards St Cleer, Josh expressed his disgust at the attitude of the Kit Hill miners.

The preacher shook his head sorrowfully. 'I learned long ago not to be surprised or disappointed at anything. When there should be gratitude there is complete indifference. Good deeds are repaid with bad, and there sometimes seems very little sense in preaching the fellowship of man. But it must be done or the world will slide back into darkness. It's a new experience for you. One not easy to accept. But don't blame the Kit Hill miners too much. They came close to losing their livelihoods. It brought them face to face with the realities of its consequences. They don't care to risk it again for fear their luck might not hold good.'

'What about the men who have been sentenced to transportation for their sakes? Don't they count for anything?'

'Of course they do. But they knew what might happen to

them because of their beliefs. They accepted it. There will be others who'll suffer for the same cause. But one day we'll win. We must win in order to stop miners risking their lives thousands of feet below ground without getting reasonable pay and conditions. That's what this is all about, Josh. Each tiny victory, no matter how small, is another step closer to that goal.'

Josh did not go on to St Cleer with William Thackeray. Instead he turned off and took a short cut to Sharptor.

Sarah was busying herself in the kitchen, and the exaggerated clatter of tins told Josh that she was not in the best of moods. Nevertheless, he told her the results of his trip to Kit Hill with William Thackeray.

'Well! What else did you expect?' she snapped. 'You don't think anyone will thank you for meddling in their affairs, do you? They burned down the store and they know that someone must be punished for it. You are a fool to get yourself involved with them. Mother thinks so too.'

Josh paused in the act of putting a mug of water to his lips.

'What has your mother got to do with it?'

'We spoke about it when I was home.'

'Oh?'

Sarah flushed. 'Isn't it natural for a girl to talk over her problems with her mother?'

'I hadn't realised I was a problem.'

Sarah looked hurt. 'You know very well what I mean, Josh. It worries me to see you mixed up with something like this. It's dangerous.'

'It worried Theophilus Strike too. But at least he heard me out and tried to understand why I feel so strongly about the union. That's more than you'll do. You've decided to close your mind to anything connected with unionism and that's the truth of it.'

'I have more important things to occupy my mind,' said Sarah.

'What sort of things? Whether to do the washing on a Tuesday instead of a Monday? Wondering whether the blue dress looks nicer than the pink one to wear into Launceston market?'

It was spiteful and he knew it, but it was out before he could bite it back.

Sarah placed the pan she was holding carefully in the cupboard and dried her hands upon her apron before answering him.

'No. The sort of thing that is occupying my mind at the moment is whether I will bear you a son or a daughter.'

Josh's expression of utter astonishment was very satisfying.

'You – you're pregnant?'

'Yes.'

'But why didn't you tell me? Why didn't you say something about it before?'

'You have been so involved with this silly union business that I was scarcely able to gain your attention for long enough to tell you anything. Anyway, I wasn't absolutely sure. That's why I went home to see Mother.'

'You could have spoken to my mother about it. She would have told you anything you wanted to know.'

'I couldn't have asked her about something like this, Josh. It was difficult enough to discuss with my own mother. Dr Scott examined me and told me for sure, though.'

'Why did you see the doctor? Is something wrong?'

His concern brought an answering smile from Sarah and she was no longer angry with him. 'Of course not. It is usual for a woman who is having a baby to see a doctor. And I have known Dr Scott all of my life.'

'Jenny didn't see a doctor when she was expecting.'

'Well, I am not Jenny,' said Sarah sharply. 'And I want a doctor to be with me when I have my baby.' She looked suddenly unhappy. 'You haven't even said you are pleased about it!'

'Of course I'm pleased.'

He took her into his arms and kissed her very gently. 'And I think you're very clever. What's more, if I like it I'll allow you to have lots more . . .'

*　　*　　*

Jesse and Ben Retallick were delighted with the news when Sarah and Josh visited the cottage the following evening and told them.

'I've expected it for some weeks,' exclaimed Jesse as she beamed at her daughter-in-law.

'How?' Sarah glanced quickly down at her stomach. 'There is nothing to see yet.'

'I've seen it in your face. That's where it shows first.'

'You'll find life is a bit different with a baby around,' said Ben Retallick, grinning from the comfort of his arm-chair. 'You can forget what a good night's sleep is like for a start.'

'Nonsense!' Josh said. 'You're forgetting I was here when Jenny had little Gwen with her. She was no trouble at all.'

'Not to you, she wasn't,' said Jesse. 'You slept through most of her crying. You can't do that when it's your own.'

She put a tea-pot on the table and looked pointedly at Josh. 'And perhaps having a child around will keep you home in the evenings.'

'What's that supposed to mean?' asked Josh.

'You know well enough. Gallivanting off with that preacher from St Cleer. I breathed a sigh of relief when you came back from Hayle and saw nothing of him for a while. But from what I hear you've taken up with him again, riding around to meetings of miners and stirring up trouble. It's a pity he doesn't spend more time preaching and less time urging miners to do things they wouldn't think of left to themselves.'

'Then you'll be pleased to hear he is holding a special prayer-meeting tomorrow,' said Josh. 'Outside Bodmin Jail. To pray for the five men who have been sentenced to trans-portation. He hopes to gather as many people as possible so their singing might give encouragement to the men inside.'

'That sounds as though it has all the promise of a mob,' said Ben Retallick seriously.

'No, Preacher Thackeray will keep it in hand. There'll be no violence.'

'You are not going?' This from Sarah.

'Yes. I've promised Preacher Thackeray I'll be there. But I'm so certain nothing bad is intended that you can come along with me and see for yourself.'

'I'll have no part of any of Preacher Thackeray's meetings,' declared Sarah, and Jesse agreed with her.

On the way home that evening Sarah asked, 'Will Preacher Thackeray's wife be going to the meeting tomorrow?'

'I doubt it. Why do you ask?'

'No special reason,' said Sarah, much too casually. 'But I heard she often speaks at meetings. I wondered . . .'

'This is a prayer-meeting, a service,' answered Josh. 'I expect Miriam will have other things to do. But why don't you come along and see for yourself?'

Sarah did not go, and Josh was wrong. Miriam was very much in evidence.

She had persuaded Mrs Reeve, wife of the imprisoned union leader, to come with her, together with three score miners' wives.

There was a huge attendance at the 'prayer-meeting'. By the time Preacher Thackeray was ready to begin the service there must have been close to a thousand miners standing in the shadow of the high grey prison wall. They had come from Kit Hill, Caradon, St Austell and as far west as Redruth. On the edge of the crowd, their cloaks and dresses rustling in the wind, the women formed a small group.

A number of interested townspeople hung about the fringe of the gathering, curious to hear what Preacher Thackeray would have to say. They did not stay long. News of the proposed service had reached official ears, and no sooner had the preacher called, 'Let us pray,' than the huge iron-studded gates of the prison swung open and an infantry officer marched out at the head of forty soldiers. The townsfolk immediately scattered to watch the proceedings from a safer distance.

The soldiers left the prison in a double file, marching along the road into Bodmin town until they had cleared the edge of the crowd. Then, at an order from the officer, they wheeled left, keeping a distance of twenty yards between themselves and the miners. The officer barked out another order and one file of twenty men began marking time while the other column carried on. When they formed one single line with the others they too began marking time until the whole line was called to a smart halt.

At the command 'Left turn!' the soldiers faced inwards towards the miners. Only the spongy grass prevented the precision of their movement being fully appreciated as their feet stamped down in unison.

Ignoring the military presence Preacher Thackeray called upon his vast congregation to pray with him.

They had hardly begun murmuring the Lord's Prayer when the harsh parade-ground voice of the officer rang out.

'Attention there! By assembling here today you are breaking the law which forbids such gatherings on a Sunday. As an officer of Her Majesty's Army I order you to disperse peaceably in the name of the Queen. If you refuse I will carry out my duty and break up this illegal meeting.'

Preacher Thackeray continued in his prayer until the 'Amen' was said.

'Do you hear me? I order you to disperse immediately.'

There was a long silence before the officer called his men to come to attention and 'order arms', a command which brought their musket-butts down on the ground.

Quietly and deliberately Miriam led the women to form a line between the soldiers and the miners. The move caused the soldiers to glance uneasily at their officer.

'At the command "Take up firing positions" . . .,' the officer called, but Preacher Thackeray interrupted him in a voice as authoritative as his own.

'By what law do you seek to break up a service of divine worship?'

'The by-laws of this borough. I am empowered to order you in the Queen's name to abandon this meeting and go home in an orderly and quiet manner.'

'Do the by-laws of this borough override the laws of England? Since when has the misuse of Her Majesty's name been sufficient to flout the will of Parliament? This is not a "meeting" as you will persist in calling it. I am a minister of the Methodist Church and am conducting a perfectly legal religious service. Furthermore, if you persist in your interruptions I will call the Constable and have you arrested for the contemptuous disturbance of persons assembled for religious worship. Since you appear to be sadly lacking in knowledge of the Law I will tell you. It is an offence punishable at the Court of Quarter Sessions and you will be held in custody until the day of the trial.'

There was nervous laughter from a section of the miners. It ceased immediately when Preacher Thackeray frowned in their direction.

The officer was perplexed, but he had started something and his training told him that once a course of action had been decided upon it should be carried through to a conclusion, however wrong it might ultimately prove to be. He barked out an order and forty muskets came to the firing position, albeit reluctantly and with less precision than the soldiers had shown until now.

The women in front of the miners closed ranks determinedly, and their move caused more unease among the soldiers.

'We can't shoot at women . . .'

'Silence!' It was the same voice, but the face behind it was the pallor of the granite walls.

'If you fire and kill anyone in this congregation you will hang for it. Each one of you who pulls a trigger will be guilty of as foul a murder as any to have been tried in the courts of this country.'

The breeze was not strong, and the forty muskets waved more violently than the ribbons of the women who faced them.

'Sarge, we can't shoot them, can we? He can't order us to do that.'

'Shut up!' The soldier with three gold stripes on his arm spoke in a hoarse whisper that carried to the miners. 'He's the one who's giving the orders. If anyone's neck is going to be stretched it'll be his, not yours.'

The uncertain silence that followed was broken by the even voice of Preacher Thackeray.

'We will sing our praises to the Lord.'

He began to sing, taking the first line on his own until the clear voice of Miriam joined him. Other women and miners followed, and the words of the hymn hung heavy in the air.

Halfway through the second verse the singing swelled to a powerful and triumphant crescendo. The soldiers were leaving! Looking neither to right nor left the officer led his men back on to the road. Pausing only to form twos, the bright-coated infantrymen marched back into the jail and the heavy doors banged shut behind them.

The service went on for another hour and a half but it was now something of an anti-climax. The miners had witnessed an incident that would be told and retold in every mine in Cornwall. Inside the forbidding jail, in that mysterious way imprisoned men have of gleaning and passing on every single crumb of information from that faraway world outside the high walls, the prisoners knew of the miners' triumph over the military long before the service had ended.

It was news that would have gladdened the hearts of Henry Reeve and his fellow-unionists had they been there to hear it. But, unknown to those outside Bodmin Jail, they had been moved the previous day and were now being held in the foul-smelling, rotting prison-hulk lying off Devonport. They had set foot on Cornish soil for the last time.

The miners had scored a small point. The game had gone to the other side.

Chapter Twenty-One

By December in that year of 1844 the exiled miners were three
months distant from England. Cornwall had experienced more
than twice its normal winter rainfall, and it still wanted a week
to Christmas. The clouds hung around the crags of Sharptor
like a veil. For months there had not been two consecutive
dry days. Water poured from the high moor in a thousand
angry rivulets, forming deep dangerous ponds in the 'old
men's' ancient diggings. In the depths of the working mines
the water oozed from wall and roof as though the rock were
a sodden sponge.

Josh should have been leaving with Sarah to spend Christmas
with her parents at Hayle, but the abnormally wet state of
the deeper shafts was causing some concern in the Wheal
Sharptor. The great engine was pumping at twice its normal
speed yet barely managing to hold its own against the water.
A pump-rod cracked with the extra strain placed upon it,
threatening to tip the scales against the men who worked the
mine. Had it broken without warning it would have wiped
out the mine's profits for a whole year. As it was, Josh and
his helpers had the pump-rod changed inside two hours.

In these conditions, Josh felt he could not leave the mine
without an engineer. In spite of Sarah's sulking and bad
humour he decided to stay on at the mine for a while longer.

'You don't *have* to stay!' she said for the fifth time that morning.

'I *do* have to stay,' he repeated patiently. 'If the pump stopped for very long the mine would flood beyond recovery. You've left Hector for me. I'll ride him to Hayle on Christmas Eve to join you.'

'I shouldn't have to travel alone in my condition,' Sarah said petulantly. 'Anything could happen.'

'You'll be in a coach with other people. The baby isn't due for nearly five months. If the travelling worries you so much, then don't go. Stay here and we'll have Christmas in our own home.'

'No. It has been ages since I saw my family and I have had enough of Sharptor this winter. If I don't get out of this cloud for a few days I will go insane.'

Some women glow with a new vitality and happiness when they become pregnant. Sarah was not one of these. She felt heavy and awkward, and tired very easily. It had not helped her humour when old Mary Crabbe came up to the house to pay her customary pre-natal visit. It was part of local tradition. No village woman was ever entirely convinced she was going to have a baby until Mary Crabbe had been to the house.

But Sarah was impressed by neither the old crone's reputation nor her appearance.

'I will not have that woman delivering my baby!' she declared when Mary Crabbe had left the house. 'Did you see her hands? They were absolutely filthy; her nails looked as though she had been sorting ore!'

'Those were the hands that delivered me,' replied Josh, 'and just about every other baby in the district.'

'That may be so, but she won't be delivering my baby!'

Whether or not Sarah's undisguised displeasure was the reason, Mary Crabbe paid only the one visit to the house. Some days later she was talking to Jesse Retallick and, when the coming baby was mentioned, Mary Crabbe turned away without a word, leaving Josh's mother standing alone in the village street looking after her.

A light carriage sent by Theophilus Strike took Sarah to St

Cleer. There she transferred to the bulky post-carriage that would carry her the remainder of the way. Josh loaded her cases and fussed about her, settling her into her seat with a blanket wrapped about her legs.

'Now, you take care,' he said, 'and keep well wrapped. I'll be with you on Christmas Eve and will bring your presents with me.'

'I wish you were coming with me now,' declared Sarah. All at once she looked very young and vulnerable.

'So do I,' said Josh honestly, 'but it won't be long. In the meantime you'll be surrounded by your family. They'll make you feel like the Queen.'

'Not until you join me, Josh.' She kissed him and clung to him for so long he became embarrassed for the coachman standing waiting patiently. But Sarah had seen the door of the preacher's house swing open and, though she could not see who was standing back from the doorway, she did not release her hold until the door was closed again.

Josh waited until the coach swayed from view at the bottom of the hill before turning and heading back to Sharptor.

Sarah will feel better for a few days' rest, he thought as he arrived back at the house and changed into his working clothes to go to the mine. She'll be her old bright and happy self when I see her again on Christmas Eve.

But for the second time in his life the weather spoiled his Christmas plans and decreed that it would be longer than a few days before they met once more. The day after Sarah left the wind changed direction and the temperature dropped rapidly. The snow began to fall at dusk and gradually put a covering on the sodden ground. It snowed until the rivulets were no more than thin cracks of water a foot below the crust of the snow. Then the wind increased, and snow and wind vied in their efforts to outdo each other.

The equal battle raged for five days before a brief truce was called on Christmas Eve. From the bedroom window of the house Josh looked down the slope of the moor and along the valley beyond. It was a pure white featureless world, with neither track nor hedge showing through the snow. The wind had banked the snow against the walls of the few cottages within view. Had he not known exactly where they were situated he would not have been able to pick them out from any other mound of snow.

Josh had tried to leave the house and make his way to the mine earlier. For half an hour he had dug from the front doorway to clear what he at first thought was a drift, only to discover that the snow was lying to a depth of four feet on that east-facing slope. He had never known a snowfall like it.

At ten o'clock Nehemeziah arrived at the house, plodding behind two big shire-horses harnessed in line to stamp out a path from the mine to the house.

'Never known such weather,' said the wizened old hostler as they made their way together to the mine. 'And there's more'n a bucketful up there.' He raised his eyes to the heavy dark sky.

Ben Retallick was warming his hands at the boiler fire when Josh arrived.

'There will be no Christmas at Hayle for you this year, Josh.'

'No,' Josh agreed. 'And Sarah won't be too pleased about that. She tried hard to get me to go with her last weekend.'

'You couldn't have done that – not with the weather we've been having and the water in the mine.'

'That's what I told Sarah. She wasn't convinced then – and she certainly won't be today!'

'Never mind, Josh.' Ben Retallick could not suppress a sympathetic smile at Josh's forlorn expression. 'If women weren't so contrary they wouldn't be women. I was going to add that you'd learn that one day, but you won't. Your mother can still surprise me by taking off after something I've said in all innocence. You'll be spending Christmas with us, of course?'

Josh nodded.

'Good! That will please your mother. Jenny and Tom will be there with young Gwen. And Wrightwick.'

'I won't be down until midday,' said Josh. 'If I'm not going to Hayle I'll come down here and spend the morning firing the furnace. The engine-man can have the morning with his family.'

Tapping one of the boiler-gauges he said, 'How is the water in the lower levels? I'd like to slow the pump down a bit if possible. It was never built for high-speed work.'

'We should get a few easier days before the thaw,' said Ben Retallick. 'But I'm going down there now. I'll let you know whether the water is tailing off when I come back up.'

'You'll be better off down below than outside, Cap'n Retallick,' said an old surface-worker, pounding snow from his clothing as he came into the engine-house. 'It's started snowing again.'

When he got home that evening Josh cleared a path to the stables across the old farmyard and forked plenty of hay down from the loft for Hector. It was as well he did. By morning another eighteen inches of snow had fallen and Josh floundered to the mine along the path cleared by Nehemeziah the previous day.

The engine-man had been drinking, and the fire was much lower than it should have been. Josh made no complaint. He knew that the man would have spent the whole night singing to prevent himself from hearing the sound of the 'knockers', who were reputed to take over the mine workings on this special night. If the engine-man needed something to help him keep up his courage there was no one who would criticise him for it. It was a brave man who would defy generations of superstitious fear and remain alone in the vicinity of a mine for the whole of Christmas Eve night.

The morning passed quickly for Josh, and when the relief engine-man arrived at lunch-time he walked to the Retallick cottage in a light flurry of snow.

It was a Christmas like so many others that Josh had shared with his family, but his thoughts kept turning towards Hayle and the Christmas he should have been having with his wife. He could not help feeling guilty about not being with her.

'You're not going to frighten the snow away by looking out there,' said Jenny as he glanced out of the window for the dozenth time.

'No, I suppose not,' he grinned wryly. 'I only hope there's snow like this at Hayle.'

'Don't worry yourself about that,' said Ben. 'This goes a bit further than Hayle. I doubt whether there is a passable road in the country. It's worse than the time when you were an apprentice and couldn't get home for Christmas. The way the wind has set there'll be little change for a week or two.'

'Sarah will be all right, Josh,' said his mother. 'She'll be snug and warm in that nice house, with her family to look after her and spoil her a little.'

'Yes. We must all count our blessings,' said Wrightwick Roberts pompously. 'There are a great many folk in far more uncomfortable circumstances than ourselves and those we love.'

'The Kit Hill miners on their way to Botany Bay, for instance,' said Josh.

Wrightwick Roberts did not agree with unionism and he disapproved most strongly of the actions of his fellow-preacher at St Cleer.

'They received what they deserved,' he said. 'They knew the law.'

'And they broke no law.' Josh thought an argument with the preacher might take his mind off Sarah. 'It was an improper trial. Harry Reeve and the others committed no crime because they were in the Callington lock-up when the Kit Hill store was burned down. They never incited anyone else to do it because they were arrested before they had a chance to speak to their men.'

'The Law must be upheld,' said Wrightwick Roberts dogmatically. 'The courts of this land are there to administer justice. They do it well enough.'

'Just as they did with the young boy at the last Launceston Assizes,' retorted Josh. 'You remember it, Wrightwick? Thirteen years old, wasn't he? Caught stealing two gallons of potatoes to help keep his family from starving. It was the Lord Chief Justice himself who judged that case. Supposedly the fairest man in the land. What sentence did he pass on that boy? Tell us, Wrightwick?'

The preacher squirmed in his seat.

'Yes, I see you remember. It's something no man in Cornwall should ever forget. Penal servitude for life – at the age of thirteen! Some might argue that such a sentence is justice, but it was tempered with precious little mercy.'

'Now then, you two. What sort of a conversation is this for Christmas Day? Ben, put another couple of logs on that fire and Jenny will give us a verse of a Christmas hymn. One we can join in with.'

Wrightwick Roberts smiled sheepishly and the family Christmas resumed, the harmony broken only when little Gwen got a piece of Jesse's special cake lodged in her throat. She had to be up-ended while Tom Shovell thumped on her back.

It was the new year before a gentle thaw set in. Not until the sixth day of January was Josh able to send a letter off to Sarah with the coach from St Cleer. Afterwards he called in to visit William Thackeray, but he had gone to Liskeard to meet a preacher from London passing through *en route* for the port of Falmouth.

Miriam invited Josh into the house and he sat in the kitchen while she made him tea and gave him the latest news of the local unions. There was increasing support for it from the miners. But as support grew, so did the opposition of the mine-adventurers.

'They fear the power the miners will hold,' reported Miriam. 'And so they should.'

Watching her move about the kitchen Josh was once more stirred by the cross-current of feelings she provoked in him. There was something almost boyish in the free way she moved, her strides long and certain. But the masculinity ended there. Her figure was completely feminine: slim and firm.

'We've got to get every miner into the union,' she went on fiercely, unaware of his appraisal. 'When the last man joins life will begin anew for everyone. The miner will enjoy a standard of life he's not yet aware of.'

'Not all mine-owners breathe fire, and drink miners' blood for breakfast, Miriam.'

She smiled as she handed him his tea. 'Working for Theophilus Strike is inhibiting your enthusiasm. He's the one flaw in our argument against the adventurers. But mining is a family business for him. He takes an interest in the way things are run, not merely in how much profit goes into his pocket.'

She stood in the centre of the kitchen and her smile became the cheeky grin of a younger Miriam. 'But he hasn't always been a good judge of men. Do you remember Herman Schmidt and that day in Bodmin?'

'I remember. He had a very heavy hand.'

'Poor Josh!' Her look was warm. 'All to defend the honour you thought I was anxious to sell.'

'No, I realised what you were doing. I was only worried that his eagerness might prove stronger than your cunning.'

'Shame! I wasn't worth it, was I? It would have been better had you walked away, not caring whether Schmidt did what he wanted with me. It would have saved us both a lot of hurt if you hadn't cared so much.'

'Didn't you care just as much, Miriam? Or did I imagine your tears when we were returning on the wagon?'

'Yes, I cared. I cared so much that when I needed to I was incapable of thinking straight. Caring is a painful emotion, Josh. It makes you so much more sensitive and puts life under a magnifying-glass, making it larger than it really is.'

It was perhaps fortunate that there was a diversion at this juncture. It came in the form of a loud cry from another room. Miriam said, 'That's Daniel.'

Josh had not seen the boy since the day Miriam had visited the house at Sharptor, almost a year before. Usually when Josh called Daniel was 'in bed' or 'with his grandmother'.

Before Miriam returned to the room he could hear her talking in low endearing tones. When she opened the door she bore in her arms a sturdy little boy, no longer a baby but a child with stabbing fingers and big blue eyes.

'Hello, Daniel. My, but you've grown into a tough little chap!'

Daniel tucked his chin in and pretended not to look at Josh.

'I believe you're shy!'

Daniel turned and grabbed his mother for safety and she hugged him to her.

'Are you hoping Sarah will have a son, Josh?'

He looked startled and she laughed. 'Oh, Josh! Don't tell me you're surprised that I know Sarah is carrying a baby? My mother lives in Henwood. Nothing happens there that isn't immediately common knowledge.'

He gave her a sheepish grin. 'I wasn't thinking. No, Miriam, I am hoping that Sarah will have a girl.'

Miriam was about to say that she thought a man always wanted sons to perpetuate his own image but she stopped herself quickly. It might direct the conversation to dangerous ground. It was not long before the sight of Miriam hugging Daniel to her, and having the boy looking at him from his Cornish blue eyes, began to cause an emotional upheaval inside Josh that he had no wish to analyse. He stood up to go.

'Won't you stay until William comes home, Josh? He should return within the hour. He'll be very sorry to have missed you. Stay and have a meal with us.'

Josh shook his head. 'Thank you, but I've got some work to do at the Wheal Sharptor. I shouldn't have come away but I wanted to send a letter.'

'Well, if you must. But come again soon, Josh.'

At the gate Miriam said something to the child in her arms and Daniel waved to him. Josh returned the wave before swinging into the saddle of Hector and heading the horse towards the Wheal Sharptor. He had to fight the animal all the way. During the bad weather Hector had been kept inside without exercise and now he wanted to run. But the ground was in too treacherous a state for an uncontrolled gallop. So it was a thoroughly bad-tempered beast that Josh shut into the stable when he arrived home.

The house felt big and empty without Sarah. The emptiness

made Josh restless, unable to settle anywhere. He had hoped she would come home as soon as the roads were passable, but the snow thawed and a strong drying wind blew in from the east and still she did not return.

He was beginning to get anxious when a letter arrived with a wagoner. It had been sent from Hayle with one of the ore-boat captains. The sailor had scribbled a note on the outside of it apologising for the time it had taken to arrive – due, the captain had written, to conditions of the sea over which he had no control and which was as like to have driven the boat to the Americas as bring it to Looe.

Sarah's letter was a lengthy tale of woe. Her Christmas had been spoiled because Josh was not there with her. Her unhappiness had been infectious and spread to the whole family. She went on to chide Josh for not having come with her as she had begged him to before the snows came. Also, she said, she had been expecting a letter from him long before it actually arrived, as the snows at Hayle were cleared away before the turn of the year. Finally, she stated that worrying about Josh had brought her so low her mother had refused to allow her to travel until she was fully recovered in health and spirits.

The tone of the letter so alarmed Josh that he set off on Hector to ride to Hayle that weekend. Galloping across the moor and then along the open wind-swept road, he had only the turnpikes to think about. He reproached himself for not having considered Sarah more, for not leaving the Wheal Sharptor to cope without him for a few days. The mine employed enough sensible men to keep things running in the temporary absence of their engineer. Even that cracked pumping-rod might have been repaired after a fashion to await his return. There were too many other things that had occupied his mind when his main concern should rightly have been for his wife. He promised himself that he would make up to Sarah for his thoughtlessness.

After his resolutions and good intentions it came as an anticlimax to arrive at the Carlyon home and find nobody there. The shift foreman told him the family had gone out to visit friends. Who the friends were and at what time they might return the foreman was unable to say.

It was dusk and the light beginning to light up the windows of Hayle before the Carlyons' small coach rumbled in through the works gate.

Sarah did not look ill. She alighted laughing gaily with her sister. When he opened the front door of the house there was a confused silence before Sarah flung herself at him.

'Josh! What are you doing here?'

'I came because I received your letter telling me how ill you were.'

Sarah looked embarrassed, but her mother came to her rescue. 'And so she has been ill. So much so we were all most worried about her. Poor Sarah was so upset that you weren't here at Christmas she worked herself up into a terrible state. Today is the first day she has been anything like her old self. I thought a visit to St Ives to see her cousins would be good for her. And so it was. Getting out of the house and into the sea air has worked wonders. Poor child! But I expect she will be better now you are here.'

Sarah squeezed his arm affectionately. 'It's lovely to see you, Josh.'

'I'm very relieved to see you looking well,' he replied. 'I've been imagining all sorts of things as I rode down here.'

William Carlyon had been driving the carriage, and after handing it over to an hostler he came into the house and shook Josh's hand warmly. 'It's good to see you again, my boy. I've been surrounded by these women since before Christmas. I wondered how long it would be before you came to my rescue. Now, since no one else seems to be able to leave your side I'll get you a drink myself. What will you have?'

'I'll get them! I'll get them!' Mary ran to the cabinet which held the drinks and William Carlyon sighed, 'There you are, Josh. I spend a fortune educating the child and the only thing she really enjoys doing is serving drinks!'

Josh said he would have a brandy, and Mary selected the correct glass, poured the drink and handed it to him.

'I hear the weather has been quite severe on the moor,' said the works manager. 'Far worse than we experienced here – and we were unable to move far from the house.'

Josh told him of the snow and its results – of the small mines which had been forced to stop work completely, their stocks of coal exhausted; of the sheep, frozen to death and not discovered until the thaw uncovered the gullies where they had taken shelter.

'Yes, it's the worst weather in memory,' agreed the works manager. 'If we hadn't stockpiled iron ore the foundry would have been out of business. For ten days not a ship moved in or out of Hayle. It was a ghost port.'

'How is the house?' asked Sarah. 'Is there any damage from the storms?' Josh reassured her that the house and its outbuildings had stood up to the weather.

'Will you be able to stay with us for long?' asked William Carlyon.

Josh shook his head. 'Until Sunday only.'

There was an immediate outcry from the two girls, and Sarah said, 'Why, Josh? Why can't you stay for longer? Surely the mine can spare you for a few days?'

Josh put down his brandy and turned to face her. 'I thought you would want to come back with me. If you are feeling well enough.'

Mrs Carlyon threw up her hands in horror. 'It would be madness. The poor girl has been so ill. She shouldn't make a long journey while she is carrying a child.'

Since his arrival Josh had been nursing a suspicion that Sarah's mother was trying to arrange things so Sarah should have the baby at Hayle.

'The journey would be worse for her next week. Even more so the week after. I think the sooner she comes home the better.'

'Why not let her have her baby here, Josh?'

He had been right. Now it was out in the open.

'It would be much, much better from Sarah's point of view.' Mrs Carlyon waxed enthusiastic. 'Just think. Someone would be here to care for her *all* the time. Dr Scott would be on hand. He's known Sarah since she was a child, and he's very good at delivering babies. Not only that; she would be more comfortable here. I mean no offence, of course. Your house is lovely and you're lucky to have it. But there are things here it takes years to gather together.'

'You have a very nice home, Mrs Carlyon. But it's not *our* home. That's at Sharptor. When it's near the time for the baby to come I'm sure my mother won't spend much time away from the house. And we have doctors there too.'

'I hope you're not referring to mine doctors,' Mrs Carlyon snorted. 'I wouldn't trust one of them to deliver a litter of pigs.'

'Josh is right.'

William Carlyon stood up and went to the drinks cupboard. On the way he paused by Sarah and gently ruffled her hair. 'Your mother finds it difficult to realise you're not still a little girl. You are a married woman now and your place is with your husband. Especially for the birth of your first child.'

He refilled his glass and looked towards his wife. 'Can you imagine what I would have said to your mother had she suggested you go home to her when you were expecting Sarah?'

It looked as though Mrs Carlyon was thinking up a further argument, so Josh said quickly, 'You are quite welcome to come and stay with us when it's nearly time.'

'No, Josh.' William Carlyon shook his head. 'It's your life. Yours and Sarah's. And it's your child. Nobody has the right to interfere with your arrangements for that. Sarah will come home with you on Sunday. The works hostler will take her in my carriage.'

He held up a hand to silence his wife as she was about to speak. 'I know Sarah hasn't been too well, but there's nothing wrong with her now.'

'Well! I'm only trying to do my best for Sarah. If that's going to be considered interference there's nothing more to be said, I'm sure! Come along, Mary. Upstairs and change your dress before you get it filthy playing about.'

She swept out of the room followed by Mary, who gave Josh a shy smile of support before she too went out.

'I think that could be termed a "royal exit",' commented William Carlyon. 'Now, if you'll excuse me, I need to check with the foreman that everything is well in the foundry.'

Sarah and Josh were silent for a few minutes after he left the room.

'Don't you want to come home, Sarah?' Josh said at last.

'Oh, Josh, of course I do!' Her eyes filled with tears and she gripped her hands in her lap. He reached for them and pulled her around to face him.

'Then what is it? Have you changed your mind about me? Don't you love me?'

'O-o-oh!' she wailed and leaned towards him, and he held her close.

'Then what is it? Something's very wrong. Won't you try to tell me?'

She pulled away from him and looked down at her hands from eyes that threatened to overflow.

'I'm scared, Josh.'

'Scared! Of what?'

She shrugged helplessly. 'Of everything. Of spending so much time on my own in the house. Of the moor. Of having the baby. Most of all having the baby.'

'But why haven't you told me this before? I thought you were happy. Don't you want the baby?'

'Yes! Yes, of course I do. I want it more than anything. It's just. . . . Oh, I don't know, Josh. I don't seem to have got to know anyone at Sharptor. Or in Henwood village. I feel as though I am a complete stranger there.'

'But, Sarah, you've only lived there for a short while. The folk are no better and no worse than they are anywhere else. They wouldn't force themselves upon you because they're afraid they might not be welcome, but if ever you were in trouble they would help without having to be asked. They are concerned about you. There isn't one of them who hasn't asked after you since news got around about the baby. Why, they've even asked after you as far off as St Cleer village.'

Sarah looked at him quickly. 'You mean Miriam?'

'Yes.'

She continued to look at him as he explained, 'I saw her when I put your letter on the coach. She already knew about the baby.'

'Do you wish you had married her instead of me?' Her bluntness took him by surprise.

'Is that what you believe?'

'I don't know what to believe. I only know that I get knotted up inside when you are off somewhere with that preacher because I think you might be talking to her. I imagine you will compare us and wish you had married her instead of me.'

He was relieved when she dropped her gaze.

'Sarah, I married you because I wanted to. Nobody forced me to do it. I was – and am – very proud to have you for my wife. I've known Miriam all my life. I couldn't forget her if I wanted to. But you are my wife and Miriam is married to my friend. Need I say any more?'

'No. I'm sorry, Josh. It isn't anything you have done. It's me. Don't take any notice. Women get like this when they are pregnant. Come upstairs with me while I change into something more comfortable. This dress was made for a slim young girl. Not a pregnant wife. It is cutting me in two. When I have changed we will see if we can put Mother in a good mood again.'

She rose from her chair and, taking Josh's hand, pulled him to his feet. She was far more relaxed now. 'Poor Josh, I've given you a bad time, haven't I? Never mind, we'll go back to Sharptor and I will be a good and dutiful wife to you.' She managed a pale but happy smile. 'And I do love you. Husband.'

They went home to Sharptor as planned on the Sunday and the next months were very happy ones for both of them. It snowed sporadically until the end of February but the snow rarely hung around for longer than two days at a time, and it was pleasant to sit indoors in front of a crackling log-fire with snow floating down outside. During these months the house on Sharptor became a home.

There was no shortage of work at the Sharptor mine. The

main pump needed an overhaul, and Josh worked hard with his trainees to complete it in record time. Meanwhile the water was kept under control by an emergency system that Josh rigged up.

Then there was his latest man-lift innovation in the secondary shaft. It was a cage-lift with improved gearing and a sophisticated indicating system enabling the winchman to know just where the cage was during the whole winching period. The gearing also meant that at shift-change time when there was no ore being carried the men could be taken down to the working levels and the off-going shift brought to grass in record time. In an emergency it could prove invaluable.

Josh showed the plans to Theophilus Strike, describing how it would work, one afternoon when the mine-owner was visiting Sharptor. Strike waxed enthusiastic about its potential.

'It's a great piece of engineering design,' he said. 'I can see it having uses in mines far beyond the Cornish border. You must patent it.'

Josh protested that it was merely an idea and would have to be proved first. But Theophilus Strike was not to be put off.

'It will work. Anyone with the slightest knowledge of mines can see that. And because it will work well it will be copied. If you won't patent it, then I'll do it for you. You sit down and copy out that plan you've shown to me. I'll do the rest.'

He was as good as his word. Later, when the system was installed in the Sharptor mine and had proved itself, he frequently brought fellow mine-owners to watch it at work. Within three months of its first trial run a mine-engineering company in the North of England negotiated with Josh to install similar systems in mines in their area. Josh was to receive a fair percentage of the profits they made on it.

The atrocious weather of the winter and the subsequent difficulties in travelling and communications meant that unionism remained in a near-dormant state, Josh not once venturing as far as St Cleer.

This pleased Sarah, mainly because it kept him away from

Miriam. In her present condition Sarah had become obsessive about William Thackeray's wife, although she managed to keep it from Josh. But she also thought Josh foolish to dabble in such dangerous nonsense when he could be working on new designs and inventions. Her father had told her Josh would rapidly become the world's foremost expert on mine safety equipment if he devoted more time and energy to it. Sarah wanted to push him into doing what she thought was right. She was too inexperienced as a woman to understand that Josh was one of those men who might be easily led in certain directions but who would never be pushed into anything.

Then, early in March, on a day when the moorland scrub was bowing before the fierce winds, the brief period of contentment came to an end in the house on Sharptor. Josh arrived home from the mine as it was growing dark to find Sarah lying back in the rocking-chair in the kitchen. Her face was pale and frightened, beads of perspiration standing out on her forehead and upper lip.

'Thank God you are here, Josh!' She rolled her head from side to side, wide-eyed, thoroughly alarming Josh. 'The baby. I think it's coming!'

A spasm of pain gripped her as she finished speaking. 'Oh! Josh, help me. Help me! Please!' Her shoulders hunched and a cry of agony broke from her lips as the muscles of her stomach contracted with fierce strength.

Josh gripped her forearms and shared her agony until the pain passed away.

'Don't move, Sarah. Stay here and I'll go and find the doctor.'

'No!' she screamed at him as he moved towards the door. 'Don't leave me, Josh! Don't leave me!'

'I must get help, Sarah. You need someone with you who knows what's happening.'

'No, stay with me, Josh . . .' Her voice rose and ended in a cry of animal anguish as the pain came back yet again.

Josh was in a terrible quandary. Sarah needed help. The baby was not due for another seven weeks, but there seemed little doubt that it was coming now. Something was seriously wrong, yet if he left her alone even for a short while she might become hysterical and do something to cause herself injury.

Then he heard a sound from the track that went past the house on to the moor. He opened the door and in the gloom made out the shape of a cart going up the hill towards Ward-brook, the farm situated a mile away on the moor.

'Hey! Stop!' He ran from the house, waving his arms, and the cart creaked to a halt. It was being driven by a lad of about sixteen, one of the Wardbrook farmer's sons.

'I need your help,' said Josh. 'My wife is in the house and our baby is coming two months too soon. Do you know where Captain Retallick lives?'

The boy shook his head. 'No, we don't have anything to do with mine folk. Pa says they're a blight on good farming land.'

He was slow of speech and far from bright, but he was Josh's only hope.

'Never mind.' He dug into his pocket and came out with a silver coin. 'Look! Here's a shilling for you. Run down to the mine and tell them that Sarah Retallick up at Idle Farm is starting her baby and needs help quickly. Have you got that?'

'I've got it.' He snatched the coin from Josh's fingers. 'But what about my horse and wagon?'

'Leave it. It won't go anywhere except home.'

Behind him in the house he could hear Sarah screaming again. 'Hurry, now. It's very urgent. I'm depending on you.'

The boy heard Sarah too. Jumping down from the cart he set off at an awkward lope along the path to the mine while Josh rushed back into the house to find Sarah struggling to her feet.

'I thought you had gone. Oh God, Josh, I'm scared! Help me.'

He held her tight until the latest spasm passed. Then he guided her gently upstairs to their bedroom. He turned back the bedclothes, talking all the time, telling her that help was coming, that soon everything would be all right.

'I think help will be too late, Josh. The waters have already burst. The baby is coming now.'

He undressed her and helped her into the special nightdress she had set aside for this occasion. The pains came twice more before she was safely in bed. By this time he was perspiring as much as Sarah.

He lit the lamps in the room and brought in two more.

'I'm just going down to put as much water on the stove as I can. That's what they did when young Gwen was born.'

'Don't be long, Josh. Don't leave me alone up here.'

He hurried downstairs, threw logs on to the fire and put all the pots and kettles he could find on the stove. Every few seconds he looked through the window, expecting to see help arriving.

Then an agonised scream from Sarah sent him rushing upstairs again.

'It's coming! It's coming! I can feel it! Help me! Help me!'

It was the last thing in the world that Josh felt capable of doing, but there was no alternative. Sarah was looking at him from eyes as large and frightened as a cornered doe.

'It's all right, Sarah. Lie back and try not to throw yourself about too much.'

'No! The baby. It's coming. I know it is.'

Her back arched with pain and she threw the bedclothes off her body.

Josh drew them right down and saw that Sarah was not exaggerating. Her frenzied thrashing had caused her nightdress to work up about her waist, and there, just emerging from her body, was the damp dark head of a baby. There was no time for nervousness now. He went to take hold of the baby's head but Sarah's body relaxed for an instant and the head returned inside her. Twice more contractions of pain threatened to force the baby from her, and twice it returned. Then, the third time, there was no denying it. The pain had her rolling and screaming in agony, but there was no return for the baby now. Josh had its head between his hands. He was never sure whether it was his doing or whether Nature supplied the twist that turned its shoulders. But suddenly the baby was there. He was holding it. A tiny damp bloody object, attached to the body in which it had grown by a thin, ridiculously long umbilical cord.

Sarah lay back on the bed, sucking in great noisy gulps of air and Josh was left wondering what to do with the motionless baby when belated help arrived. He heard the door open downstairs and his mother called, 'Josh! Sarah! Are you up there?'

'Come quickly. The baby's here.'

Jesse Retallick ran up the stairs and into the bedroom and saw Josh crouched holding the baby clear of Sarah's legs, frightened to straighten up.

'Has it cried yet?'

Josh looked startled.

'The baby. Have you made it cry?'

'No.' Josh shook his head, not comprehending.

Throwing off her cloak, Jesse Retallick took the baby from his hands and, hanging it head downwards by its ankles, slapped it on the backside. Once. Twice. Three times.

With a frown she put a finger inside its mouth checking that its tongue was down and the throat clear. Then she smacked it again. The fourth slap brought forth a low strangled cry. At the fifth its body jerked feebly and it gave another weak cry.

Jesse Retallick looked worried and Josh said, 'What's the matter. It's all right, isn't it? It's alive. It made a noise.'

The cry had been like the feeble mewing of a weak kitten. Jesse Retallick was unhappy.

'I wish Mary Crabbe was here,' she said. 'But she went to Callington for her brother's funeral and hasn't returned yet.'

'Shall I fetch a doctor?'

'Your father's gone for the mine doctor at the Phoenix. He's the nearest.'

'Josh. What is it? Is it a boy? Have I given you a son?'

Poor Sarah, exhausted by the pain and effort, opened her eyes as though coming out of a drugged sleep.

'It's a boy,' said Jesse Retallick.

'I'm glad,' Sarah murmured wearily. 'Can I hold him now?'

'Not yet, my love.' Jesse turned to Josh. 'Get me some of that hot water I saw on the stove. And some towels. I've got to cut the cord, and the afterbirth will have to be brought away. Hurry, now.'

Josh was only too pleased to have someone else to give the orders. Childbirth was a time for women. Men should have no part in it. Besides, there was something wrong. Whatever it was, his mother was far more capable of dealing with it than himself.

He ran up and down the stairs, carrying hot water and towels up and empty pots down to be refilled and set back on the stove.

After one such trip he arrived in the bedroom to discover that the baby now had a separate existence. Jesse was winding a strip of linen about the tiny waist, hiding the bloody knot that sealed off the severed umbilical cord.

She placed the baby in the small cot that was still not fully completed. As she tucked tiny blankets about it she said to Josh, 'I want hot-water bottles filled and brought up. You hear me?'

Josh nodded.

'Good. They are for the baby. While you fetch them I'll get on and help Sarah.'

Ben Retallick came into the kitchen as Josh was filling the earthenware bottles from the large kettle.

'It's a boy,' said Josh. 'I delivered it.' Then he noticed the angry frown on his father's face. 'Where's the doctor?'

'He was too drunk to get any sense out of. I wouldn't have let him touch a moorland sheep in that state. Are Sarah and the baby all right?'

'I don't think Mum is very happy with either of them. You'd better go and see her.'

Screwing the stopper into the second bottle he went up the stairs ahead of his father.

In the bedroom Jesse Retallick was kneading Sarah's stomach as though it was a pile of dough and without pausing in her efforts she looked questioningly at Ben.

'The doctor wasn't available,' he said, going across to the cot. 'Is this our grandson? Is he all right, Jesse?'

Jesse looked down at Sarah, making sure her eyes were firmly closed before shaking her head vigorously.

She left Sarah for a minute and, taking the hot-water bottles from Josh, wrapped them up well and pushed them down the side of the cot beside the still infant.

'There's no sense in trying to hide it.' She spoke in a whisper that would not carry across the room. 'The baby has come much too soon. It's a weakling. But I'm more worried about Sarah. She must have been in labour for a long time. She's desperately tired. The afterbirth has got to come away, but I'm getting no help from the poor girl. We must get a doctor from somewhere.'

'There's a new doctor at St Cleer,' said Josh. 'I'll saddle Hector and go and fetch him.'

'Hurry, Josh. I don't want to alarm you but I think Sarah's condition is serious. Oh! If only Mary Crabbe was here.'

Josh was already out of the room and on his way to the stable. Hector was not used to being disturbed after dark and having a saddle slung roughly on to his back. He showed his disapproval in no uncertain manner.

'Steady, boy! Steady! That's better. We've work to do tonight. You'll need the speed of the west wind. Come on, now.' Leading the horse from the stable he sprang into the saddle.

Fortunately there was a good moon. Fifty yards down the track Josh swung Hector on to the narrow path he had used when he went to St Cleer for his schooling. Hector took it at a fast canter, not rearing at shadows, though he once protested when a startled badger made a noisy departure from the path ahead of them.

The door of Dr McKinley's house was opened by his wife and Josh hurriedly explained the emergency.

'The doctor's visiting Preacher Thackeray,' she said. 'Tell him I'll have his bag ready and his horse saddled by the time he gets back here.'

Miriam opened the door to Josh but her warm welcoming greeting fell away before his enquiry for the doctor.

'He's playing chess in the lounge with William. What is it, Josh? Your father? Is it a mine accident?'

'No. It's Sarah and the baby. . . .'

Both men looked up in surprise as Josh flung open the lounge door.

'Why, Josh. . . .' William Thackeray rose to his feet. 'You look as wild as the moor. What is it?'

'I came for the doctor, William. Would you ride out to Sharptor with me, Dr McKinley? Our baby has arrived nearly two months before time. My mother says it's a weakling and there's something wrong with my wife. The afterbirth won't come. My father went for the Phoenix mine doctor but he was as drunk as a tinner when he found him.'

'You can tell me about it on the way.'

Dr McKinley was new to St Cleer. He was a young man and a keen doctor. 'I'll play you again another night, William.'

'I'll fetch your coat.' Miriam rushed away and returned with the doctor's coat and hat.

'Josh.' She took his arm. 'I hope things go well for Sarah and the baby. I really do.'

'Thank you.' He was impatient to be on his way with the doctor.

'We will pray for them both,' said Preacher William Thackeray.

But God must have had business elsewhere that night. In spite of all that Dr McKinley tried the baby died before the sun rose.

Neither did he have any more success with Sarah's afterbirth. He used methods that had Sarah screaming in pain and made Jesse Retallick's tired face turn even paler. Josh and his father were keeping a vigil in the kitchen, and the shift captain did his best to talk loudly whenever the sounds from above became too alarming.

When the dawn was dusting a thin pale crust on the distant sky-line it was a very weary doctor who made his way downstairs.

'I'm sorry,' he said. 'I've done all that I can. All that remains is surgery. That will require greater skills than I possess.'

'But where can we find a surgeon?' Josh pleaded. 'She's too ill to stand up to a long journey.'

Dr McKinley shook his head. 'I don't know. The only thing I am sure of is that if she doesn't see a surgeon soon she'll die.'

'Then we must take her by coach to Plymouth,' said Josh as Jesse came into the room tying up the strings at the throat of her cloak.

'You leave that girl where she is until I come back,' she ordered in a voice that allowed for no argument.

'Where are you going?'

'To fetch Mary Crabbe,' Jesse announced firmly. 'No disrespect to you, Doctor. I saw for myself that you did your best. But Mary Crabbe has brought more children into this world than any doctor. If she can't do anything, then it will have to be the surgeon.'

'Believe me, I welcome anything that might save that girl upstairs from the surgeon's knife,' said Dr McKinley in a tired voice. 'But delay will be dangerous.'

'I won't be many minutes. Josh, go up and sit with Sarah. Keep her forehead cool. She's in a fever.'

Sarah's appearance shocked Josh. When he had last seen her she was tired after the hard childbirth. But now she was gaunt and haggard, her cheekbones unhealthily prominent and perspiration standing out on her forehead. He spoke to her, but she seemed not to hear. As he bathed her forehead he tried not to let his gaze wander to the sheet-draped cot in which lay the body of their child.

Sarah had not stirred when he heard Mary Crabbe's wheezing breathing and his mother's voice coming from the stairs.

The old lady came into the room with uncombed hair, wearing an ill assortment of clothing; indicative of the haste with which Jesse Retallick had roused her from her bed.

She stood in the doorway gazing about her and waiting for her breathing to become less laboured.

'Get out!' she snapped at Josh. 'And take that with you.'

She pointed to the draped cot. 'It's ill-luck to have death in the room with a sick mother. Hurry up! And boil up lots of water. We'll need all you can heat. And a bowl – two bowls. Jesse, help me prop up this maid. Go on, boy. What are you waiting for? Move yourself.'

Josh carried the cot into another bedroom and placed it down gently. There was something pathetic about the lack of weight in his burden and it brought a lump to his throat. Here beneath the creased sheet was the body of the child that had always been a little unreal to him.

But for Sarah it was to have been a great fulfilment. For seven months she had carried the developing life in her body and a dream in her mind.

Sarah had always held a fear that Josh was unsettled with life and with her; that he had married her but had not really settled down into a married state. The baby was meant to change that. She believed that giving Josh a child would put her ahead of Miriam and tip the scales in her favour. With his child here in the house she was sure Josh would stay at home, having less to do with William Thackeray, his unionism – and his wife.

Josh did not know all these things, but he was aware that having the baby was very important to her. Now it was dead.

Only Dr McKinley remained when Josh went down to the kitchen. When he asked, the doctor told him that Ben Retallick had gone to send a rider to Hayle. The Carlyons needed to be told of the night's happenings.

'Yes, it's right they should know,' muttered Josh, though he knew before the end of the day Mrs Carlyon would be at Sharptor with recriminations and hostile glances. He had taken Sarah from her care and the birth had not gone well.

Ben Retallick returned to the house with Jenny Shovell. She made tea for the men before going upstairs to join the other women.

The men were talking quietly among themselves, and Dr McKinley had said for the third time, 'We must get that girl

to a surgeon,' when there were noisy footsteps on the stairs
and Jenny hurried in for another pot of water.

'It's all right!' she announced. 'Mary Crabbe's done it. Sarah
will be all right now.'

The relief in the room was enormous, but in the case of
the doctor it was swamped by incredulous disbelief.

'You mean the afterbirth has come away?'

Jenny nodded. 'Yes.'

'But how? How did this woman do it? I tried everything
I'd learned at medical school . . . !'

'I think it was herbs, mostly,' said Jenny.

'I must see this for myself, or I shall refuse to believe it.'
Dr McKinley left the kitchen talking to himself and shaking
his head.

'Can I see her now, Jenny?' Josh asked.

'Not just yet, Josh. Sarah will be all right, but wait until
Mary Crabbe has finished all she needs to do.'

It was a matter of moments only before the doctor returned,
more amused than indignant at being ordered from the
bedroom by Mary Crabbe. 'She has certainly succeeded
where I failed,' he admitted. 'And after all my years of
medical training . . . ! I find it very hard to understand.'

'I shouldn't try, Doctor,' said Ben Retallick. 'I've known
Mary all my life. There are some things I've heard of her
doing that I'd be frightened of knowing too much about.'

'If she was a younger woman I would ask her to help me
with my maternity cases,' Dr McKinley declared. 'A woman
like that is worth her weight in gold.'

'Mary Crabbe never worked for any man,' said Ben Retallick.
'And she's upset as many women as she's helped.'

'All the same . . .,' Dr McKinely mused. 'But there is nothing
more I can do here.' He looked at Josh. 'I'm sorry about the
baby. There was nothing you could have done better. The
poor little chap came into the world too soon, that's all.'

'Or too late!'

Nobody had heard Mary Crabbe come down the stairs. She
stood in the doorway, hair awry, standing as solid as a toad.
'There are few eldest sons in these parts who weren't begotten

in the fern of the moor.' She cackled. 'There's more love to be found there.'

The three men looked at each other but Mary Crabbe had not finished. 'And there will be precious little love to be found in this house. Shame, yes. And more. But you'll find out. Oh yes! You'll find out soon enough!'

Pulling her dirty shawl about her shoulders she shuffled out of the house. In the silence that followed they could hear her talking to herself as she walked out to the track on her way back to the village.

'I think her mind has finally gone,' said Ben Retallick after he had cleared his throat noisily. Josh was standing pale with fatigue and shaken by the old woman's words. 'Take no notice of her, Josh. She is so old she doesn't know what she is saying half the time. Forget her words and remember only her deeds. You owe her Sarah's life.'

'Yes.'

Josh nodded his head, tiredly trying to shake out the chill thoughts Mary Crabbe had placed there. Turning abruptly from the others, he said, 'I'm going up to Sarah.'

Sarah was lying quite still. Her eyes were closed and she looked very weak. Josh felt her forehead. It was quite cool now.

'Josh?' Her lips hardly moved.

'Yes. I'm here, Sarah.'

'I'm sorry, Josh.'

'Shh! You've done nothing to be sorry about. You're a very brave girl and I'm proud of you.'

A tear crept from the corner of her eye and tracked rapidly down her face. 'No. It wasn't meant to be, Josh. It should have been Miriam here bearing your child. I've always known that. She belongs to the moor as you do. I have no place here. I don't belong. I don't! I don't!'

'Now, what kind of talk is this?'

Jesse Retallick had been gathering towels and soiled bedding. Heaping it on the floor, she crossed to the bed and gently brushed back a wisp of fair hair from Sarah's face. 'You shouldn't be thinking such strange thoughts.'

Sarah's head rolled from side to side on the pillow and, moving away, Jesse took Josh's arm and led him to the door.

'Leave her now, Josh. She's had a bad time and needs sleep. Having you here is disturbing her. Go off somewhere and rest yourself. It's been a bad night for you too. I'll stay and look after Sarah.'

When he went back to the kitchen it was empty. Dr McKinley had gone and in the distance Josh saw the broad back of his father walking wearily down the path to the Wheal Sharptor.

Josh went out of the kitchen, across the yard and up the hill to the high moor. It was a clear spring morning, the birds busy and singing. On the rocks of Sharptor two ravens croaked. A pair of buzzards drifted across the sky, disdainful of the crows who noisily and jealously defended the square of sky they regarded as their own.

But Josh saw none of the things he usually looked for on the moor.

Mary Crabbe's words had disturbed him greatly, but Sarah's had upset him more. He could not put them out of his mind.

He walked alone on the moor for three hours. Then, after looking in at the house where Sarah now lay in a deep sleep, he went to the mine.

At home he felt helpless and his mind was too active to allow him to sleep. What anguish must Sarah have been going through for her to say what she had? And what was the meaning of Mary Crabbe's predictions, so vague and disquieting? His tired brain did not want to think about them.

In the mine were things he knew, tangible things. His skill as an engineer was something of which he was sure. Here, surrounded by familiar objects, he put the pieces of his mind back into place and became less troubled.

In St Cleer, Miriam saw the weary doctor's return and hurried out to hear the news. She returned to the chapel cottage choked with grief for Josh. It was a generous and sincere emotion. She had prayed so often for his happiness.

But she also longed for the impossible – to be able to comfort Josh for the dead child another woman had borne him.

Chapter Twenty-Two

It was dark when the coach carrying Mrs Carlyon rolled into the yard of the old farmhouse. Seconds later Sarah's mother swept through the house and up the stairs to the bedroom where Sarah still lay in an exhausted sleep.

Jesse Retallick met her at the bedroom door and held a finger to her lips. With only the briefest of nods Josh's mother-in-law went directly to the bedside. It was with difficulty she restrained herself from tucking in the corner of blanket that hung to the floor.

Tight-lipped, Molly Carlyon shook her head in a gesture of displeasure and walked from the room ahead of Jesse Retallick.

Jesse closed the door and in the passageway outside said, 'I'm pleased you're here. I only wish it was in happier circumstances.'

'Where is the baby?'

Jesse Retallick hesitated and the other woman said impatiently, 'I know the child is dead. But I would like to look at my first grandchild.'

'*Our* first grandchild,' Jesse Retallick corrected her quietly. The fact that Sarah's mother had not even greeted her civilly had not gone unnoticed. 'He's along here. Such a tiny scrap of a boy.'

Standing by the other woman as she turned back the sheet covering the baby, Jesse Retallick felt intense sadness at the sight of the cold wrinkled little face. It was such a terrible waste of a new life. The baby had left behind so many undiscovered things.

Mrs Carlyon replaced the sheet and the two women went downstairs. Josh had been in the outhouse having an all-over wash when the coach drew up. Now, dressed in clean clothes, he was making some tea.

'A fine mess you've made of looking after my daughter. . . .' Mrs Carlyon launched straight into the attack.

The kettle banged and popped noisily as Josh replaced it carefully on the stove.

'"We have doctors at Sharptor too", you said when I wanted Sarah to stay at Hayle. What of your doctors now?'

'There was nothing the best doctors in the world could have done . . .,' Jesse began, but Josh waved her into silence.

'Mrs Carlyon, the baby was so early that nobody was ready. It all happened so quickly I had to deliver the baby myself. I did my best. If that wasn't enough, then I must be responsible for the death of my own son. But I don't think I could have done more.'

'He did well,' said Jesse. 'I held the baby when he made his first cry. I knew then he was too tiny to live.'

'And what about Sarah? She is lying up there a very sick girl.'

'Sarah is an exhausted woman,' said Josh. 'She had a very difficult time. But she'll be all right if you don't upset her.'

'Upset my own daughter!' Molly Carlyon bristled with rage. 'I came here with a reckless coachman, bounced about until I'm covered in bruises, and I arrive here to be told I mustn't upset Sarah!'

'Sarah is your daughter. She's also my wife. In your present mood I can see nothing but harm from this visit. My father sent to tell you what was happening because he thought you had a right to know. But Sarah has lost our baby and that's distressing enough. If I thought you were going to add to it, Mrs Carlyon, I'd put you back in your carriage and order the coachman to return to Hayle this minute.'

Mrs Carlyon appeared to be actually swelling with rage as Jesse moved in to smooth things down.

'That's quite enough nonsense from you, Josh. Go and fetch some logs for the fire while I pour Mrs Carlyon another cup of tea. Go on, now!'

When he went, reluctantly, Jesse Retallick said, 'Josh is upset and doesn't mean anything by his bluntness. Remember he hasn't been to bed since this whole business started. He is tired. On top of that, he's had an experience to unnerve a far older man. He had to deliver his own child and it died. I think he blames himself—'

'And so he should.'

'No, he shouldn't.' Jesse Retallick silenced the other woman. 'He did as much as anyone could. Had he not kept his head you might not have a daughter now. Here's your cup of tea, Mrs Carlyon. If I seem ungracious it's because I too am tired. I'll tidy up here then go to my own cottage.'

'Leave what you have to do here,' said Molly Carlyon. 'I'll attend to everything. You go home to your husband.'

She gave a tight forced smile. 'I'm a worrier and there was little else to do in the coach on the way here.'

'You don't have to explain to me. There wasn't one of us – Josh, Ben or myself – who wasn't worried sick all night. It must have been dreadful to travel all that way not knowing what you would find when you arrived.'

'Yes, and I'm sure Sarah's father won't sleep tonight, either. I said I would send for him immediately if I felt he was needed.'

'Ben will get word to him tomorrow,' Jesse promised. 'Now I really must go. I'll be back in the morning to see how Sarah is.'

Outside, Jesse met Josh coming across the yard.

Before she allowed him past her into the house she made him promise to hold his tongue and not quarrel with Sarah's mother. Not until he gave his word did she go down the path to her cottage, satisfied that all was well in the old farmhouse, albeit temporarily.

Meanwhile, Mrs Carlyon went upstairs to Sarah's bedroom before Josh came in. She tucked in the blanket and straightened the pillows.

Josh made himself up a bed in a small bedroom before going in to see how Sarah was. She was still sleeping and looked very pale and fragile.

'Your bed has been made up in the room next to this one,' Josh said to Mrs Carlyon quietly.

'I'll stay here, thank you. In case Sarah wakes during the night.'

'If you need anything you'll find me in the end room.' Josh had the uncomfortable feeling that he was an interloper in his own home. He laid a gentle hand on Sarah's forehead, pleased to feel it cool; then he went to his own makeshift bed. He was asleep within a minute of laying his head on the pillow.

Waking in the morning light, Josh heard the murmur of voices from the bedroom along the corridor. Flinging back the bed-clothes he dressed and hurried along to Sarah's room. She was lying propped up against the pillows, her eyes dark hollows in her bloodless face.

The smile that she gave him was brief, but for a moment he felt its warmth. Then it was replaced by an expression that made him remember her last words before she had fallen asleep.

'Hello, love.' He kissed her and took her hand. 'How are you feeling this morning?'

'Much better, thank you.'

'I'll go and freshen myself up.' Mrs Carlyon had not thawed from the previous evening.

'No. Don't go!' Sarah cried, struggling to sit up. Without warning she burst into tears. Josh's arms went about her and he held her to him. But he could not stop her sobbing. It seemed that whatever he said only caused her to cry more bitterly.

Determinedly, Mrs Carlyon eased her from his arms and laid her back against the pillows. 'There! There! Don't cry like that. You're all right now.'

To Josh she said, 'Leave us now. She's too upset to reason with. She must rest.'

Bewildered, Josh left the room and readied himself for work. He could still hear her crying as he passed the room on the way out but dared not go inside again.

He worried about her all that morning and went home at lunch-time to see her, but she was asleep once more. Jesse Retallick and Mrs Carlyon were both in the house and agreed that it would be better not to disturb her again. He returned to work having caught no more than a glimpse of her through the partly open bedroom door as she lay snuggled down in bed.

That evening he rushed straight home. Finding no one downstairs in the kitchen, he went up to the bedroom where he was greatly relieved to see Sarah sitting up in bed looking far more cheerful than she had been before. But as soon as he spoke to her she began weeping uncontrollably once more.

For two days this state of affairs continued. Nothing he said or did could prevent her from crying whenever he entered the room where she was. He tried talking to her, telling her that losing the baby was not her fault, that it was nobody's fault; but she would not listen. He tried holding her and saying nothing, but the crying sounded even louder in the silence. Always in the background was the disapproving tight-lipped presence of Sarah's mother.

Sarah left her bed for the baby's funeral, the Carlyon coach brought into use to take her to the chapel. Josh hoped with the brief simple ceremony behind them Sarah would begin to improve, but nothing changed. Sarah sank into a morass of unhappiness that nothing Josh did would disperse.

After a week he dreaded returning home. He despaired of life ever returning to normal. He had a guilty feeling of relief when Mrs Carlyon announced she was taking Sarah home to Hayle for a long period of convalescence.

'What do you mean by a "long period"?' asked Josh.

'I mean for just as long as it takes her to become a healthy happy young woman again.'

'Yes. All right. Sarah will be better with someone to talk to her all the time. Here there is nobody but Jenny of her own age, and having me around doesn't seem to be helping her. I'll miss her, though.'

'If you miss her that much you can move to Hayle to be with her. Sarah's father will find a place for you in Harvey's works. Why don't you do that? I understand you're quite a clever design-engineer and could go far. Why on earth you choose to waste your life as an engineer in this God-forsaken place I don't know. It's enough to give anyone the melancholies.'

Mrs Carlyon's opinion of Sharptor had been coloured by the bank of low cloud and drizzle that had descended three days before and showed little sign of lifting.

'It's a tiny mine, Mrs Carlyon, but God probably spends more time here than he does in most other places. Sarah was happy here in the few months before the baby came. She'll be happy here again.'

I doubt that. Molly Carlyon would have said it aloud but she did not want to antagonise Josh now. She would make quite sure that Sarah never returned to this backward part of the county.

'When are you going to leave?'

'Tomorrow. We'll make an early start and take the journey slowly.'

'Tomorrow!'

'Yes. The sooner Sarah reaches home, the sooner she'll begin to mend. I'm very worried about her state of mind.'

Josh had no intention of baring his feelings to Sarah's mother but he knew Sharptor would never be a happy place again without Sarah.

'I'll go and tell Mum and Dad so they can come up and say goodbye to Sarah.'

He walked slowly down the hill, ignoring the drizzle. He was deeply unhappy. During their brief time together Josh had learned to love Sarah. It was a quieter, less devouring love than the one he had shared with Miriam, but he accepted that there were degrees of love. Now the bonds between Sarah and himself were being cut like their pathetic child's umbilical cord he feared it would shrivel into nothingness.

Later that night, when his mother and father went home and Mrs Carlyon had retired to her own bedroom, he went quietly in to Sarah.

A small oil-lamp was burning on a table across the room from her. Although she was lying quite still, her eyes were open and they followed his progress to her bedside.

'Hello, Sarah!' He smiled down at her gently, desperately eager for her to understand. 'Tomorrow you're going back to Hayle for a nice long holiday. You'll get yourself fit and well again.'

She stared up at him and said nothing. Encouraged, he went on, 'I'll miss you, Sarah. The house is going to feel very empty without you. This week has been a nightmare for both of us, but you mustn't think you are in any way to blame. You were a very brave girl. I'm proud of you.'

He choked with emotion and could not stop himself from dropping to one knee beside the bed and kissing her. He thought she yielded to him briefly, but then she flung her head to one side violently.

'No, Josh! No! I don't want to have another dead baby. No more, Josh! Please, no more!'

'Shh!' He tried to gather her into his arms, wanting desperately to hold and comfort her, but she struggled and fought him off, shouting the whole time.

'Leave me alone! Leave me alone!'

The door banged open and Sarah's mother rushed across the room to the bed, her hair tied in rag-curlers.

'What's going on? There, now! There!' She held her daughter and glared above her head at Josh. 'What do you think you're doing? Why must you upset her tonight? She has a strenuous day tomorrow and needs all the rest she can get.'

'I wanted to say a few words to her, to tell her to hurry and get well. I don't know when I'll see her again.'

'That's entirely up to you. Now leave us. I'll quieten her down. You can see her in the morning before we go.'

He would see her in the morning, but they would not be alone. Jesse and Ben Retallick would be there, and Jenny and Tom Shovell, all waving goodbye to the shell of the girl who had been his wife for such a brief time – the bright intelligent girl who had come to Sharptor as a bride and was now leaving, a near-demented woman, with only a tiny tombstone in a village graveyard to record her stay.

Chapter Twenty-Three

With Sarah gone, Josh lost all purpose in life. For the first few weeks he leaned heavily on his family and friends. He visited Jenny and Tom Shovell and spent hours playing with young Gwen. With his own family, he talked about everything except Sarah.

He called on people he had scarcely spoken to for years. When his visits were over he walked back to the old farmhouse to sit composing letters to Sarah. Most of them travelled no further than the fire in the kitchen. But he sent off three letters in the first fortnight after Sarah left and received replies to none of them.

Then, as suddenly as it had begun, his mood changed. Josh stopped calling on friends. Instead, he began to spend his evenings at the Cheesewring Inn in Henwood village.

At first he was a welcome customer. A popular figure among the miners of both Sharptor and the Wheal Caradon, he was known to the men of the Wheal Phoenix and the many other smaller mines dotted about the moor.

At the inn he could forget the lonely house on the tor and the girl who was no longer there. While he bought the drinks he was never short of ready listeners. He learned that if he drank enough alcohol it blotted out memories as thoroughly as a hill fog wiped Kit Hill from the horizon.

If the drink failed to fulfil its purpose it was possible to find other diversions – such as the night he got into an argument with two tin-miners from west Cornwall. Afterwards he had no recollection of how the argument started, or even what it was about, but it ended with Josh skinning his knuckles on the nose of one of them and banging both their heads together so hard they were unconscious for half an hour. After this incident, the crowd about him was never quite so thick.

His father sought him out at the mine and tried to talk him out of his drinking, but Josh brushed the advice aside.

He was more shame-faced about it when Jesse Retallick confronted him one Sunday morning at the old farmhouse. She interspersed her sentences with such words as 'shameful' and 'disgusting', but that same evening he stumbled his way home with the stars reeling above him and the path eluding him. He woke in the bracken below the house the next morning to the soft nuzzling of a inquisitive moorland pony.

Not until the days had lengthened into early summer did Josh's drinking come to an end.

It was late when he roared his goodbyes from the inn doorway and took an exaggerated stride across the stone step, before lurching out into the uneven village street.

For a long swaying minute he allowed his eyes to become accustomed to the gloom, then a soft voice at his elbow said, 'Hello, Josh.'

Startled, he turned towards the voice and, losing his balance, stumbled backwards. The hands that gripped his shirt-front were slim and long-fingered, but they were strong enough to halt his backward progress and jerk him upright.

'Who's that? Miriam! What are you doing here?'

Stupidly drunk as he was, he still made an effort to overcome the slur in his words.

'I've come to see you. But I'm not going to talk to you outside this place. I gave up waiting outside inns when I was a very young girl. Let's walk.'

He tried to shake her hand from his arm. 'Leave me alone. I can get home on my own.'

'That's not what I've heard. Come on, now. Don't cause a scene and embarrass me.'

'I wouldn't want to embarrass the Reverend's lady.'

It was foolish, childishly foolish. He knew it.

'Why aren't you home with your husband and Daniel? What are you doing here in Henwood?'

'At the moment I'm trying to move you in the general direction of your home. Without very much success.'

'I can get home very well without your help, thank you.'

He straightened his shoulders and stepped forward determinedly, making almost twenty yards before hooking his toe into the mud-scraper beside the door of Henwood shop and dropping to one knee.

'Damn!' If it weren't so dark he would be able to see and not make such an idiot of himself.

He imagined that Miriam was laughing at him. Shaking her hand away roughly, he got back on to his feet unaided.

'Go home,' he said. 'I don't need your help. Or anyone else's. I'm quite capable of looking after myself.'

'It would serve you right if I did walk away and leave you alone, Joshua Retallick. Do you think I enjoy seeing a man I admire fall about as though he was an imbecile child? I've memories enough of my father to last me until I go to the grave. I don't need to watch you behave like it.'

Her anger got through to him. Although he could not keep the impediment from his speech, he felt able to think sensibly.

'I'm sorry, but I honestly don't need your help. I'll get home all right.'

'Fool yourself if you want to. You're not convincing me.'

She grabbed his arm and steered him on a course forty-five degrees from the one he was pursuing. 'That ditch you were heading for is four feet deep, with enough rocks in it to damage even your head. No, don't pull your arm away. We'll get along quicker if I guide you. I have no intention of spending the night wandering in circles around Henwood village with you.'

'What are you doing here? Where's William?'

'He's at home, looking after Daniel. My mother isn't well. I'm staying with her until tomorrow.'

Josh allowed himself to be guided along the track, uphill from the village. He was all right, he told himself; but his legs seemed to be in more of a hurry than his body.

'Why aren't you with your mother now, instead of fussing with me?'

'I'm "fussing" with you because I brought something from St Cleer for you. I don't intend giving it to you until I'm quite sure you are sober and know you've received it.'

'What is it? I'm sober enough now. Give it to me and go.'

'I appreciate your gratitude, but you can keep your orders for those who have to take them. When you're safely in your house you'll get your letter. Not a minute before.'

'A letter? Where is it? What are you doing with it?'

'It arrived on today's coach. I said I would bring it with me. I thought it might be something you were waiting for.'

'I am, Miriam. It's the first one since – since Sarah went to Hayle.'

'Yes, I thought that might be the case.'

They were close to the house now and the drink and the uphill walk were causing him to breathe heavily. But he was not as drunk as he would have been had he come home alone.

Nevertheless, Miriam was hard to convince. Inside the house she kept his head beneath the kitchen pump until he felt more drowned than drunk.

Handing him a towel from the rack beside the sink, she said, 'Here. Dry your hair and I'll give you your letter.'

He rubbed vigorously until his hair was no longer dripping water before taking the sealed letter from her.

Tearing it open, he read quickly, then handed the letter back to Miriam without a word.

'I don't want to read Sarah's letter!' She thrust it back at him.

'It's not from Sarah. It's from her young sister Mary. Read it.'

Opening out the stiff sheet of paper, Miriam could see that the writing was much more childish than it was on the outside of the envelope.

'Dear Josh,' she read. 'I hope you are not too lonely living by yourself in that big house. How is Hector? I have a new pony all of my own now. I call him Bob. Sarah is looking a lot better now, but I have not been able to talk to her properly because the doctor said she must be kept very quiet. I saw her sitting in a seat by the window yesterday and I waved. I am sure she smiled so I think she will soon be all right again. I wish you could come to stay with us, but Mummy says that would upset Sarah too much. I don't know why. I am very sorry about the baby because I wanted to be an aunt. I must end now. Lots of love, Mary.'

Her signature was followed by half a line of Xs.

'Oh! I thought the letter came from Sarah. I wouldn't have made such a fuss about it had I known.'

'I'm glad you did. It might not say a lot but it contains the first news I've had of Sarah since she left here. I'll sit down and reply to Mary tonight.'

'Is that wise? I mean . . . don't you think it would be better to leave it until tomorrow when you will have a clearer mind?'

'What you really mean is "when I am sober". No, it's all right. I'm perfectly well now. Thanks to you.'

'I wish I could do something to keep you that way, Josh.' She was taken by a sudden thought. 'When did you last eat?'

'I – I don't know. I had some breakfast this morning.'

'Then I'll cook you something now, before I leave. If you told the truth I doubt whether you've eaten at all today.'

Ignoring his protests, she searched the larder, finding eggs, bread and some salt bacon.

'I'll make a start on this but the fire is getting a bit low.'

'Yes, my mother will have called in and made it up for me a lot earlier this evening. I'll put on some wood shavings. That will get it burning.'

When he came back into the house carrying wood there was a delicious smell rising from the cooking-pan. Ten minutes later he was seated at the kitchen table demolishing a meal that would have satisfied three men like William Thackeray.

Wiping the plate clean, Josh leaned back and gave Miriam a sheepish grin.

'Miriam Thackeray, you may be a hard bullying woman, but there's no disputing that you're a fine cook.'

Her answer was a loud snort. 'Huh! You had such a hunger on you it would have made no difference had I burned it black.'

Their eyes met for a warm second but Miriam dropped her gaze immediately and smoothed the waist of her dress. 'Now I've seen you safely home and fed I must go.'

He looked at the big clock on the shelf above the fire-place and started guiltily. 'I didn't realise it was so late. You'll be getting yourself gossiped about in Henwood. Even at this hour there's bound to be someone to see you coming from Sharptor. I'll put on my coat and walk down to the village with you.'

She laughed. It had been a long time since he had heard a happy sound in that room.

'You do that and the gossips of Henwood will have something to talk about. No, Josh. You stay here. I'll go on my own. There's nothing on the moor to bother me. I'm happier walking here after dark than I am in St Cleer.'

'Thank you for the meal, Miriam. And for sobering me up.'

She stopped at the door and without looking at his face said, 'You don't know what it did to me to see you in that state, Josh. It was as though a knife was going into me, cutting open the bag of bad memories I have there. When I was a very small girl my father enjoyed a drink, but it hadn't yet possessed him entirely. In those days he would know I was waiting outside the inn and wouldn't stay late. When he came out he would swing me up on his shoulder and give me a ride home. It was only as I grew older he began to stay inside longer and longer and forget I was waiting. When he did come out I sometimes ran away from him because he was shouting or swearing at the other miners. One night my mother came down for him. It was pay-day and she wanted money for food. I saw her jostled and man-handled by drunken miners before someone told my father she was there. He was angry, very angry, because she had come looking for him. He was also very drunk. When she asked him for money he hit her. She still held out her hand so he hit her again. He hit her and hit her until she fell to the ground and stayed there. Then he went back inside the inn. All this came back to me as I waited outside the Cheesewring Inn for you to come out tonight. When you came through that door reeling-drunk it was as though I'd made a journey back in time. I felt physically sick.'

'I'm sorry, Miriam.'

'Oh, you needn't be.' She shrugged. 'You're quite entitled to tell me it's none of my business. But I hate to see a good man destroying himself. You have your problems, Josh. I might be partly to blame for them. But you won't find any answers inside an inn.'

'Where do you suggest I start looking for the answers – Hayle?'

'That's up to you, Josh.'

'Yes. I know I still owe Theophilus Strike a few years here, but if I thought it would be for the best I'd leave Sharptor and go to work for Harvey's. That's what Sarah's mother wants. But it wouldn't work. Mrs Carlyon would have too much control over our lives. It's out of the question at the moment, anyway. I can't get near Sarah. She bursts into tears at the sight of me. I'll think about it and discuss it with Sarah when she's well again.'

He made a helpless gesture. 'I hope it won't take too long. There was a time when I enjoyed the thought of having Sarah for my wife because she is the daughter of William Carlyon, the manager of Harvey's. But during the last few months I became very fond of her. We were happy during the time we were waiting for the baby.'

'Poor Josh. . . .'

'No, don't pity me. I couldn't bear that coming from you. Anyway, Sarah is back with her sort of people now. She'll be visited by friends who know which tie to wear for a wedding, who can sit down at a table and know which knife, fork and spoon to use without having to wait and watch what everyone else is doing. I only wish she was well enough to enjoy it.'

'She's being looked after, Josh. But what about you? Will you cease being Josh the engineer now and become Josh the Sharptor drunk?'

'No, Miriam.' He was serious. 'This talk with you has done me good. I'll be able to manage without the aid of the Cheesewring Inn.'

'Then I don't care what the Henwood gossips have to say. I'll have done something worth while.'

When she reached the far edge of the yellow light reaching out through the open kitchen door she stopped. 'If you're feeling the same way tomorrow evening perhaps you'll walk me back to St Cleer. Have supper with William and me.'

'Yes, I'd like that.'

'Good! I'll give you time to come home and clean up from work and wait for you at the edge of the village.'

He took Hector and suggested that Miriam ride while he walked beside her, but she objected. In the end they compromised by both riding on the uncomplaining horse, Miriam occupying the saddle with Josh behind, arms about her, holding the reins.

Just before they entered St Cleer he put the horse into a trot. Jogging and bouncing they arrived at the gate of the chapel house, red-cheeked and laughing.

From the window of his study William Thackeray watched the arrival of his wife and Josh with a frown. The frown deepened as Josh swung Miriam to the ground with his hands about her waist.

But minutes later William Thackeray's smile was as welcoming as any loving husband whose wife has been away from home.

'It's nice to have you home again,' he said, kissing her. 'Daniel will be pleased. He's playing in the back garden. And Josh! How nice to see you after such a long time – an unhappy time for you, I fear.'

He grasped Josh's hand in both his own. 'I can't tell you how sorry I was to hear about the baby and poor Sarah. How is she? I heard she was very ill.'

'Yes. She's staying with her parents at Hayle.'

'For long?' The question was accompanied by a calculating look.

'For quite some time, I fear.'

'He's been on his own for too long,' said Miriam. 'I thought it was time he had a good meal. That's why I invited him here tonight.'

'I hope it wasn't only the promise of food that persuaded him to come.' He smiled at Josh. 'Mind you, I'm forced to admit you look as though you need a good meal.'

'I'll go and find Daniel. Then I'll start the cooking.' Miriam smiled at the two men as she went towards the back of the house.

'Come into the lounge, Josh,' said William Thackeray. 'We have a lot to talk about. Have you heard about the miners' benefit scheme? Sixpence a week collected from each miner guarantees him ten shillings a week if he's home because of an injury received in the mine. Think of the peace of mind that will give to an injured miner. He'll be able to give himself time to get well without his family starving.'

'Educate the miners and adventurers in the meaning of mine safety, rig a man-lift in every mine and you eliminate most accidents. That way the miner and his family stay happy and don't have to try to manage on ten shillings a week.'

'True, Josh. Quite true. But you must admit this is a start. Build up the Union, let the miner see he has a strong movement behind him and he can demand that your safety measures be implemented.'

This was what the preacher enjoyed – having someone to talk to, to argue with, shaking the argument around and looking at it from every possible angle. Josh had always been able to satisfy this need. Miriam had the intelligence to carry on a discussion with him but she was unable to see every fact as a multi-sided prism, the argument shifting with each facet. Miriam was too positive in her approach. She saw one point of view and stayed with it, unwilling to concede half a point against it.

William Thackeray and Josh discussed the Union until Miriam called them into the kitchen for the meal she had prepared. The discussion halted for a while as Daniel was to eat with them. He provided the topic for conversation until the meal was over.

Daniel was a bright attractive child in his third year. His presence both fascinated and embarrassed Josh. He became unusually tongue-tied, wanting the boy to talk to him, yet not sure of his own ability to reply to him.

At last the meal was over and Miriam led Daniel away to bed, ignoring his vigorous protests.

'That young man has a strong will,' commented Josh.

'I suspect it's an inheritance from his mother,' replied William Thackeray. 'Now, we've discussed the benefit scheme. What do you really think of it, Josh?'

'It can do nothing but good. Unless the mine-owners think because the miners are getting paid by someone else for injury time they have no need to improve mine safety. That's likely to happen on some mines.'

'Ah! Now you are coming to the second part of my scheme, Josh. After a few months we'll have a good sum of money in the fund. When we have reached that happy state we can extend it. One thought I have in mind is that if there are too many accidents at a particular mine the fund committee will ask the mine captain to improve safety measures. Should he refuse the men stop work and receive benefit as though they were off through injury.'

'The fund won't last long if you call out the work-force on a large mine,' said Josh.

'But that won't happen.' William Thackeray's face lit up with the fervour of a crusader. 'We're not likely to get trouble from the large mines. They know poor safety only leads to lower profits. It's the smaller mine that tries to cut costs. We can beat them.'

He held up a hand before Josh could speak. 'I know what you're going to say. Such a state of affairs doesn't exist at Sharptor. And you're quite right. But Sharptor is a one-man-owned mine and few mines are as efficiently run. Even so, I don't think Theophilus Strike deserves all the credit for it. It was not such a good place to work when Herman Schmidt was mine captain. The good Sharptor record is due to your efforts and those of men like your father and Captain Shovell. Nevertheless, we will need to have the Sharptor miners in the benefit scheme. To be a complete success it needs the co-operation of every miner in the district – in the whole of Cornwall if we can extend it that far.'

'I can't see anyone raising objections,' said Josh. 'Theophilus Strike is anti-Union, but he will see this is for the good of every miner and his family. The fact that it will not cost him a penny will help.'

But Theophilus Strike did not see it that way when Josh put it to him a few days later.

'We don't need such a scheme in the Wheal Sharptor!' he declared. 'Our accident rate is lower than any other mine in the county.'

'One roof-fall at the wrong time would alter that,' replied Josh. 'I thought you'd welcome the scheme.'

'Welcome it! I welcome nothing that has the smell of unionism behind it. Who thought of it? That St Cleer preacher?'

'As a matter of fact he did.'

'I thought as much. No doubt he will administer it and call the tune. Unionism is gaining more ground than is good for anyone. Don't let yourself be fooled by high ideals, Joshua. That preacher would not be pushing it so hard if anyone else controlled its affairs. He wants to become a power in this part of the county. This is his way of doing it. To me it's no more than a matter of personal annoyance. Others feel far more strongly and will stop at nothing to stamp it out. When they're ready to make a move someone will suffer. This preacher friend of yours is far too slippery for it to be him. Make sure it isn't you.'

'Then you agree to the men contributing to a benefit fund?'

'Would it make any difference if I didn't? No, Joshua. The unionism fever is gripping every miner at the moment. If I said I'd deduct the same amount from the men's wages and give them *fifteen* shillings a week injury pay I wouldn't be considered a humanitarian. The men's first thought would be "What's Theophilus Strike getting out of it for himself?"

Nobody would join. But I have no doubt they'll jump at your offer. I won't stop them. But I do have a word of warning for you. I've always tried to run a good mine and be fair with the men who work for me. Make sure they're joining a benefit scheme and not a union of miners. A Sharptor miner serves only one master – me. I'll not have any preacher coming here to tell me how to run my mine.'

'I don't think it will ever come to that, Mr Strike.'

'Think! Boy, you stop thinking when you walk away from an engine. Now, be damned to your unionism. Go find your father and tell him I want to inspect the new deep level. You can take us down in your latest toy. Come down with us. I've been getting reports about lack of air down there. If it's true you might be able to think of a way to improve it.'

Outside the mine office it was a wet and blustery day. The davits over the shafts creaked and groaned and the wind sang mournfully in the taut cables.

The man-lift had been adjusted to perfection. After travelling two hundred and forty fathoms from grass to the bottom of the shaft, Theophilus Strike had a step down of less than a foot to the damp ground below him.

The airless humidity was immediately apparent to all of them. The slow monotonous thumping of the water-pump was like the beating of a giant heart above them. But all the body heat was down here in the deep darkness at the bottom of the mine.

They ducked into the working adit which was still in a largely exploratory state. It had not been widened or heightened for easy working. Before they had gone thirty yards they were gasping for breath, the candles on their hard hats spluttering and groping for oxygen.

The three men were in the adit for less than twenty minutes but as they ascended in the lift it seemed to Josh he had been working a full shift below ground. His clothes were wet with perspiration and his head sang from the lack of oxygen he had experienced. Looking at his father and Theophilus Strike he could see they were feeling the same.

The effort of breathing oxygen back into their systems kept

them speechless until they reached the surface. It was not until they stepped on to the ground at the top, grateful for a grey overcast day with a cool miserable wind, that any of them spoke.

'The reports are not exaggerated, Ben,' said the mine-owner, running a white linen handkerchief around the neck-band of his shirt. 'Unless we can do something about it we won't be able to get anything out from that level. It looked like prize ore too.'

'The best in the mine,' agreed the shift captain. 'But a man would be overcome by foul air inside an hour, even if I could persuade him to work there.'

'Then what would you suggest? An adit through the side of the hill?'

'No.' Ben Retallick shook his head. 'We're too deep for that. Too deep even for a sloping shaft.'

'How about you, Joshua? Can you think of anything that might help?'

Josh nodded thoughtfully. 'Yes, I have a vague idea in my mind of something that might work. I'll fix up an apparatus along the lines of the water-pump. If air is pushed down through a long pipe fitted with a non-return valve it should work. It's worth a try.'

'The lad's a genius!' exclaimed the mine-owner. 'But won't it mean another engine?'

'A very small one,' replied Josh. 'There's one for sale at the West Caradon we could get for next to nothing.'

'Then buy it. Do whatever you think is necessary. Let me know when you have it working.'

He turned to Ben Retallick. 'Make him work at it, Ben. It will keep him from that so-called preacher and his radical ideas.'

Josh smiled. 'I'll have that tunnel fit for working in two weeks, Mr Strike. I don't want the men wasting their hard-earned benefit money.'

Theophilus Strike grunted as he walked away and Ben Retallick could not hide his amazement.

'I never thought I'd live to see the day when anyone would

use the word "benefit" in front of Theophilus Strike and still work for him.'

'In a few years everyone will know about "benefit", and I hope there will be far less need of it.'

Ben Retallick's expression was serious. 'Perhaps. But Strike was right about one thing. Preacher Thackeray. You'd be well off staying away from him, Josh. There's little good in anything Thackeray does, unless he benefits from it too.'

'If it wasn't for him miners in these parts would be a lot worse off than they are now,' retorted Josh. 'He's the fire behind the movement.'

'And like every fire he needs to burn fuel,' said Ben Retallick. 'Make sure you aren't thrown on the heap for burning. It's no good shaking your head at me, my lad. Preacher Thackeray may be some sort of a hero to you, but he is as human as anyone else. Staunch unionist he might be, but he has no cause to love you.'

'What do you mean by that?'

'You don't have to raise your hackles with me, Josh. I'm your father. I don't think I have to spell out anything I say to you. You were more than friendly with Preacher Thackeray's wife before they were married. I wasn't the only one who thought she'd be part of the family one day. Then she ups and marries Preacher Thackeray as sudden as any wedding I've known. Too soon after that to be decent a babe was born. Nice folks will say it was born before its time. There's others who don't. Most of them would wager that the preacher didn't have anything to do with fathering it, either.'

Josh's face paled and then the blood rushed into it angrily, but his father stopped him before he could speak. 'Just a minute. Let me finish. I'm not saying that I, or any other decent person, has taken any notice of what they say. I'm only telling you it's been said. And if I've heard it you can be sure Preacher Thackeray has too. It's the sort of thing that festers in a man's mind, Josh. And I've heard from some that the preacher isn't the most forgiving of men.'

It was quite true. Josh knew it. But it was something more than anger that burned within him.

'I've never heard anyone say it. If I did they wouldn't repeat it to anyone else!'

'I've no doubt of it. That's why the rumours have never reached your ears,' said Ben quietly. 'I only mentioned it now because I felt you ought to know and adjust your friendship with Preacher Thackeray accordingly.'

'My friendship with Preacher Thackeray will be what it's always been,' declared Josh. 'If he takes notice of rumours of that sort he's not the man I believe him to be.'

'I hope time proves you right and me wrong.'

Ben Retallick walked out of the office, leaving Josh looking after him. Josh had argued strongly for the preacher, but he knew even more than his father how dangerous the preacher could be if he chose. Soon after Harry Reeve and the other Kit Hill miners' leaders were transported there had been an ugly rumour circulating that Preacher Thackeray had arranged their arrests. It was said he was jealous of the stature they were gaining in the eyes of the Kit Hill men.

But, as quickly as he remembered, Josh shrugged it off. What he had said to his father had been the truth. Preacher Thackeray had done a great deal for the cause of the Miners' Union. To doubt him now would be totally unworthy.

It was as much a result of this guilty feeling as for any other reason that Josh rode to St Cleer that evening. He found Preacher Thackeray working in his study. The welcome he gave Josh was as warm as ever. Josh immediately resolved to put any last lingering doubt about the preacher behind him.

'It's always a pleasure to see you, Josh,' said William Thackeray as he ushered his guest into the house. 'Let me make some tea for you. I'm alone for an hour or so. Miriam is taking a class for older girls this evening.'

'I didn't realise she was a teacher these days,' said Josh.

'Oh, there isn't much that Miriam can't turn her hand to,' smiled William Thackeray. 'She's the perfect wife for a minister of the Church. She teaches, stands in for me during my absences, corrects my sermons, and can hold her own in a union meeting against any man foolish enough to doubt her capabilities. I tell you, Josh, she's one in a million.'

'Yes.'

'But, talking of wives, what am I thinking about? There's a letter here for you. It came on today's coach. Miriam asked me if I would take it over to Sharptor for you tomorrow. Now, where has she put it?'

He began searching through the compartments of his bureau. Finally he held a sealed letter up in triumph.

'Here we are! I hope it contains good news for you, Josh.'

Josh took the letter and to his surprise and delight recognized Sarah's handwriting. It looked more irregular than usual but there was no doubt about it.

Tearing it open he began to read excitedly. Gradually the expression on his face changed from delight to surprise, then through disbelief to dismay.

The preacher was watching him closely. 'Is it bad news, Josh? Is something wrong?'

'It's. . . . She. . . .' His mouth opened again but instead of speaking he handed the letter to William Thackeray.

On the opened-out page the unevenness of the writing was even more apparent than on the envelope. The scrawled words wandered untidily across the page. But their meaning was clear enough.

'My Dear Josh,' the letter began. 'Forgive me for what I have to say. I cannot tell you how much it upsets me to write so, but I feel it is the only honest thing I am able to do. You know I was never really happy at Sharptor. After all that has happened I could not bear to live in that house again. That is why I am writing now. Mother has said many times it would have been better had we never married. Although there was a time when I bitterly resented her words, I now realise it is true. I have brought only unhappiness to you, dear Josh. I was not even capable of giving you a child. This is not a part of my illness; the doctor says I am almost over that now. My tears threaten to wash away every word that I write, but it must be said. The sooner I tell you, the quicker you can begin a new life without me. I do not want to see you ever again, Josh. Whatever you

decide to do with your life I wish you the happiness and
success I know you can achieve. I cannot write more now.
God bless you. Sarah.'

'You can't take any notice of this letter, Josh. The very
writing shows that the poor girl is far from well. I'm amazed
her mother allowed such a letter to be sent to you. Sarah must
have worked herself up into a piteous state to have penned a
letter like this. Ignore it, I implore you.'

Josh looked at the preacher with unseeing eyes. 'I wish I
could. If only I could. There's too much truth in it to be
ignored. I knew she wasn't happy at Sharptor, but that would
have changed with time. Now, with her mother feeding her
every thought, it can never be.'

Punching a fist into the palm of his left hand he spun on his
heel and reached for his coat.

'Where are you going?'

'To Hayle. There's no answer to be found here, and no peace
in me until I've seen for myself how well Sarah is. Whether
things really are over between us.'

'Josh, is that wise? Go home and think about it. Leave a
decision until tomorrow.'

'No. There are times for thinking and times for action. I've
been thinking for too long.'

Without another word Josh strode from the house, and
William Thackeray made no further attempt to stop him.

Josh untied Hector from the rail outside the chapel and
reined the horse's head around. Then he rode out through
the village at a fast canter and was soon out of sight beyond
the houses.

Within an hour of leaving St Cleer it was dark and great caution
was needed. The road was pot-holed and rutted for most of
its length. It was impossible to distinguish road from verge.
The slow journey gave Josh ample time to think of what he
would do when he arrived. He had no intention of storming
into the Carlyons' house like a marauder and carrying Sarah
back to Sharptor by force. It was quite probable she would
never return there, as she had declared. But he wanted to be

sure it was her own decision, made without any interference from her mother.

He rode even more slowly as he neared Hayle. He could have arrived before dawn. Instead, he stopped, and seated on a granite milestone watched the sun rise and colour the countryside.

The day shift was settling in at the foundry when he reached the house. His unheralded appearance brought a variety of reactions from the Carlyon family, ranging from Mary's unreserved pleasure to open hostility from Mrs Carlyon. Sarah was not downstairs, and Mrs Carlyon made it clear she had no intention of allowing Josh to go up to her.

'It was that foolish letter!' she exclaimed angrily. 'I knew I should never have allowed her to send it.'

'It was a letter from Sarah to her husband,' Josh said equally angrily. 'She had every right to send it. There was no need to ask your permission.'

'Husband, indeed!' Mrs Carlyon's snort would not have been out of place in a stable. 'And where has my daughter's "husband" been these last weeks while she's been lying upstairs? Her mind has been in such a turmoil I doubted whether she would ever be sane again. And who nursed her through nightmares so frightening they brought me out in a cold sweat? Answer me that if you can, Joshua Retallick.'

'It was because I thought it would be better for Sarah that I allowed her to return here with you. At your insistence,' replied a thin-lipped Josh. 'I have no doubt she has had the best attention possible. I'm very grateful for that.'

'Gratitude has never paid bills,' snapped Mrs Carlyon. 'When a man takes a wife it's usual for him to support her.'

'You can send every bill that Sarah has incurred to me,' flared Josh. 'They'll be paid.'

'What's all this talk of payment?' William Carlyon came into the room and shook his son-in-law's hand warmly. 'What sort of greeting is this for a man who looks as though he's ridden through the night?'

'I don't care if he's ridden for a week. He has not done his duty as a husband to Sarah and I don't think it's in her interest to see him now.'

'That's a most unfair statement,' the works manager protested. 'If Josh had felt he could have helped in any way I'm sure he would have been here with Sarah. Why, it was you who said he would only hinder her recovery. Josh has shown great strength of mind to have stayed away for this long.'

'Sarah is still not well enough to see him,' Mrs Carlyon persisted.

'She's well enough to write to me,' said Josh. 'And apparently quite well enough to have her mind poisoned against me by you.'

'That's a disgraceful assertion . . . !'

At that moment the door from the hall opened and Sarah came in. She looked quite normal and healthy until she saw Josh. Then she froze, her hand flying to her mouth.

Although at first glance she appeared to be the same Sarah he had known, there was something in her eyes that disturbed him greatly. It was a lost unreal look.

'Sarah!' As he moved towards her she shrank back. 'Sarah, I won't hurt you. I've just come to see you. . . .'

She looked around, seeking some way of escape, her face twitching as though she was in physical pain.

'There! Don't you see? You're terrifying the poor girl.'

Mrs Carlyon could hardly keep the triumph from her voice.

'Sarah, it's me. Josh.'

Sarah cringed back until she was touching the wall, then she edged her way along it sideways, moving towards the door.

'Sarah, please! I came because of your letter.'

'Leave her alone. I told you this would do no good.'

'Sarah! Josh has travelled all night to see you. Don't be silly now.'

'Sarah, Josh wouldn't hurt you.'

'Leave her alone. Go away.'

'Sarah!'

'Sarah . . . !'

Everyone was talking to her, looking at her. Their words beat in upon her like waves in a storm, pounding her brain into a thousand pieces. It was more than she could endure. Her hand touched the door-handle. She turned it – and was gone.

Josh rushed to follow her, but Mrs Carlyon barred his way.

'Leave her! Haven't you done enough? I told you this would happen.'

'Now, Molly, you're not being fair to Josh. He came here to see Sarah because he is worried about her. Had anyone asked me I would have sworn that she was well enough to see him again.'

'Mummy, you said yesterday that Sarah was almost better.' This came from Mary, and Mrs Carlyon rounded on her. The argument continued bitterly until Mary burst into tears and rushed from the room.

'All right! All right!' said Josh wearily. 'You've proved your point, Mrs Carlyon. Sarah is still a sick girl. But when is she going to be better? When am I going to be able to see her and talk to her properly?'

'When I and the doctor say so,' replied Mrs Carlyon. 'Not one minute before.'

Josh's night without sleep was beginning to catch up with him fast. He felt weary and sick. Whatever he said, whatever anyone said, there could be no arguing with the look on Sarah's face when she saw him in the room, no way of explaining away her subsequent behaviour.

'You'll let me know when that time comes?'

'When she's quite well again, I will.'

'Very well. If you'll check to make sure she's all right now, I'll leave immediately and return to Sharptor.'

'Nonsense, Josh! You must stay for a meal and get some sleep.'

Josh shook his head. 'Thank you, but no. I was at St Cleer when I received Sarah's letter. I didn't stop to let anyone at the Wheal Sharptor know I was coming here.'

'Sarah isn't in her room. Mum! Dad! Sarah isn't here.'

The cry came from Mary.

Molly Carlyon ran from the room and Josh and William Carlyon followed as far as the hall.

Josh could hear the sound of doors being opened and slammed shut as Sarah's mother searched upstairs. Then she appeared at the head of the stairs, a frightened Mary beside her.

'Sarah isn't up here anywhere. Quickly now, search all the downstairs rooms. Mary, you look in the garden. Don't forget the shed.'

She advanced down the stairs. There was sheer hatred on her face as she looked at Josh. 'If anything has happened to that girl it will be all your fault.'

'That's enough, Molly,' said her husband. 'Had we not spent so much time arguing, this wouldn't have happened. I expect she's quite safe. Perhaps in the garden.'

But she was not in the garden. By now everyone was thoroughly alarmed. The search spread to the foundry where one of the apprentices said he thought he had seen her on a horse, leaving the works through the main gate.

'She turned right, as though she was going up towards the downs,' he said.

'It's a fine day. She'll come to no harm up there,' said William Carlyon.

'That's assuming she's gone to the downs,' said Mrs Carlyon. 'She hasn't been out of the house since she came home.'

It was Josh who noticed that Hector was not where he had left him near the front gate to the Carlyon house.

'The hostler might have put him in the stable,' said William Carlyon. 'I'll go and ask.'

'I hope he has,' said Josh. 'Hector doesn't get enough exercise these days. It's as much as I can do to hold him in check. Sarah would never control him.'

But Hector was not in the stables, and in the street outside Harvey's they spoke to an old man who had seen a girl with flowing golden hair galloping a horse out of Hayle along the St Ives road.

Josh and William Carlyon were the first to get mounted on horses belonging to Harvey's. Before they rode away from the works the manager left orders for every man who could ride to follow them and join in the search for Sarah.

'Have you any idea where she might be heading?' William Carlyon flung back over his shoulder as they sped along the open road. 'Was there a special place you were both fond of?'

'There were many,' Josh shouted back. 'But only one along this road, and I pray to God she hasn't gone there. It's dangerous enough for a well person.'

But his fears were soon realised. They found Hector with trailing rein and heaving sides, blowing, at the top of a steep and narrow track that clung to the sheer side of jagged cliffs. Below was a tiny patch of sand scarcely large enough for a smuggler's boat to ground on.

Twice on the way down Josh slipped. He prevented himself from falling only by clinging to the coarse grass growing in the crevices of the rock.

There was nothing to be seen at the bottom of the cliff, only the water of the high tide lapping at the rocks. Further out the swell from the Atlantic lifted over the natural breakwater and fell away again to reveal the ragged black teeth of rocks.

Josh was to remember those black rocks.

As more men arrived from Hayle the search extended for miles along the coast. But it was not until after midday, when the tide had ebbed away, that a man standing on the cliffs above called that he could see something caught in the rocks.

A fishing boat from St Ives, one of half a dozen called in by William Carlyon to join the desperate search, went perilously close to the rocks while Josh and the works manager watched helplessly from the shore, each hoping this would not be the end of the search.

They saw the boat swing broadside on to the rocks, the men at the oars straining to hold it off. Then one of the young men put down his oar, stripped off his jersey and plunged over the side. Twice he dived down into the water. The first time he came up for a moment to draw in a deep breath before diving again. The second time he was down a longer time and when he surfaced he was dragging something behind him.

The men in the boat leaned over the side to take it from him. As they pulled it from the sea those on shore could see it was the body of a girl.

Sarah Retallick had been found.

*   *   *

'You mustn't blame yourself, Josh. It was her state of mind. She didn't know what she was doing. It wasn't your fault.'

In spite of his own deep grief William Carlyon was far kinder than his wife had been. There would be nights when Josh would wake in a cold sweat hearing her voice screaming, 'Murderer!' At him.

'Whether it was my fault today or sometime in the past I'll never know,' said Josh.

He was mounted on Hector and ready to return to Sharptor. He was desperately weary with the events of the last twenty-four hours, but he could not bear to stay at Hayle for a moment longer. Sarah would be buried in the little Hayle cemetery and Josh did not want to be there. She would be buried bearing his name but that was all. Here, in this place, he was an interloper, not a part of the Carlyon family. He wanted to keep his own memories of Sarah. A beautiful girl with long fair hair who had shared a brief part of his life. He did not want to remember her as the battered disfigured body lying in the house behind him.

'Goodbye, Mr Carlyon. You've always been very kind to me. I thank you. I'm sorry to have brought such unhappiness to your family. But I grieve for Sarah too. . . .' He would not trust his voice further.

'I know you do, Josh. Don't take what Sarah's mother said to heart. She's very distressed. She doesn't really believe you are to blame. Come back and see us in a few months' time. You'll be made welcome. I promise you that.'

Josh shook his head. 'No, Mr Carlyon. I don't think we'll meet again.'

He reined the horse around and rode away from Harvey's works. Taking the road to the east, he was as tired as any man who had travelled the road before him.

Chapter Twenty-Four

The news of Sarah's death was doubly distressing for Jesse Retallick. She had been very fond of her son's wife and the suddenness and manner of her death came as a great shock. More, she dreaded what it would do to Josh. She believed he would resume the way of life he had taken up after Sarah had left Sharptor. She doubted whether her influence was sufficient to prevent him drinking himself into an early grave.

But, contrary to her expectations, Josh did not begin drinking again. Instead, he threw himself into his work with a vigour that awed those who were obliged to work alongside him.

He constructed the pump to force clean air into the newest working shaft in the Sharptor deep level, though the problems associated with it took a long time to solve. The greatest difficulty was to make the whole length of the tube airtight. But when it was completed the miners declared that the air brought in by Josh's air-pumping machine was fresher than any to be found elsewhere in the mine workings.

With this behind him, Josh set about making modifications to his man-lift. The royalties from it were beginning to come in regularly now.

There were other problems that summer. It seemed the politicians in London never learned by their mistakes.

There was a reversion to the corn policy which had resulted

in such hardship a few short years before. It meant that the bulk of the coming harvest would be sent to the towns and cities of the south-east and the new industrial centres of the Midlands. The Cornish farmer was expected to put the maximum acreage under corn, then send off his whole crop in accordance with Parliament's wishes.

This time it was not only the miners who raised their voices against the Corn Laws. The fishermen and farmworkers were also angry.

Because he had nothing to stay home for in the evenings, Josh was prepared to go anywhere to address a Miners' Union meeting. He threw himself wholeheartedly into their cause. He became a harder, more positive man. There were few hecklers at any of the meetings who would have cared to argue with him face to face.

All through that hot summer of 1845, Josh, William Thackeray and Miriam travelled around Cornwall addressing meetings. The Miners' Union was now an accomplished thing. At one evening meeting on the sands at Par, three thousand miners turned up to hear Josh and William Thackeray spell out what the corn policy would mean to the mining community.

'This has been a good harvest year,' shouted the preacher. 'The best we've seen this century. But what happens to the corn when it's harvested? Will the stomachs of our families be full? Will the miners of Cornwall go to work with enough food inside them to keep going through the long shifts ahead? No! The Cornish miner and his family will stay hungry. He'll watch the crops in the fields ripen, see them harvested and the corn gathered in; then he'll watch as it's loaded into wagons and hauled to the ports to be carried to the cities of England – and even to other countries! Are we going to stand by and allow such idiocy?'

There was a roar from the huge crowd. Cries of 'No!' 'Never!' Then a voice from their midst called, 'But what can we do about it?'

This was Josh's cue. Moving forward he towered above the small preacher.

'See your own Mine Union Committee. Join the benefit fund

so we know how many men are supporting us. If there's no committee in your own mine, start one. When the right time comes we'll tell you what to do. If we all stand together we'll succeed. There will be no corn leaving Cornwall until we're sure as much as is needed remains here.'

His words were received well. After a few more questions were answered the meeting broke up. Josh and William Thackeray left with a feeling they now had a large and organised movement behind them, one where its members were pulling in a single direction. It was no mean achievement, as any man who had ever tried to organise Cornishmen would know.

'Well, Josh,' said William Thackeray as they set their horses up the slope through Tywardreath, 'I think Parliament in London has done our task for us. The Cornish miners are united as never before. If only we can keep them together we'll be able to improve their lot a hundredfold.'

'That's if the militia doesn't interfere,' said Josh.

'What if they do?' declared William Thackeray jubilantly. 'The militia won't be able to keep the mines running if the men down tools.'

'The adventurers won't starve if the mines are closed for a while. The men will. The fund money won't last for ever, and with tempers running as hot as they are now someone will get hurt.'

'Don't be so parochial,' said William Thackeray. 'We must think of the cause as a whole. If the militia are called in and miners are hurt – or killed – public sympathy will swing to our side. Parliament and the adventurers will become so alarmed they'll have to give the men what they demand.'

'Tell that to the families of those who die,' retorted Josh.

Preacher Thackeray looked at Josh in exasperation. 'There are times when I find it difficult to understand you, Josh. You stand up in front of three thousand men and tell them what they want to hear. They roar their support for you, make it clear they would follow you if you took up arms against the Queen. Then you turn around and tell me you're concerned because a miner or two might get hurt. We're taking part in a revolution, Josh. A revolution of the workers. In revolutions men get hurt. That's accepted. These men are fighting for the future of all miners. We mustn't get squeamish now.'

'It sounds to me as though we are fighting for different causes,' said Josh. 'You're dreaming of some great movement of the future, a power to influence Parliament and change laws. That doesn't interest me. I believe in unionism for the same reason I built the man-lift. Because the lot of the miner is unnecessarily hard and dangerous. I want to see it made easier and safer.'

'Admirable sentiments, Josh. And extremely limiting to real progress.'

Josh smiled. 'Had anyone told you a few years ago that three thousand miners would attend one of your meetings, you'd have been delirious with joy. Today you've witnessed it, and you talk of "limited" progress.'

The preacher shrugged. 'When you have three hundred you dream of three thousand. When that's achieved you look for thirty thousand. That's ambition, Josh.' He kicked the horse into a canter. 'Miriam has a rabbit pie waiting for us tonight. Tomorrow will take care of itself.'

The subject came up again during the meal. Miriam agreed with Josh on the aims of the Miners' Union, but she was well aware of the ambitions of her husband and it was to him she spoke.

'What happens on the day you have your thirty thousand miners gathered together? You know well enough what they're like. If one says go north there will be three who want to go south. They will never be able to agree on a single policy.'

'Not if the matter is thrown open to discussion.' William Thackeray poured himself some more wine. 'But given the right leader they will do whatever he says is necessary.'

'And you will be that leader?' asked Josh.

'Who else? Unless yourself. Outside this room there is nobody with either the ability or the inclination to lead them.'

'For how long do you think you would be allowed to exert this power?'

'I'm sorry, Miriam. I don't understand.'

'No, because you've been too carried away by your successes to wonder where it might end. Calling meetings and discussing ways of improving the living standards of the miner is all right. It's part of a minister's work. Although there'll be a great many grumbles from the employers, nobody in authority can fault you for it. But march at the head of thirty thousand men with the intention of forcing Parliament to change the laws of the land and I think there will be a very different reaction.'

'I don't think you understand. I have no plans to put myself at the head of thirty thousand men and march anywhere.'

'No?' This from Josh. 'How else will you stop the grain from being exported from Cornwall?'

'Now you are both joining forces against me. We don't have thirty thousand men. Even if we had I've no intention of taking the miners anywhere. My plan is for the miners to blockade the ports peaceably, to prevent grain from being taken away until adequate provision is made for the Cornish miner and his family.'

'How do you propose to stop the grain from being moved? With words? Farmers are Cornishmen too, William. They can be as stubborn as miners. We don't like these corn policies, but they mean money for the farmer. He's not going to see that slip out of his hands because someone throws words at him.'

'The policy will change long before force becomes necessary,' said William Thackeray, a trifle too casually. 'Parliament is bound to see they are wrong. They won't allow women and children to starve. The united determination of the men will be sufficient.'

'That's not what you were saying when we left Par,' said Josh. 'You told me violence in revolution is acceptable. Yes, you did! And what is opposing the will of Parliament if not revolution?'

'Yes, and don't think you're going to appear at the ports of Cornwall with your miners and take everyone by surprise. It's too late for that. There has been so much talk of the miners uniting, the adventurers have become alarmed. Rumour has it the Somerset militia is being mustered for service in Cornwall. I spoke to a coachman today who saw part of a Welsh regiment passing through Bristol, heading this way.'

'Then I hope they have the sense not to interfere with any peaceable action taken by the miners,' said William Thackeray. 'That would certainly precipitate violence.'

'It would never come to that,' said Miriam. 'The Army will arrive first and arrest the men who lead the miners. That means you and Josh. I doubt whether you'll be as lucky as the leaders of the Kit Hill incident. They were only rebelling against the mine-owners. Your fight is with Parliament. They hang men for that.'

'I fail to understand you, Miriam!' Preacher Thackeray got up from the table abruptly. 'I thought you were as strong for the Union as I am. You've even spoken out for it at my meetings. What's happened to bring about this sudden change of heart?'

'I haven't changed, William. I'm as much for the Union as ever. But I think it would be better for everyone if you preached for law and order at your meetings. Made it quite clear you wouldn't condone violence under any circumstances.'

'What absolute nonsense!' Josh had seldom seen the preacher angry. 'What do you want me to do? Drop out of the movement at this critical stage? Are you telling me I should desert the miners because there might be trouble?'

'No.' Miriam was as calm as he was angry. 'I am merely saying that you should restrict what you say in public to matters affecting miners' welfare. Anything else should be discussed with a selected few of their leaders. In private.'

For a moment William Thackeray looked as though he had been struck dumb. Then he banged his fist on the table and let out a roar of approval.

'Did you hear that, Josh? Did you hear what she said? She has more brains in her head than you and I put together. She's right, of course. Absolutely right. I should have been the first to see it. If we carry on the way we are there will be a confrontation with the militia. That can have only one end for you and me. On the other hand, if we are heard to preach moderation what grounds could they possibly have for arresting us?'

'I've always favoured moderation. If a policy is bad the sooner it's abolished the better. But not at the cost of men's lives.'

'Of course, Josh. I agree with you. If the magistrates think trouble is simmering they'll order the arrest of those who are stirring it. From now on were going to do some very clever and serious planning.'

But changing the surface image of the Union was not easy. When public meetings were called, the men attending them expected to hear scathing attacks on the iniquitous corn policy. Instead, they received glowing reports of the benefits to be gained by belonging to the Miners' Union, were told of the safety measures provided in mines as a result of union representation. Questions about the Corn Laws were carefully side-stepped. If any answers were given they were variations on a theme of non-violence. For the ordinary miner it was a frustrating and baffling period. But on most nights of the week the chapel at St Cleer was occupied by groups of their leaders from mines in east and central Cornwall. And messengers galloped the roads of Cornwall with news and instructions for the masterplan that was being formulated.

What that plan was soon became clear. One farmer, more efficient than his fellows, eager to obtain a good price in the Bristol market, brought the first creaking wagon-load of corn down the steep lane to Boscastle harbour. He found the way blocked by two hundred grim-faced miners. There was no violence and little argument. But so impressed was the farmer by their determination he promptly turned around and sold the whole of his wagon-load in Camelford market, contrary to the orders of Parliament. The whole load was eagerly snapped up by buyers who paid a price equal to any he would have received elsewhere.

The news was hailed throughout the county as a miners' victory. The more naïve among them awaited the changes in the law they were sure it would bring about.

Parliament had other ideas. The rumours from Bristol had not been false. The Monmouth militia arrived. It was first billeted in Launceston, then split into smaller units to garrison other Cornish towns. The Somerset militia too moved into the county. But by far the most ominous threat to the hopes of the miners came when the 32nd Foot – Cornwall's own regular regiment – returned from overseas duty and moved into garrison at Bodmin. The men of the 32nd were disciplined battle-hardened soldiers who scorned all civilians, Cornish or not. On pay-nights they caused the citizens of Bodmin to shutter their houses and cower inside until the barrack gates closed on the last rowdy warrior.

One of these soldiers was Morwen Trago. He arrived at Preacher Thackeray's gate in St Cleer one evening as Josh was leaving.

Morwen looked very smart in the red-coated uniform with white cross-belts. The army life evidently suited him; he looked extremely fit and bronzed.

Josh expressed pleasure at meeting him and held out his hand, but Morwen Trago ignored it.

'What are you doing here, Retallick? I would have thought marriage had got you out of my sister's system. But perhaps her husband's away and you're just sniffing around.'

Josh had almost forgotten the tragic circumstances that had preceded Morwen's enlistment into the Army. He was unprepared for the sheer hatred that showed on Morwen's face.

'That uniform has done nothing to improve your manners, Morwen. Try not to disgrace Miriam when you meet her husband.'

Morwen Trago's eyes blazed angrily and Josh tensed, expecting the hot-headed Morwen to launch an attack on him. Instead, the soldier slammed the gate shut and stalked away along the path to the house. Morwen Trago was aware that his sister had achieved status in the community by marrying a preacher and he was keenly aware of his own lack of education. He had tried to make up for it by ensuring his uniform was immaculate – the white webbing cross-belts pure white, brass buckles gleaming. So determined was he to arrive in this state that he had ridden in the coach from Bodmin sitting upright, not allowing his back to rest against the seat lest his coat crease or dirt find its way on to his cross-belts.

Miriam was overjoyed to see him. William Thackeray stayed smilingly in the background while they reminisced about imagined good times in the past, intruding only to keep Morwen's tankard filled.

There was much to tell. Morwen had been away for four years and was not aware that Miriam had a baby. For her part, although she knew her soldier brother was abroad, Miriam did not know where he was serving. Morwen came into his own telling of the countries he had seen and battles he had fought and won there.

When the conversation between brother and sister showed signs of flagging Preacher Thackeray joined in.

'You've led a very interesting and active life since you left the mine, Morwen. You'll find things very much quieter in Cornwall, I'm quite sure.'

'Don't you believe it!' Ale and brandy coupled with the warmth of the room caused his cheeks to glow fiery red. 'They don't pay soldiers to sit on their backsides and play cards in the barracks, Preacher. They've got us down here for a reason.'

'A reason for the Army here in Cornwall?' Preacher Thackeray smiled.

'Ah! You'd be surprised if you only knew. We've been told this outcry against the Corn Laws is just an excuse to start a revolution, to overthrow Queen and Parliament – just as they did in France. But they'll have a surprise when they start here.'

'I'm quite sure they will.' Preacher Thackeray leaned back in his chair and looked at the half-drunken soldier. 'But I doubt whether your regiment would be sufficient to defeat the whole of the county should they choose to rise.'

'It isn't only our regiment.' Morwen waved his tankard unsteadily before his face. 'There's the militia – for what use they might be. They're coming from Wales, Somerset and Devon. Then there's the Navy.'

'The Navy!' It was difficult to see how the fleet could be used.

'Yes. The miners are trying to stop corn from leaving from the ports, aren't they? Well, they aren't going to succeed. The

Navy has its men-of-war sailing just outside the ports. At the first sign of trouble they'll come in and land their marines. With a regiment of foot soldiers and the marines against them the miners won't last a day. You can be damned sure of that!'

'Men-of-war, eh?' Preacher Thackeray mused. He looked at Morwen, who was now staring ahead of him glassy-eyed, the tankard dangling from a finger and dripping ale to the floor.

'I think I'd better help our guest up to the spare bedroom,' he said.

'No. He's my brother. I'll do it.'

'Then we'll both help him.'

Between them they got him up the stairs and laid him on a bed. Miriam removed his boots, undid his coat and covered him with a blanket.

'Poor Morwen,' she murmured when her husband had left the room. 'What a legacy our father handed on to you.'

When Miriam returned downstairs, William was pacing the floor of the lounge. 'So Parliament is expecting big trouble? Sending marines, militia and a regular regiment against us. They're taking this far more seriously than I thought they would.'

'You'll have to cancel your plans now, William. This makes things far too dangerous.'

'Cancel my plans? Nonsense! It will alter them, of course. But there's absolutely no question of cancelling anything.' He looked at her quizzically. 'Do you think Morwen could be persuaded to help us?'

'Never! You heard him yourself. He's overjoyed at the chance of fighting miners. He seems to imagine they are all responsible for the death of our father. No, he won't help us.'

'Then we'll just have to manage without him. One thing is clear. He's not aware of my involvement or he wouldn't have said as much as he did.'

'What does that mean?' Miriam gave him a curious look.

'It means that it might already be accepted my interest is purely in the welfare of the miner. Should that be the case I'll be able to lead them quite safely, in the manner suggested by yourself.'

'You can't intend opposing the export of corn now. Not after what has been said tonight? The miners will have no chance against soldiers and marines.'

'How long is Morwen staying with us?'

'Only until the morning. Then he's walking to Henwood to spend a day with Mother before returning to Bodmin.'

'Good. I'll call a meeting for tomorrow night. I have an idea.' A few days later Preacher Thackeray's plans began to take effect. A farmer loaded up two wagons of wheat for Charlestown harbour but at the end of the lane from his farm he was surrounded by forty tough and determined miners. Despite his protests he was escorted to St Austell market square where the load was disposed of for cash in a mere fifteen minutes. The farmer reported it to the magistrate only because he would otherwise have been held to account for the corn he had grown but not 'exported'. The price was a fair one and he returned home well pleased. The same thing happened to the next farmer. And the next. Then the militia was divided into even smaller detachments with orders to patrol every market town and prevent the sale of corn.

This too failed. The farmers were intercepted as they left their farms and taken to a nearby open space where buyers were waiting. The corn was auctioned off, transferred to waiting wagons, and the farmer escorted home to his farm to prevent the magistrates being alerted before the corn was spirited away to a safe hiding-place.

It was at this point that the angry military authorities brought a plan of their own into operation. The farmers were ordered to inform the nearest magistrate when corn was almost ready for delivery to the nearest port. A small party of militiamen would then accompany them to one of many large barns hired specially for the purpose throughout the county. A guard was placed on the barn until all the corn for that area was gathered in. Then, under full escort, it was taken to the nearest port. The idea worked. It was so effective that the authorities in the county told Parliament the matter was now fully under control. As a result the ships were withdrawn from around the seaports of Cornwall.

The miners too saw it as a defeat. At the open meetings where only two weeks before they had boasted of their victories they now condemned the Union for not staying one step ahead of the soldiers. There was anger and recrimination too at the secret meetings held in the chapel at St Cleer.

At first, William Thackeray shrugged off the setbacks suffered by the Union. They had achieved modest success and obtained some corn. They had stretched the resources of the military, forcing them to guard every load of corn all the way from the fields to the ports.

But this was not enough for the miners' leaders. When Thackeray saw the strength of popular feeling, he went along with it. He began to prepare for a more violent form of protest against the corn policy.

Josh was appalled. At one meeting he stood up and told the miners' representatives why.

'There is absolutely no excuse for the use of force now. Most families have corn. While it may not be as much as they might normally use, properly husbanded it will last the winter. There was corn rioting last weekend in Tavistock. Soon it will spread to other towns in Devon and Somerset and the whole of the West Country. If we remain patient we shall win. Parliament will have to change the law.'

John Kittow agreed. But miners have never been the most patient of men. Cornish miners were no different. They jeered at Josh's apparent timidity. They were not content to wait any longer. They wanted a showdown and now was a good time.

Had Preacher Thackeray sided with Josh they might have turned the tide of the argument. But recently the two men had failed to agree on many union principles. There were times when Preacher Thackeray felt jealousy at the respect the engineer commanded. He voted against Josh's moderate policy.

Perhaps there were other reasons too for the cooling-off in their relationship.

Before Morwen Trago had left the preacher's house after his first visit he had walked with William Thackeray in the garden. They spoke of many things, of the troubles in the country and the changes that had occurred in the mining industry since Morwen left it and joined the Army. When William Thackeray mentioned Josh's inventions in the field of mine safety, Morwen expressed his misgivings about the preacher becoming too friendly with the Sharptor mine-engineer. It was not wise, he said, in view of Miriam and Josh's close attachment in the past. Then he dropped his bombshell. He had heard some of his officers talking, he said. Josh's name had been mentioned in connection with the Union.

William said nothing then, but both reasons for Morwen's concern nourished seeds that were already planted in the preacher's mind.

After the latest meeting in the chapel at which much heat was generated without any firm decision being made, the miners' leaders dispersed to go their separate ways. Josh followed his established custom of going to the preacher's house for a drink and talk with William and Miriam. There the main points of the meeting were argued out again.

'Josh, I respect your reasoning and your concern for the Cornish miner, but yours is a short-term policy. You are interested only in the "todays". I am looking ahead towards the Union to which the sons of today's miners will belong. And their sons after them. Believe me, Josh, I know what I'm talking about. I've spent a lifetime dedicated to this cause. You're a mine-engineer and far too close to the men to know what might ultimately be best for them.'

'As a preacher you should be equally close to them. Promises for the future are words. Those who employ the Cornish miner have never been mean with talk. Your argument about the future is mere speculation. If we have patience we'll gain what we want. In this case sufficient corn to feed the men's families. Ordinary people all over the country are taking an example from our actions here. The corn policy will crumble and become history before the year is out. To use tactics that can only bring about a fight between the soldiers and the miners will damage your cause. They can't hope to win in a direct fight with authority. There would be bloodshed, arrests and transportations. Why, the soldiers could strike such a decisive blow it might cause resistance to the corn policy to fizzle, becoming nothing more than a bubble of angry words.'

But Thackeray had made up his mind which side he was backing. He would not be moved.

'On the contrary, if we don't take action now a stubborn Parliament could retain their policy for years to come. A direct confrontation with the soldiers and the militiamen would force their hand. Public outrage at the death of even a single miner would swing the opinion of the whole country to our side.'

'And what of the man who is dead?' asked Josh. 'He might become a symbol, a martyr. Will that help his family? And the others – those who are crippled or maimed in the fighting. Will people be so grateful they bring them a week's pay every Friday? No, William. Your ideas may help the cause of unionism. They won't help the miners of Cornwall.'

'I agree with Josh,' said Miriam, who had listened to the argument.

'Agreeing with Josh seems to be a habit with you,' snapped her husband angrily.

'I'm quite capable of forming opinions of my own,' retorted Miriam equally angrily. 'And I believe he's right. If I thought you were right I'd say – as I have so often in the past.'

'I wish I could believe that,' snorted William Thackeray. Turning, he left the room. A few seconds later Josh heard the front door slam shut. He started after the preacher, but Miriam stopped him with a hand on his arm.

'No, let him go, Josh. There'll be no reasoning with him while he's in this mood.'

'How do you know? Has he said things like that before?'

'Yes, but I say nothing and it soon passes.'

'Perhaps it would be better if I stayed away for a while. William and I no longer agree on what is best for the miners.'

'No, Josh. Don't desert me – us – now. William is ambitious to keep firm control of the Union. It's reached a point where he'll go along with whatever the majority wants. But, although you may not think so at the moment, he has great respect for your judgement. He's in need of your advice more than ever before.'

Her hands were gripping his arm tightly and she looked pleadingly up into his face.

'I *know* your way is right. I'll do my best to convince William of that. But I need your help.'

'All right.' Josh nodded his agreement. 'But it won't be for William's sake alone. The action the miners want to take would be disastrous for all of us.'

Chapter Twenty-Five

Late in August of that year Jenny Shovell gave birth to a son. News that she was in labour came to the Retallick house shortly after dusk. Jesse threw a shawl about her shoulders and gathered up a bag of all the things she considered to be necessary at a childbirth. Josh went along to the mine captain's house with her.

There was a light coming from every window. It looked for all the world as though Jenny were having a party instead of a baby. Some of the women from the village were already there, as were two shift captains and a number of the more senior Sharptor miners. Josh went in to wish Tom Shovell well and found the middle-aged mine captain as edgy and nervous as any young prospective father.

They were all talking in the kitchen when old Mary Crabbe came in. As her part in what went on upstairs was second only to that of the principal, the men stepped back respectfully to allow her through. She went to the wide iron stove and checked the water, speaking to none of the men and not looking at their faces. Satisfied that the water was sufficient she turned, making her way across the kitchen towards the door that led to the stairs. She had almost reached it when she stopped, her hand outstretched. It was as though someone had spoken to her. Turning, she looked at the faces of the men for the first time and her wild dark eyes came to rest on Josh.

Pointing a shaking bony finger at him, she shrieked, 'Out of this house, Josh Retallick. I'll deliver no baby beneath the same roof as you, or the curse on you will be laid upon the child.'

There was a horrified silence until someone at the rear of the room gave a nervous laugh. The sound enraged the old woman.

'Laugh if you will,' she screeched. 'But either Josh Retallick leaves this house or I do. And if I leave there'll be nothing to celebrate tomorrow.'

Tom Shovell looked apprehensively from the woman to Josh and back again, utterly bewildered.

'It's all right, Tom. I'm going,' said Josh.

'You'll leave because a crazy old woman says you must?' This from one of the younger miners who had no more superstition in his body than he had brains in his head. 'Ignore the old fool, Josh. It's the full moon. You know what she's like at such times.'

'Yes, there's a grown moon,' cackled Mary Crabbe, as though confirming the miner's judgement of her. 'But before there's another you'll have reason to know how crazy Mary Crabbe is.'

'Oh, come on, Mary!' This from one of the shift captains. 'Josh has had his troubles. Give the boy some luck now.'

'Troubles? They haven't begun for Josh Retallick yet.'

'You go upstairs and tend to Jenny, Mary,' said Josh. He was as superstitious as his father and his calm voice did not reflect his true feelings. 'Perhaps sometime you'll tell me what the future has in store for me.'

'If I thought it would do any good I would,' said the old crone. 'But if you mind the business of others you must expect to inherit their troubles. That's all I have to say.'

With that she shuffled from the room. When the door closed behind her everyone began talking at once.

'You don't really have to leave,' said Tom Shovell awkwardly.

'It's all right, Tom. I never intended staying. I came here with

Mother to wish you and Jenny well. I've done that. Now, since this is a night for predictions, I'll make one. I predict that you and Jenny will have a fine son who'll grow up to be a great mine captain. Like his father.'

The other men in the room chorused their agreement and Josh left the house. He waved back at them cheerfully but felt less happy inside. Mary was a true witch. He could not recall one firm forecast she had made that had not come true.

There had been too many witnesses in Tom Shovell's kitchen to keep Mary Crabbe's words secret. The following day a worried Jesse Retallick spoke to Josh about them.

'It's this stupid union business. There's been no sense in you since you finished your time at Hayle. I hoped when you married poor Sarah – God rest her soul! – you'd settle down. Instead . . . !' She made a gesture of resignation.

'I don't know what will become of you, Josh. You're a young man. Why don't you find yourself a nice girl and marry her? You could have the choice of any girl in the country. You've got a good job, money coming in from that lift-machine you made, and that fine house on the tor. I don't suppose you've been near there for more than a month – unless it's to feed and exercise that horse of yours.'

'The house was bought by William Carlyon for his daughter,' Josh replied with a scowl. 'I want no part of it. There's been little happiness there for me.'

'That's not the fault of the house. And didn't you tell me Mr Carlyon had written to say he'd bought the house for you and Sarah and it was now yours alone?'

'I don't want the house, and the last thing I want is to marry another girl and take her there. But if you want me to leave here I'll find somewhere else to live.'

'Now, what sort of a thing is that to say, Josh?' his mother flung at him. 'This has always been your home and will be for as long as you want it. I'm only thinking of you and your future. I want to see you settled and raising a family, not wasting your time with a crowd of no-good miners who are intent on stirring up trouble. These are uncertain times, Josh. We don't want any trouble with the soldiers.'

While they were talking Ben Retallick had appeared to be sleeping in his chair but now he stood up and crossed to the window.

'I thought I could hear something unusual while you two were arguing. It seems the soldiers aren't content to stay in their barracks waiting for trouble. They've come looking for it.'

Jesse hurried to join Josh and her husband at the window.

'Well I never! Now, there's an omen for you. One minute I'm talking to you about them. The next thing you know is they're outside. I can't ever remember seeing them about here before. I don't like it. It gives me a bad feeling.'

'Nonsense,' Josh laughed. 'They didn't just drop out of the sky. They've marched here from Bodmin.'

'I wonder what they're after?' frowned Ben Retallick. 'Even with the present troubles there is nothing for them about here.'

'I would say they're marching through the mining areas to remind us the Army's in Cornwall,' said Josh. 'But it's a stupid thing to do. The miners are in an ugly mood. It might well be the soldiers who are made to realise they are not fighting helpless savages.'

There were about sixty soldiers marching up the road from Henwood village. They made a smart formation, keeping time to a lone drummer. Taking the road below the cottages, they headed southwards towards the Phoenix and Caradon mines.

The steady monotonous beat of the drum travelled ahead of them, and along the way they had collected a motley following of miners' sons and farm-boys. The boys ran alongside, jeering and catcalling, or swaggered behind in ragged mimicry. There was none of the hero-worship of only a few short years before, when the army that had beaten Napoleon's soldiers was a welcome sight anywhere in the country.

'Let's take a walk up to Wheal Sharptor,' Ben Retallick said to Josh. 'I won't rest easy until I see the soldiers clear of the mine.'

But the soldiers appeared to have no designs on the Sharptor mine. As Josh and his father climbed the hill beyond Sharptor they saw the uniformed men turn down the track to the Phoenix mine, the drummer silent as the men broke step on the uneven surface.

'The fools!' exclaimed Josh. 'What do they think they're doing? They could hardly have chosen a worse time to visit a mine. If some of the Phoenix hotheads are still above ground there'll be trouble.'

'Then we'd best go down and see what we can do to stop it,' said Ben Retallick.

'No. You stay here and make sure none of the Sharptor miners go down and interfere. I'll see what's happening at the Phoenix.'

Josh set off through the ferns and heather of the steep hillside at a run. It was only a couple of hundred yards to the mine track but the soldiers reached the Phoenix before Josh.

The officer allowed the men to break ranks, and they stood around, arrogant in their smart uniforms, passing derisive comments about the state of the mine and the men and women working within their view. Some twenty surface-workers, young boys for the most part, watched them with wary curiosity.

'You there!' the officer beckoned to one of the lads. 'My men want a drink of water. Is there somewhere near at hand?'

A grizzled old miner limped from a nearby shed to give them their answer. 'We get ours from a pump outside the engine-house. But there's a horse trough along the way; that should do for you.'

There was an angry murmur from the soldiers and nervous laughs from the surface-workers. It was fortunate the mine captain arrived upon the scene at that moment. He was under-ground on one of the upper levels when the soldiers started down from the road. One of the young boys working on sorting ore had hurried to fetch him.

He left the officer in no doubt as to who was in charge of the Wheal Phoenix and let him know he and his soldiers were not welcome.

'What do you want here? And tell your men to stay clear of the machinery. Apart from the danger to them the crusher they are leaning against cost a lot of money and it's difficult to obtain spare parts.'

'I came here for water for my men and a place where they could rest and eat a meal,' said the officer.

'Water they are welcome to,' replied the mine captain and turned to one of the boys. 'Jimmy, go and fetch two buckets of water and a couple of mugs.'

He turned back to the officer. 'As for a rest and meal, this is a working mine; I'll not have my boys distracted while your soldiers lounge around eating. There's a whole empty moor around us. I suggest you find a place to camp and eat there.'

'That's hardly a sociable attitude to take,' said the officer. 'We are your county's own regiment just back from service abroad. We even have a man from your own village in our ranks. Indeed, I understand he worked in this very mine. And you tell us we are not to remain here for one minute longer than is necessary!'

'That's exactly what I'm telling you,' said the Phoenix captain firmly. 'And I've already seen Morwen Trago. He's welcome to come visiting at any time. But not when he's wearing the uniform of a soldier.'

'Then I think we'll go to the mine on the hill.' He nodded in the direction of Sharptor. 'Perhaps we'll receive more civility there.'

'Don't waste your time,' said Josh. 'The Wheal Sharptor is also a working mine. Soldiers would be as much in the way as here.'

'Oh!' The officer's eyes glittered angrily. 'Are the men of the Phoenix mine spokesmen for every mine in Cornwall?'

'I'm not from the Wheal Phoenix.' Josh moved to stand beside the Phoenix captain. 'My name is Retallick. I'm the engineer at Sharptor. My father is a shift captain and we both came out to make sure you didn't come visiting.'

'Retallick? I've heard that name before.'

'It's likely. Retallick's a common enough Cornish name. More Cornish, I should think, than your own.'

The officer flushed angrily. Although he had made the comment about it being a Cornish regiment, his accent placed him as coming from far to the east of the Tamar.

'Well, I have no wish to put a strain on the hospitality of such generous hosts,' said the officer. 'Fall the men in, Sergeant.'

He half-bowed towards them. 'Goodbye, gentlemen.' Looking directly at Josh, he said, 'I feel quite sure we'll meet again, Mr Retallick. I look forward to it.'

Placing himself at the head of his soldiers, he rapped out a command. The drummer started to swing his drumsticks and the soldiers marched from the Wheal Phoenix.

'I think we convinced them they aren't needed here,' said the mine captain.

'No doubt,' replied Josh. 'But they didn't tell us their reason for the visit. I'm sure they had one. Furthermore, I think they might have achieved it.'

He did not explain further but turned and made his way up the hill to Sharptor.

The harvest that had been going well was disrupted by a fortnight of heavy rain at the turn of that month. With a third of their crops still to be gathered in the farmers fumed impotently, swearing they could not remember a worse harvesting season, muttering about ruination. But it was only in the south-western counties of England. Throughout the remainder of the land the harvesting went ahead, and Parliament realised it was not only the Cornish who were upset by the unfair corn policy. Rioting took place throughout the land. What Josh had foreseen quickly came to pass. The men of the Monmouth militia were recalled to Wales. There the fiery Welsh coal-miners were showing their displeasure in a far more violent manner than the comparatively placid Cornish.

During this period the meetings held in the St Cleer chapel became even more divided about the form of their future action. A few came over to Josh's side, sensing that the increasing national unrest must mean a reversal of Parliament's policy on the corn issue. The others, following

Preacher Thackeray's lead, clamoured for more violent action to be taken in Cornwall.

The division between the two opposing groups became so deep and the arguments so bitter that, in spite of his promise to Miriam, Josh no longer visited the preacher's house. Because he missed the stimulus of conversation with William Thackeray and the pleasure of being in the same room as Miriam, he tried once to bridge the gap between them. But the preacher would not unbend. The easy comradeship that they had once known perished in the bitterness of their opposing convictions.

When the rains ceased and the muddy water-filled tracks became passable once more, the farmers resumed the harvesting of their crops and forgot their prophecies of doom.

It was now that rumours began to circulate among the miners that they had obtained far less corn than had been thought. They were told there was insufficient to keep their families fed through the winter months.

This was not true. Josh knew it and so did the miners' leaders. But still the rumours persisted. The clamour to keep the remainder of the corn harvest in Cornwall grew.

Quite how they would achieve it nobody seemed to know. Despite their reduction in numbers the soldiers were still escorting farmers' wagons and their grip on the situation was as tight as before.

Inevitably, it seemed, the scene was being set for violence. It came on a beautiful hot day in late September. There was hardly a cloud to scar the blue sky. A pair of lazy buzzards wheeled and dipped high over Twelve Men's Moor. Above the red waste of the Sharptor mine a pair of very late swifts screamed in a breakneck dive, skimming the dusty earth with their scythe-like wings, gathering insects and building up strength for the long flight south.

Josh had been helping the engine-men to renew the padding in the main piston of the whim-engine. He was cleaning his hands in the tub outside the engine-house when a convoy of coal-laden wagons creaked into the mine, returning from the canal-head at Moorswater.

'They've got themselves a parcel of trouble up at Wheal Caradon,' called old Nehemeziah Lancellis as he climbed stiffly down from the lead wagon. 'Someone along the way told me to tell you the whole blessed mine be closed.'

'Oh!' Josh was instantly interested. 'What's happened? Have the adventurers cut their pay and caused the men to walk out? They should be working extra time up there. They've a flooded shaft to clear.'

'Ain't nothing to do with the mine.' Nehemeziah spat into the dust. ''Tis this damned corn business. Whole lot of 'em downed shovels. Gone to Looe to stop a corn boat leaving. Damn fools, the lot of 'em.'

'That's ridiculous!' Josh was alarmed. 'They know the soldiers are at Looe. They would as soon shoot a miner as a rabbit.'

'Don't know about such things,' said old Nehemeziah. 'But I was to tell you where they'm heading. Spoiling for a fight, I was told.'

'The idiots! Who was leading them, do you know?'

The hostler snorted. 'No. Might just as well ask which starling leads a flock. They'd be just a-going. Shouting and calling with no leader at all.'

'I wonder whether Preacher Thackeray is with them?'

Nehemeziah's laugh was short and derisive. 'Preacher Thackeray? He won't raise his head 'bove water when trouble's around. Thought you'd a' known that. He's the spoon as does the stirring, not the pot as sits on the fire.'

'Have you any idea what time they left?' Josh's mind was racing ahead. The men were on foot. If the Army had not got wind of their approach and made moves to intercept them it might be possible to take a horse and head them off.

'Don't know. I got news of it an hour ago. They'd be well on the way now.'

The chances of preventing the miners from reaching the port were very slim indeed, but Josh would try.

'I've got to get out of these greasy clothes, Nehemeziah. Send someone to saddle Hector for me and bring him down here.'

'You're not going to Looe? 'Tis mad! If they're stupid enough to want trouble, let 'em have it. It need be none o'your business.'

'They are miners, Nehemeziah, the same as us. Go and get my horse saddled.'

Nehemeziah walked away, muttering to himself and shaking his head. There were problems enough in earning a living without getting involved with men from other mines who wanted to fight soldiers.

Josh was not the only one worried about the Caradon miners. He was a mile out from Looe, with the steep wooded slope on one side, the muddy brown tidal waters of the Looe river on the other, when he caught up with John Kittow. The Caradon miner's leader was bouncing along on a pack-horse that had seen better days.

'Fools! Bloody fools!' was all he seemed able to say when Josh reined in beside him.

'What are their plans?' asked Josh. 'What are they hoping to do?'

'Plans!' exclaimed John Kittow, sweating and angry. 'They've no plans. They're going to keep the corn from being loaded on to a ship. That's all I know. I doubt if they've thought beyond that.'

'Weren't you able to stop them? They usually listen to you.'

'They might have listened to me, had I been at the mine.' The shift captain swore. 'I was over to Callington to hire a couple of blacksmiths. When I got back it was a mine without miners. How did you find out about it?'

Josh explained. 'And I hope we'll be in time to avoid bloodshed.'

John Kittow kicked the pack-horse with renewed vigour, provoking it into an ungainly trot.

Rounding a bend down the hill into Looe town, Josh and John Kittow became aware they were already too late. The roar of a large crowd of angry men greeted them. The sounds came from the wharf just beyond the arched bridge. On the bridge itself were farmers' wagons, tailed back to the western bank of the river. The soldiers who had been acting as escorts were forming up close to them. But these were not foot-soldiers.

They were mounted, wearing the blue jackets and plumed helmets of Dragoon Guards.

Josh kneed Hector forward, passing the dragoons as the order was given for them to draw sabres. Beyond the bridge the scene at the dockside was even worse than he had feared. There must have been six or seven hundred miners, the Caradon men having received support along the way. They were packed in a tight swaying mob on the open jetty, spilling out into the narrow streets and alleys of the town.

The small harbour was crammed with shipping, and sailors swarmed the rigging of the ships the better to view the shoreside happenings.

There were fifty wagons of corn drawn up at the water's edge, white-faced farmers and farmers' men fingering the reins of their horses uncertainly. Between the wagons and the angry miners a line of red-coated soldiers stood with guns held at the ready.

An officer was arguing with a small group of miners, none of whom Josh recognised as from the Wheal Caradon. But the officer was the same one who had led his men into the Wheal Phoenix. Josh spurred his horse forward into the crowd. After offering initial resistance, the men moved aside for him and John Kittow. He heard miners call their names as they arrived at the far edge of the crowd.

Even at this late stage it might have been possible to avert bloodshed, although a magistrate had already been to the wharf and proclaimed the Riot Act to the miners, declaring them officially a 'riotous assembly'. This was sufficient in a court to justify any violence that might be used against them. It is doubtful whether any of the miners fully realised the seriousness of their position. They had no capable leader, only hotheads like those who were arguing with the officer on the quayside.

Josh and John Kittow had hoped to persuade the miners to return to their homes peaceably once they had made their protest. They never had an opportunity to try. Exactly what was said to precipitate the disastrous scenes that followed was never clear. But in the middle of the heated argument the officer grabbed the shirt-front of one of the miners. He attempted to drag him back towards the soldiers. The miner struggled and struck out wildly. At the same time, two of the men with him began raining blows upon the officer until he fell to the ground with one of the miners on top of him.

This was sufficient for the sergeant with the platoon. At a hoarse command every second man in the line dropped to one knee. Rifles aimed at the seething mass of miners. Before a horrified Josh could do or say anything, a volley of shots rang out. When the drifting acrid smoke cleared, a second volley followed.

There were alarmed shouts and screams. Half a dozen miners lay sprawled on the ground. Those immediately behind them turned and pushed away from the red-coated soldiers. Slowly, as realisation of what had happened dawned on the miners, the whole crowd began to move forward with them – only to find their retreat barred by the mounted Dragoon Guards. They had advanced from the bridge with drawn sabres and now bore down upon the totally defenceless miners.

The mounted dragoons began hacking about them as soon as their horses were among the miners, and the crowd broke, the miners trying to escape as best they could.

Josh rode at the foot soldiers, calling on them not to fire as their guns came to the aim position once again. He was too late. Another volley was fired and more miners slumped to the ground. Josh kneed Hector forward among the soldiers, bowling some over as they fired yet again. Some of the miners found an escape route through two narrow alleyways at the side of the jetty. They fought and struggled to get away from the scene of carnage behind them.

Josh turned his horse again, pleading with the soldiers not to shoot, only to find himself caught in the charge of the dragoons. Frightened by the noise, Hector reared, crashing down against the horse ridden by one of the dragoons. The soldier's mount slipped on the smooth cobblestones and crashed to the ground, carrying its rider with it.

Then Josh was in the middle of the hacking, slashing sabres

of the dragoons. A steel blade slashed across his back and a burning pain seared through the great muscles of his shoulders. Then Hector too stumbled and Josh was thrown to the ground. He clambered to his feet and in front of him, not fifteen feet away, was the officer in charge of the foot soldiers. Bloodied and bruised, he pointed in Josh's direction and called upon his men to shoot.

'Get him! Get that man! I want him!'

All was utter confusion now. Men were running in every direction. Foot soldiers, horse soldiers and miners running or fighting all over the wide jetty. There were also a great many still figures lying on the ground – not only miners but also blue-coated dragoons and hatless scarlet-coated soldiers. Josh saw an opening between the horses of the dragoons and ran for it. From somewhere close behind a gun roared and it felt as though someone had struck him a hard blow in the left arm. He spun about and a horse collided with him, knocking him to the ground again. Picking himself up, he clutched his left arm just above the elbow. Hot blood oozed between his fingers. Then, miraculously, John Kittow appeared beside him, still mounted and with Hector's reins held in his hand.

'Quick, Josh! Get up. Hurry!'

Josh swung himself into the saddle. Urging his horse forward he clattered after the Caradon miner, ducking his head low as they swung through a passageway between houses. Then they were out on a street with shuttered shops on either side and people running beside them.

Josh followed John Kittow along the road. They galloped past the bridge and out of the town, back along the road that had brought them into Looe a scant fifteen minutes earlier.

Soon they were clear of the fleeing miners but they rode hard for another mile before John Kittow pulled his horse in alongside Josh. By now the fire in Josh's back was burning fiercely, his arm throbbing alarmingly.

'My God, Josh! You're a bloody mess. Get off here. Let me have a look at those wounds. No, further down by the river. I'll need water to clean you up.'

They walked the horses down to the water's edge where Josh

swung from Hector's back, staggering as his feet touched the ground.

'Sit down while I get your shirt off.'

The miner stripped Josh's shirt from him without ceremony, ripping it away from his body; then he dipped his neckerchief into the river and began cleaning Josh's wounds. The river was tidal, the water salt. It stung. John Kittow grunted in sympathy. The wound in Josh's arm was quickly cleaned. The musket-ball had gone straight through cleanly, without touching the bone. Josh's back was a very different matter. It was laid open from the left shoulder to the right of his waist, laying bare the large muscles around his shoulder-blade.

'I don't like the looks of this, Josh. You must see a doctor as quickly as we can reach one.'

'It had better be a doctor well away from here,' said Josh, gritting his teeth against the pain of the salt water, 'or I'll have more than a wound to worry about.'

He gasped as John Kittow wrung more water into the wound.

'There was something I didn't understand back there, Josh. I heard the officer call your name just before you were shot, and I'd swear it was Morwen Trago who fired. Why?'

'That officer brought his men on a march around the mines,' explained Josh. 'I told him he wasn't welcome at Sharptor. I told him my name and he said he'd heard of me. I doubt very much if the wound in my arm was the result of a chance shot.'

'No. It was you they were after. And if they know your name they'll come for you at Sharptor.'

'We'll worry about that when we get there. The only good thing to be said for it is if they were so interested in me it might mean that you weren't recognised. Can you bind my back, John?'

John Kittow stripped off his own shirt and began tearing it into strips.

'I'll do what I can, but it won't last long, Josh. It's no more than an attempt to staunch the bleeding.'

They heard a ragged crackle of musket-fire in the distance and both men looked back towards Looe.

'God! It sounds as though the slaughter is still going on. Who were those fools arguing with the officer, John?'

'I don't know. They weren't from the Wheal Caradon. Most likely they came from the St Austell area.'

He laid a strip of damp cloth along the line of the sabre-cut, binding the remainder of the two shirts around Josh's body to hold it in place.

'That will have to do for now, Josh. Can you get back on your horse?'

Josh nodded, with more assurance than he felt. When he stood up the countryside swung about him. With John Kittow's help he managed to climb back into the saddle and cling there.

They set off again, following the line of the canal towards Moorswater. They were almost there when they heard the clatter of horses' hoofs on the road behind. Pulling their horses off the bridle path they hid in a small copse and watched six dragoons ride past at the gallop.

'Do you think they're looking for us?' asked John Kittow when the soldiers were out of sight.

'Probably. If they are they'll warn the militia at Liskeard. We'd better stay well clear of the town.'

By the time they reached the head of the canal, Josh was reeling in the saddle.

'You can't possibly ride any further, Josh. We must find somewhere for you to rest while I go on ahead and fetch a doctor.'

'No.' Josh felt sick. The blood from his back had run down inside his trousers and dried, making him stiff and uncomfortable. But he knew they had to keep moving.

Two miles further and the sun had almost disappeared over the western moor. The trees cast long shadows across the narrow lane along which they were riding. Suddenly Josh slumped over the pommel of his saddle and would have fallen had it not been for John Kittow.

'You're in no fit state to ride any further Josh. . . .'

'I'll be all right in a few minutes.' It came out as a mumble. Josh rested both hands on the horse's neck, trying to ignore the pain that burned through his arm and back.

Another mile put them on to the moor west of St Cleer and Josh could ride no further.

'We'll make those rocks up ahead,' said John Kittow. 'I'll leave you there and go on for the Caradon doctor.'

'No. Keep clear of the mine,' gasped Josh. 'There will be soldiers there by now. Go into St Cleer and fetch the doctor. The young one. I know him. Tell him what's happened.'

At the rocks he tumbled from his horse into the arms of John Kittow, who lowered him to the ground only half-conscious. John Kittow propped him up and left him with his good shoulder resting against one of the rocks. Hector's reins twisted about his wrist.

'I'll be back in half an hour,' promised the miner.

Josh could do no more than nod.

It was a clear night with a full moon balancing on the horizon when John Kittow rode off.

Hector woke Josh from an exhausted sleep by shaking his head and jerking on the reins. Looking up, Josh saw the moon high in the sky above him. It must have been well after midnight. John Kittow had been gone far too long. Something was wrong.

Then he heard the sound which had disturbed Hector. It was the jingle of harness. Painfully and stiffly he rose to his feet and held Hector's head still, relying on the shadow of the rocks to hide him as horsemen passed along the track not twenty yards away. They were troopers. He felt sure they had something to do with the non-return of John Kittow and were now searching for him.

When they disappeared from view and he could no longer hear the sound of their horses' harness he mounted Hector, the effort causing the blood to flow once more from the wound in his back. He kneed the horse forward, heading away from the track, out on to the moor. He was not familiar with this particular area and trusted to luck and the intelligence of his horse to keep them clear of moorland bogs. Luck was with him. It was not long before they arrived at a part of the moor he knew well. Now he could move forward with more confidence. Here he had no need of tracks or paths and travelled in a straight line across the moor, heading for Sharptor and the cottage of his parents.

It was fortunate he had stayed clear of the paths. As he picked his way down the last hillside close to the cottage Hector slipped, dislodging a stone. Josh heard an exclamation of surprise from someone standing in the shadows to one side of the cottage.

'Who's there?' It was the soldiers. They had been expecting him and were waiting.

Josh pulled Hector about in a tight turn, hoping they were foot soldiers. His hopes were swiftly dashed. He heard the creak of leather as the dragoons mounted hurriedly. A single shot was fired at him but the ball sped harmlessly through the undergrowth twenty feet away.

Then horses were crashing through the bracken and he coaxed Hector into a canter. The movement jarred his wounds unmercifully. He would be unable to keep going in this manner for very long. When Hector broke clear of the tangled moorland undergrowth on to a path, Josh urged the horse to move faster still.

Another shot hummed past him, closer this time. The dragoons had also found the path. He could not outrun them with a tired horse. His only chance lay in outwitting them. Crouching as low as the pain in his back would allow, he coaxed Hector into a gallop in an effort to gain some distance. In spite of its tiredness the big horse responded magnificently and Josh risked a quick glance behind him.

He could not see the dragoons but he could hear them shouting. He had to act now.

Pulling the horse to a halt he jumped awkwardly from the saddle. Slapping its haunches, he called, 'Go, Hector! Give them a run, boy.'

It was as though the big horse understood. With head high it set off at a gallop into the night, leaving Josh to sink down into the tall ferns, a few feet from the path.

The dragoons were well spread out as one by one they passed the place where Josh was hiding. When the last of them had pounded into the distance Josh stood up and weaved his way across the hillside.

He knew where he was going. He had not been there for some years but he had no trouble finding it. He was wider across the shoulders than he had been years before and the tunnel through the gorse was slightly overgrown. As he crawled through it, a stiff needle-loaded branch scraped along his back, touching a part of the wound from which the rough bandage had slipped. He almost fainted with the pain of it. But he made it to the shelter of the rock hideout safely and collapsed on to his face in relief. The soldiers would not find him here. He was safe. Here a man could live with his freedom. Or die with it.

Josh was right in assuming that something had gone seriously wrong with John Kittow's quest for a doctor.

When the miner galloped into St Cleer he became immediately aware that news of the fight at Looe had reached the village ahead of him. Few of the houses did not have lamps glowing brightly in their windows. People clustered around doorways, talking excitedly. They were mostly women, for a large percentage of the men from here were Caradon miners. Their fate would affect the community deeply.

Dismounting at the doctor's house, he tethered his horse and banged heavily on the door. It was opened by the doctor's wife. She shook her head in answer to his question.

'No, the doctor is not in. He heard about the shootings at Looe and went there in case he should be needed. He rode off almost two hours since.'

'The news must have arrived very quickly,' said John Kittow. 'Who brought it?'

'Soldiers. They were here looking for some of the miners' leaders who had escaped on horses.

As he and Josh were the only two men belonging to the mining community who had been on horseback at Looe, John Kittow knew that it meant that the soldiers were looking for them.

He thanked the doctor's wife and turned away at a loss as to his next move. Josh needed a doctor urgently but it would be difficult to find one at this time of the night – especially one he could trust. None of the mine doctors would risk incurring the wrath of the adventurers by treating anyone associated with the militants of the Miners' Union.

Leading his horse along the St Cleer road John Kittow suddenly thought of Preacher Thackeray. Even if he were unable to recommend a doctor he might take Josh into his house to await the return of the St Cleer doctor.

John Kittow was a sound reliable shift captain. He knew mining and he knew miners. But he did not have a quick enquiring mind. If he had, he might have wondered about the number of horses tethered near the preacher's house. As it was, his mind was too full of other things. He hurried to the door, banged hard upon it and when it was opened by a pale wide-eyed Miriam he immediately blurted out, 'Where's Preacher Thackeray? I must see him. Josh is badly hurt.'

When the uniformed figure of Morwen Trago stepped into the light behind Miriam, John Kittow was stunned. By the time he recovered his presence of mind it was too late. Morwen Trago pushed his sister aside and grabbed the miner, at the same time calling for assistance. Two dragoons rushed from the shadows alongside the house and John Kittow was a prisoner.

They dragged him into the house and pushed him into a chair in the kitchen. Triumphantly, Morwen Trago said, 'So my shot didn't go astray. Where did I hit Josh? Where is he now?'

'Don't tell him!' The cry came from Miriam Trago. Her brother strode across the room and bundled her into the passageway outside. Returning, he made one of the dragoons stand against the door. He continued his questioning with Miriam banging helplessly on the other side.

'I'll ask you again. Where's Josh Retallick?'

John Kittow glared at him and said nothing.

'Don't be stupid, Kittow,' said Morwen Trago. 'Trying to protect him will do no good. We'll catch him sooner or later.

It won't be well received at your own trial if it comes out that you protected him.'

'My trial for what? All Josh and I did was try to stop the miners causing trouble. We arrived too late. You and your murderous soldiers fired on them before we could speak to them.'

'That's a likely story,' grinned Morwen Trago. 'You and Josh Retallick were there leading them, inciting them to violence, causing them to attack us. If we hadn't fired when we did they would have overrun us.'

'You're a liar, Morwen Trago. A true son of your father.'

Morwen Trago's eyes blazed and he moved as though to strike the shift captain.

Instead he shrugged and said to the dragoons, 'You'd better take him off to Liskeard lock-up. We'll find Josh Retallick sooner or later. Dead or alive.'

'Wait a minute,' John Kittow shouted. 'I came here to see Preacher Thackeray. He'll know I'm telling the truth. Where is he?'

'I doubt whether my brother-in-law would prove anything of the sort,' replied Morwen Trago smugly. 'He was here when everything was happening. He heard of the troubles only when we arrived and told him. Now he's gone to see what he can do to comfort the miners you and Josh Retallick misled into such a stupid venture.'

He signalled to the dragoons. 'Take him away. Enough has been said.'

John Kittow and the dragoons were halfway along the pathway before Miriam caught up with them.

'Wait!'

The dragoons halted.

'John! Do you know where Josh is now? Is he very badly hurt? Please tell me. I want to help him.'

'As your brother helped him – with a musket-ball?' asked John Kittow, both scorn and sadness on his face. 'Or as your husband would have helped him? He knew this was going to happen, didn't he? He could have prevented it had he wanted to. But I doubt whether there'll be any sorrow in his heart when he learns Josh has landed himself in trouble. Yes, Josh is badly hurt. He's lost a lot of blood. But I don't think he'd thank me for telling you and these soldiers where he is. If he's going to die he'll die a free man. Not in some stinking prison.'

If John Kittow had seen the look of anguish on Miriam's face as she watched the dragoons ride away with him between them he might have had more sympathy.

But in the place to which he was going thoughts of self-preservation had a habit of submerging all sympathy for others.

The Reverend William Thackeray was feeling well pleased with himself and the feeling blossomed into elation before he reached St Cleer. The miners had lost a fight today, it was true. The soldiers had beaten them in a bloody one-sided battle. Miners had died.

Yet in death they had turned defeat into victory. When the bodies of the dead miners were being carried home from the port Thackeray had witnessed whole villages turning out for them. Not understanding what it was about, young children, roused from sleep, stood in their night attire. Alongside them the older members of the families stood with bowed heads, flickering candles in their hands, paying respect to the murdered men of Cornwall.

The soldiers out in strength patrolling the lanes and roads around Looe town saw it too and were uneasy.

William Thackeray's elation stepped across the threshold of his cottage with him but went no further.

'Where's Josh? What's happened to him?'

'My dear, how can I have seen Josh? I've come straight from Looe town. I did what I could to help the miners I met on the way. Josh was not among them.'

'Are you saying you had nothing to do with Josh going to Looe to try to turn back the miners?'

'If Josh went to Looe with the miners for any reason whatsoever it was foolish in the extreme. It would be difficult for a man to profess he was peaceable if he formed part of the mob that fought in Looe today!'

'And his being out there somewhere badly hurt is not a result of your scheming? You swear it?'

'*My* scheming! My dear Miriam, it was you who advised me to preach peace and not violence. You and Josh – remember? I can hardly be blamed for the outcome of Josh ignoring his own advice.'

'So you know of no reason why Morwen should come straight to this house to boast of shooting Josh himself?'

'Should I know what goes on in the mind of *your* brother? Why, I don't understand you much of the time. Now, for instance perhaps you'll explain why you accuse your husband of all manner of treacheries and work yourself up into such a state about one who should be part of your past? Do I have to remind you that you are my wife?'

'No, William. I need no reminding. But when it's my turn to compete with your ambitions I doubt I'll fare any better than your friends.'

Before William Thackeray could make a reply Miriam turned and ran upstairs to Daniel's bedroom and he heard the bolt being secured on the inside of the door. Josh slept fitfully through the night. His wounds were paining him. John Kittow had been telling Miriam the truth when he told her Josh had lost a lot of blood. Twice he heard horses passing along the path beyond the gorse-passage. The soldiers had caught Hector and were back-tracking in an attempt to find the place where he had escaped from them. But they would find nothing in the darkness. By the time the sun rose they would have so confused any tracks he might have made they would never find them. They would probably not even be sure which track they had been on. He was quite secure where he was for the moment. Later he would make his way to a place where he could obtain food and medical attention. He realised that would only be the beginning of his problems. But he was in no state to start thinking about his future.

When next he woke the sun was high in the sky above him. This time it took him a few minutes to place where he was. He felt stiff. Painfully stretching his limbs he tried to stand. But during his exhausted sleep he had moved, causing his back to bleed excessively. There was blood on the earth beneath him and he was much weaker than he wanted to believe. After much painful effort he made it to his feet. He stayed upright for a few seconds only before feeling so sick and giddy he sank to the ground again.

It was another hour before his mind cleared sufficiently for him to be aware of the sounds about him. In the distance was the steady thump-thump of the Sharptor mine-engine. Still further away the mixed noises of the Wheal Phoenix. Somewhere above him he could hear the mewing of a buzzard, and at least two larks hovered on the wing nearby.

Out there it was a normal moorland day. Life was going on without him as though nothing had ever happened. But Josh was aware his life would never be the same again. It was all a bad dream. Only the severe pain in his back and the dull throb of his arm effectively convinced him it was all very real.

He wondered what his mother was doing. She would be worried to distraction. Ben Retallick would be going about his work at the mine, replying to anyone who asked that Josh knew what he was doing, that he would be safe somewhere waiting for all the excitement to die down. But what of John Kittow? What had happened to prevent him from returning from St Cleer?

The questions went through his mind in quick succession, but of more immediate concern was what was likely to happen to himself. He hardly possessed the strength to stand, let alone leave the hideout to forage for food. But without food he would only lie here growing steadily weaker. With these thoughts in mind he tried once more to get to his feet. This time he used the rocks as support. It was easier. He shuffled the few steps necessary to see out through a small aperture between the rocks that gave him a view over the needle-spined gorse beyond.

He saw soldiers, red-coated ones, beating through the undergrowth five hundred yards distant. But they were beating up the slope, working steadily away from his position. That was hopeful. They could have no idea of his possible whereabouts, might even have already searched the area where he now was. But it did mean he could not risk leaving the hideout yet.

He looked up at the sun. It was still early afternoon. There was no hope of contacting anyone during daylight. It would be risky enough in the dark. The soldiers would be expecting him to come out of hiding then. He sank back on to the dry earth, tired and with a strong feeling of hopelessness. Tucking his good shoulder into a crevice in the rocks he rested his face against the rough granite warmed by the sun. He was in a desperate mess and could see no way out of it.

He was still crouched in that position when Miriam found him soon after sunset that evening. Word had come back to St Cleer that he had been chased into the darkness above the Retallick cottage, that the soldiers had taken his horse only a mile away. Immediately, Miriam had known where Josh was hiding.

She had brought food with her. When she saw Josh lying so still her first thought was that she was too late, that he was dead. But when she dropped to her knees and touched his face his eyelids flickered open. He looked at her with uncomprehending eyes.

When he tried to speak Miriam whispered, 'Shh! Keep your voice very low. I've got some food and some bandages. Are you badly hurt, Josh?'

'I don't know. I think my back's on fire, although my arm throbs more. But how . . . ?'

'John Kittow told me you were hurt last night before they took him away.'

'Took him away? Who? Why? He did nothing wrong. He went to Looe to try to stop the miners. We both did. . . .'

He sank back against the rock. 'But I don't expect the soldiers to believe that. I knocked a dragoon from his horse.'

'No, they don't believe it. They are saying you led the rioting. That John Kittow was with you. He's to appear before the magistrate tomorrow. He'll then go to Bodmin Jail to await trial – when they've caught you.'

'But William knows the truth of it. He knows I've always

been against any form of violence. John Kittow felt the same way. William can tell them. He will tell them.'

Miriam's expression changed. 'No, Josh. You mustn't expect William to say anything, for or against you.'

'But he must, Miriam! He knows John and I are innocent.'

'He *knows* nothing, Josh. He wasn't there when the rioting took place. You were.'

'But he can tell them what went on before. He knows the arguments I've put forward at meetings. That I've always declared against violence. He can tell them that.'

'And admit to the court that he's one of the leaders of the Union, Josh? No, expect nothing from William and you're not likely to be disappointed.'

There was bitterness in her voice which she made no attempt to hide from him. 'Besides, I don't think he'll be in Cornwall very much longer. He's been called to London to appear before the Conference. I believe the Church wants to know about his activities here.'

'Will he go?'

'To answer the charges, yes. But wherever they send him he'll always be a union man. So he intends leaving here as the leader of a successful campaign. There's already news that Parliament is so alarmed by what's happening that they've stopped the export of corn from Cornwall and other country districts.'

Josh sagged visibly. 'Then the miners were right after all. Their way was the only way to get results.'

'No!' Miriam was trying to unwind the cloth from about Josh's body. She was having difficulty in separating it from the wound where the blood had dried through it. 'No, Josh. There wouldn't have been time for news of the fight at Looe to have got to London and action to have been taken because of that. I believe you were right. That Parliament had made their decision before the miners marched on Looe. If only they had been a little more patient there wouldn't be seven of them lying dead and many more wounded. Parliament doesn't care what's going on here in Cornwall. We're so far away that by the time the news of what's happening reaches them it's no longer news. It's the general unrest throughout the land that's forcing them to change their policies. That and farmers who are refusing to grow corn again because of the danger it's put them into.'

Josh gasped in pain as Miriam pulled out a piece of cloth embedded in the wound.

'I'm sorry, Josh.'

Miriam tried to keep her feelings hidden from him. What she was looking at, in the light of a stub of candle pushed well back into a crevice in the rocks, was a terrifying wound. Across the small of his back it was little more than a scratch. But from the shoulder to the bottom of his ribs it was a wide open gash. She had brought water with her and some herbal balm which old Mary Crabbe made up as an antiseptic. She dressed the wound as best she could.

'You should really see a surgeon and have this wound drawn together. There's little I can do to help it heal. Now, let me have a look at that arm.'

She treated the bullet wound in a similar manner but this worried her even more than Josh's back. The musket-ball had passed straight through his arm, but around the hole it had left behind the flesh was puffy and inflamed.

Miriam bound him up again and gave him the food she had brought. He ate it greedily, but it tasted dry in his mouth.

Miriam sat back on her heels watching him. When he had finished she said, 'What are we going to do with you now, Josh?'

'There's no need for you to do anything more, Miriam. I'm grateful to you for coming here. Very grateful. You've probably saved my life. But you mustn't become any more involved in this. None of this trouble is of your doing. You must think of yourself and young Daniel. How were you able to get away to come to me today?'

'My mother isn't a healthy woman these days. I don't need an excuse to come to Henwood to visit her.'

It reminded him of his own mother. He asked Miriam to get word to her, telling her not to worry about him.

'Yes, Josh. But first we must get you away from here. Far away.'

'I'll be safe enough for a while. Leave me some food. When I've eaten that I'll be able to move.'

'Josh, I can't leave you here like this. You once saved my life by coming up here to find me. Remember?'

'Yes, Miriam. There was another time. A night that changed both our lives. I'll never forget that night, either. This place seems to have a special significance in our lives. All the same, I'd rather you weren't mixed up in this mess.'

'I'm already involved. Far more than I would like to be. In fact, the whole of this might be more of my doing than you realise, Josh.'

'How? You couldn't have known what was going to happen.'

She looked down at him. 'William has always known how close we were as children. I thought he'd accepted that I was still very fond of you. But in recent months he's been saying things, making nasty insinuations. He seems to have become jealous for no reason at all. Then, when you disagreed with him over the miners, he thought you were threatening his authority. And he resented the way the miners looked to you as their natural leader. He has to work hard to keep their respect. You know he's a very ambitious man. I believe he began to see you as an obstacle to his ambitions. Later, when Morwen came to see us, I believe he said something to William that gave him an idea of what to do. They've talked together a great deal. Once Morwen came to the house with his officer. I am sure they must have been talking about you but they always stopped talking whenever I got close to them. But when Morwen left I heard William mention your name to him. I couldn't hear anything else.'

She looked at him unhappily. 'I believe William has a lot to do with you being hunted now, Josh. Now do you see why I'm sure he'll do nothing to help you?'

'I can't believe it! We've been such good friends in the past. For all our differences I'm sure William would do nothing like that.'

'I wish I could find some other explanation for what's happened, Josh. But this ambition of his is so all-powerful that

I'm sure he would sacrifice anyone, including me, to achieve his ends.'

'But how could he have known I'd go to Looe and get mixed up in the fighting there? He couldn't have arranged that.'

'I don't know – unless he sent someone to tell you about the miners. Anyone who knows you could guess what your actions would be. You'd rush to stop them. Once there Morwen and his officer could pick you out. You're known to be a strong union man so you would be blamed for any trouble that started.'

'No, Miriam. I don't believe anyone would do that.'

'*You* wouldn't do it, Josh. It isn't your way. But William would.'

The candle began to flicker and splutter. Miriam pinched it out between her fingers before she stood up and brushed down her dress.

'I'm going now, Josh. You'll be safe here for tonight. I'll return tomorrow morning with more food. No, don't argue. I want to. I only wish I could pick you up and carry you to safety as you once carried me.'

She stooped, kissed his forehead and rested her hand against his cheek for a moment. 'Goodbye, Josh. Stay as still as you can. Try not to start the wound in your back bleeding again. If it's no better tomorrow I'm afraid we're going to have to find a doctor to treat it. Whatever the danger.'

'We'll worry about that tomorrow. Thank you, Miriam.' Already he was feeling tired again.

When she had gone he thought about what she had said. Although he had expressed his doubts to Miriam, William's involvement would make sense of a lot of things that did not otherwise fit together. But he did not want to believe it.

During the night, Josh had an unexpected visitor. He woke suddenly and thought a soldier had stumbled upon his refuge, but it was an old boar badger grunting and snuffling as he led his family through the gorse-tunnel. He stopped to crunch a snail he found there, then herded his family back down the tunnel, oblivious of Josh's presence.

That was the only incident in an otherwise thoroughly miserable night. Around midnight the wind rose and within an hour it began to rain – a miserable skin-soaking drizzle that the moor was able to call up at a moment's notice. Huddled in the angle between two rocks, Josh was protected from the wind but there was no way of escaping from the rain. He lay shivering until dawn arrived wrapped in a cold grey mist.

Miriam came early, worried about the effects of the night on his weakened body. She found him cold and shivering, crouching like some sick animal. She had set out from her mother's house with some hot broth in a covered bowl. It was no more than luke-warm when she fed it between his chattering teeth, but it was sufficient to stop his shivering.

'Did you manage to get news to my mother?' he asked when the broth had stilled his teeth.

'No. I would have sent Uncle John to your cottage last night but it was too dangerous. Morwen is one of the soldiers guarding your house. He would have known what it was about. But John is going to get word to your father at the mine this morning.'

'Good!'

Josh leaned his head back against the rock and closed his eyes. 'I'm not going to recover very quickly unless this weather improves, Miriam. The muscles in my legs wouldn't support me when I tried to stand earlier. Another night like last one and I'll either die of pneumonia or my coughing will be heard by the soldiers.'

'I know. I lay awake worrying about you. We must get you inside somewhere so I can get a doctor to look at your wounds. Your back has been bleeding again and the inflammation in your arm has spread beyond the bandage. We'll have to take advantage of this mist and get you beneath a roof.'

'Yes, but what roof?' asked Josh. 'Anyone who shelters me will be in trouble if the soldiers find me. I'm a fugitive.'

'I know one place where you'll be safe. In your own house. The old farmhouse up on the hill.'

'But the soldiers must know about that.'

'They've already searched it and found it to be empty, so they're not guarding it. They're expecting you to make for your parents' cottage. I came past the farmhouse on my way here this morning, so I know there are no soldiers there. Isn't there a hay-loft above the stables?'

Josh nodded.

'Then that's the place. You'll be warm and dry there. Even if the soldiers were to search the house again I doubt whether they'd go up into the hay-loft – not if I remove the ladder when I leave you there.'

Josh managed a faint smile. 'The idea is fine, Miriam. But how do I get there? You said yourself you couldn't carry me. I haven't become any lighter during the night.'

'We'll manage somehow. If you can stumble along I'll support you. It isn't far if we go straight across the moor. You've got to make the effort, Josh. If this low cloud lifts we'll not be able to do it without being seen.'

'All right. Let's start now.'

The crawl through the tunnel was not too difficult, although it pulled the edges of his wounded back apart yet again. Once outside he got to his feet with Miriam's help. He stood with her shoulder beneath his armpit, his arm draped heavily about her.

They staggered drunkenly for about twenty-five yards before he fell, dragging her down with him.

'I'm sorry,' he gasped. 'I don't think I can make it.'

'Of course you can. You've *got* to do it now we've started. The soldiers will be out searching again soon. They'll find you here if you stay.'

Painfully he regained his feet. This time he managed to cover twice the distance before tripping.

As he lay face down in the bracken she looked at the dressing on his back. The blood was coming through, but it was not as bad as she had feared it might be. Once more she helped him to his feet and they managed another fifty yards.

So it went on. Fifty yards, twenty yards, once a mere fifteen, but always onwards and upwards, through the gorse and fern. Then after what seemed an eternity they arrived at the wall behind the old farmyard. Miriam heaved Josh over and pushed him up step by step as he made heavy work of climbing the ladder to the loft.

With a groan of relief he cleared the final rung and dropped gratefully into the sweet hay. Miriam's breathing was as heavy as his own but she dropped down beside him and cradled his head to her.

'We've done it, Josh! I told you we would.'

He could only grin weakly, too exhausted to reply.

That night she brought a doctor to him. He was a drunken little mine doctor from the North Hill district who asked no questions and seemed to have very little idea where he was.

He dressed the wound, soaking it with a strong antiseptic that Josh later swore would have burned the bristles from a pig. Then he drew the edges together with rough stitches that brought the perspiration pouring from Josh. When it had just reached the point where he thought he would either scream or faint, the job was done. Then the doctor turned his attention to the wound in Josh's arm. His method of cleaning the bullet-hole involved a swab and an iron rod. This time Josh did faint with the pain. When he came to, Miriam had led the alcoholic medical man away into the night.

But the doctor's crude methods marked a turning-point in Josh's recovery. The inflammation left his arm and the following day he devoured every scrap of food that Miriam brought for him.

His mother was aware that he was safe, Miriam told him, but she had not been told his whereabouts and would not be until the soldiers had gone from the area.

But that day never came. On the third day after the doctor's visit, Miriam brought him a basket of food in the evening, pleased to see him on his feet as she came up the ladder into the hay-loft.

'You're looking like the old Josh today,' she said to him.

'I'm beginning to feel like the Josh you once knew,' he replied. 'But isn't William wondering why you are in Henwood for so long? Or is he too busy with other things?'

'No. He came to my mother's house today.'

'And?'

She shrugged her shoulders. 'My mother *is* ill. I told him I wouldn't return to St Cleer until I felt happy about leaving her.'

'Did he accept that?'

'He had to.'

Miriam broke open a loaf of bread and put a large piece of cheese with it. She was about to hand it to him when there was a sound in the yard outside. Her hand froze halfway to him.

As Josh and Miriam looked at each other apprehensively there were footsteps at the door of the stable below them. A voice called, 'We know you're up there, Josh Retallick. Come down without giving us any trouble or I'll take great delight in coming up and shooting you again.'

It was Morwen Trago.

Miriam's eyes showed disbelief that was as quickly replaced by terror.

'He must have followed me!' she whispered. 'But I was so careful!'

Josh nodded.

She looked at him tearfully. 'What are you going to do? You can't give yourself up.'

'There's nothing else I can do. Even if I managed to escape from the back of the hay-loft I couldn't run far.'

'Then let me speak to him.'

She stood up, but Josh pulled her down on the hay beside him. 'No. I don't want you involved.'

Holding her arm to prevent her from getting up, he called, 'Morwen! You know I'm here alone?'

There was silence as the implication of Josh's words sunk in.

'If you say so,' Morwen answered.

'I do say so. Because I'm alone and have no wish to see my property torn apart I'll come down and give myself up.'

'Then come down.'

'There must be some other way, Josh,' Miriam whispered.

'No. You've risked too much already. I'm going now. Stay until we're clear. Morwen won't allow any of the soldiers to come up. Thank you, Miriam. I only wish things could have been different for us. . . .'

He kissed her quickly, then walked to the ladder. 'I'm coming down now.'

Soldiers are not renowned for their gentleness and Josh's captors made no exception of a man they believed had led a mob against them. They handled him roughly as they tied his hands behind his back and pushed him out of the stable ahead of them. Fortunately, only his arm began to bleed. He managed to keep most of their blows from his back.

For all that, he was a sorry sight as they marched him past the Retallick cottage. Seeing him from the window, Jesse Retallick screamed and ran outside. The soldiers pushed her back roughly, but Ben came out behind her and his booming voice stopped them.

'Take your hands from her! That's our son you have there. If you hope to get out of mining country with your lives you'll let his mother speak to him.'

Tom Shovell and the off-duty miners from the small group of cottages had come from their homes, drawn by the commotion. They formed up behind the shift captain as though preparing to back up his words.

Before the soldiers could get assistance they would have to pass the Wheal Phoenix, Sharptor and Caradon. They realised the truth in Ben Retallick's words.

Only Morwen Trago had anything to say. 'If I thought that was a threat . . .,' he began.

'You can take it for whatever you want,' said Ben Retallick. 'But Josh's mother will speak to him before you move on.'

'Then she'll have to make it brief,' said Morwen, giving in surlily. 'We want to make St Cleer before nightfall.'

'Josh, what have they done to you? How . . . ?'

'Everything's all right. My arm is bleeding a little, that's all. It looks far worse than it really is. Don't fuss over me. Everything is going to be all right. I'm not guilty of anything. As anyone who was at Looe knows. The court will find me innocent.'

'That's what John Kittow told the magistrate,' replied Jesse. 'But he was sent to Bodmin Jail to await trial.'

'Then the truth must wait to come out at the trial,' said Josh. 'Don't upset yourself.'

The soldiers were showing signs of impatience, and Josh said, 'I must go now. Please don't worry.'

Jesse reached up to kiss him and as he brought his head down to her Josh whispered, 'I owe a great debt to Miriam. Without her I wouldn't be alive today. Remember that.'

She drew back her head to look at him and he shook his head, 'Say nothing now.'

'Come on. We've a long march ahead of us.'

One of the soldiers pushed Josh away from his mother and set off along the track. Ben Retallick called to Josh that they would obtain the best lawyers in the county for him.

By the time they arrived at St Cleer, Josh had fallen many times and had to be helped by two soldiers. It was only the jeers of Morwen Trago that had kept him on his feet. He was determined not to give Miriam's brother the satisfaction of seeing him collapse completely.

The soldiers had a van at St Cleer. Josh was thrown roughly inside. As the other soldiers stood around boasting how they had captured the ring-leader of the rioters to any villager who would listen, Morwen Trago stepped into the van to check Josh's bonds.

Breathing heavily, Josh asked, 'How did you come to find me?'

'Because of something I should have realised all along,' hissed Morwen. 'It wasn't your mother we should have been watching, but my own sister. I always suspected you'd laid her in the fern when she was running barefoot on the moor. Now I'm sure.'

His inspection ended, he jumped from the van and slammed the door behind him. As he lay in the dark, Josh heard a bolt rammed home. Then the van lurched off and rumbled its way to Liskeard and the lock-up.

Later, well into the night, Josh was awakened by the opening of the lock-up door as a noisy sour-smelling drunk was thrown inside.

He tried to ignore his new companion by pretending to be asleep but it was not long before the shouting ceased and in the quiet of the darkness Josh felt the fingers of the stranger fumbling over his body, exploring his pockets.

Josh brought his hand up in a clubbing blow that sent the man crashing against the wall of the lock-up. The drunk fell to the floor and spent what remained of the night crying softly to himself and talking to the grotesque creatures who dwelled in a mind tortured by delirium tremens.

Chapter Twenty-Six

Josh's appearance before the magistrate was the merest formality. He was asked to confirm his name, the officer in charge of Morwen's company gave a brief version of what he alleged had occurred at Looe, and Josh was remanded to Bodmin Jail to await trial.

Bodmin Jail was a comparatively modern prison, the stones having not yet acquired the smell of decay and dirt found in most other prisons of the realm. Here was only the smell of imprisoned man – his sweat, his filth, and his fear.

There were women in the prison too. Demoniac women with tangled hair who screamed and shouted at the new arrival, beckoning to Josh through crowded bars as he climbed stiffly from the hard-sprung prison van.

In the large communal cell shared by those prisoners awaiting the circuit judge, Josh was reunited with John Kittow and nine miners who had been arrested on that violent late-summer day. All the others were strangers to him and came from mines well to the west of Bodmin Moor, adding further to Josh's growing belief in what Miriam had told him – the march on Looe had been planned well in advance.

'I'm not going to say I'm pleased to see you,' said John Kittow, leading Josh into a comparatively clean corner of the huge cage, taken over by the miners for themselves. 'As each day went by my hopes rose that you'd made good your escape. Even though part of me was worried lest you'd died in the spot where I left you. How are your wounds now? And what's been happening to you?'

Josh told the Caradon shift captain of his adventures since the night of the Looe battle, leaving out reference to Miriam. But he told him he had heard a rumour that William Thackeray might have been responsible for much of the misfortune that had befallen them.

'Now you mention it,' mused John Kittow, 'the miner who told me the men were on their way to Looe said something about going on to tell you. I wondered at the time why he should be bothering. He wasn't a man I knew well. He could have been following Preacher Thackeray's orders. But why? Why would Thackeray do such a thing?'

Josh shrugged and said nothing.

'To think that I actually went to his house for help. Had I kept away I wouldn't be locked up now.' He went on to give Josh the details of his capture before repeating, 'What can Preacher Thackeray hope to gain by betraying us?'

'I think it was your misfortune that you decided to make for Looe,' replied Josh. 'Preacher Thackeray couldn't have anticipated that.'

He inclined his head towards the other miners. 'I haven't seen any of these men before and I don't recall seeing any of the men who regularly attended Preacher Thackeray's meetings among the crowd at Looe town.'

'No, not now you mention it. But don't worry, Josh. Our own miners won't allow us to rot away in here. They'll force Preacher Thackeray to take some action to get us out.'

'You're fooling yourself if you believe that, John. The miners were marching upon Looe to score a great victory for the Miners' Union. They were going to prevent the corn from leaving the harbour, to force the soldiers to back down. None of these things happened. They not only lost – they suffered a humiliating defeat. Now they'll be too busy licking their wounds to think about doing battle on our behalf – especially as we weren't even with them. Oh yes! Preacher Thackeray will call his meetings and use brave words. He might even use some of the Union's funds to secure a lawyer for us. But nothing he does is going to make any difference. I'm quite sure he's aware of that. The judge must make an example of us. It wouldn't do for miners to believe they can take the law into their own hands. No, John. The soldiers have won. Preacher Thackeray has won. Only the miners have lost.'

'The soldiers have been putting it around that some of us were armed,' said John Kittow. 'Have you heard that?'

'I've heard nothing. But such a claim is absurd. Miners don't possess guns.'

John Kittow shrugged. 'We know that. But two of the soldiers were shot. They were probably shot by other soldiers, but nobody is likely to admit to that, especially as one of them is said to be in a serious condition.'

'That makes our chance of receiving a fair trial even more remote,' agreed Josh.

The situation looked hopeless. Then, as an evil-smelling greasy meal was being distributed that evening, Josh had an unexpected visitor. It was Dr McKinley from St Cleer. He had come, he said, to check on Josh's wounds and change the dressings on them.

As he went about his work, Josh asked him who had sent him.

'Well, it wasn't the soldiers,' said the doctor. 'Let's say I'm here on behalf of some of your friends and leave it at that. There are a great many people who are worried about you.'

He eased the dressing from Josh's back and grunted. 'Did you go to a sail-maker's assistant to have these stitches put in?'

'Do they look that bad?'

'It will heal. But you'll carry a scar like a herring-bone for the rest of your life.'

He seemed more pleased with the arm. 'That's clean enough and is healing nicely.'

Binding up the wounds he stood up and looked at Josh with sympathy.

'I've been asked to check on you every other day,' he said.

'As a doctor I'm not involved with either side. Neither am I for or against the Miners' Union. But if there's anything you wish me to bring for you, or any messages to be taken to anyone, I'll be happy to be of service.'

'There's nothing I can think of at the moment,' replied Josh. 'It will suffice to tell whoever engaged you that I'm well, and that I hope certain persons can be prevailed upon to come forward at the trial to testify that John Kittow and I had nothing to do with the march on Looe.'

'I wouldn't be unduly optimistic,' said the doctor. 'But I'll certainly pass on your message.'

He also promised to convey a report on John Kittow's well-being to his family.

The prison food was every bit as unpalatable as it looked, but all that Josh spurned was grabbed and gobbled up by other inmates of the common cell.

The following day Josh's meals underwent a radical change. He was brought a meal of beef, vegetables and even ale. When he expressed his surprise he was informed by the jailer that Theophilus Strike had arranged for him to have meals brought in from outside. There was enough food for Josh to share his good fortune with John Kittow. Somehow this small privilege made them feel like individuals again, not simply part of an anonymous mass.

That same day a cheerful roly-poly little man was escorted into the jail cell and he introduced himself to Josh as Reuben Button. He was a solicitor engaged by the mine-owner to examine the question of Josh's defence.

Button oozed confidence from every pore. 'Now,' he said, seating himself on a stool that he insisted the warder bring in for him, scorning the grubby bench that was at first offered. 'Tell me exactly what happened. From the very beginning.'

Josh told him. At the end of his story the solicitor frowned, looked quizzically at his client. 'You are quite sure you are leaving nothing untold?'

'I have told you everything,' replied Josh. 'Apart from knocking the dragoon from his horse – and that was hardly a premeditated act – I did nothing. My sole object in going to

Looe was to prevent violence, to stop the miners from doing something stupid. But they never had the opportunity; the soldiers fired first.'

'I understand the Riot Act had already been read out by the magistrate prior to your arrival,' said Button. 'That makes the whole matter far more serious. You understand that, of course?'

Josh nodded.

'But one thing confounds me. If what you have told me constitutes your sole involvement in this sorry affair, why were the soldiers so anxious to apprehend you?'

'There are two possible explanations for that. The first is Morwen Trago. We were boys together and he has no reason to be fond of me or my family. He was one of the soldiers at Looe, the one who put a bullet through my arm.'

'I see.' The solicitor was busily writing. 'We must bring that out in court. And the other reason?'

'The officer in charge of the soldiers brought them around the mines recently. He took them to the Wheal Phoenix and he was told he wasn't welcome. While he was there I warned him to keep away from the Wheal Sharptor. He asked for my name and I told him.'

'Well! Well! Well! Previous bad blood between yourself and the officer in charge of the soldiers.' He spoke slowly and deliberately as he committed each word to paper. 'I'm sure we can make something of that. Now, when were you informed about the miners marching to Looe?'

Josh told him, and the solicitor wrote his reply down.

There were many such questions and answers, and Mr Button called on John Kittow to verify certain parts of Josh's statement.

Finally and cheerfully the solicitor folded the papers and tucked them away in the bag he was carrying.

'How do you think the case will go? Is there any chance we'll be set free?' Josh asked.

'I think we have a very strong case,' said Mr Button guardedly. 'But of course this *was* a riotous assembly. That is looked upon by the courts as being most serious. However, we have an interesting defence. Very interesting. Do not become too depressed. Now, before I go I have another little matter to attend to.'

He waved a scented handkerchief in front of his nose as a door leading to the main section of the prison was opened and the odour from within escaped.

'Mr Strike – who I must say I have found to be a very generous man – personally believes in your complete innocence. He wishes that you be made as comfortable as is possible during the period prior to your trial. He has authorised me to obtain a private cell. I have an appointment with the governor in a few minutes to discuss the matter.'

'I'm much obliged to him,' said Josh. 'But would it be asking too much for John Kittow to enjoy the privilege with me?'

'Provided little extra expense is involved I foresee no problem,' said Mr Button. 'I'll make the necessary arrangements for both of you.'

Before nightfall that day Josh and John Kittow were lodged in a cell on the first floor of the jail. From the tiny barred window they were able to see the moor, rising beyond the ugly granite walls.

The days passed with very little to disturb the monotony of jail life, apart from the visits of either Mr Button or the solicitor engaged by the Miners' Union to defend John Kittow and the other miners. Josh's wounds healed to the satisfaction of the St Cleer doctor and his visits soon stopped. They had one bad day when they were told that an additional charge was to be brought against them, that of being party to a conspiracy contrary to the Treasonable and Seditious Practices Act. It was on such a charge that the Kit Hill miners had been convicted and transported when the mine store was burned down. Immediately after this Mr Button brought word that one of the wounded soldiers had died. He said the soldiers in the town were in such an ugly mood that a miner dared not venture abroad after dark for fear of being murdered. Although none of the miners in Bodmin Jail was actually being charged with responsibility for the soldier's death, it would no doubt weigh heavily against them when the evidence was produced to the jury.

The day after this, Jesse and Ben Retallick came to the jail to visit their son. The meeting was a painful one for all of them. Jesse looked old and grey with grief. All her fire had drained from her. The grim prison surroundings seemed to weigh heavier upon her than they did upon Josh. Even Ben Retallick, a man by any standards, somehow shrank in stature within the prison walls. He did little more than twiddle his hat between his fingers during the whole of the uncomfortable visit.

In sharp contrast, the later visit of Theophilus Strike was a very different affair. He was escorted to the cell by the governor of the prison. When the mine-owner demanded to know whether Josh was being treated well the governor's look practically implored Josh to say that he was.

After satisfying himself that Josh was as comfortable as could reasonably be expected in the circumstances, Theophilus Strike turned his attention to the matter of Josh's arrest and impending trial.

'The whole thing is preposterous,' he fumed. 'I've warned you in the past about the stupidity of meddling in the affairs of the miners, but that doesn't make you a criminal. You're an engineer and I need you back at the Sharptor mine.'

He was so positive in his belief in Josh's innocence that for the duration of his visit even Josh could not help but believe that he would be acquitted. Only after the mine-owner had gone did Josh realise he had said nothing new. Nothing had changed.

But the visit of Theophilus Strike had brought a breath of fresh air into the fetid prison surroundings. Josh felt better for it.

The day before the trial was to commence at Bodmin Assizes, Josh had a very special visitor. This time it was Miriam and she brought Daniel with her.

At first Josh was appalled. 'You should never have come here. It's not right for Daniel to be in such surroundings.'

'I feel the same way about you,' Miriam replied with a forced smile. 'How are you, Josh, and how are your wounds?'

For a long time they spoke of nothing in particular and there were long awkward silences before John Kittow called for the jailer and asked to be taken out for exercise. Such was Theophilus Strike's influence and open-handed generosity that the two men were able to take exercise periods whenever they wished.

Josh and Miriam protested that John Kittow should stay, but their protestations were not so strong that they might have persuaded him to change his mind.

When the Caradon mine leader had gone, Josh asked, 'Does William know you're here?'

Miriam shook her head. 'No, I haven't told him, and I won't. But it would make little difference if I did. He and I have been going separate ways since your arrest.'

'You mean you've left him?'

'No, we are still living under the same roof, but that is all.'

'Miriam, you've already done a great deal more than you should for me. I won't have you ruining your whole life on my account.'

'You're not the sole reason for things being the way they are, Josh. William knew I wasn't in love with him when we married, but I liked him a great deal, and I respected him. That was very important – to be able to respect him. Respect has gone now, and without it I find our relationship well-nigh impossible.'

'I'm sorry.' It was totally inadequate.

'You needn't be. I've accepted it and William has many other things to occupy his mind at the present time. There are meetings and committees to be formed – and more meetings. All of them full of talk about the solidarity of the Union and the defence of its members who are facing trial for their ideals. The whole thing is so hypocritical, Josh. I have listened and pried and checked every detail that I could. I'm more convinced than ever that William plotted with Morwen to have you involved in the disturbances at Looe.'

'Is it possible to get any proof? Something that my solicitor would be able to use?'

'No. There can be no proof unless either William or Morwen admit it. They are hardly likely to do that.'

'I suppose not.'

'What do you think will happen at the trial, Josh?'

He shrugged his shoulders. 'My solicitor says we have a strong case on everything but the riotous-assembly charge. I hope he's right. I understand the prosecution will be asking for the death penalty if we're found guilty of all charges.'

He saw the look of horror on her face and hurriedly added, 'But he's quite sure we needn't fear that.'

'I should hope not! You're innocent. Neither you nor John had anything to do with what happened.'

'But we were there during the trouble. I have the scars for them to prove it. No, I feel sure we'll be found guilty on the riotous-assembly charge and transported for a few years.'

'Josh, I don't want you to go away. We've both wasted more than enough of our years already.'

He took her gently by the shoulders. 'Miriam, you've already done enough to find yourself in this prison, if the facts came to light. You have Daniel to think of. Yes, you may have wasted a few years of your life. Please don't throw away the rest of it.'

Daniel was engrossed in an illustrated book Theophilus Strike had sent in, and as Miriam clung to him Josh kissed her hungrily. The fire was still there between them, but a cell was no place for romance.

'Miriam, please go now. Let what's happened between us remain one of memory's secrets. Don't allow it to destroy your life.'

'But, Josh, if they acquit you we could be together, with nothing to stop us. We could go away and start a new life.'

'If only we could! I fear it's a wistful dream, Miriam. One we can't afford. I know what's going to happen when we appear in court. You must face up to it too. Go now – please! And, whatever happens, take care of yourself and Daniel. Thank you for everything.'

Tears were commonplace in Bodmin Jail, and the jailer

avoided looking at Miriam as he let her and Daniel out of the cell.

When John Kittow returned he made no comment about Miriam's visit, until Josh told him of the suspected alliance between William Thackeray and Morwen Trago.

The miner looked at Josh quizzically. 'She told you of this though one of the men involved is her husband, the other her brother?'

'We've known each other since we were children. Had it not been for the incidents that led to the death of Moses Trago we'd have been married. As it was she married William Thackeray.'

'In itself a good enough reason for Preacher Thackeray to want you out of the way.'

'Perhaps. But I doubt if a judge would accept it as evidence. I hope those speaking for us in court tomorrow will have a stronger defence to place before the jury.'

'Amen to that!' said John Kittow.

More than two months had passed since their arrest and it was a dull sullen November day when Josh, John Kittow and the other miners went on trial.

In the early morning they were hustled from the cell block and into the tiny prison van to be taken to the Assize Court. It was the busiest time in the jail calendar. Vans trundled through the great gates one after another with their cargoes of fearful prisoners *en route* for the Assize Court.

The other nine miners had not had such a privileged period of confinement as Josh Retallick and John Kittow. They looked pale-faced, tired and unkempt. They did not resent the special treatment given to the two friends. They accepted it – just as they accepted that they were on trial for something they did not look upon as a crime. It was simply part of their lot in life – the lot of a miner, to whom life was sometimes harder than at others, but always hard.

They were eager for news and pleased that Josh knew something of what was to happen in the court-room. He represented authority as the miners knew it, and they were desperate for something familiar. Their solicitor had seen them, but, as one miner put it, 'The likes of he don't understand about the likes of we.'

They were convinced they would be transported and were already talking about their prospects in Australia. Many exaggerated rumours had come back from that far continent.

Arriving at the Assize building they were hustled below and placed in a cell with the other prisoners. On the way down they noticed soldiers on guard in every part of the court-house. The authorities were taking no chances.

During the morning the judge dealt with a few of the less involved cases. It was not until after they had been given a totally unpalatable midday meal that their names were called. The eleven men were taken along a passageway to wait in line on the stairs leading to the court-room above until a red-coated sergeant signalled to their jailers. Then they were hurried up into a dark-panelled court-room with flickering lights and a packed gallery. Outside, through the leaded windows, the November sky showed a promise of rain.

They were all squeezed into the long prisoners' dock that had steel spikes adorning the rail around it. Before them was the raised bench and the deep-red padded chairs for the mayor and county dignitaries, the large central chair being reserved for the judge.

To one side of them the jurors formed a double line, uncomfortable on their hard benches. In the well of the court, between the judge's bench and the prisoners, were the tables reserved for the barristers, solcitors, clerks and others for whom a court of law was a place of employment.

Behind the dock where the light was dimmest the public benches were packed to overflowing with miners and families of the accused men. As they filed into the dock a cheer had gone up, only to be quickly stifled by the soldiers guarding the doors. It died away to be replaced by loud whispers and the coughing of jurymen.

Then a door at the rear of the judge's bench opened and a black-gowned court usher appeared. 'Silence for His Lordship Judge Denman.'

The occupants of the court-room rose with scraping of feet and chairs. A short bulbous-nosed man with flowing grey wig and red robes swept in. After glancing at the prisoners, at the blurred faces in the public gallery and the legal representatives bowing and bobbing in the well of the court, he took his seat.

'Be seated!'

The bowing ceased, the scraping was repeated and everyone sat down again. The prisoners sat down with them but were immediately prodded to their feet.

The clerk of the court cleared his throat noisily and, reading from a sheet of paper held in front of him, called out the names of the accused men. Each had to indicate acknowledgement until, satisfied they all stood before him, the clerk read out the charges.

'You stand before this court charged that on the twenty-fourth day of September you did, in the Borough of Looe, in the County of Cornwall, riotously and unlawfully assemble to the disturbance of the peace of this realm and the terror of the people, whereby divers persons were injured. This after a magistrate of that Borough had commanded you to disperse in the name of the Queen.

'You are further charged with, that on divers dates you did treasonably and seditiously conspire against the State. . . .'

The dull voice droned on, detailing in legal jargon statute and section against which they were alleged to have offended.

When he had finished he called upon each of them in turn to state whether he were 'guilty' or 'not guilty'.

One after another the men declared their innocence. On the first occasion the reply brought a small cheer from the public gallery. The judge, in a hoarse stern voice, informed the court in general that he was not conducting a public show. Unless the members of the public refrained from voicing their feelings he would have the court cleared. There was no further sound from the miners' friends while the pleas were taken.

Now the prisoners were allowed to be seated and the case against them began to unwind.

'It is', the prosecuting barrister declared, 'quite simple and straightforward! Prior to this unhappily eventful day the miners had been stirred up by men like the defendants Retallick and Kittow. Doubtless there were others who unfortunately are not in custody. They were misled into forming unconstitutional alliances, such as the Miners' Union to which all these men belong. Such a union would not be unlawful if it restricted its activities to mining matters alone. Instead, it has taken upon itself the task of changing the laws of the land. Our land. And violence is advocated as a means to obtain that unlawful end.

'They – the men in this union – disagreed with Parliament's policy on the sale of corn. They deliberately set out to use force in order to change it, were prepared to go outside the Law to achieve their selfish and dangerous aims. It is well known to all of you that the activities of these men, representing a mere handful of Cornishmen, led to the military presence in Cornwall throughout the summer months. Farmers going about their lawful business had to be protected from these unionists. The use of threats, coercion and physical assault formed part of their campaign. They deliberately set themselves above the Law—'

'My Lord, I must object!'

This was the barrister briefed by Mr Button. 'My client is not charged with leading a revolution! I submit that my learned friend is not giving evidence that will be substantiated. He is reciting a story to the jury, for pure effect.'

'My Lord, the defendants, and in particular my learned friend's client Retallick, are charged with conspiring treason and sedition. If that is not plotting revolution I do not know what is!'

'Objection overruled.' The judge appeared to be bored already. The prosecution continued.

'There have been meetings, some held in secret, others addressed openly by the prisoner Retallick. At these meetings violence was frequently suggested – I go further, *demanded*. Yes, because the military had foiled them in every other way, the Miners' Union decided to resort to violence in a bid to achieve its ends. There can be little doubt that its members were aware that by so doing they were committing treason, that their actions would lead them into direct conflict with soldiers of the Queen.

'This disgraceful day at Looe, the rioting and terrifying lawlessness – it was not a thing decided upon a few hours before the event, or even a few days. It was part of a well-thought-out plan. Only the brave determination of a handful of soldiers prevented the citizens of Looe from witnessing the destruction of honest people's property, and with it the collapse of law and order in this county. Gathered together were men from mines throughout east and central Cornwall. Caradon, Phoenix, Kit Hill, St Austell and Par. They knew exactly where to go. They knew because the plans had been prepared beforehand. Proof beyond any reasonable doubt of a treasonable conspiracy.

'As to the incidents that arose out of this conspiracy, I shall be calling only sufficient witnesses to prove the Crown's case. A similar story could be told by every inhabitant of that unfortunate town. You will hear evidence from innocent shopkeepers. They will tell you of their terror at beholding this unruly mob. You will hear from the brave magistrate, called out when the mob was seen approaching, who, in fear for his very life, stood boldly before them, calling on them to disperse in the Queen's name. He even warned them of the consequences of their actions. They paid him no heed, doubtless scornful of the few soldiers who stood between them and their unlawful intentions.

'But the soldiers who opposed them were men of the 32nd Foot Regiment, themselves loyal men of Cornwall. They took up defensive positions to protect the ships, and the grain belonging to honest Cornish farmers. To aid them they had a small troop of Dragoon Guards.

'The officer in charge of the foot soldiers tried to reason with the rioters, but they were beyond reasoning. They attacked the officer in front of his men and, fearful for his life, the soldiers were forced to open fire in order to effect a rescue. Then the miners in their overwhelming numbers attacked the soldiers. So fierce did the fighting become that the dragoons had to be called in to assist them.

'The miners standing before you in this court were – with

two exceptions – no worse and no better than any of their fellows in that riotous crowd. The two exceptions, Joshua Retallick and John Kittow, are not simple miners. They were important members of the mining community and so must accept great responsibility for what went on about them. And so they should! For, mounted and in clear view of the others, they led that cowardly unlawful mob. Retallick attacked a trooper of the dragoons. Witnesses will be called who saw him personally knock a trooper to the ground, with utter disregard for the trooper's safety beneath the hoofs of the milling horses.

'Yes, gentlemen of the jury, so close to the fighting was the prisoner Retallick that he was himself twice wounded. But with the aid of the prisoner Kittow he made his escape. Yes, these two "leaders" deserted the miners they had led into sordid battle and fled. Indeed, Retallick was not apprehended until he had been at liberty for a number of days. That is briefly the case for the prosecution. Now I will proceed to call witnesses who will prove it beyond any shadow of a doubt.'

The first few witnesses were tradesmen from Looe, required merely to say that on the day in question they feared for the safety of their property and were terrified by the miners who marched upon their town.

Next came the magistrate, pompous and eager to impress the judge with his courage in standing up before 'hundreds of miners bent upon mischief and disturbance of the Queen's peace'. He went on to tell how, disregarding all the insults hurled at him, he completed the reading of the Riot Act before hurrying away to safety.

Mr Button, seated beside the barrister defending Josh, leaned over and whispered something. The barrister stood up to cross-examine the magistrate.

'Magistrate Phipps, I am quite sure you behaved with commendable courage. Indeed, would I be right in saying that you behaved with composure? That you assessed the situation in a calm and brave manner?'

The surprised magistrate beamed. 'I did my best, sir.'

'Then no doubt you were aware of the exact composition of the crowd?'

The magistrate looked puzzled.

'Come, now, Mr Phipps. Were they all afoot or all mounted?'

'Why, they were afoot, of course.'

'All of them?'

'Yes.'

'You are quite sure?' The barrister had to speak loudly because of an interested stir in the public gallery.

'Quite sure.'

'And yet the prosecution has informed the court that my client Mr Retallick and Mr Kittow were both mounted. Am I correct in assuming that neither of these men was present when you read out the Riot Act? They were not members of this riotous assembly?'

The magistrate opened his mouth and closed it again. He appeared to think, a puzzled frown on his face. 'We-ell. . . . They might have been at the back of the crowd. There were a lot of people there.'

'But you did not see them? You cannot point a finger and say, "Yes, those two men were present on their horses"?'

The magistrate was forced to agree that he could not.

'Thank you. There would appear to be a discrepancy between the evidence of a reliable witness and the fairy story the prosecution told to the court. Far from my client standing out in his leadership, he seems to have been most noticeable by his absence!'

There were laughs from the gallery and the judge called for order.

The counsel employed by the Miners' Union used his questioning time trying to make the magistrate say that the miners were in fact behaving in a quiet and orderly manner, that at no time was there any necessity to read the Riot Act. His argument was remarkably lacking in conviction.

Next came the evidence of the soldiers. It followed more closely the story told by the prosecuting counsel. They spoke of being ordered to fire into the crowd to save their officer, of defending themselves. Some went on to describe the arrest of one or more men in the dock. Their evidence was well rehearsed. Although a couple of them were noticeably uncomfortable when being cross-examined, they could not be tricked into going back on what they had already said. They all disagreed strongly with the suggestion that their action in firing into the crowd was more offensive than defensive.

Nobody, unless it was a miner who had been at the scene, would have doubted their evidence.

The dragoons' evidence was far more damning. They told the truth as they had seen it. When they arrived on the scene, Josh and John Kittow were part of the crowd. One dragoon told of being attacked by Josh and falling beneath the feet of the horses. It was, he insisted, a deliberate and determined attack.

'Surely not,' argued the barrister representing Josh. 'Was my client armed?'

The dragoon grudgingly admitted he did not believe so.

'Then perhaps he was holding a stave – or something you thought might have been a weapon?'

'No.'

The eyebrows of the barrister were a statement in themselves.

'Yet you had a sabre drawn and were prepared to use it upon my client?'

The dragoon showed some hesitation now.

'Yes.'

There was a loud and angry murmur from the public gallery.

'Silence!' The judge emphasised his order with the aid of the wooden gavel on the bench in front of him.

'And you are telling us that Joshua Retallick – unarmed, with nothing in his hand – *attacked* you? Attacked a soldier with a sabre clear of its sheath? A sabre raised and ready for use? You are suggesting this in all seriousness?'

'Yes.'

'Come, now. Is it not more likely that my client found himself trapped in a dangerous situation not of his making. That in trying to extricate himself from it he accidentally knocked you from your horse?'

'No, sir. It was deliberate.'

'You are quite sure?'

'Yes, sir. He had his arm raised to strike me.'

'I submit it was far more likely his arm was raised to protect himself from the blow of an up-raised sabre. That had your horse not slipped you would have split his skull open?'

'No, sir. It was a deliberate attack on me.'

The barrister shook his head. 'If such an assertion were true, it would make my client a fool. I will be proving later that he is far from that.'

The next witness was the dragoon who had slashed Josh's back. He too gave evidence that Josh was 'laying about him'. He further stated that John Kittow had also struck him.

Josh's barrister commented that John Kittow had undoubtedly saved Josh's life, that there was not a scrap of evidence to suggest that John Kittow had assaulted anyone – a point which was followed up by the Miners' Union barrister.

The dragoon was followed by the officer of the company of foot soldiers. He began his evidence by making vague allusions to Josh's position in the Miners' Union, to his having preached treason and sedition.

Josh's barrister was quick to object to such evidence on the grounds that it was 'hearsay'.

This time his objection was sustained and the officer was told to restrict his evidence to that which he knew and not that which he believed to be true. The officer then spoke of Josh's 'belligerent' attitude when they had met at the Wheal Phoenix. He swore that he had seen the Sharptor engineer with the miners when they marched into Looe.

This brought forth another flurried exchange between Mr Button and the barrister and this point was taken up with the officer. He remained adamant. He *had* seen Josh arrive with the miners and, *yes*, he was quite sure. He would not admit to any possibility of being wrong.

Then it was the turn of Morwen Trago. Like his officer he swore that Josh had been with the miners at the time they entered Looe. Further, he said Josh was urging the men to attack the soldiers. He had seen him strike down one dragoon, and when Josh had been about to attack another he, Morwen Trago, had fired at him, wounding him in the arm.

Morwen told of searching the moor around Josh's home and of capturing him in the barn. Josh was greatly relieved that no one said anything that might possibly have brought Miriam into the case.

Then it was Morwen's turn to be cross-examined by Josh's barrister.

'Is it true', asked the barrister, 'that you knew Joshua Retallick as a boy?'

'Yes. We lived close to each other on the moor near Sharptor.'

'Were you friends?'

Morwen shrugged. 'I wouldn't say that. We knew each other.'

'And did you like him?'

A shrug again. 'I neither liked him nor disliked him. I knew him, that's all.'

The barrister hitched his gown up on his shoulders. 'That is not the truth, Morwen Trago. The fact is that you hate Joshua Retallick as you hate no other man – unless it be Joshua Retallick's father.'

'No.'

'No? Really, Morwen Trago? You must be a special kind of human being, someone with a remarkable talent for forgiveness. Is it not true you believe Joshua Retallick's father to be responsible for the death of your own father?'

'He *was* responsible.'

'Surely not. Didn't your father rape a girl who lived with the Retallicks? When pursued I believe he slipped and fell into a disused mine shaft and was killed?'

'No! He didn't fall. He was pushed.'

'There is proof of this allegation, of course? Your father's – er – "murderers" were tried by a jury? And found guilty?'

'No, but that's what happened.'

'That may be what you choose to believe, Morwen Trago. It is certainly not corroborated by the known facts. But, be that as it may, do you still claim that you have no hatred for anyone who bears the name Retallick?'

The court was hushed as the jury waited for Morwen Trago
to reply. He said nothing.

'Never mind,' said the barrister. 'There are certain silences
that shout louder than words. We will allow that matter to
rest. But I put it to you that you did *not* see my client arrive
with the miners. That you have concocted your own version
of the day's events, carrying it off with such conviction you
have persuaded others they saw it too. What is more, if you
told the truth about what you saw on this fateful day – and
I have not the slightest doubt that you saw exactly what did
occur – I repeat, if you were to tell the truth, not only would
Joshua Retallick be acquitted but he would leave this court
with the praises of the learned judge ringing in his ears, for
attempting to prevent the bloodshed that took place on that
September day.'

'No! That's not true!'

But Morwen Trago's cries were drowned by the noise from
the public gallery. This time there was no silencing them.
The efforts of the court ushers brought only stamping feet
and howls of support for Josh Retallick and the miners in
the dock.

It was at this stage that the judge adjourned the proceedings
for the day.

On the return journey to the jail the accused miners were
in an optimistic mood, convinced that the mood of those in
the public gallery represented the view of the jury. Even John
Kittow's morale had been boosted by the final demonstration
of support. Only Josh would not allow himself to be fooled.

The next day only two more soldiers were called to give
evidence. Then it was time for the defence to present its case.

It soon became apparent to Josh that his pessimism had been
well founded. There were few defence witnesses and their case
was held together by a very frail thread.

Of those in the dock only Josh was called into the witness-
box to tell his story. He told of riding to Looe, and meeting with
John Kittow on the way. How both of them had ridden into
Looe town in a vain attempt to head off the miners, and of the
scene in the square when they arrived. He told how the soldiers

had fired before they had been attacked and, when pressed by his barrister, said except for the scuffle involving the officer he had not seen the miners use violence at any time. More. Once the soldiers had opened fire on them the miners were far too busy dodging musket-balls to offer violence to anyone.

Yes, he admitted, he had knocked a dragoon from his horse. But the fault lay with the horses rather than their riders. He had not fought the soldiers, although he considered their actions to be unnecessary and cowardly. Their first volley had been sufficient to strike terror into the ranks of the miners. After that their only thought had been escape.

His manner in the witness-box was quiet and straightforward enough to impress the jury. But then it was the turn of the prosecuting barrister to cross-examine him.

'Joshua Retallick, you have told the court you were not with the miners when they marched upon Looe.'

'Yes.'

'You rode there in great haste when you were told of their action?'

'Yes.'

'I won't go into your reasons, but is it not true you set off knowing when you caught up with them you would be able to influence them?'

'I hoped they might listen to me.'

'You "hoped they might listen". No doubt you had good reason to believe they would. They had listened to you many times in the past, when you addressed their meetings?'

'I addressed very few meetings.'

'You agree there were some?'

'Yes.'

'So you are not denying that the miners regard you as, for want of a better word, a leader? A leader of this union movement?'

'It is a miners' union and I have spoken to them at meetings.'

'And they listened to you with considerable deference, no doubt?'

'They listened.'

'Thank you, I think we are in complete agreement on this point. You are a leader of this so-called "union" of miners. Now, let us pass on to some of the things you have told the court. They do not seem to agree with what has been said by the many witnesses who came before you. You say you went to Looe in a vain attempt to prevent the miners from doing something which you now agree was "stupid", something for which the laws of this country have a much stronger word?'

'Yes.'

'But when you discovered they intended to carry out their unlawful plan of attacking the soldiers and seizing the corn wagons, you decided you would join with them.'

'No.'

'Further. When you saw the dragoons moving in to quell this riot you personally led an assault on them, attempted to beat them off to allow the miners to carry out their unlawful intentions.'

'No, I have said what happened.'

'You have told us what you would dearly like this court to believe, Mr Retallick. If the jury and I choose not to believe your version of the day's happenings I trust you will forgive us.'

With this the prosecuting counsel sat down.

'There is only one further question I would like to put to my client in re-examination, My Lord,' said Josh's barrister. 'Joshua Retallick, your intention when you went to Looe was to prevent the miners from breaking the law. Had you been successful you would not be standing in the dock now. Is that not so?'

'Yes.'

'Thank you. I have no further questions.'

Curiously, the Miners' Union barrister had few questions to put to Josh. Josh was asked only to confirm that John Kittow rode into Looe with Josh and that he had struck no blows.

His questioning over, Josh was returned to the dock with the other prisoners.

Then the character witnesses were called to speak on behalf of the miners. Shift captains in the main. But two adventurers came from the Caradon mine to speak for John Kittow. They praised his diligence and reliability and spoke of him as a man of integrity and loyalty.

When it was the turn of the character witnesses to speak on Josh's behalf it was the beginning of a series of surprises for him. The first was Theophilus Strike. His commanding presence rose above the grim court-room surroundings. In his usual forthright manner the mine-owner called the charges against Josh 'preposterous!' 'Joshua Retallick,' he said 'is a brilliant engineer. His contribution to mine safety is recognised far beyond the borders of his own county as being far ahead of his time. He has patented a mine-lift to bring miners from the depths of the deepest mine to the surface that will revolutionise current safety standards.'

Theophilus Strike went on to say that in all the time he had known Josh he had heard him neither preach nor practise violence. His interest in the Miners' Union was a humanitarian one. The mine-owner said that he was well aware of Josh's passionate interest in the welfare of the miners. He had in fact discussed it with him. He was perfectly satisfied that Josh was concerned with the well-being of the miners and nothing more.

Theophilus Strike was so positive in all his utterances that the prosecuting barrister chose not to take up a single point with him.

The next witness was William Carlyon.

The Harvey works manager smiled sympathetically in Josh's direction as he took the stand. He too spoke of Josh as a brilliant engineer with a great future. Further, he said he would rate him as possessing the potential to become one of the country's greatest.

'I believe it is true to say your relationship with the prisoner is closer than that of two engineers?'

'Yes.' William Carlyon's voice was pitched low. 'He was my daughter's husband.'

'Was?'

'My daughter died as the result of childbirth. This spring.'

The statement brought Josh sympathetic glances from the jury.

'It may be painful for you to talk about it, Mr Carlyon, but I am sure you are aware of the importance of your evidence. Will you tell us the tragic circumstances leading to your daughter's death?'

'Yes.' Despite his assurance William Carlyon's face showed strain. 'Josh – Joshua Retallick – and my daughter Sarah had a baby in the spring.'

'I am sorry, Mr Carlyon. You are talking about the spring of this year?'

'Yes.'

'Please go on.'

'It was a difficult birth. Josh was alone with my daughter and had to bring the baby into the world by himself. The baby was before its time and lived for only a few hours. My daughter was also very ill.'

'What sort of illness, Mr Carlyon?'

Josh could not look at the strained face of the works manager. He stared instead at the wooden floor at his feet.

'She became mentally unbalanced as a result of having to endure prolonged pain. . . .'

'And then?'

'She returned to Hayle to stay with her mother and myself, in the hope she would make a full recovery.'

'Did she make the hoped-for recovery?'

'No. One day Josh came to visit her. While he and the rest of us were talking in the house she rode off to the cliffs not far away. Soon afterwards her body was recovered from the rocks off-shore.'

'So, in the course of a few weeks Joshua Retallick lost both his wife and his child. It left him a lonely man, I would imagine?'

'Yes.'

'It would doubtless deeply affect the most hardened man among us,' said the barrister. 'In order to overcome such desolation most intelligent men would probably devote themselves to something that would, of necessity, occupy both their time and thoughts. A cause, perhaps. Something like a miners' union?'

'I would say that was highly probable.'

'Do you think he would become involved to such an extent that he would advocate violence, Mr Carlyon?'

'No. Josh is not a violent man.'

'That is what I too believe. Thank you, Mr Carlyon.'

The prosecuting barrister asked William Carlyon a few questions in an attempt to overturn his evidence that Josh was not a violent man, but he failed to shake him.

There were no more witnesses after William Carlyon. It was time for the prosecution to conclude its case. The prosecuting counsel stood up to address the court.

'My Lord. Gentlemen of the jury. You have listened to the evidence in a case of the utmost seriousness. A case involving a section of the community placing themselves above the Law. Attempting to impose their will upon others. This has always been regarded as one of the most serious offences in the land. It is a crime aimed at the very structure upon which our way of life depends. The upholding of law, and an ordered society. You have heard the evidence of honest men. They have told you how these men in the dock, with others, marched upon Looe with the express intention of seizing corn. They knew soldiers would be guarding it. They knew they would have to fight to have their way. This did not deter them. It could be that the orders given by Parliament to send the corn to other places was not wise. We cannot be sure of that. Parliament alone is aware of the needs of the whole country. They will stand or fall by their decisions. The laws of this land are made for *all* its people. It is of the utmost importance that they are obeyed. Not undermined in any way. I repeat. They must not be undermined. This is a mining community. The wisdom of that saying should be clear to everyone.

'This attempt to impose the will of a small minority upon the majority was more than folly. The way in which these miners sought to do it was both criminal and *treasonable*.

'The men in the dock before you come from a number of mines – irrefutable evidence that this was not a sudden storm that blew up in the heat of a summer's day, the result of an explosion of anger. This was a well-thought-out and well-planned – albeit ill-executed – uprising. That it was the result of a conspiracy must surely be beyond dispute. This treasonable folly was conspired at. There was a conspiracy to commit treason.

'When this mob arrived at Looe their behaviour was such that the Riot Act was read to them by the courageous magistrate whose evidence you have heard. The very wording of the Act is calculated to bring home to such men the seriousness of the situation, to persuade them to disperse quickly and peacefully.

'They did not disperse. They had no intention of so doing. Having gone to this peaceful town for an unlawful purpose, they were determined to see it through. Furthermore, they attempted it. Because of that one soldier died and others were injured. It can only be considered fortunate that innocent citizens of Looe were not amongst those who lost their lives.

'There is no disputing that nine of the men before you formed part of that riotous crowd. They have not attempted to deny it. They could not. Instead, they have tried to escape justice by throwing the blame for the violence upon the soldiers.

'Forget such considerations. That is not a point at issue.

'From two of the accused prisoners, Retallick and Kittow, we have heard protestations of innocence, and arguments as to whether they were at Looe when the Riot Act was read. They must be allowed to plead their case. That is justice. But I would remind you that these two men have much to lose. *Everything* to lose should they be found guilty here today.

'Against them you have heard the evidence of an officer, an honourable gentleman, and the men under his command. Men who have fought nobly in foreign lands for our country, in the ranks of the regiment Cornwall is proud to call its own. They have no reason to lie. They told you what they saw, honestly and convincingly.

'From his own lips you heard Retallick admit he was in the habit of addressing meetings of miners. "Union" meetings. Those of you who know something of this movement might refer to it by another and less pleasant name. An unpatriotic name. Retallick did not admit he was responsible for conspiring that the miners march to Looe. We could not expect him to do that. After all he pleaded not guilty.

'But I am sure that you, the members of the jury, will recognise the truth and find him as guilty as he assuredly is. His companion Kittow is perhaps more misguided than evil, but he is as guilty as Retallick. You will – you must – find him and all the other prisoners guilty as charged.'

In a heavy silence the counsel for the prosecution sat down.

The miners' defence barrister made a long speech that was repetitious and dull and had the jurors fidgeting on the hard benches. He said nothing new and his speech was delivered with a faintly apologetic air. When he ended he sat down abruptly and it was the turn of Josh's counsel.

'My Lord. Gentlemen of the jury. My learned friend for the prosecution spoke at length. Some of you may feel he spoke at *great* length. This is a barrister's privilege – indeed his duty – *when he presents a weak case.*

'I have no intention of taking up so much of your time. Neither is it necessary. Allow me only to remind you of the facts that have emerged.

'There was a disorder at Looe on the twenty-fourth of September, in this year eighteen hundred and forty-five. That is beyond dispute. But the magistrate who read the Riot Act, a cool, calm, observant citizen, did not see Joshua Retallick. Of course he didn't. Joshua Retallick was not there!

'Ah! you might say, but the soldiers saw him. Of course they did. All I dispute is *when* they saw him. I am not suggesting they are lying. Simply confused. They were excited, perhaps fearful – and who can blame them? They were greatly outnumbered. But what a pity they did not allow Joshua Retallick to talk to the crowd. Had he done so there might have been no blood shed on either side.

'He was himself wounded by a ball fired from the musket of a man who had reason to hate my client's family. About that I will say no more. Intelligent men can draw their own conclusions. But imagine, if you can, Joshua Retallic. Wounded and unarmed in the middle of a terrified crowd. Fired upon by muskets on the one side and hacked at by sabre-wielding dragoons on the other. In the *mêlée* is it surprising that he knocked a dragoon from his horse? He has told you in all honesty it was an accident. I venture to suggest he could in no way be blamed were it otherwise!

'He had gone to Looe in a vain attempt to prevent the miners from behaving foolishly. It was an action in keeping with his character. His concern for the miner was well known. It was not a secretive thing. His employer knew it, and came here to inform this court in no uncertain manner that Joshua Retallick was no criminal but a man and an engineer held in high esteem by colleagues and employer alike. William Carlyon confirmed Joshua Retallick's standing in the world of engineering. He also gave us an insight into the tragedies that have overtaken my client in the recent past – gave, if any was needed, a reason for him to have thrown himself wholeheartedly into the cause of the miner. In so doing might he not dull the sorrows that have cast such a heavy shadow over his own life?

'This is the man you are asked to judge now. A brilliant engineer. A man who cares for the miner. No stranger to personal tragedy. Is it feasible that he would act in a manner so completely out of character, as the prosecution would have you believe? No, gentlemen of the jury. I ask you that justice be done this day. That you allow Joshua Retallick to leave this court as a free man.'

The deep silence that followed his speech was broken by the judge.

'Thank you. If you've finished I will sum up the case for the benefit of the jury.'

He went through the case in a somewhat haphazard manner, missing out portions of the case he felt disinclined to emphasise, then he came out with a pronouncement that was more damning to Josh's case than anything that had gone before.

'You have heard character witnesses speak for these men, especially the prisoner Retallick. They were men who are used to speaking, men used to commanding. They did their duty as they saw it. The law of the land allows them that privilege. But what they have said about the prisoners before you does not constitute evidence. You must base your verdict on evidence such as that given you by those who were present at the sad events in Looe town that day, those who were involved in the violence that took place. You have to find the prisoners "guilty" or "not guilty" on that evidence alone. Was there a riotous assembly? There would appear to be little doubt of it. Were all the prisoners in the dock present during that riot? Once again you will have heard evidence that should answer the question beyond any reasonable doubt. Was there a treasonable or seditious conspiracy? You will take into consideration all that has been put to you on this point, paying particular attention to the places at which the accused normally worked and their distances from each other. I do not think it will be difficult to arrive at a just verdict. I trust your deliberations will not be overlong. We have a long list of cases yet to be heard and I wish to conclude these Assizes this week.'

Finishing his speech the judge rose, the prisoners were prodded to their feet and the judge bowed from the court as the jury filed off to their room.

The jury stayed out for an hour, during which time the prisoners were kept in the cells beneath the Assize court building.

Then, with a flurry of excitement, they were hustled back into the court-room to stand fidgeting in the dock as the jury returned to their places.

'Gentlemen of the jury. Have you reached a verdict on each charge?'

'We have,' replied the foreman of the jury.

'And how do you find the prisoners?'

The foreman of the jury cleared his throat noisily. 'On the charge of riotously assembling, we find the prisoners Retallick and Kittow "not guilty". All the others "guilty".'

There were some gasps from the public gallery, but the ushers were quick to silence them. The judge frowned. Whether it was due to the verdict or the noise in his court it was difficult to tell.

'And on the charge of being parties to a treasonable and seditious conspiracy?'

'We find all the prisoners "guilty".'

This time there was no denying the shouts of 'No! No!' from the public gallery.

'Silence!' This from the judge.

He looked at the men standing before him in the dock.

'I shall deal first of all with those of you found guilty of being part of a riotous assembly.' He read out the names of the miners. 'This is a most serious crime. One which cannot be tolerated in any civilised country. You are all grown men and fully responsible for your own acts. I sentence you to transportation for a period of seven years.'

There were groans and cries from their relatives.

'Now I come to the other charge on which you have been found guilty. Conspiring to commit treason. This is something which is aimed at the very foundations of the land. Allowed to go unchecked such actions can have only one outcome. In the land just across the English Channel we have seen it happen. I can think of no more serious crime. Those men I have just named will serve a further fourteen years' sentence of transportation, to run concurrently with their previous sentence.'

This provoked more cries from the public gallery. When the court ushers and some of the soldiers moved in to stop it there was some scuffling at the rear of the court-room.

'Take the men I have already sentenced down,' ordered the judge. As they were being escorted below, two persons were ejected from the public part of the court.

When all was quiet again the judge looked at Josh Retallick and John Kittow and his lips drew to a tight thin line.

'Kittow. You are, I feel, a man who has allowed himself to be led by his companion. Possibly you are more sinned against than a sinner. Nevertheless, I cannot overlook your part in this grave offence. I therefore sentence you to be transported for a period of fourteen years.'

John Kittow swayed in the dock and Josh gripped his arm in sympathy. For a few minutes he had thought there might be a chance of John Kittow escaping with a light sentence. Now, after the judge's words, he had no illusions of his own fate.

'For you, Joshua Retallick, I can find little to say in your favour. I consider your part in this disgraceful affair to be a major one. It is possible you are the actual instigator of this march upon a law-abiding town. You have been found guilty of a crime which a man of your intelligence could conceivably have carried through to its logical conclusion. The complete overthrow of organised government. Such an offence carries with it the death penalty. I will tell you quite openly that it was my determined intention to pass such a sentence upon you should you be found guilty. That I do not do so may be a mistake on my part. I may be failing in my duty. But the evidence of William Carlyon moved me, for even judges have emotions. He suggested the personal tragedies that have fallen upon you during this year may have impaired your judgement, that you may have done things not normally a part of your character. For these reasons alone I will exercise my mercy. Joshua Retallick, I sentence you to be transported for life.'

'That's not justice! He's an innocent man! You're sentencing an innocent man!'

Josh recognised Miriam's voice raised in loud protest before pandemonium broke loose in the court. He turned to see her but was hustled down to the cells below the court-room as soldiers, ushers and constables moved in upon the shouting, screaming, stamping crowd in the public gallery.

As furious fighting broke out in the public gallery Judge Denman called angrily for order. When it became increasingly apparent that his authority was being totally ignored he remained only long enough to ensure the Clerk understood his demand that the court be cleared. Until order was restored he would wait in the safety of his chambers.

Outside the court building Theophilus Strike, himself angry at what he considered to be a gross miscarriage of justice, watched the more vociferous objectors to the verdict being bodily hurled into the street from the steps of the court building.

When two soldiers appeared carrying Miriam between them

and taking advantage of her struggles to indulge in crude fondling, Strike stepped forward to her rescue.

Not stopping to argue with the mine-owner, the soldiers released Miriam and hurried back inside the building.

Miriam stood on the steps dishevelled and furious. The anger had nothing to do with her rough handling. It was her inability to do anything to reverse the monstrous judgement that had been passed on Josh.

'Young lady! Aren't you the Trago girl who married Preacher Thackeray?'

In her present mood Miriam might have said much to a man whose fellow mine-owners had helped to put Josh where he was now by their hatred of the Miners' Union, but she appreciated that Theophilus Strike had personally put more into trying to prove Josh's innocence than she had herself. She managed a simple 'Yes'.

'I thought I recognised you in the court-room.' At that moment he saw William Carlyon appear from a smaller door further along the court building. 'Will you wait here for me? I would like to have a talk with you.'

Waiting only for Miriam's nod of agreement, Theophilus Strike hurried away, and he and William Carlyon went into the now quiet Assize courts.

In the cells below the court John Kittow could only keep shaking his head, unable to believe they had really been found guilty. The other miners had received the punishment they had expected. In fact, there was little effective difference in their sentences. It was doubtful whether any of them would ever return to Cornwall.

Theophilus Strike and William Carlyon came into the cell and tried to reassure Josh.

'Try not to worry too much,' said the mine-owner. 'I'll do all in my power to help you. We'll lodge an immediate appeal.'

Josh shook his head. 'It would be a waste of your time and money. The judge had to do this. You must see that. My sentence is intended as a deterrent to others. I'm sorry about it only for my mother and father's sakes. For myself it's not such a great tragedy. There's very little here for me now. Perhaps I'll be able to make use of my engineering knowledge somewhere else.'

William Carlyon took his hand and there were tears in his eyes as he spoke.

'I find it difficult to express my feelings at seeing you in this situation, Josh. If only I could have helped more. You and Sarah. . . .'

His voice failed and he turned away.

'Nobody could have been of more help to me than you were, Mr Carlyon. I repaid your kindness by bringing tragedy into your life. Now, I would be grateful if you would both go before I start feeling too sorry for myself.'

'I'll do what I can for you,' said Theophilus Strike. 'Don't abandon hope yet. I have a great many friends to call upon. There will be justice for you yet. I'll be back with good news before very long.'

When Theophilus Strike parted company with William Carlyon outside the Assize courts he looked round for Miriam and found her waiting in a nearby doorway. Her anger had boiled away, leaving her cold and dispirited. It showed in the dejected way she stood, and the mine-owner took her arm and led her away along the street. Any resentment she might have had towards him was dispelled by his first words.

'I refuse to believe I see defeat in your face. No child of Moses Trago could possibly have heard of the word. Do you have a horse or carriage to take you home?'

Miriam shook her head.

'Good! I have a carriage at the inn along here. I'll give you a ride home and on the way we'll have a nice long talk together. You can tell me why you are so sure of Josh's innocence.'

William Thackeray was writing a letter seated at the desk in his study when the carriage drew up outside the chapel cottage. He watched in amazement as Theophilus Strike stepped from it and handed Miriam out. The mine-owner chatted seriously to her for a few minutes before climbing back inside the coach and waving the coachman on.

When Miriam entered the house her husband met her at the foot of the stairs in the hallway and demanded to know why she had been travelling in a carriage with the Sharptor mineowner.

'He brought me back from Bodmin Assizes. That's where all Josh's friends have been today – together with those of his enemies with the courage so to declare themselves.'

'And who won the day? Your Josh – or his "enemies"?'

'He was sentenced to transportation for life.' In spite of her promise to Theophilus Strike not to give up all hope, Miriam choked on the words.

'How tragic.' At that moment Miriam hated him fiercely for his sardonic hypocrisy. 'The Union will miss him. Poor Josh did much for the miners.'

'Then why weren't you in court to tell that to the judge? You could have helped him without too much risk to yourself.'

'I would have been pleased to help had it been possible. But who would have taken my word against all those witnesses who actually *saw* what went on?'

'You would never have gone into that court-room. You would have been far too worried that your part in the matter might come out. The conspiracy to involve Josh that you, Morwen and his officer were part of.'

'What an incredible suggestion, my dear. But in view of your distraught state I'll ignore it. I'm sure you'll feel better in the morning.'

His calm mocking air of superiority goaded her beyond discretion.

'You ignore it if you wish. I doubt if Theophilus Strike will.'

'Strike! You told him of your wild imaginings?'

It was the first time she had ever seen genuine fear on his face and it told her as much as words might have. William had deliberately involved Josh in the Looe riot.

'Far more than that, William. I gave him facts. I told him of the meetings between you and Morwen, gave him the date the officer came here with him to meet you.'

Now she called on her most calculated bluff. 'And I told him of the conversation I overheard between you and the officer.

Strike intends seeing that justice is done, William. You'll have
little cause to celebrate your success.'

Miriam watched the battle between fear and anger being
fought on William's face. The victory went to anger. Without
any warning the preacher's arm swung in a wide arc and his
hand struck her across the face.

It was the suddenness of it as much as the power behind the
blow that caused her to stagger sideways against the wall.

'You Judas harlot! This is the thanks I get for taking you into
my home and giving you my name. Don't you think I knew
what had gone on between you and Josh before? Oh yes, I
knew – but I forgave you. I was sure you'd put your wild
ways behind you when I married you and gave you a place
in decent society. I was wrong. You've lusted for Josh since the
day of the wedding. You don't think I've been blind all these
years? I've watched the way you looked at him – and he at
you. Now you would sacrifice me for the sake of it. Give up
all you have here – all that's decent – for someone who would
be best forgotten.'

'I gave up all that was decent years ago, William Thackeray,
for something I wish I could forget.'

She fingered the side of her face where he had struck. 'I did
my best to make you a good wife, William. It wasn't always
easy. You knew my feelings when you married me. I told you I
never loved you, but I respected you and because of that I tried
to be the wife you wanted and needed. I have no respect for you
now and no amount of beating will change that. As for lusting
after Josh – yes! It's quite true. And like the harlot you called
me Josh could have had me whenever he wanted me. Here in
your house, on the moor – anywhere. If he would take me now
he could have me even in the filthiest prison cell.'

William Thackeray recoiled as though she had struck him.

'I'll be leaving your house in the morning, William. Daniel
will go with me.'

William Thackeray looked as though he would argue, but
Miriam was in full command of the situation now.

'I'd rather you didn't make things difficult for me, William.
If I were to write a detailed letter to Conference you wouldn't

remain in the Church one day more. Now, if you'll stand aside, I have things to do upstairs.'

For a moment Miriam thought he would hit her again and she threw up her head, braced for the blow.

It never came. William Thackeray turned away and scurried from the house.

As the door banged behind him Miriam's knees sagged and she caught at the hand-rail on the stairs. It was done. For months she had realised that the day had to come when she would tell William Thackeray she was leaving. She had dreaded the scene it would provoke. Now it was over. Now she could look forward, to face the hardships that lay ahead. Alone.

But Miriam had one last distressing meeting with her husband to come before the break became final.

It was after he returned from London and his long-awaited appearance before the Conference. It had been a stormy and unsatisfactory meeting for Preacher Thackeray and it showed in the way he slouched in the saddle riding into Henwood village in the last light of evening.

Miriam opened the door to him herself, leaving Daniel inside with her mother and John Trago.

William Thackeray had not anticipated a doorstep confrontation but he did his best to project some of his old authority.

'I've come for you and Daniel, Miriam.'

'Then you've had a wasted journey, William. We're not leaving here.'

'You're my wife, Miriam – and Daniel is my son. If necessary I'll seek recourse to the courts to have you return to me.'

'No, you wouldn't. You fear what I might say in a court-room.'

'I fear nothing that might be said here in Cornwall. It would not follow us to London, and that's where I've been ordered.'

'What I have to say would follow you to the grave, William Thackeray, so don't make me say it.'

'He'll not make you say or do anything.' John Trago pushed

past Miriam with no apologies for eavesdropping. Glaring down at the preacher he added, 'She'll stay here as long as she's a mind to and Daniel stays with her.'

'It's all right, Uncle John. I'm going nowhere with William. Go inside and leave this to me.' As John Trago hesitated she said, 'It will be all right. I promise.'

'If you say so.' He continued to glare at the preacher for a few more seconds. 'But if you need me, then you just shout. I'll be right out.'

Miriam waited until he had gone into the house, then pulled the door closed before turning back to her husband.

'There is nothing more to be said between us, William. Too much has happened to be undone. I'm not blaming you. I married you for too many wrong reasons and I must bear the shame of that. . . .'

'Miriam, forget what's gone. Let's try to start again. I have to return to London but that's not the end of the world. We can work together for others as we did here.'

'Did we? No, William. I *thought* that was what we were doing but it was all to build your reputation. The price of it was far too high. I don't want to see you again – ever. Your going to London will help to remove many of the difficulties for both of us.'

'But you can't have really thought about this. What will you do? And Daniel? You must consider him.'

'I have. I'll work on the mine for his food and clothes and he'll get a better education from me than any other boy about here.'

'Miriam, don't let our marriage end like this. I need you both. I love you. Come with me. . . .'

'There's nothing to be gained by this discussion. It can change nothing. Go, William. Please.'

'I beg you, Miriam. Don't let it end like this. For Daniel's sake if not mine. Where is he? Let me see him. Just once. . . .'

'No!' The cry was torn from her as William Thackeray's composure disintegrated before her eyes. Turning, Miriam fled into the house.

The understanding John Trago let her run upstairs to her

bedroom before he went outside to confront the now pathetic figure of Miriam's husband.

'Preacher, you've had your say and Miriam's told you what's in the future for her and the boy. Many years ago I told Josh Retallick to leave her be to pick up the pieces of her life again. I was telling the wrong man that day and many's the time I've regretted it. But I'm telling the right one now. Go away, Preacher. I don't want to see you here again.'

Miriam watched from the window as William Thackeray rode away. She despised him for what he had done, hated him for his betrayal of Josh. She should have been able to glean some satisfaction from his abject misery. Instead, it saddened her. The candle of greatness had burned within William Thackeray but it had not been strong enough to drive away the darkness of his jealousy and ambition.

Chapter Twenty-Seven

Josh knew nothing of the things that were going on in the world he had once known, and Theophilus Strike was unable to pay him his promised visit. For Josh never returned to Bodmin Jail.

It was normal for prisoners to spend a couple of weeks in jail before being sent to one of the convict hulks anchored off various ports and dockyards around the coast of Britain. There they would be held until a transport was available to take them to Australia. But the military authorities in Cornwall believed there would be demonstrations if the prisoners sentenced for the Looe riots were held at Bodmin. So, instead of accompanying the other prisoners back to prison, all eleven of them were taken in chains from the court to the prison hulk *Captivity* lying off the naval dockyard at Devonport. The hulk was the battered shell of an old Trafalgar man-of-war.

The communal cell at Bodmin Jail had been bad. The *Captivity* was an absolute nightmare. The boat carrying them out to it approached from down-wind. When they were still fifty yards from the dark shape the stench was enough to make a weak-stomached man puke.

The boat bumped heavily against the side of the hulk and the sentenced miners made their way precariously up a slippery gangway in the darkness, clanking heavily and wearing the broad-arrowed clothing hurriedly acquired at Bodmin.

Their names were ticked off in the uncertain light from a lantern by a jailer who peered shortsightedly at a list of names. They were then split into three groups, each man fettered by chains at his ankles and attached to the others by a second chain joining them at the waist.

It was now that Josh was parted from John Kittow. It happened so quickly that he never had time to say so much as 'Goodbye'. One minute, they were being pushed around by swearing jailers fixing and checking chains. The next, the groups were being pushed along the deck in the darkness, each bound for a separate hold.

He never saw John Kittow again. Three months to the day after he climbed aboard the *Captivity*, the ex-shift captain died, the victim of a typhoid outbreak on the foul hulk.

Josh and the three men with him were pushed down a steep wooden ladder into a dark and indescribably stinking hold. Here there were no lights. But all around were the sounds of men, moaning, snoring and coughing. The hatch cover was slammed shut and the miners left to grope their way forward in the blackness, seeking space for themselves. As they trod upon protesting, squirming bodies their progress across the crowded hold was measured by curses and oaths. They finally found a small space, and by easing out other prisoners they made room to sit down.

Sleep was out of the question. They were part of a walking nightmare. Only when the grey light of dawn filtered reluctantly through cracks between the rotting boards that secured port-holes did the miners realise the darkness had been kind to them. There was filth and scattered rubbish everywhere. Convicts lay chained together like wild beasts, their faces reflecting the same desperate likeness. Red-eyed and unshaven, they put gruff questions to the newcomers, resentful of their recent freedom. They asked about the world of which they were no longer a part. The half-real world that belonged to another lifetime. Here they were chained captive creatures, something to be shouted at, abused and baited.

If a man had to stay in the hulks for a long time he looked upon death as a friend and hurried to greet him. But not all were granted this release.

Men sentenced to short terms of transportation often spent the entire period on a prison hulk. There should have been employment for them in the royal dockyards, but since the end of the war with France the fleet had been allowed to dwindle in size. There was little for prisoners to do in the dockyards. All they could do was endure the reeking, floating garbage-ship and envy the men who shared their habitat only until a transport was available to take them to a new land.

For five ghastly weeks Josh was on the *Captivity*. Many times he feared for his very sanity. He learned to fight like the worst of his fellow-prisoners for the abominable food that was lowered to them twice daily. Once he gloated for a whole day when he was able to steal two handfuls of tasteless porridge instead of the usual one.

He had to learn to accept the most base instincts of the men around him during those five weeks of abject degradation.

Then one day the hatch cover was removed at an unusual hour and one of the jailers called his name. He kept calling until Josh, dragging his chained companions with him, reached the bottom of the ladder. The warder made him climb halfway up before he would come down to loose the chain attaching him to the others. The jailers were for the most part as ignorant and brutal as the prisoners in their care. One would not dare venture alone into a hold full of vengeful men who had little to lose by murdering a jailer.

With only the chains about his ankles, Josh awkwardly climbed the rest of the way. He breathed deep of salt air as he shuffled after the jailer to the cabin that was the hulk overseer's office.

The overseer looked at Josh in distaste as he stood before him, dirty and with five weeks' beard on his face.

'Your name Joshua Retallick?'

'Yes.'

The overseer sniffed. 'You're not my idea of a brilliant engineer.'

Josh's hopes took a sudden unreasonable climb. There must be some word from the outside world. How else would anyone on this prison hulk know that he was an engineer? To them he was just an anonymous dirty prisoner in an arrowed suit of clothing.

'I was an engineer,' he said.

'There'd better be no "was" about it,' said the overseer, waving a piece of paper at Josh. 'I've a letter here which says you're to be sent to Australia, going on a regular immigrant-ship with a warder on his way to Botany Bay with his family. Seems they've found copper in Australia and need someone out there in a hurry to install some engines. It's all in this letter that you'll take with you. It's written by William Carlyon, manager of Harvey's foundry at Hayle. Some of his engines are being sent on the ship with you. There's another letter from a Theophilus Strike, promising to pay all expenses incurred in your transfer. This isn't the right way to send a prisoner to the penal colonies, and I'll complain about it in my next report, but the release order has come from London, signed personally by a Minister of the Queen. Why he needs to bother himself with a convict I don't know.' He sniffed his disapproval. 'Your ship is lying at Falmouth. You'll get cleaned up and out of those stinking rags and then be taken there under escort. But remember, Retallick. You may be travelling on a ship with free men, but you'll still be a prisoner. Whatever your warder tells you – you do. Understand?'

'Yes.'

It was unbelievable. Josh was unable to accept the truth of it – not even when he stood on a cold jetty, shivering in a chill east wind, the stinking hulk a dark smudge on the river behind him. He had wanted to ask to see John Kittow before he left, but was terrified that if he stayed on the *Captivity* any longer a letter would arrive to countermand the previous one. And after five weeks in a prison hulk one did not ask for favours.

The two escorts travelling with him said very little along the way. When they stopped at an inn he went inside with them. Although handcuffed, he ate food such as he had not seen since leaving Bodmin Jail. He even shared ale with them and wondered at their generosity, until he realised that Theophilus Strike was footing the expenses bill.

As the coach rolled along the long straight road into Liskeard he could see the rounded hill that was Caradon Tor. He strained his eyes hoping to see Sharptor, but it was hidden from view by Caradon. Even so, for as long as it was visible he watched Caradon and its gorse-covered slopes.

They spent the night at Lostwithiel, the warders putting up at the coaching inn and Josh being lodged in the town's lock-up.

They set off at dawn and arrived at Falmouth in the early afternoon. The streets of the town were crowded with people, the shops and vendors doing a busy trade. During the time he had been in the hulk time and dates had meant nothing to Josh, but when he asked his escorts they told him it was the day before Christmas Eve.

Josh had one moment of uneasiness as they set off from the jetty in a small boat, suddenly afraid that the whole thing would turn out to be a cruel hoax and the promised ship another prison hulk. His mind was put at rest when the boat was brought up alongside a sailing vessel larger than any other he had seen. It was more than twice the size of the ore carriers that put into Looe and Hayle.

Once aboard he was escorted to a windowless cabin well down in the bowels of the ship. Here his escort handed him over to the warder who was to be his jailer on the long journey to Australia.

The warder was a very different man from the jailers on the hulk, or even in Bodmin Jail. Samuel Evans was a family man. He looked the part and spoke to Josh as a man would speak to another man, not as a warder to a prisoner.

'Hello, Joshua. I've heard a great deal about you and even had Mr Carlyon journey across from Hayle to speak with me about you. I can do nothing about the fact that you're a convicted prisoner. While we're in harbour you'll be locked in this cabin. Once we put to sea you are free to wander about the ship as though you were any other passenger. I had to ask permission from the ship's captain, of course, but he agreed. However, he reminded me that I'm responsible for your good behaviour. I've learned something about your background and the crime for which you stand convicted and I'm willing to take a chance on you. But I want your word not to attempt to escape or do anything to interfere with the running of this ship while you're at large. Do I have that assurance?'

'You have it – and my deep gratitude,' said Josh.

'Good, then it's settled. Mr Carlyon brought some clothes for you to wear on the voyage, but I fear you've lost some weight since he last set eyes on you. I'll have a meal sent down to you tonight. We should sail on the morning tide, bound for the new life that lies ahead for both of us. You're fortunate to have good and wealthy friends, Joshua. But if the hulk you've left is like those I've seen you'll already appreciate that.'

When the warder left, Josh sat down on the narrow bunk. He felt like weeping. There were still many problems ahead of him but the nightmare, the dreadful nightmare of the hulk, was over.

His cabin, though narrow and with no port-holes, was as good as most of the others on board, better than the accommodation provided for the emigrants travelling steerage.

The ship did not sail on the morning tide. More cargo arrived to delay its departure. It did not leave Falmouth until the late evening.

There was a fairly strong cold north-easterly wind blowing from the land. In no time at all the vessel was well out into the Channel.

When the evening meal was brought to the cabin, Warder Evans arrived with the clothes that William Carlyon had obtained for Josh. The two men talked as Josh ate his meal and changed into his new clothes. The following day was Christmas. The warder told Josh of the toys he had brought

aboard for his children. There would, he said, be a service on
the after-deck. He hoped to see Josh there. Then the warder
took Josh on a tour of the boat, pointing out places he would
need to know. Then, aware that Josh would want to savour
his new-found freedom, the warder left him alone on the
deck. From now until they arrived at their far destination,
Josh would be treated as a free man.

It was dark on the deck, with only a few lanterns swinging
in tiny islands of light around each gangway. It was bitterly
cold too. The decks were deserted.

Josh made his way to the stern of the ship. From here he
could see the light of the Lizard lighthouse in the distance.
Along the coast of the scarcely discernible land that was
Cornwall were the lights of small cottages. Occasionally,
huddled beneath towering cliff shadows, a cluster of lights
showed where a fishing village prepared for Christmas.

Josh felt a deep feeling of loneliness well up inside him.
He thought of his parents in the cottage on the slopes of
Sharptor, getting ready for a lonely Christmas without him.
There were miners too whose companionship he had taken
for granted. And Miriam. . . .

He shivered. It was cold. He could have gone below but
he wanted to stay here with his thoughts, looking back until
the land and the life he had known disappeared for ever.

He sensed rather than saw the figure that came up to
stand close to him. Close, but back from the rail. He half-
turned but could make out only a pale shadow that was a
face.

'Josh, is that you?'

He could not believe it! It was not possible!

'Miriam!'

'Oh, Josh!' She was in his arms, holding him as though
the north-east wind might tear him away from her.

But how . . . ? What . . . ? It couldn't be true! Now he
was certain the whole thing was a dream. He would wake
up soon and find himself back on the *Captivity*.

'What are you doing here?' he asked at last. Suddenly he
stiffened. 'William! Is he here with you?'

'No, Josh. And don't let's mention him after tonight. William is in London.'

'And Daniel . . . ?'

'He's here on the ship with me – with us. Come down to my cabin and see him. I have a lovely cabin, Josh. Theophilus Strike got it for me.'

'Strike? What has he to do with you being here? Miriam, will you please tell me what's happening?'

She laughed at his bewilderment and squeezed his hand happily. 'I'll tell you the whole story when we get below. I'm surprised you didn't know I was on board.'

'How could I?'

'Well, I came down to your cabin last night and put my hand on the door. I heard you moving inside and I wanted to touch you so much I felt sure you would have heard my heart crying out for you.'

Her cabin, though not large, was very comfortable. It had two bunks, on the smaller of which Daniel lay sleeping.

Miriam took off her cloak and began to explain her presence on the ship.

'I was at your trial,' she began.

'I know. I heard you,' Josh smiled.

'Theophilus Strike heard me too. I was thrown out on to the street by the soldiers and he came outside to find me. He'd recognised me as Morwen's sister, he said, and had heard I was Preacher Thackeray's wife. In view of this he couldn't understand why I should be standing up in court risking arrest to shout your innocence. I told him what I believed had happened – that William and Morwen had arranged for you to become involved in whatever happened at Looe. He was very interested. He said he would cause some enquiries to be made. We discussed a lot of things when he gave me a ride home to St Cleer in his own coach.

'William saw me alighting from the coach and demanded to know what I was doing with Theophilus Strike. I told him exactly what I had told Mr Strike.'

'Wasn't that a foolish thing to do?'

Miriam shrugged. 'I was so angry it didn't matter. But it

mattered to William. He was so frightened he struck me. It was the first and last time. He also called me a lot of names and said things about you and me. They were a lot of very nasty lies but I let him believe they were true. The next morning I got some clothes together and took Daniel with me to Henwood to stay with my mother.

'William came there once to try to make me return with him, but he couldn't do much with Uncle John there and I simply refused to go. It was all very upsetting.'

'But that doesn't explain how you came to be here. . . .'

'Patience, Josh. You have the whole of a very long journey to learn about it.' But she continued with her story.

'Theophilus Strike wasn't able to obtain any further evidence and asked your father to tell me. Incidentally, both your father and mother know I'm here with you.'

'And they approve?'

'I think they were deeply shocked at first, but the day before I left Henwood your mother came to see me. She asked me to give you the love and blessing of both of them. She said she'd be happy knowing you would have me to look after you.'

'Poor Mum. But. . . .'

'I know – the story of why I'm here. . . . Two weeks ago Theophilus Strike came down to the village to speak to me again. He wanted to know what I intended doing with my future. He asked me a great many very personal questions. Then he told me the great news. He said William Carlyon had received an order for mine-engines from a man who had discovered copper ore in Australia. It was a rich find and many men in London were prepared to back the scheme. Parliament too were very interested. They thought it would help open the country up to settlers. Anyway, the man who had found the ore not only wanted the engines but also wanted a good engineer to set them up and keep them running. William Carlyon and Theophilus Strike discussed it and Theophilus Strike journeyed to London. When he returned he had a letter with him which said you could go to Australia and work the engines. It was as simple as that. I think Theophilus Strike has some very important friends in London. All that had to be done was for your fare to be paid in advance. Theophilus Strike did that immediately.'

'Thank you. That explains why I'm here! I am still no wiser about you being here too.'

'Well,' said Miriam, 'among the questions that Theophilus Strike asked me was why I was so concerned about you. I told him.'

'You told him what?'

'I told him I loved you, that I'd always loved you and that I only married William because in some horribly confused way it seemed that I was being loyal to my father.

'He asked me whether I believed it possible for you and I to make a new life together if we had the opportunity. I told him "Yes". That was all. He arranged for me to come as a passenger on this ship.'

'If I live to be a thousand I'll never be able to repay Theophilus Strike for all he's done for me,' said Josh. He looked at Miriam. 'You know I love you too, don't you?'

Miriam's answer was to cling to him fiercely.

Josh shook his head. 'God! What a mess we made of our lives. If only we'd accepted that as the only really important thing from the very beginning.'

'But we can start our new lives from now, can't we, Josh? I have a lot of money here for you. Theophilus Strike gave it to me. He said it's royalties on the patent of one of your inventions.'

'He's a good man,' said Josh. He suddenly held Miriam away from him. 'But what about Daniel? What will you tell him?'

'What is there to tell him, Josh? He's still little more than a baby. *You* are his father. You've known that all along. I told Theophilus Strike about that too. It's never been an easy thing to keep locked inside me.'

She looked at him with tears of happiness on her face. 'Now there's no need to keep anything locked away inside me. My passage was booked on this ship in the name of Mrs Retallick. We have our son Daniel Retallick with us and are heading to a new life together. Far away from the troubles of the old one.'

'You mustn't forget I'm still a convict, Miriam.'

She waved his words aside. 'Only in name. When we get there you'll find that Theophilus Strike has sorted everything out for you. You'll start work on the mine as their engineer. In a short time everybody will have forgotten you were ever a convict.'

Slipping away from him she took down a small tin box from a shelf by her bunk. Opening it she took out a piece of crumpled paper which she smoothed out and laid before him.

'Do you remember the day you wrote this for me?'

Written on the paper in a childish handwriting was a single word. 'Miriam.'

He nodded. 'I remember. You made me write it so you could copy it. Then you persuaded me to teach you to read and write.'

'Write it again, Josh.'

He looked at her in surprise and she knelt down beside him and brought his hand up to her lips. 'Just write "Miriam" for me again, as you did that day on the moor.'

Still not understanding he took the paper and a pencil from her and carefully wrote 'Miriam' on the paper. Beneath the name he had written many years before. When he had finished, Miriam took the paper from him and looked at it with as much pleasure as she had shown on that moorland day when they were children.

'That's beautiful, Josh. But now you have something far more important to teach me than how to read and write. You have to teach me how to live, to give without holding back, to be a complete person again and have so much happiness inside me it bubbles over and engulfs those I love. Will you do that, Josh? If I promise to give you my love for ever in exchange will you teach me all the things I want to know.'

'I can only teach you the things I know myself, Miriam.'

He trembled a little as he drew her, soft and yielding, to him.

'We'll both have to learn about them together.'

BEN RETALLICK

E. V. Thompson

The first book in the bestselling Retallick saga

In the tin mines of Cornwall during the first decades of the nineteenth century, death is the constant companion of the working man.

Ben Retallick has grown to sturdy manhood among the miners and fisherfolk, through the hard and hungry years when blood was often the price of bread.

When cruel fate steals away Jesse, his dark-eyed love, Ben searches the hiring fairs to find her again, knowing nothing of her parentage and caring only for the day he'll make her his wife.

'A lot more historical than romance – you will not be disappointed' – *The Times*

FLOWER OF SCOTLAND

Emma Blair

'Emma Blair is a dab hand at pulling heart strings' *Today*

In the idyllic summer of 1912, all seems rosy for Murdo Drummond and his four children. Charlotte is ecstatically in love with her fiance Geoffrey; Peter, the eldest, prepares for the day when he will inherit the family whisky distillery, while Andrew, gregarious and fun-loving, is already turning heads and hearts. Nell, the youngest, contents herself with daydreams of a handsome highlander. Even Murdo, their proud father, though still mourning the death of his beloved wife, is considering future happiness with Jean Richie, an old family friend.

The Great War, however, has no respect for family life. As those carefree pre-war days of the distillery fade, with death, devastation, revenge, scandal and suicide brought in their wake, the Drummonds are plunged to the horrors of the trenches in France. Yet those who survive discover that love can transcend class, creed and country . . .

HALF HIDDEN

Emma Blair

'Emma Blair is a dab hand at pulling heart strings' – *Today*

The news of her fiancee's death at Dunkirk was a cruel blow for Holly Morgan to suffer. But for Holly – forced to nurse enemy soldiers back to health while her beloved Jersey ails beneath an epidemic of crime, rationing and the worst excesses of Nazi occupation – the brutality of her war has only just begun.

From the grim conditions of the hospital operating theatre where Holly is compelled to work long hours alongside the very people responsible for her grief, unexpected bonds of resilience and tenderness are forged. When friendship turns to love between Holly and a young German doctor, Peter Schmidt, their forbidden passion finds sanctuary at Half Hidden, a deserted house deep within the island countryside. A refuge where traditional battle lines recede from view in the face of more powerful emotions, it nevertheless becomes the focus for the war Holly and Peter must fight together – a war where every friend may be an enemy . . .

Other best selling Warner titles available by mail;

☐	BEN RETALLICK	E. V. Thompson	£5.99
☐	HALF HIDDEN	Emma Blair	£5.99
☐	FLOWER OF SCOTLAND	Emma Blair	£5.99
☐	TREVANION	David Hillier	£5.99
☐	STORM WITHIN	David Hillier	£5.99
☐	THE DANCING STONE	Evelyn Hood	£5.99

WARNER BOOKS

WARNER BOOKS
Cash Sales Department, P.O. Box 11, Falmouth, Cronwall, TR10 9EN
Tel: +44 (0) 1326 372400, Fax: +44 (0) 1326 374888
Email: books@barni.avel.co.uk

POST AND PACKING
Payments can be made as follows: cheque, postal order (payable to Warner Books) or by credit cards. Do not send cash or currency.

All U.K Orders	**FREE OF CHARGE**
E.E.C. & Overseas	20% of order value

Name (Block Letters) _____

Address _____

_____

Post/zip code: _____

☐ Please keep me in touch with future Warner publications

☐ I enclose my remittance £ _____

☐ I wish to pay by Visa/Access/Mastercard/Eurocard

Card Expiry Date
